Frank P. Ryan is a multiple-bestselling author, in the UK and US. His other fiction includes the thrillers *Goodbye Baby Blue* and *Tiger Tiger*. His books have been translated into more than ten different languages. Born in Ireland, he now lives in England.

Visit him at www.frankpryan.com

The
Snowmelt
River

FRANK P. RYAN

Jo Fletcher

BOOKS

First published in Great Britain in 2012 by

Jo Fletcher Books
an imprint of Quercus
55 Baker Street
7th Floor, South Block
London
W1U 8EW

A CIP catalogue record for this book is available
from the British Library

ISBN 978 1 78087 738 9

10 9 8 7 6 5 4 3 2 1

Typeset by Ellipsis Digital Limited, Glasgow

Printed and bound in Great Britain by
Clays Ltd, St Ives plc

For William

It is rumoured from sources older than history that once these were happy lands, fruitful and bounteous as any heart might desire. The Arinn were the masters then, a race of magicians of unparalleled knowledge – but that very knowledge rather than wisdom was their undoing. In their arrogance, they wrought a malengin wondrous beyond understanding, yet so perilous that even today few other than the very wise or the very foolish dare utter its name. In such folly lay the seeds of our tormented world . . .

Ussha De Danaan: last High Architect of Ossierel

Contents

PART I:
The Enchantment

PART II:
The First Power

PART III:
Ossierel

PART I

The Enchantment

The Kiss

It was a beautiful Sunday morning, early and quiet, before most people were awake. A special day, so special the fifteen-year-old boy astride his stationary bicycle felt overwhelmed by it. Lately he had often dreamed about this day and his dreams always led him here, to the tree-shadowed lane outside the twin gates that led into the Doctor's House. Alan Duval's excitement centred on a mountain now out of sight but looming ominously in his imagination. Slievenamon was the name of the mountain. Beyond the small Irish town of Clonmel, over its streets and the decaying ramparts of its medieval walls, the mountain soared, shrouded in legend, two thousand, three hundred and sixty-eight feet above the horizon. And now on this special morning the mountain beckoned, casting an enchantment on the air like a thickening scent, intoxicating and heavy, so he couldn't help but be drawn to it even though it chilled the blood in his veins.

The left half of the gates was opening in the high ivy-covered wall. He listened attentively but heard none of the usual creaking. They had oiled the hinges last night, in readiness. He saw the front wheel of her bike roll through, then the flash of her auburn hair, like a warm red flame, and even as his heart began to leap, he saw the excitement in her eyes, the soft green of evening light on the meadow that sloped down onto the far side of the river.

Kathleen Shaunessy lived in the Doctor's House with her uncle, Fergal, and his housekeeper, Bridey. Nobody called her Kathleen except her uncle. Everybody else called her Kate.

Alan held her bike while she closed the half gate. Fourteen years old – she wouldn't be fifteen until 6 November – Kate wore blue jeans, tight-fitting over worn trainers, and her upper body was hidden under a thick white sweater. This early in the morning, even at the close of a particularly hot summer, it would be cold. Over one shoulder she carried a denim backpack, just as he carried one on his back: a change of underwear, toothbrush and toothpaste, sandwiches and fruit. All they needed for a brief adventure.

'What did you tell Bridey?'

'I left her a note. Sure, she won't believe the half of it anyway!'

She spoke with the soft singsong accent that had so bemused the American youth when he had first arrived in Clonmel, an accent that in Kate he had come to love. Kate was so excited by the mission she didn't appear to notice his own shakiness. He knew she had crept out through the first-floor bathroom window and climbed down the fall pipe with its convenient bends, as she had many a time before, because if she had left by the door her dog, Darkie, would have barked Bridey awake. He had no need to make furtive arrangements back at the sawmill since his grandad, Padraig, knew all about it. Padraig had helped them plan it. But Alan had worried about it all the same, tossing and turning through the night, with his bedroom window open to the cool night air, fitfully sleepless, as his puffy face now testified, and struggling to come to terms with his own fears.

He said, 'Let's check out the others. See if they're ready!'

Kate switched on her mobile, sending the text message:

RedyRNot

The answer flashed to her screen within moments, and with a shaking hand she held it out for Alan to see:

WotDyuTnkRevoltinGrl

Only Mark could have thought it through so quickly. Revolting had more than one meaning. It was typical of Mark's sarcastic sense of humour.

So it was really happening. The excitement no longer

bearable, Alan did something he had never done before, something at once shocking and wonderful: he hugged Kate across the bikes. Then he kissed her on the lips, feeling lost and weightless with the ecstasy of the contact, the quickness of her surprise. He could not have moved a muscle again until Kate, with the same blossoming of friendship into love, kissed him back there in the shadowed lane, the bicycles interlocking like a promise between them.

Now, his heart racing with the thrill of her response, he saw the flush invade her face, an expanding tide about the roots of her auburn curls and down into her throat above her sweater, with its monogram opening letter from the *Book of Kells*.

Wordlessly, they wheeled the bikes around so they faced the town. The road was empty and they cycled side by side, Alan's jittery legs moving around in their own automatic motion, to the crossroads, with the slaughterhouse on the corner and the memory of animals bellowing in the trucks as they trundled in through the gates and the river tributary soon turning red with their blood. They wheeled right around the corner, picking up speed as they crossed over the first of the old stone bridges and then slowing momentarily at the second bridge, with the steps leading down to the river. With every turn of the pedals, the Comeragh Mountains loomed closer, their patchwork of green and yellow fields studded with whitewashed farm cottages, and, below them, extending southwards and westwards, the forests that fed Padraig's sawmill. They rode on into the sunrise in silence. All of a sudden, time was running away with them. And there was the scary feeling that it might never slow back to normal again.

The Swans

It had begun only a few months earlier, although now it seemed more like years. Alan had been fishing the River Suir upstream of some small islands opposite the big fork in the river. The morning was misty and cool, and the water meadow, which the locals called the Green, was overgrown, with grasses and rushes way higher than his knees. People said it was unusual. The plants were running wild that summer. The drier parts, up close to the riverbank, were dense with meadowsweet, floating over the ground in thick clouds, and filling his nostrils with its sweet scent. In his hands was the old bamboo three-piece he had borrowed from his grandfather, Padraig. He wasn't expecting to get a bite. Just looking for some space away from the bustle of the sawmill – and away from Padraig's intrusive fussing.

He hadn't got any closer to finding answers since arriving in Clonmel two months earlier. If anything the despair had relentlessly increased. It was there right now, as it was during every waking moment. Like the fire had gone out at the heart of him.

He had done his best to get it together. But he had nothing in common with the other kids here. He'd enrolled at the local high school thinking maybe he could connect with them through sport. He had always been pretty good at games. But even the games they played here were very different from back home. There was no American football, no baseball, no basketball, nothing. Football here was Irish football, where, as far as he could make out, they just slugged the daylights out of each other. That or the hurling, which was even worse. He must have looked half crazy to the other kids at times, his thoughts going blank on him, just standing there in the playground or sitting at his desk, his eyes staring, his limbs suddenly weighted down, like he was suited with lead. He just couldn't get his mind around the fact that Mom and Dad were gone, really gone, gone for good – period. How did you make sense out of something that couldn't possibly make any sense? With their loss came a great anger. He wanted to know why they had died. There had to be a reason – somebody who was responsible. He must have drifted into another of his blank spells, his eyes wide open but seeing nothing, when, abruptly, he came to with a sense of danger. There was a *homp-homp* noise from somewhere nearby, something strange cutting through the dreamy morning. And whatever it was, it was heading his way.

Then he saw the swans.

He had noticed their nest, with three huge eggs in it, on one of the small reedy islands that dotted the shallows. Something, maybe the toss of his line, had made the birds panic. The homp-homp was the beating of their wings as they took off, still only half out of the water and rising into the air like two white avenging angels. He saw every detail highlighted as if in slow motion: the pounding wings, the prideful black knobs on the upraised orange bills, the eyes all-black. He could hear the power in those webbed feet as they battered the surface. For several moments, as they cleared the water just thirty feet from where he was standing, he was overwhelmed by a sense of paralysis. He did nothing at all to save himself. He just stood still, returning, stare for stare, the rage in those alien eyes.

He felt a sudden blow, but from an altogether different direction to what he expected. He offered no resistance to being dragged to the ground in a confusion of bodies, arms and legs, hearing the splintering into pieces of the fishing rod, only distantly aware that he had ended up on his back with somebody else on top of him.

'Holy blessed mother – are you out of your mind?'

A voice, hot in his ear. A girl's voice!

He glimpsed a face, pallid as goat's cheese in striking contrast to the furnace of auburn hair. Immediately above them the swans clattered over their ground-hugging figures. His ears were full of a low throaty hissing. And then they were gone.

Alan just lay there for a while, the stuffing knocked out of him.

She spoke again. 'Did you hear the sound of them hissing?'

He swallowed.

She added, 'They're supposed to be mute!'

His neck felt stiff. He had to turn his head through a painful ninety degrees to look at his saviour, who was now sitting up beside him. He sat up himself, seeing they were both covered by the creamy petals of meadowsweet.

All of a sudden she laughed, staring after the swans, which were sweeping low over the gentle rise of the Green, clearing by inches the hedge at the top, and continuing the slow ascent until they dwindled to specks against the mountains.

'I . . . I guess it was my fault. My fishing must have spooked them.'

But she wasn't even listening to him. He heard her whisper, as if to herself, 'Sure, it's a sign.'

'A sign of what?'

'Like maybe they sensed something different about you.'

He didn't know what to say to that.

Climbing to his shaky feet, he must have looked even more awkward and gangly than usual. Alan had topped six feet on his fifteenth birthday, two weeks earlier. He kind of hoped he would stop growing soon so he wouldn't end up having to bend his neck to get through doors like his beanpole grandfather. He thought about helping her up but he wasn't sure she'd like it. Instead he extended his hand to shake hers.

'Hi! I'm Alan.'

She slapped his hand away instead of shaking it. She hopped to her feet with a grin and said, 'Kate Shaunessy!'

What had he done that was funny? There was an awkward silence. He could see in her eyes that she was weighing him up.

Man! He was useless at dealing with girls. And that made him feel even more awkward than ever. And now he was looking at her, very likely staring, and it was making her blush a bright scarlet. She whistled to a small black and white sheepdog, which came bounding up. She plucked at its coat, brushing it free of grass stalks and petals, like she was getting ready to leave.

He said, 'Thanks!'

He saw her eyes flash, like she had made up her mind about something. 'I've seen you out here before. Pretending to be fishing.'

'I never noticed you.'

'Why would you notice me? I've been watching you, moping around, feeling sorry for yourself.'

'I – I wasn't feeling sorry for myself.'

'I already knew who you are. I know you're an orphan.'

He shook his head, slowly, not knowing what to say.

Then he saw how she was trembling. She had been freaked out too. She blurted out, 'Oh, you needn't get embarrassed. I'm an orphan too.'

He stared at her for a long moment, wordless. Then he began to pick up the broken pieces of his grandad's rod, making the best he could of the tangle of line, so he could hold the bundle together in his right hand.

She walked about a dozen paces but then she stopped and patted the dog. He had the feeling she was waiting for him.

Alan caught up with Kate and her dog. He was thinking about what she had just told him: *I'm an orphan too.* The way she had said it, kind of defiantly. It made him hope that somehow you really did come to terms with the bad things, even if they never made any sense.

She said, 'I'm taking Darkie home. You can come with me, if you want. I'd like to show you something.'

'Show me what?'

'Are you interested in herbs?'

'I've never thought much about them.'

'Hmph!'

The mist had melted away from the morning and he hadn't even noticed it going. It felt like maybe a little of it had invaded his senses. His mind was groggy and his limbs felt numb, so he hardly registered the grassy bank under his feet as they passed by the island with the swans' eggs.

'Well I'm very interested. I've been learning about them. Teaching myself, really. With some help from Fergal.'

They abandoned the Green to enter the beaten dirt track that ran southwards along the riverbank.

'Fergal?'

'Fergal's my uncle. But he's a zoologist and not a botanist.'

They continued to chat and to stroll, following the dirt track, limited on their left by the slow-flowing River Suir and to their right by the hoary limestone wall that separated the river from the Presentation Convent School.

'Here, Darkie!'

Kate cracked open the right half of the gates, ushering the dog through, and then she waited for Alan to follow after it into a big, overgrown garden. They were within sight of a very strange-looking house.

A woman paused in emerging from a stonewall outbuilding, to take stock of them. Alan guessed that she must be the housekeeper for Kate's uncle, Fergal. She was about mid-sixties, stocky and aproned, with thick grey hair held back in a bun. Under one brawny arm she carried an enamel basin filled with newly washed bedding.

Kate said, 'Oh, Bridey – this is Alan.'

'Gor! I know who he is! Don't I see for meself Geraldine O'Brien looking back at me!'

Alan caught Kate's whispered, 'Sorry!' Geraldine O'Brien was his mother's maiden name. Dad had called her Gee.

'You knew Mom?'

He didn't know if his question embarrassed Bridey, or if she heard it at all. She was suddenly caught up with shaking her fist into the sky. 'Them blessed yokes, with their perpetual thundering!'

Alan glanced up at a jet passing high overhead. The sound might, at a pinch, be described as a thundering, however faint and distant.

Kate said, 'I'm showing Alan around the place. But you could tell him more about the house.'

'Sure he's not interested in this auld ruin.'

'Ma'am, I am interested.'

Bridey peered back at him with a look of suspicion. 'And why is that now? Because it looks so contrary?'

He couldn't help but smile at her choice of word for the house, which captured the look of it perfectly. 'Is it Victorian?'

'It started off as Georgian, but they went through a fit of overhauling it during Victorian times.' Bridey talked into the air, as if half-bemusedly to herself. 'That was the time when it got its name, the "Doctor's House". The Doctor in this case being the medical superintendent of what in them days was known as "the madhouse".'

Kate tugged at his arm to haul him away from Bridey's reminiscences. 'We're going to take a look at the garden.'

'Ah, be off the pair o' you! Leave me to feed Darkie! But mind you keep clear of them greenhouses. Sure that uncle of yours is as stubborn as the tide.'

Kate waited until Bridey and Darkie had disappeared through a side door into the house before explaining, 'My grandmother died when Fergal and Daddy were young.

Bridey became their nanny. Then when Daddy died at the mission in Africa, she blamed the planes.'

'She blamed the planes?'

'For taking him to Africa.'

Alan shook his head.

'She's convinced the house is cursed.'

'Cursed?'

'By what went on – in the old asylum.'

He smiled. 'You've got to admit it's a weird-looking house!'

'All the time I was growing up here I thought I was living in the same world that Lewis Carroll wrote about.'

The original house must have been compact and square, with sash windows divided up into small Georgian panes. But somebody, maybe the Victorian asylum keeper, had inserted an octagonal tower on one corner. Alan was standing right outside it, looking up at a structure of wooden frames filled with small glass panes, capped by an amazing minaret-style tower that soared to a tiny flagpole, bearing the Irish tricolour. On the gable ends of the house he saw other additions, very likely arising out of the same fantastic imagination. Ornate canopies topped fussy bay windows and porticos surrounded the front and back doors. There were additional dormer windows on the roof adjacent to soaring chimneys. The surrounding gardens were a labyrinth of arbours for roses, honeysuckle and stuff, so you could wander out of the house into a fairyland of scents and colours.

They carried on round to the back, taking a course that avoided some large greenhouses, with peeling paintwork and several broken panes.

He murmured, 'Looks to me like Bridey had a point!'

'It's nothing that a bit of fixing wouldn't make safe. They were properly cared for when Grandad was alive. He was interested in plants, an amateur like me. But Fergal is too busy to take proper care of them. Bridey wants to knock them all down. We're the only Shaunessys left of the family. She's terrified something bad will happen. But there are old memories, like when Daddy and Uncle Fergal were growing up. So Fergal can't bring himself to do it.'

She led Alan along a neglected path, overgrown with elderberry and nettles, bringing them face to face with a tunnel big enough to drive a car through. When they stepped inside, it was dank and gloomy. A hesitant light hovered around the entrance, as if fearful to penetrate deeper.

'I used to hide here from Bridey, playing hide-and-seek. It cuts right under the main road. Then there are all sorts of secret carriageways and tunnels before it finally comes out in the grounds of the hospital.'

'This still leads to the asylum?'

Kate nodded. 'It's a mental hospital now. Once I saw a picture of the old superintendent. He had huge side-whiskers and a beard like Father Christmas. The whole place was arranged so patients never left it even when they came to work here in the gardens.'

'Creepy!'

Kate hooted with laughter at the expression on his face. 'Some of the mad people still try to escape this way. Oh, I know I shouldn't call them that. There are times I feel madder than any of them myself. But Bridey could tell you stories. Those poor souls, they wade out into the river until it comes up to their chins. Then they shriek to the nurses that they'll drown themselves if anybody tries to come and save them.'

'Shee–it!'

She led him back to the house where they did a tour of the downstairs rooms. Bridey appeared with two glasses of orange juice, then left them to it. They carried their drinks into a study with collections of tropical insects mounted in frames.

'Your uncle works with insects?'

'He's an entomologist at University College Cork. He's off right now counting new species in the African jungle before they become extinct.' Then, with what seemed a clumsy abruptness, she just came right out with it and asked him how his parents had died.

Alan was startled into silence.

'You don't have to tell me, if you don't want to.'

'There isn't much to say. It was an accident.'

'What kind of accident?'

He looked down at his feet. Would she never stop asking him questions? 'It was in March – just a lousy accident.'

She slumped down into a chair and toyed with

her orange. She said, 'I'm sorry! I didn't mean to upset you.'

He remained standing, annoyed with himself for letting his feelings show. 'How about your folks?'

'Mammy and Daddy were murdered.'

'Oh, man!'

'You don't need to worry. I've got used to it.'

He took a deep breath. 'I'd been on a school skiing trip. It was snowing a bit but it wasn't any kind of a snowstorm. Dad and Mom were coming to pick me up. A special treat in a chopper. Dad was an experienced pilot. He wouldn't have taken any risk. A bunch of us, school friends, we wanted to get one more run on the slopes. I look back and I think it was a really stupid thing to do. I keep thinking, what if we hadn't gone back for that last run? A kid called Rudy Forrester broke his leg. It was a really bad break, with his shinbone poking out through his skin. Mom and Dad – they had to take him to the hospital about thirty miles away. They were supposed to come right back for me.'

The silence between them lasted several seconds.

'All my life, well, I guess I was your typical American kid. You could say I was one of those laid-back guys. To tell you the truth–!' Alan's right hand suddenly came up and he slapped it against his head, like he somehow wanted to just punch sense into it.

She jumped to her feet and grabbed at his arm. 'Please, Alan! Don't do that. Don't blame yourself.'

His brown eyes grew distant. 'I guess . . . I guess I was some kind of a stupid jerk. The kind of kid who just goes through life without really thinking all that much about anything.'

She held onto his arm, almost hugging it to her. 'What happened to them? Was it an accident?'

'That's what the wreck report said. They made a big thing about the fact it was snowing – and the fact Dad wasn't familiar with the area. But he was a really good pilot. I just don't buy it.'

'You don't think it was an accident?'

'My grandfather, Padraig, doesn't think so. He's downright paranoid about it.'

'What? He thinks it was suspicious?'

'I know it sounds kind of crazy. But that's what he thinks.'

She took him into a large sitting room, with its big chintzy lounge suite and dark mahogany furniture. The strange tower came off it on one corner, and there was an upholstered window seat so you could sit in there and look out into the garden. There were photographs on the walls of waterfalls, and safari shots of lions, zebras, elephants and crocodiles. In between the photographs, Alan saw rusty iron spears and big wooden clubs. He looked at pictures of a younger Kate with her parents outside single-storey buildings with white walls and red-tile roofs. They were surrounded by palm trees and colourful tropical plants. Kate's parents looked slim, medium height. Her father was black-haired and her mother was red-haired, like Kate herself, but a lighter, more golden, red. There was a boy, who looked younger than Kate, with the same red hair.

She brushed her finger over the glass in the frame. 'My brother, Billy.'

'And all that's what – some kind of medical mission?'

'It was a Belgian Catholic Mission, with a school and a small hospital. Mammy was the matron of the hospital and Daddy was the doctor. They worked in the Democratic Republic of the Congo all of the time I was growing up. Billy and me, we lived here with Uncle Fergal and Bridey.' Her green eyes filled with longing. 'We used to really look forward to going out there and joining Mammy and Daddy in the long holidays. The mission was close to the gorilla forest. There were palm trees in the grounds and all sorts of fabulous plants. Right outside our bungalow was a giant aloe that sent up seed flowers as tall as a tree. Then, when they seeded, the whole plant just withered away and died. Sister Marie Thérèse, she was like the Bridey over there. She had such a sense of fun. She used to tell us stories of what the patients did behind the doctors' and nurses' backs. They still believed in spells and potions. She called them *les petites feticheurs*! I loved the Africans too. They needed so very little to make them happy. Mammy used to say that the best smiles she ever saw were African smiles.'

Alan saw that the living room was like a mirror image

of the living room back at the sawmill. Bridey and Padraig had each made a shrine to happier times.

'What happened, Kate?'

Her head jerked and her eyes darkened. 'There was a lot of trouble going on. There were enough bad people locally already without others coming out of Rwanda. Mammy and Daddy had been told to leave. But they knew if they abandoned the hospital the mission would have been finished. And they thought they were safe because they were a hundred and fifty kilometres away from the border.' She hesitated, blinking a little fast, still staring at the photographs.

'Good job you weren't there!'

'I was there and so was Billy.' Kate inhaled and her nostrils dilated. 'Sister Marie Thérèse saved me. She was in charge of the kitchen gardens. We were out there gathering vegetables when we heard the trucks drive in and then the shots and the screaming. I wanted to run back but she stopped me. There was a . . . a kind of pit. An underground store where she kept yams and stuff. She pushed me into it.' Kate sniffed and rubbed at her nose. 'I hid there all through it.' He could see she was doing her best to fight back tears. 'I was still there when government soldiers came around, I don't know how many days later. They found me in the pit. They . . . they told me the rebels had killed them all . . . everybody . . .'

'Hey—!'

'I had counselling. I couldn't bear to go out. I couldn't

face meeting people – nobody. Not even my friends.' Kate's face was flushed and her eyelids were blinking so fast they were fluttering. She looked very different from the girl who had pushed him out of the way of the swans.

He touched her shoulder, spoke to her softly. 'C'mon, Kate! Let's go explore the garden!'

She scampered back out through the door, half running. He gave her a little space to recover her composure. When he caught up with her he found himself standing at the top of a gentle slope of lawn leading down to the open river. Alan followed her gaze across the forty yards of reed-strewn water to the Green, and beyond that, to the mountains, which were so close you felt you could put out your hand and touch them. He realised that they were almost exactly opposite the place he had been fishing, but closer to the big fork in the river.

'A good job Bridey wasn't watching us earlier!'

Kate managed a nervous laugh. 'Bridey would have needed binoculars. But if she had, she'd have had a heart attack.' She was hurrying on again. 'Come on – I told you there was something I wanted to show you!'

'Show me what?'

'You won't know about BSBI.'

'What's that?'

'The Botanical Society of the British Isles. I'm helping them with a project on rare and threatened plants.' She stopped in front of a small tilled piece of the garden, right by the water, about as far away from the house as you could possibly get. It was divided up into tiny beds, each about a foot square, separated from its neighbours by uneven rows of bricks. He guessed that Kate had laid out the bricks.

'You see?'

The beds were empty except for one.

'Are you kidding me?'

'Go on! Take a closer look!' Kate went down onto her haunches and so he did the same. He saw a flower that looked a bit like a dandelion. The label read 'Irish fleabane (*Inula salicina*) – rare. K.S. Clonmel, Tipperary'.

'K.S. – that you?'

She nodded, proudly. 'It's on the threatened list. I'm waiting for the seeds so I can send them to the gene bank people in Dublin.'

'Huh!'

She glanced across at him with a wry smile. 'If you're really interested, maybe you could help me.'

'I know nothing about this stuff. If you hadn't told me what it was, I'd have looked at that plant and I'd have seen a weed.'

Kate's eyes turned to the Comeragh Mountains, to the forests that clambered over the lower slopes. 'I just knew it was fate. Your grandfather's woods cover half of those foothills. There are bits of the old original forests up there on the slopes. Bogs, even!'

From the chatter of words she had flung into the air like seeds, Alan's mind plucked out one more curious than all the others: fate.

The Blooming

Mark Grimstone was glad he had agreed to keep his sister company while Mo was looking for crystals. They had scouted a few rocky fields before cutting in to explore the dense woods off the Dungarvan Road. After three-quarters of an hour of walking through shadows and being bitten by midges, they came out into a natural clearing, with a white rocky scarp at one edge. Mo went to investigate while Mark passed a moment or two looking around him, swivelling on the heel of his left trainer. Her squeal of delight meant a discovery had been made.

They would spend an hour or two here. Mark sat in a patch of grass, lounging back against a heather-covered outcrop, whipping at insects with a switch of ash and wondering why the Reverend Grimstone, his adoptive father, had brought them to the Irish backwater of Clonmel.

Grimstone would play his usual games, pulling in the more gullible locals – those hoping for salvation from their personal demons – into his rituals of head-touching and shouting their sins aloud. This was all in a day's work for Grimstone's style of hellfire and brimstone. But why Clonmel? Mark couldn't fathom it. He gave up trying, and slumped back against the outcrop, watching his sister search for treasures against the sun-bright scarp of pearly rock.

Mo was happy poking around among the crystals, or finding something that caught her eye in a single flower head or an insect scuttling among the stems and roots. She'd take ages examining her finds before sketching them into her album. Mark dropped his head, plucking a battered harmonica from the breast pocket of his short-sleeved shirt. His fingers caressed it, as if the feel of it was comforting, and he played a few riffs to while the time away. His eyelids never completely closed, but he relaxed into a daydream, lulled by the peacefulness of the woods and the image of his sister searching for crystals. He so abandoned himself in mind-mazing that he lost track of time. Only when he noticed that his face and forearms were burning did he swear aloud, causing Mo to lift her head.

'Mo! You might have warned me.'

'I – I've guh-guh-guh . . . guh-got the cuh-cuh-cream.' Her stammer worsened because he was annoyed with her.

'Oh, it's all right! I'll come and get it.'

He climbed back up onto his knees, rubbing the skin of his face with hands that were also growing increasingly lobsterish. He was burnt all over. And now he saw, with a start of alarm, that they were not alone. A man was watching them from the far edge of the clearing. Dressed in worn denims and leather boots that were laced to just below his knees, he was as lean as a scarecrow, with a face that looked like a weather-beaten mask pulled tight over a long bony skull. It was with a thrill of alarm that Mark noticed his eyes. They were an intense bright blue, so luminous that even from a hundred feet away they seemed to glow with an inner source of light.

Suddenly the man stepped out of the shadows and, with a long-legged amble, he closed in on Mo.

She abandoned her backpack and notebook and, scuttling over to Mark's side, she clutched his arm so fiercely he winced with pain from his sunburnt skin.

'Are you aware this is a private wood?'

The words were spoken in a bass growl. And now he stood over them, the stranger was as tall as a door.

'We're sorry! We didn't know we were trespassing.'

'English it would seem, judging by your accent.'

'Stop buh-buh-buh-bullying muh-muh-my brother!'

The old man's cheeks were lined with vertical wrinkles so deep they could have been gouged by a chisel. His eyes, swivelling from Mark to his sister, were like searchlights.

'You don't much resemble brother and sister.'

Mark muttered, 'We're adopted, if it's any of your business.'

The tall man paused a moment, as if to reappraise Mo

anew. 'And your names, if you please, without the boldness?'

'I'm Mark Grimstone and this is my sister, Mo.'

'Yes, and if I'm not mistaken, you must be the brood of the visiting Reverend Grimstone?'

'You've met him?'

'Met him? I certainly have not. Nor would I ever wish to do so. Just what do the pair of you think you're doing in my wood?'

'My sister is interested in crystals.'

The man gazed down at Mo, focusing the intense blue eyes on her cowering shape. 'It was crystals then you were drawing in your notebook?'

Mo nodded glumly.

'Well then, go and fetch it. Show me your drawings.'

Mo ran to fetch both her backpack and the notebook. She handed the book up to the stranger.

The man plucked some iron-rimmed glasses out of the breast pocket of his shirt. His gnarled hands thumbed through the tiny pages and the blue searchlights passed over the drawings and words. His frown turned to curiosity. 'Strange and potent images, for all that they are in miniature! And these words that go by them, if words they might be at all, are in no language that I recognise.'

'Mo writes in a language of her own.'

The old man shook his head. 'Why would a child go to such extremes?'

'So nobody else can read it.'

The blue eyes were softer now as they confronted Mark's own. The obvious question lay in the air between them. But the old man was prudent enough to leave it unasked. Instead he turned back to the notebook and carried on browsing. Suddenly he stopped, his finger tracing one of the images. Whatever the old man had seen, it was enough to turn him from the book to Mo, studying her with the same intensity of scrutiny he had previously focused on the book.

'Perhaps your presence here is not without purpose?'

Mark was curious as to what the old man had seen in Mo's notebook. He was still eyeing Mo, with intense interest. 'Sure you're as elegant as the famous boy pharaoh.'

Mo lifted up her hazel eyes to confront his blue. 'Cuh-cuh-cuh-can I have muh-muh-my notebook back, please?'

'On a condition! Will you be so good as to show me what it was you were so busy sketching by the white rock?'

He held the notebook low enough for her to point out her most recent drawings and secret writings, which covered two pages. Then he studied the pages again through the iron-rims, glancing from her drawings to the white rock and back again. He whistled. 'Well now – aren't you the most remarkable creature. Here I recognise quartz and pyrites, here purple amethyst and ultramarine turquenite. You have the geometry of their structures – that's a fact. But you've captured something deeper than any ordinary eye might see.'

Mo flushed.

'And did you plan to take away some crystals in your satchel?'

It took Mo a second or two to recognise he meant her backpack. She shook her head vigorously. 'That wuh-would be suh-suh-suh-stealing.'

'Not if I were to give you permission. An artist of your skill demands that much respect. So take what you will of them. Explore my woods wherever you will, or must.' He returned the notebook to Mo.

Mo nodded her thanks, although her whole body was trembling.

'A final question. How long have you been here, in Clonmel?'

Mark answered, 'A little over a week.'

'Yet still time enough for one gifted with such vision. Tell me, Mo Grimstone, have you been surprised by what you've observed here?'

Mark said, protectively, 'What kind of question is that?'

'Let your sister answer for herself, if she has a mind to.'

Mo gazed back up at him again. 'Whu-whu—?'

The tall man leaned closer to Mo, so he could see the true expression in her eyes. 'Take your time to find the words. I'm interested to know what might have captured your attention.'

'In nuh-nuh-nature?'

'In nature maybe – or in the nature of things?'

'Nuh-nuh-nature is buh-buh-buh . . .' Mo shook her head, frustrated in her attempts to express the word.

Mark hissed, 'I've had enough of this. Just leave her alone.'

A huge hand descended over Mark's left shoulder. 'Patience just a moment longer. Leave her room to speak her mind.'

'. . . buh-buh-blooming.'

'Nature is blooming?'

Mo nodded.

The tall man held his face close to that of the girl a moment longer before he straightened up and gazed about himself at the ring of trees.

'These woods are a confusion of trails and half-trails. Will you be able to find your way back the way you came?'

'Of course we will.' Mark turned on his heel as if to walk away, but Mo put her hand on his sunburnt arm.

'Your sister is not so sure?'

Mark sighed. 'Okay. So why don't you show us the way out?'

The old man looked down at their anxious faces and abruptly turned on his heel, his long paces already creating such a lead they had to run after him. He called back over his shoulder without breaking stride. 'Oh, I think I'll do better than that. I'll escort the pair of you to meet a matching pair of scallywags. You might find you have mischief in common.'

Kate's notion of fate had come to interest Alan a lot more over the days that followed that first meeting by the river.

The loss of Mom and Dad had certainly made him wonder about fate. But he wasn't sure he believed in it. At least not the superstitious notion of it that Kate and his grandfather had in mind. Over the ten days since then he had enjoyed getting together with her at the sawmill. They had agreed to a daily ramble, planning a route the night before. So far they hadn't saved any threatened plants from extinction, but they had found a fleabane that was heading towards vulnerable and a cudweed that, if it wasn't threatened, was still kind of interesting, at least to Kate. Enough to plant two more beds in the garden of the Doctor's House.

Then, sometime in the middle of all this, Kate had clapped her hands and exclaimed, 'We need to get better organised!'

'What do you mean – like some kind of place of our own?'

She clapped her hands. 'A den!'

He had talked to his grandfather about it, and only yesterday Padraig had finally agreed that they could use the former dairy, a detached red-brick outhouse in the shade of a dilapidated old pear tree that was peripheral to the main house and the sawmill complex of buildings. And today, after Kate had arrived, they went to have a good look at the place, finding it filthy, with outdated wiring and old lead plumbing, and chock-full of rubbish.

Alan pulled a face. 'Boy – what a mess! It looks like it's been abandoned for half a century.'

But Kate was more enthusiastic. 'We'll just have to put off rambling for a few days and get it sorted out.'

They had only just begun the clearout when Padraig came striding in off the slopes with two strangers in tow: a slim flaxen-haired boy with a bad case of sunburn, and a girl with strikingly bronze skin and shoulder-length dark brown hair. The boy looked fifteen or sixteen, maybe the same age as Alan and Kate, but the girl looked more like twelve or thirteen.

'Company for you!' Padraig tossed the comment into the air and was gone.

Kate was as surprised as Alan with the appearance of the two strangers, who were peering curiously at the cluster of buildings that stood back from the road, including Padraig's plain two-storey Victorian house, built of the same liver-coloured bricks as the dairy, and the labyrinth of corrugated iron sheds, surrounded by piles of logs. Padraig's return to work was announced by the high-pitched scream of an industrial wood saw.

'Hi!' she said, smiling. 'I'm Kate.'

The youth blinked at her, looking embarrassed. 'Hi!' he said. 'I'm Mark and this is my sister, Mo.'

'And that's Alan.' She waved to where her newfound American friend was lounging against the trunk of the pear tree.

Alan lifted an arm in greeting.

'You're English – over here on holiday?' Kate enquired.

'We wandered into the woods and got lost. The old man found us and brought us back here.'

Alan shoved himself off the tree and came to stand next to Kate. 'He's my grandfather, Padraig.'

'You don't sound local, either. You're American.'

'Yeah, I'm American. Padraig is an O'Brien, my mother's father. Or I should say was – my folks are dead.'

'Mine too,' Kate added. 'We're both orphans.'

Mark looked as if he didn't quite know what to say to that. He exchanged glances with Mo, whose eyes widened. Kate thought she had amazingly beautiful eyes, a pearly hazel in colour, and nothing like the blue eyes of her brother. They appeared lambent against the bronze tones of her skin.

'Whu-whu-whu-what you suh-said about being orphans?'

Kate blinked, taken aback by Mo's stammer. 'It's true. We're both orphans. But, well, you know, it was a lot more recent for Alan – only months ago.'

Mo's eyes shifted fleetingly to Mark, but they returned to look directly at Kate. Her face was tense, her look questioning as she added, 'Muh-Muh-Mark and I, wuh-wuh-we're . . . adopted.'

Alan exclaimed, 'What? Like you're not really brother and sister?'

'Oh, I can't believe this,' Kate implored. 'Don't tell me – you're not saying that you're orphans too?'

Mark shrugged. 'We think we are. But we don't really know if we're orphans or not.'

'You don't even know – sure that's awful,' muttered Kate'

'We're used to it.'

Alan groaned, 'I can't believe this. It's all getting like too much of a coincidence!'

For several moments an uncomfortable silence pervaded the company. Then it was Mo who was the first to break the tension, shoving past Mark, to peer into the outhouse. Her gaze took in a jumble of old furniture and pieces of outdated woodcutting equipment. The place stank, as if generations of cats had used it for a toilet. 'So whuh-whuh-whuh-what are you planning?'

Alan shoved a clump of brown hair off his brow. 'We're going to make the dairy into a den.'

Mark and Mo couldn't fail to notice that, under his fringe, Alan had a red triangular birthmark in the centre of his forehead.

Kate added, 'And we could do with some help.'

Mark seemed to be the last of them to shrug off the tension. Judging from the look on his face, he wasn't sure that he wanted to spend the rest of the day shifting rubbish.

Mo appeared to read her brother's mind. She said, 'Cuh-cuh-can't we help them, Mark? Oh, cuh-cuh-cuh . . . c'mon.'

Alan nodded up to the ceiling where there was an antiquated electric light fitting. 'Looks like we've got juice. And there's an old porcelain sink over there. So we've got water too, if maybe just a cold faucet and lead-piped, so definitely not drinkable. This place used to be a real dairy, back whenever. You've got to watch the floor because it slopes away to the corner where you see the sink. But hey! We get the junk shifted and we've got space for stuff, like maybe a table and chairs and even a phone line.'

Mark sniffed at the green-stained sink. 'You really think you could rig up a connection?'

'I don't see why not. There are two separate lines going into the house and the sawmill. All we've got to do is to hook up to one of them.'

'We could set up a computer station?' Mark's spirits were beginning to lift. He and Mo only had another week, but even a week could become interesting.

'Don't see why not.'

'We could download stuff – music?'

'Sure! We could party!'

Kate cut through the exchanges. 'Partying wasn't what I had in mind.'

'Kate here is saving Ireland's plants from extinction. I've been recruited to help her. The den will be our headquarters.'

'Wow!' Mark pretended to be impressed.

Mo muttered, 'Shu-shu-shut up, Mark!'

The two youths grinned, struggling to control themselves.

Mark lifted his eyebrows at Kate. 'Maybe we can work out a compromise?'

Kate shook her fist at him. 'The only compromise I'll give you is a meeting between this fist and your scalded English face!'

The two boys fell into uncontrollable laughter.

Mo raked her fingernail along Mark's spine as Kate blushed a furious red. For a moment the two girls looked at each other. Then Mo's lips pouted and she waved Kate to join her. 'Cuh-cuh-cuh . . . Oh, come on, Kate!'

There was no getting out of the chore after that. Mark, still laughing at times, threw himself into it as hard as the others. Clearing the dairy of junk took several hot and sweaty hours. All four of them ended up covered in dirt and spider webs. Alan tugged and hammered at the single cold tap until he got it working, and they washed their hands and faces over the white porcelain sink. They filled up some empty bottles so they could sprinkle water over the concrete floor, getting ready to broom it clean. A careless sprinkle and they ended up throwing the water over each other amid hoots of laughter. An hour later, with the sun heading west, they found an old wooden table and an assortment of chairs, so they could settle down and rest in a little more comfort, feasting on Irish ham sandwiches and ice-cold orange juice from Padraig's kitchen.

A sweat-streaked Kate rested her face on her interlaced knuckles and looked across the table at the fair-haired English boy. His short-sleeved shirt was muddied and streaked. Could it really be that all four of them were orphans? And if so, was Alan right – was this too much to put down to coincidence? The thought caused an anxious fluttering of her heart. She noticed Mark lifting a battered looking harmonica from his shirt pocket and she watched how he toyed with it on the scratched bare wood of the table.

'Are you going to give us a tune?'

His face flushed an even deeper red with embarrassment and he stuffed the harmonica back into the shirt pocket. But from time to time, as they munched and got to know one another, Kate noticed that he would glance her way, as if mentally assessing this bossy Irish girl with her green eyes and a temper to match the colour of her hair.

The Sigil

Mark and Mo were late in getting back to the rented house, formerly a Church of Ireland parsonage, where their adoptive mother, Bethal, was impatiently waiting. Bethal was tall, grey-eyed and bony, with long mousy hair plaited like a show horse's tail and long unshapely hands that always looked raw. Now, in the gloom of the oak-panelled entrance hall, she shrank from the grimy appearance of their clothes.

'Filthy toads!' Her lips were inadequate to cover her gravestones of teeth. 'Filthy! *Filthy* in body and soul!'

With her ribs thrust out, she blocked entry to the tunnel-like corridor that led to the ground-floor washroom.

'Get up there! Let Sir see for himself the state you're in! He'll know what to do about it!'

So saying, she harried them upstairs with raps of her knuckles against the backs of their skulls, on through the tiers of chairs in the Meeting Hall and the tabletop makeshift altar, and through the heavy door into the office-cum-sacristy at the back. Here she abandoned them with a slam of the door. Late as they were, evening worship had not long ended and the pungent odour of sweat still permeated the Hall and chased them into the inner sanctum. Sweat, lots of it, was an integral part of Grimstone's services, which had little to say about the gentle Lord Jesus. The Lord he venerated skulked away from the light in deeper and darker places, devoid of anything a normal priest or vicar would have recognised as Christian caring and kindness.

On entering the sacristy, they saw that his soiled dog collar had been flung onto the desk surface. They also saw, with a slender hope, that he had little or no interest in their lateness, or, for that matter, the dirtied state of their clothes. Ignoring the clatter of their arrival, Grimstone leaned against the sill, while staring out into the fading evening through the wide round-topped window. As usual when he was coming down from the high of a service, the black silk shirt was stuck to him with sweat, sculpting his heavily muscled body.

They waited in silence for more than a minute, listening to the deep methodical rasp of his breathing.

'You've been wondering why I brought you here? I know you have, so don't bother to deny it.' His voice was quiet, a sonorous growl, but they knew him well enough to sense danger.

'Well, much as it surprises me too, this town is of

growing interest.' He inhaled a deep draught of the cool air of evening. 'There is the reek of old power here. Not that you would catch the whiff of it. It is almost buried and forgotten, yet lingering, the way heavy stinks do. Maybe you girl, with your whore-witch heritage, can actually smell it? I've seen you scribbling into that book. So tell me what you've discovered.'

'The nuh-nuh-nuh . . . the name is Cuh-Cuh-Celtic.'

'Cuh-Cuh-Celtic! Of course it's Celtic. Clonmel in their degenerate tongue means the Vale of Honey. But this stink is older . . . far older still. Pah! Why do I waste my breath on the likes of you! What can you tell me that I don't know already?'

'I'm nuh-nuh-nuh . . . nuh-not sure, Suh-Sir.'

'You're nuh-nuh-nuh-not sure? Well, let me explain then what is to be done. We face a more formidable challenge than I realised when I came here to proselytise this backwater. Why, then, I hear your small minds wondering, does he bother to share the good news with us? Why? Because it is my Lord himself, my sacred Master, who senses the threat. The threat is to Him. Oh, yes, indeed. He senses a threat to Him, here in this town, in the old power that still lingers here.'

Mark muttered, 'A threat, Sir?'

Grimstone's head was nodding slowly, his hair glistening with an opalescent sheen of sweat. 'I had anticipated every sewer of Papist heresy, with its confessionals and slothful delusions. But this is far worse. What's at the bottom of it? A lingering relic of the old paganism? I wouldn't be surprised.' His voice rose, throaty and rasping. 'Old power! Old power, and a threat to My Lord, that by His blessed will, I will expose and crush.'

Only now, as he spun round to face them, did they see that the black metal cross, the symbol of the church Grimstone had personally founded, was clasped in his right hand. He lifted it lovingly against his brow, pressed its embossed sigil against the scars of many such impressions, a new branding. Although the cross did not look hot, the smell of his burning flesh pervaded the room. Then he intoned the mantra:

'My own Lord! My beloved Master! My personal salvation!'

Mark and Mo shivered, their eyes averted from the repulsive sight. The cross was matted and gnarled with great age. He never tired of recounting how he had acquired it, when, as a young man, he had been a wastrel, heading for perdition. He had rescued the cross from an elderly antiquarian, a greedy robber of graves. Yet the very moment he first held it in his hands, he had his first vision. So forceful was the shock of revelation, he had lost consciousness. When he came round, the collector was dead, drowned in his own blood. Grimstone had staggered from the antiquarian's home, already glimpsing his destiny in the truth and power of the cross. He had dismissed the antiquarian's claim – sometimes there were hints that he had tested that claim on the antiquarian's lips in more violent forms than mere words – that it had come from a barrow grave that dated to long before the Christian era. Instead Grimstone pretended that it was a Templar relic, dating back to the Crusades.

He had kept his discovery to himself for some years, immersing himself in ancient learning. Only when he felt ready did he present himself as witness, to begin the foundation of the Islington Church of the Sigil, named after the silvery shape embossed into the metal where the figure of Jesus would normally be, a shape that resembled the symbol for infinity, but comprising three twisted circles of silver instead of two.

No one other than Grimstone was allowed to hold the cross. It was brought out at the high point of conversion for every new flock, a blessing for their eyes, but not their kiss or their touch, and only when they had proved their devotion through weeks of induction leading to a final service of proclamation and dedication, ready to be born again in veneration of Grimstone's unforgiving Lord. It was usually put away after the service ended. But the fact Grimstone had kept it out this evening, that he was still venerating the sigil after the service, was ominous.

Knowing this, Mark's and Mo's hearts quailed as Grimstone turned his back on them, looking down the fall of the gentle hill into the town, where twilight now clothed the rendered walls and slated roofs, his eyes finally alighting on the river.

'The river should also interest you, witch-foetus. Its name suggests a paganish worship by a race much older than the Celts. Half savages, like your whore of a mother. Now I know you haven't missed the lingering signs in your scratching and searching in the dirt?'

'Nuh-nuh-nuh-nuh . . . nuh-nuh . . .'

'Quack-quack-quack! Enough of your quacking! Three rivers – evocative of the foulest pretence – the stink of a heathen trinity?'

'I . . . I duh-duh-duh-don't know.'

'Liar!'

His growl deepened. 'Old power! Its grip long vanquished, yet such is its hold on the very landscape, it has endured.'

Grimstone inhaled, a deep breath, then, deeming his body sufficiently cooled, he turned away from the open window. His eyes, almost coal-black in the gloom, confronted them.

'I will have no more lies – not a single word! I know where you have been today, from moment to moment, and who you met. I want you to describe every detail of it to me. Not a morsel omitted!'

Mo spoke first, risking his anger. 'I tuh-tuh-tuh-took us into the woods . . . like yuh-you asked me to.'

Mark felt a stab of horror, realising now that the day had been manipulated by Grimstone. The trespassing and, very likely, everything else that had come from it, had been planned. But why?

'Don't keep me waiting!'

Mark described the clearing in the woods where Mo

had found some crystals, and drawn them in her notebook. The appearance of the old man, Padraig.

'I know you had a lengthy conversation with this man.'

Mark blinked with a second shock of realisation; somebody must have followed them, watched them constantly, closely enough to see what was happening but not close enough to overhear the conversation.

He described how Padraig had warned them they were trespassing. How he had questioned them.

'He asked you your names?'

'Yes.'

'Did he recognise your names?'

'Yes, Sir! He knew about you.'

'What did he know? His precise words?'

Mark did his best to imitate the deep-throated local accent. '"You must be the visiting brood of the Reverend Grimstone?"'

'Brood indeed!'

'I asked him if he had met you.' Mark tried the accent again. '"Met him, I certainly have not. Nor would I ever wish to do so."'

Grimstone's eyes widened. 'But he didn't immediately order you out?'

'He saw the crystals Maureen had drawn into her notebook. He was really impressed with them. He went on a bit – I didn't understand all of it.' Mark did a fair imitation of Padraig, '"You have the geometry of their structures, that's easy to see. But you've captured something deeper than ordinary eye might see of them."'

Grimstone's hand fell on Mark's left shoulder. 'Something deeper? What was the old fool alluding to?'

'He didn't explain. He said something like . . . an artist of Maureen's skill should be treated with respect. He said she could help herself to the crystals, if she wanted to take them.'

The hand squeezed harder. 'His exact words!'

'"So take what you will of them. Explore my woods wherever you must." Then he gave the notebook back to her.'

'Yet still he did not send you away?'

'No, Sir.'

'You've missed something out. You know what will happen if you continue to try my patience!'

'He asked how long we had been in Clonmel. I told him, one week. Then he said something really odd. Something about time enough for somebody like Maureen.'

A hard slap on his sunburnt cheek jerked Mark's head to one side.

He bit his lip, continued with what he recalled of Padraig's exact words, '"Time enough for someone gifted with . . . with vision." Then he asked her another odd question. "Have you been surprised by what you've observed here?"'

'Ah!'

'He didn't explain. He just told Maureen to take her

time to find the right words. "I'm interested to know what might have captured your attention."'

'I knew it! I knew there was something else. And what had caught our little witch's attention?'

Mark glanced at Mo, a mute blink of apology. 'She said something stupid, or at least it seemed stupidly obvious. She just said, "Nature is blooming."'

'That's it? "Nature is blooming"?' The dark eyes swung over to confront Mo from a distance of a foot or so.

She nodded.

Before Grimstone could turn his full attention onto Mo, Mark continued, 'He took us back to the sawmill, where we met an American boy called Alan Duval and a local girl called Kate Shaunessy.'

'He made a point of introducing you to this pair?'

'Yes, Sir.'

Mark went on to explain what had happened at the sawmill, the hard work of clearing out the room for a den. Grimstone demanded every detail. Mark didn't mention computers, music or partying. When his story was finished, Grimstone remained thoughtful for several seconds, during which time he held Mark in the intense focus of his gaze.

'I want you to cultivate this friendship.'

Mark was astonished. 'You want us to spy on them?'

Grimstone merely stared.

Mark felt bewildered. All the interrogation, and now this! He wondered if Grimstone had finally gone stark raving mad. But even in madness he saw the glimmer of an opportunity.

'Does this mean, Sir, that we'll be staying here in Clonmel for longer?'

'My flock is growing. I have become aware of the real challenge here. We shall stay until I am satisfied that my work is complete.'

Mark hesitated, then blurted it out. 'It – it might help if I had a mobile phone.'

'Are you bargaining with me?'

'No, Sir! They would expect it, Alan and Kate. Mobiles are equipped to take pictures, capture images, even video images. If I'm seen to take pictures with a camera, they'll be suspicious. But they'll take no notice of a mobile.'

Those eyes still glared into Mark's, as if reading his mind.

'There's some ulterior motive?'

'No, Sir.'

Grimstone pinched a fold of Mark's sunburnt right cheek, squeezing the inflamed skin hard enough to make him wince.

'It's that caterwauling you call music, isn't it?'

'No, Sir!'

'You mean, "Yes, Sir." You'll find some way of stuffing the gadget with that sluttish screeching. That's what it is. Don't lie to me.'

Grimstone's pinch tightened until it brought tears to Mark's eyes, but still he defied his adoptive father.

Grimstone drew back his right hand, still holding the cross. His eyes widened and he almost seemed ready to strike.

Mo wailed, 'Duh-duh-duh-duh-duh . . . duh-don't huh-hurt him!'

For a moment Grimstone's eyes were unfocused with rage. But then, abruptly, his expression altered. His eyes refocused. He brought the cross back into contact with his brow and pressed it hard against the overheated flesh. For what seemed like ages he held it there with his eyes clenched shut. When he opened them again he patted Mark's swollen cheek, as if it had all been no more than a game between father and son.

'Very well! Have your gadget if it's what you really want. Even the most righteous of fathers must show a little indulgence.' He reached down and drew Mo close to him. His arms enfolded them both in a single sweat-soured embrace. 'Why do you provoke me? Are we not a loving family in this, the most sacred of tasks?'

'Yes, Sir!'

'And you, daughter! What can we not contemplate?'

Mark reached out, unseen, to find Mo's hand, to hold it as he had done a thousand times before.

'Fuh-fuh-fuh-fuh-fuh . . . failure, Sir!'

Friends

Mo's observation proved to be prophetic. Nature really was blooming. And as July grew hotter the world grew more lush. Even Bridey remarked on it. 'Sure Mother Nature's abandoned her modesty.'

To get through gaps in the hedgerows they had to battle their way through thistles six feet tall, with bristly stems as thick as fall pipes, fighting for space with hogweed, ragwort, and the purple-headed fountains of giant stinging nettles. The untilled fields became lakes of wild flowers. Even in the thick woods around the sawmill the trees were so heavy with leaves you only had to walk into the woods and you were plunged into twilight. The air shrilled so loudly with birdsong it hurt your ears. Even the little grassy glades, where growth was usually scant, were waist-deep in grasses, the air so heady with scents, so clouded with swarms of butterflies, it was like wandering into an enchanted garden.

Meanwhile the four friends worked at getting their den in order, at times going at it almost frantically, as if, instinctively, they sensed that time was short. For days they scrubbed and hammered, all the while getting to know each other.

They emulsioned the walls and the ceiling and covered most of the floor with a mat. Padraig indulged them with whatever they asked for, including the paint and the floor covering. An electrician arrived to replace the old wiring, putting in a working light and a deck of wall sockets close to the table. With a little more persuasion, he put in a phone line.

When they arrived on the fourth sunshiny morning, they found a battered little electric oven and a fridge waiting for them outside the door. From now on they could heat pizzas and cool their drinks. Alan humped over the desktop computer he normally kept in his bedroom.

Within minutes Mark was parked in front of it. He had already figured out how to connect it to his new state-of-the-art mobile phone.

Alan quizzed him, 'What are you up to?'

'Begging, stealing and borrowing dreams.'

'Like what?'

'Like Stevie Ray Vaughn, *Couldn't Stand the Weather*.'

'Never heard of him!'

'Had a big patch on his left arm – just here.' Mark tapped about halfway up his forearm. 'Where the skin was missing.'

'Yeah?'

'He played a mean guitar, hard steel strings. The strings took the skin off the tips of his fingers. He'd put superglue on the worn-out tips. Then, when the glue was still tacky, he'd touch his fingers against his other arm, to put on new skin.'

'No shit?'

Mark grinned at the expression, which he so identified with American films and television. 'Yeah! Really – no shit!'

Mo, who had entered the dairy without any of them noticing, said, 'Mark knows a muh-muh-million buh-buh-blues stuh-stories.'

Alan shook his head, playing dumb. 'But you still haven't told me what makes a song into a dream?'

'Dreams are private.'

'That says nothing.'

'You can't explain "private". Private is private.'

'I give up with this guy!'

Kate and Mo eyed one another, also broadly smiling. Kate shoved Alan out of the dairy. 'Leave the poor idiot to his dreams.'

Mo followed Kate and Alan out into the sunshine. Mark hardly noticed the fact they had gone. In dreams, the first thing you lose track of is time. And the next thing you lose track of is your worries and cares.

It was many hours later before he came out of the dairy, looking exhausted but exhilarated. He just slid down the wall and sat on the grass. Mo, who was leaning with her back to the pear tree, looked at him. Mark took his harmonica from his pocket and, without a word, he began to play his own interpretation of the blues track, 'Ain't No Sunshine'.

Mo danced.

Kate and Alan just watched, transfixed. Brother and sister appeared lost in a world of their own. Mo's eyes were closed, her movements as delicate and natural as the flight of a butterfly.

When Mark stopped playing Kate clapped her hands.

Even Alan laughed with amazement. 'What the heck was that?'

Kate murmured, 'I think we just caught sight of a dream.'

Mo said, 'He cuh-cuh-cuh-can remember any kind of muh-muh-music, like a-nuh-nuh-nuh-nuh . . . like an in-suh-sane Muh-Muh-Mozart!'

All four friends dissolved into laughter.

Emulsion-spattered, in gaps between working, they talked and bantered as if they didn't have a care in the world. All the while they kept clear of the real stuff, like fate – or how life just doesn't even pretend to be fair. The bad stuff, the stuff you just couldn't bear to talk about, they left to brood on its own outside of the den.

From time to time, over the following days, Padraig would appear with a moth or a butterfly cupped in the cradle of his hands, exotic creatures that none of them had ever seen before. He'd let them go for Mo to watch them take flight. She'd squeal with delight, like a child half her age, watching their zigzag progress until they disappeared. Then she'd capture the images in her notebook. Other times it was beetles, myriad different shapes, sparkling with rainbow iridescence. Or the skulls of tiny animals. Or collections of feathers. Other times they would arrive in the morning to find a collection of crystals waiting for them, or a piece of amber containing the stem of a tiny plant, or a single petal of a flower, or an insect entombed within it. Mo's eyes would sparkle with every new piece of what Mark called her 'weirdiana'. She would study and draw them, before adding them to her altars to nature, placed at strategic points around the perimeter of the den.

It was a little eerie. As if Padraig knew exactly what would interest Mo. Kate, sitting on the grass outside the dairy, couldn't suppress her curiosity. The three of them, other than Mo, were cooling off outside, with hot noon hammering down on the leaves of the old pear tree over them. 'What's really going on, Mark? Do you think they're communicating, or what?'

'I don't have a clue.'

Kate looked down at a lodestone she had picked up from one of Mo's altars. It felt as heavy as lead. She showed it to Alan. 'Honestly! It's as if they're on some common wavelength.'

Alan shrugged. 'I warned you guys, Grandad's superstitious.'

'Yes,' she murmured, 'but you never really explained what you mean.'

Alan lifted up his brown fringe and Kate saw the triangular stork-beak birthmark. 'Grandad even thinks this is a sign – something that marks me out as different.'

Kate chuckled at Padraig's daft ideas. 'Has it ever given you some strange ability? Like some sixth sense?'

'All it's ever brought me is an avalanche of dragon's piss right down on my head. With the other kids making out like I was some kind of a freak.'

Kate shook her head. 'But I always thought superstitious people were – well, a little bit simple. And Padraig is far from simple.'

'I'm not saying he's simple.'

Mark, who had been following the conversation, met Kate's gaze with a wry smile. 'Mo's just the same. She's as superstitious as hell. But she isn't simple either. She's just different.'

Alan looked down at the daisy-strewn grass between his feet. 'You know what she reminds me of? I'm not claiming to be arty or anything, but I recall this teacher who was trying to explain stuff like Picasso and modern art to us. She talked about some natural ability we all had when we were kids. The thing is, we lose it. Somehow that happens to most of us. We lose it when we grow up. That's the difference between us and these great artists. They manage to keep hold of it. That's what I imagine is going on with Mo. She's one of those who keep it.'

Mark looked at Alan.

'Hey, I like Mo. No offence. Okay?'

'No offence taken. I think you might even be right.'

On one occasion Padraig brought Mo a finger-sized chunk of bog oak, as black as liquorice. Mo cooed with delight when she accepted it from his hand. It looked like nature had sculpted it already so it resembled a female form with one body that was the stem and three knots at one end that looked for all the world like separate knobbly heads. The heads, when you looked up close, were all different, like the three ages of womanhood. Mo stared and stared at it. But she didn't sit down and draw it. Nor did she place it on one of her altars. Instead she kept it with her constantly, to be taken out and fondled, like a talisman.

Nobody, not even Mark, understood this new twist. And if Padraig had an inkling he kept it to himself.

All of a sudden, it was the last day of July and it felt as if the whole month had been simply too gorgeous to hold onto. Mo was squinting skywards, as if in a final appeal to the sun, where it was peeping in and out of cotton-wool clouds that seemed in no hurry to move along. How she wished this last month could have gone on forever, days so full of sunshine and laughter you wanted to slow them right down. But they just melted away anyway, one day merging into another, so that in the end the whole month of July had gone hurtling by in what felt like no time at all. A time spent building sandcastles on sunny beaches. But the trouble with sandcastles is they stand only until the waves come in and sweep them away. And, today, on this exceptionally sultry day, that wave was coming. Mo had sensed it build up, little by little, not out there in the Atlantic Ocean off the beach at Clonea, but within the bodies and spirits of her friends, and the terrible thing was that even though she knew what was happening she was utterly powerless to prevent it. It was there, already, in Alan's angry expression as he put down the paperback he had been reading, pushing Mark and his mobile-phone-cum-camera away with his foot.

'Knock it off, will you, Mark? Don't do that.'

'Oh, look out!' Mark muttered as the phone fell from his grasp into the sand. 'It's hardly a crime,' he remarked while spitting on a tissue and attempting to clean it.

'Hey – it's not very nice to take pictures of Kate when she doesn't want it.'

'Oh, give it a rest, Alan!'

'Grow up – both of you!' Kate mumbled at the squabbling boys, wiping sand off her arm where it had become embedded in her suntan protection.

Mo stared, her gut squeezed in a spasm of worry about Mark. For weeks her brother had been developing a crush on Kate. Was Mark so stupid he couldn't see that Kate had eyes for nobody other than Alan?

Today's trip to Dungarvan had just been another of the bike trips that were originally supposed to be about hunting down threatened plants. Mo had been keen enough on the idea because, while Kate scoured the hedgerows and wild spaces for threatened plants, she intended to carry out her own searches for crystals. Alan and Kate already had their own mountain bikes and it had proved to be no problem borrowing two more. Being the smallest, Mo had lowered the saddle as far as it would go to fit her short legs, and so, all too predictably, short-leg jokes became the fashion for the first few trips. She had just shrugged off their banter and surprised them all with her toughness and endurance, pedalling hard to keep pace with the others. But, given the glorious weather, they soon abandoned all pretence at plant or crystal collecting and headed for the beaches south of the Comeragh Mountains along the Waterford coastline. Dungarvan, with its numerous beaches, and Clonea beach in particular, with its two-mile crescent of beautiful golden sand, had become their favourite.

And so it was here, at Clonea, on this serene afternoon, Mo sensed the change in her friends, as obvious to her inner senses as an unexpected gust of icy wind, or a cloud moving across the sun, might be to her physical senses. She remembered what Alan had said about fate: that the four of them coming together was too much to be explained away by coincidence. She also realised, with a certainty that none of her friends appeared to share, that the blooming had something to do with it. And more than anything she was sure that the same fate, whatever it implied, was closer – that all the time it had been creeping up on them.

'I'm warning you, Mark!' Alan insisted. 'I mean it. I've had it with that phone following us around all the time.'

Kate and Mo exchanged looks. It was an argument that had been brewing for weeks.

She talked urgently to Mark, after Alan and Kate had gone in for a dip.

'Yuh-yuh-yuh-you should stop whuh-what you're doing.'

'Tell me – what am I doing?'

'You're muh-muh-muh-making eyes at Kuh-Kate.'

'Don't be ridiculous.'

'Yes yuh-yuh-you are. And know very well that Kate has no fuh-fuh-fuh . . . feelings like that for you.'

'Oh, Mo – you're just being silly.'

'Why are yuh-yuh-yuh-you being so stupid?'

'I'm not making eyes at her.'

'Yuh-yuh-yuh-you know Kate and Alan are ah-ah-ah . . . an item.'

'So what if they are? Girls can change their minds.'

'Duh-don't even thuh-think it.'

'Oh, come on – you know I'm just pulling your leg.'

'No.' Mo shook her head. 'No, no – *no*!'

'Do you think I'm deluding myself into believing that Kate will fall for me if I just play some kind of long-term strategy?'

'Yuh-yuh-yes!'

Their eyes met – hers aglitter, his shifty. 'Okay! I can

see you're getting all wound up and it's making your stammer worse.'

His words just wound her up even tighter. 'Yuh-yuh-yuh-you're absolutely buh-buh-besotted with Kate.'

'I just want her to like me.'

'Luh-luh-liar.'

'All right – okay! Let's you and me not fall out about it.'

'Fuh-Fuh-Forget it, Mark.'

'Mo – for goodness sake!'

'You're muh-mad.' She put out her finger and tapped, like a cautioning whisper, against the mobile phone.

He sighed. He understood the caution perfectly. Grimstone would kill him if ever he found out!

'Okay, so I'm being stupid, Mo. I'm dreaming of Conan the Barbarian warrior sagas, in which I end up saving Kate's life.'

Mo turned away with a snort. She just couldn't bear his looking at her with that flushed puppy-dog look on his face.

'I know I can't compete with Alan. That's the maddening thing. He doesn't even have to try. They have all that recent orphan stuff in common.'

It was pathetic to watch how he mocked himself. He made a game out of the fact that his attentions only succeeded in making Kate laugh at him. But it was a dangerous game because he was so utterly lost in it, like the one thing he couldn't bear even to think about was for the game itself to end. Mark was dipping his bare toes into the sand and flicking it in little frustrated gestures in the direction of Alan and Kate. 'Oh, Mo – don't you so hate the fact we have to spy on people? I can't stand taking the pictures back to Grimstone.'

She could see how, in betraying their friends, he was turning so much of the hate on himself.

'I don't even know why he wants me to do it. It's not as if he even listens to what I have to tell him. It's just our stuff, the little things that are personal to us. That just makes it all the more awful. I want it to stop. But I'd go on doing it forever if I could go on playing games with Kate and at the same time keep Grimstone off my back.'

While Mark headed into the sea to join Alan and Kate, Mo stayed on the shore and watched him, fearful and tense, observing that he had been stupid enough to take the phone with him.

She heard Kate's voice raised in outrage. 'How many times have I told you not to take pictures of me in my bikini!'

Mo heard Alan and Mark's voices raised in argument. Alan was defending Kate, and Mark, as usual, was trying to make a joke out of it. She heard the idiot tell Kate that he had been having Conan the Barbarian dreams about her. The arguing got worse. Mark was laughing, full of self-mockery, 'How could I compete with a fellow whose name is an anagram of dual naval?' Then Mark was splashing out towards the shore with Alan chasing him. They faced each other off at the edge of the surf.

'Oh, come on!' Mark shouted. 'You telling me, Alan, you haven't been having Conan dreams about Kate?'

'You're asking for a punch on the nose!'

They locked in a wrestle and fell over in the middle of a breaking wave. Mark was struggling to escape, trying to save his precious phone. But Alan didn't give a damn about the phone. He grabbed Mark again and they rolled over and over in the surf. Alan got an arm free and he punched Mark on the nose. They separated, Alan jumping to his feet while Mark sat in the tide with his phone held against his face, blood trickling through his fingers.

'Enough!' cried Kate. 'Stop it this instant!'

Alan suddenly looked sheepish. He extended his hand to Mark, to help him up. 'Hey, I'm sorry – right? It just got out of hand.'

Mark took his hand but he followed with his head, butting Alan in the centre of the face, so it was Alan's turn to end up sitting in the surf with a bloody nose.

Alan pushed away Kate's consoling hand. 'Okay – if that's how he wants it. He's nothing but a goddam idiot. I've had it with him.'

Mo burst into tears. There was such a look of mortification on her face that Kate ran to her and hugged her. 'Take no notice of those eejits. It'll be all right. Honestly, it will. I know that Alan doesn't really mean it.'

Alan stormed off down the beach while Mark sat down

FRANK P. RYAN | 63

in the sand, drying off the mobile phone with a towel and making sure it still worked.

Kate muttered to Mo, 'What's his problem with that stupid phone?'

Mo's trembling turned into a fit of uncontrollable shaking. Her teeth chattered.

'Ah, sure, come on now, Mo. It was just a few stupid photographs.'

Then Mo said something strange. Her voice was a guttural croak, each individual syllable forced out, as if she were struggling to speak through a throat that was shackled with iron.

'Guh-guh-Guh . . . Guh-Grimstone – wuh-wuh-wuh . . . !'

'Grimstone will what?' Kate helped her down, so they were sitting together on the soft wet sand by the water's edge. Kate called to Mark, who was about ten feet away, 'Mo's really upset. Will you please tell me what's going on, Mark?'

But Mark wasn't listening. His blue eyes were staring out to sea.

Old Power

Mark hardly slept that night, too shocked at how close he had come to being found out. And Grimstone added to it, as if he sensed that something was wrong, becoming more sarcastic than usual when he made them stand in front of him in the sacristy and provide the daily summary. He warned them both that their days of tomfoolery were close to an end. Then, when they arrived at the den the next morning, the situation got a whole lot worse. Padraig was waiting with Kate and Alan, all three sitting on the hummock of grass under the old pear tree in the warming light.

The old man's eyes seemed to blaze clearer and bluer than ever as he fixed them with his wide-open gaze. 'Now then, young Mark and Mo! We know that something is not altogether right in this situation. I've been hearing one or two disturbing things. But I want to hear it from you in person. Will you tell me what ails you?'

Mark felt his throat tighten, and he couldn't hide his panic. 'Nothing, Sir! There's nothing wrong.'

'Ah, now – Sir, is it?'

Mark tried to bluff it out but there was no escaping those eyes.

'Your father would do something if you stopped coming here? Meaning it was Grimstone himself that put you up to it?'

'Muh-muh-muh . . . !'

Mark put a restraining hand on Mo's shoulder, to try to shut her up. 'Mr O'Brien—!'

But Mo shook his hand off. 'If yuh-yuh-you won't tell him, I wuh-wuh-wuh-will.'

Mark shook his head violently at Mo, his eyes pleading for her to stop.

Alan confronted Mark eye-to-eye, clearly still rattled from yesterday, in spite of the handshake. 'I don't know what's going on. But one thing I know for sure is we've got to be honest with each other.'

Mark didn't care what Alan thought. He wasn't going to explain just to please Alan. He tried to steer Mo away. But Mo wriggled free. Stutteringly and painfully, she began to explain. She told them the truth about the so-called Reverend Grimstone, and they listened to her in a shocked silence.

Kate got up off the grass and put her arm round Mo's shoulders. 'Oh for goodness sake – I simply can't believe it. Is this true, Mark?'

Mark shrugged. 'Mo and I, we grew up to be told that our biological fathers were drunkards and druggies.'

'He cuh-cuh-cuh-cuh-calls us wicked nuh-nuh-nuh . . . nuh-nuh-names.'

'Such as what?'

'Mo is half aboriginal. Grimstone says that she only has to look in the mirror to see the face of her savage whore mother.'

Kate gave Mo a huge hug. 'You're mother was nothing of the sort. If you look anything like your mother, she must have been gorgeous.'

Mo's face fell, her fingers writhing in a heap. 'Muh-Muh-Muh-Mark and I . . . we – we wuh-wuh-wuh—!

'What she's trying to say,' Mark added quietly, 'is we were abandoned. Tossed away like pieces of rubbish on Sir's doorstep – me at about eighteen months old and Mo less than a year old.'

'Sure and that's awful.'

'You don't know the half of it! You really want to know what he would say to Mo when he felt like hurting her?' Mark smiled, but there was no humour in his smile. 'He'd say, "Now why do you think your mother couldn't stand the sight of you the very moment you were born?" He'd tell Mo that everybody hated her, even when she was a baby, because she didn't look like a Christian child. "Anyone can see that at a glance," he'd say, pinching her cheek so hard his nails would leave a mark. "Go to the mirror," he'd say. "Go take a good long look at your gipsy whore face."'

Kate just hugged Mo tighter.

Alan was outraged. 'Who the hell is this guy?'

'The Reverend R. Silas – familiarly known as Arseless – Grimstone. Our adoptive father!'

'Your mother . . . your adoptive mother . . . couldn't she stop it?'

'What? Dear sweet Bethal – the werewolf?'

Padraig shook his head. 'That blackguard sounds worse than a Puritan.'

'What he really is . . . there's a better name for it,' Mark hissed between his clenched teeth. 'But Reverend isn't the word I'd use.'

Kate said quietly, 'He must be mad.'

Mo's face fell. 'Cuh-cuh-clever – clever and wuh-wuh-wuh-wicked more than muh-muh-mad!'

Mark added, 'Recently he's been getting worse. It's something to do with the reason he came to Clonmel. But we don't really know why he came here.'

Kate held Mo at arm's length. 'Why he came here? Here to Clonmel?'

'To spy on you.'

Padraig barked a laugh. 'You're pulling my leg.'

'He thinks that you, Mr O'Brien, are some kind of druid.'

'And what does he mean by that?'

'A pagan . . . or something like that!'

'Well now, isn't that quite an accusation? What then is a pagan? Is a pagan someone who believes in ghosts? Or a child who discovers the meaning of magic? The druids were more than priests. These days they would be regarded as great thinkers . . . like a mixture of priest and philosopher.'

'So you're not a pagan?'

'What were the auld religions but an attempt at understanding . . . maybe at understanding things that might better have been left alone.'

'Grimstone talked about power. Old power.'

'What old power?'

'Don't ask me. I know how weird it all sounds. But it's the way his mind works. He appears to be an old-type preacher but he doesn't really mention Jesus, only the old hellfire and brimstone stuff. All he seems to care about is controlling people. He sets up some new branch of his church somewhere, converting gullible people. He goes looking for scapegoats. Somebody to attack. It brings him publicity and frightens still more into joining him.'

'And that monster, he's here and up to something like that?'

Mark's head dropped.

Padraig stiffened. 'Didn't I sense there was something about you both, but I never imagined such nonsense in my wildest dreams.' He was silent for several seconds. 'But then, maybe we can turn the tables on him. Mo, will you show me your book again? Sit yourself down here on the grass while I take another look at some of your beautiful pictures.'

*

The four friends sat on the hummock while Padraig leafed through the pages in Mo's green-covered notebook. Mo watched the old man's face, his features half-hidden in the shadows and the long hawk-like nose almost touching the paper. She jumped when he pounced on one drawing. He dropped to one knee to point it out to her.

'There!' he exclaimed. 'This is what caught my eye when I first looked through it.'

Mo glanced fearfully at the drawing. Fear made her stammer worse. 'It's thuh-thuh-thuh – it's the suh-suh-suh . . .'

Mark spoke for her. 'It's the sigil. On Grimstone's black cross.'

'Sigil? D'you mean some kind of symbol?'

'It's part of the cross. Where the figure of Jesus would be, but this is definitely not Jesus. It's silvery in colour instead of black, like the rest of it.'

'Like suh-suh-suh-something very . . . vuh-vuh-very old.'

'That's right. The cross is made out of a black, twisted kind of metal. Like iron, but I'm not sure it's really iron.'

'Will you tell me everything you recall of it, Mark?'

'It's . . . well, it's kind of gnarly, just like Mo has drawn it, only a lot bigger . . . and heavier.' Mark held out his hands, to give an idea of the dimensions.

'Cuh-cuh-cuh-cuh-creepy!'

'The worst thing, the most repulsive thing about it, is the sigil in the middle.'

'It guh-guh-guh-glows!'

Mark nodded. 'Honestly – it's true. The sigil really glows, so you can see it shining in the dark. When Grimstone is talking to it.'

Alan interrupted, 'This guy talks to it?'

'He calls it his Lord – his Master.'

'No way!'

'Muh-Muh-Muh-Mark and I . . . wuh-wuh-wuh-we think . . . we think he kuh-kuh . . . kuh-kuh-killed . . .'

Mark took up what Mo was trying to explain. 'We don't know for certain, but from the way he talks about it sometimes, we think, maybe, he might have killed some old man for it. The old man claimed that it came from a barrow grave.'

'Which would hardly be Christian, since barrow graves are far older than Christianity.'

'He suh-suh-suh-says he had a buh-buh-blackout.'

Kate murmured, 'It gets worse and worse!'

'We think Grimstone was a thief when he was younger. He stole stuff for the old man, who was an antiquarian. But when he saw the cross with the sigil embossed on it, it . . . well, it took some kind of possession of him. He says he had a blackout. But we think he killed the old man to get the cross.'

Padraig looked deeply worried. 'It came from a barrow, you say?'

Alan turned to his grandfather. 'What's wrong?'

Padraig placed his hands on Mark's and Mo's shoulders, as if hardly able to believe what he was hearing.

Alan snorted. 'Hey – the guy's loopy!'

Kate looked at Alan with a frown. 'But you heard what they said. They've seen how this thing glows when he talks to it.'

'Silver can look like that.'

'Nuh-nuh-nuh-no! It buh-buh-burns.'

'Burns?'

Mark agreed with Mo. 'When Grimstone holds the sigil to his brow. When he's calling it Master, it burns his skin. You can hear it sizzle – you can smell it.'

Alan shook his head. 'Mo? Is this true?'

Mo nodded.

Mark added, 'Grimstone won't allow anyone else to touch it. Or even to go near it.'

'Grandad, have you any idea what's going on here?'

'I'm not altogether sure. I know a little about such things. Maybe now I wish I knew more.'

'But what are you thinking?'

'Well, I'm thinking we need to grasp what's really going on here. We have the four of you coming together here, with what appears to be important aspects of your lives in common. Happen it's fate.'

Alan scoffed. 'Hey – come on!'

'Don't you be telling me you haven't wondered for yourselves?'

Mark objected. 'That's as crazy as Grimstone.'

'There must be something happening to you – all of

you. Are you getting unusual thoughts in your heads? Or unusual dreams?'

Kate blurted, 'Mo and I, we've been sharing the same dreams.'

'What dreams?'

'We keep seeing a mountain. But it's not one we recognise. It towers up, like a great pillar of rock, with a figure on the top of it.'

'You're sure you don't recognise it?' There was a light in Padraig's eyes, now examining Kate's expression.

'No. It's nowhere I remotely recognise.'

'What about you lads?'

Mark shook his head.

But Alan looked thoughtful. 'If it's dreams about places you guys want, the only place I ever dream about is the River Suir. I dream about the river a lot.'

Padraig was thoughtful. 'Mountains and rivers! It certainly seems as if something is building up around you. Something – or someone – is trying to communicate with you, perhaps.'

Mark lifted his eyebrows. 'I suppose I'd better go check my emails.'

Kate thumped him. 'Don't you dare mock this, Mark Grimstone!'

Padraig cleared his throat, as if making up his mind about something. 'Well now, isn't it time we all were a little more honest with each other? And that goes for you too, Mr Tricky-the-loop.' He tapped Mark's shoulder.

Mark exchanged glances with Mo. 'There was something Grimstone said. He was talking about some kind of old power that was a threat to him. Stuff about the town being old but the power was older.'

'Ancient power?'

'Suh-suh-something about a puh-people from before the Cuh-Cuh-Celts.'

'I'm trying to remember how he put it. Like an old power, almost buried and forgotten, yet still lingering.'

'Huh-huh-huh-he talked about the ruh-ruh-rivers, too.'

'Ancient power to do with rivers?'

Mark said, 'I'll give you his exact words, Mr O'Brien. "It is my Lord himself, my sacred Master, who senses the threat – the threat is to Him . . . here in this town – in the old power that still lingers here."'

'What manner of threat?'

Mo spoke softly. 'Thuh-thuh-three ruh-ruh-ruh-rivers!'

Everybody looked at Mo, astonished. Then Mark nodded. 'Something about a heathen trinity. Its grip long vanquished, yet such is its hold on the very landscape, it has endured.'

Alan looked at his grandfather in bewilderment. 'Is this guy the pits, or what?'

Padraig's brow was deeply furrowed. 'I'm not sure at all as to the nature of Grimstone.'

Kate cut in, 'So how do we find out more about this . . . this power?'

'I think you won't have to look very far before the power finds you!'

She sighed. 'What on earth does that mean?'

His face reddening with embarrassment, Alan said, 'Grandad sees fate in everything that's happening.'

'Maybe he's right, Alan.'

Alan snorted. 'We're just like the butterflies and birds, following our instincts! That's what you think. Isn't it, Grandad?'

'Four orphans! And you kid yourself it's merely happenstance?'

Kate countered, 'Two orphans – and two adoptees!'

Padraig stared at her, then glanced with a gentle sympathy at Mark and Mo. 'Kate, both you and Alan assume that your parents were the victims of accidents, or deliberate killings by wicked people. But what if it was you yourselves who were the targets?'

'But that . . . oh, for goodness sake – it's ridiculous!'

'Kate, were you not with your parents when they died? And Alan too! Weren't you meant to be in the helicopter when it crashed?'

Alan couldn't help raising his voice in protest. 'So how come we're still here, then, Grandad?'

'Maybe there were other forces protecting you?'

'Aw, c'mon!'

Mark shook his head. 'I don't know anything about what Mr O'Brien is saying. But I can tell you that when Grimstone talks about our biological parents, he uses the past tense.'

'You mean he knows they're dead?'

Mo was shaking her head violently.

'I'm sorry, Mo, but he doesn't say that your mother *is* a whore. He says she *was* a whore. Always the past tense.'

Alan shook his head. 'How – I mean, what . . . Aw, heck – I don't rightly know what to think any more.'

Mark shrugged. He looked at Padraig. 'This force, I think you're suggesting it's got something to do with us? If so, can you tell us what we ought to do?'

'Maybe it's fitting to caution you that you're standing in a wood, where you can't see the wood for the trees. If I were to advise you, and I'm not sure I even want to advise you, I would suggest you get above it.'

Kate blurted, 'Above what?'

'Above what's too close to your noses, young Kate!'

'Above the world?'

All four friends stared at Padraig as he shook his head at their lack of comprehension. He spun through a quarter circle and he lifted his face to the mountains that rose to the south of where they were gathered, their lower slopes cloaked in his own woods.

Kate said, 'You mean, above the Comeraghs?'

'Not just these foothills. The proper mountains that lie behind them.'

Kate stared up at the foothills, which seemed quite mountainous in themselves. She had lived in the shadow of the Comeraghs all her life but she had never attempted to climb them, not the real mountains.

On the Roof of the World

Setting out before eight, they cycled the five or six miles to Ballymacarbry. They had planned it all yesterday, with the best route highlighted on the Ordnance Survey map which travelled with them in Alan's backpack. They took the turning for the Nire Valley. Then, in single file, with map-reader Alan leading, they cycled another two or three miles through the cool morning sunshine until they came to the bridge. After another twenty minutes of twisting and turning, they found their way to the car park at the base of the mountains, where they padlocked the bikes and started out on foot. Here, in the long shadows of morning, they sipped the piping hot coffee from Kate's mammoth flask, high-fived with nervous laughs, and then set to climbing straight away.

Of course not a single one of them really knew what they were doing here. On the compass, which was Kate's contribution, they took a bearing on 76 degrees, northeasterly towards the Gap. Within minutes they were out of the shadows and squinting up into the face of the sun, weaving a path through mauve bell heather still soaked with overnight dew. They filed one by one over a stile made of lichen-coated stones and stopped to look upslope. Alan pointed to a series of white posts in the distance which indicated the way to the Gap.

Mark offered to high-five Kate.

She hesitated. 'No more stuff about Conan the Barbarian.'

He grinned. 'You want to know the truth? You were supposed to melt when I saved you – like throw your half-naked and bleeding body into my arms. But even in my fantasies you wouldn't play along. You'd say stuff like, "We'll always be friends".'

Kate quivered with suppressed laughter.

'Don't ever stop laughing at me, Kate.'

She punched his arm, then accepted the high-five.

Mark couldn't help but be pleased at this. But Alan looked questioningly at Kate, who was now carrying on climbing. He quizzed Mark. 'You tell Grimstone why we're here?'

'It's the only reason we're still with you.'

'He wasn't suspicious?'

'The whole idea was to get him suspicious.' Mark did a pretty good take on the Grimstone growl. '"What were his words – I want the very words, and the manner he spoke them – when the old man asked you this?"'

'What planet's this guy on?'

'All I know is he has suddenly taken it into his head to go back to London. He's going to be away for two weeks, leaving Bethal in charge.'

'Huh-huh-hooray!'

The boys turned to look at Mo, who had been trailing behind at this point but had taken advantage of the exchanges with Kate to catch up to them.

'But it was a close thing. I could see he was thinking maybe he should take us back with him if for no better reason than he knew we wanted so much to stay. Look, I'm really sorry, Alan, but I told him he was probably right about your grandfather. You know he thinks he's some kind of pagan. Like a druid or something. I told him there was something going on – a lot more than Padraig is telling us.'

Alan pinked with anger.

'We couldn't let him take us away, not now. And I could see it in Grimstone's face, he was really thinking of doing that.'

Mark didn't add Grimstone's words, as those eyes came close to peering directly into his own. *You trollop's whelp! Do you think I haven't sensed the lust in you whenever you've been within a mile of that red-haired Jezebel? You've filled that confounded camera thing with pictures of the harlot.'*

'Kate isn't a harlot. You see yourself in everybody!'

Grimstone had taken hold of his ear on one side and slapped his face with all of his might on the other. Mark's ear was still swollen, and there was a sound in his head like a high-pitched whistle.

Mark pressed on into the breeze, which was bowling towards him through the heather and making a yowling cat's duet with the whistling in his ear. Forcing the memory of Grimstone out of his mind, he followed in the wake of Kate, taking comfort from her well-filled-out blue jeans ahead of him.

From where she had once again fallen twenty or so yards behind the others, Mo watched Mark increase pace to catch up with Kate. Mo's blue anorak was already stained with the gold of pollen from the heather. They were all approaching the pass Alan had circled in red highlighter pen on the map. Thankfully, she had escaped last night's interrogation. But she had seen poor Mark's face when Grimstone had finished with him, and she hated the price her brother had paid for the fact they were here.

But now, gazing about her at the increasing drama of the mountains, inhaling the scents of wild flowers, Mo wondered what it was that Padraig had been hinting at yesterday. What were they supposed to find up here? Was Padraig really some kind of pagan priest? The truth was that she had no answer to those questions. Yet it seemed to her that Padraig did not talk or behave like somebody steeped in any kind of religion. He talked about nature more the way she had felt about it all her life. Where most people saw, or heard, or even smelled, the seasons – Padraig lived them. She recalled Padraig's words: *I think you won't have to look very far before the power finds you!*

As the morning wore on and the heat increased, they took to a rhythm of climbing in silence. Alan wondered if Mom had climbed these same mountains at his age. It was another way in which he felt the sickening intensity of her loss. Step by step, he found himself mulling over the deaths of his parents. Had it really been an accident? Or was there, as Padraig believed, some . . . some what? Some kind of conspiracy?

Oh, my God – what if Grandad was right and the idea had been to kill him and not Mom and Dad!

But why would anybody want to kill him?

It absolutely made no sense. You go down that road and you were in danger of getting hooked on paranoia. The problem was he could try to dismiss it as superstitious nonsense, but then the whisper would start up again in his mind. He just couldn't shake the idea that weird things were happening – they really were happening – things that seemed to stretch coincidence.

Well, okay! So weird things did happen. It didn't mean you had to believe in unseen forces, or murderous conspiracies.

But then the little voice began to whisper again. It said: all right, but you know Grandad has a point because you really were supposed to have been in that chopper with Mom and Dad when they crashed. And you know that

Kate was actually right there too. She was with her parents when they were murdered. She had only escaped being murdered by a whisker. She lived because an African nun cared so much about her that she shoved Kate out of sight and died herself. And Mark and Mo – what was the real truth there?

Oh, man!

Alan shook his head, trying to blank the confusion from his mind. Then, when he looked around him he realised that they had arrived at the Gap. He sat down on the heather and opened the backpack so he could take another look at the map. The Gap was a pass between the Comeragh Plateau to one side and the Knockanaffrin Ridge on the other. The Plateau would take them higher, but the climb was going to get more difficult.

He waited for Mark and Kate to catch up with him before asking them, 'Guys, what do you think? Do we head left? Make for the Ridge?'

They agreed to do that. Meanwhile the slope got steeper and the going tougher. In places you were almost forced to climb on all fours. But the scenery was worth it. The view was just breathtaking.

The blue of the sky seemed to have washed over the ground so the sheen of high summer glowed in the rocks, as if the very crystals were showing off their purple and gold, indigo and lilac. Alan waited a little longer so Mo caught up.

'Look over there!' He pointed to a peak in the distance,

dotted with what looked like tiny puffs of steam. 'Mountain sheep?'

Kate corrected him. 'Goats – not sheep!'

'Yeah?'

'Oh, but isn't it glorious!' she exclaimed. 'I wish we'd brought binoculars. The goats look really cute. I've seen pictures of them in classes at school. They have these long curved horns. And just look at the flowers!'

Alan grinned. 'You spot any endangered species?'

'Ah, knock it off! You just don't have a clue. I bet you couldn't name a single one of them?'

He shrugged.

'I knew it!'

'So – enlighten me.'

She nodded at a spot a few feet from where they were standing. 'You've been putting your outsize feet within inches of squashing these. They're bee orchids.'

'What's that mean – bee orchids?'

'The lowermost petal is shaped like a bee.'

'Which part of the bee?'

She was too smart to be caught with that one. 'Even their scent is designed to mimic the female bee pheromone. So the bees are confused into thinking it's the female!'

'This I got to sniff for myself!'

She saw where it was leading and slapped his shoulder. 'You boys only ever have your minds on one thing!'

The way he was grinning at her made her smile back in turn.

'I really like it when you smile like that.'

'Get lost.'

'Honest, I do. It reminds me of the day we met. When you were showing me the single plant you'd rescued, in the bed down by the river.'

'Oh, isn't it just ravishing!' She threw her arms wide at the Suir Valley far below them, like a gigantic folded counterpane of pea-green and flag-yellow oblongs and stripes.

'It sure as hell makes me giddy.'

By the time they got to the top of the mountain, it was after eleven. They sat around and got their breaths back, gazing down onto Coumduala Lough, so far below them the waves on the surface looked like threads of fine white cotton. The sun and breeze had had a few hours to dry the dew out of the heather and they were comfortable sitting in it, fishing for sandwiches and the drinks from their backpacks. Kate lay flat on her belly and just drooled over the panoramic view of the Suir Valley heading eastwards towards Waterford.

Alan asked her, 'You seeing or feeling anything of what Padraig was hinting at?'

'I don't care any more. I just want to lie here and soak it up.'

Hunching forward, Alan began to rub the aching muscles of his calves. 'Me too. To tell you the truth, the only thing I'm feeling is my legs complaining. And here comes Mo – five feet nothing and not even a hint of flagging.'

'So what do you really think?'

'I think maybe Grimstone is a crazy-livered bully and Grandad is just a mite eccentric, like I've been telling you guys all along.'

Kate glanced over at Mo, who was resisting Mark's attempts to get her to listen to a tune on his phone. 'Mo – isn't she what dear old Bridey would call a "quare one"?'

'She's different – I've got to grant you that.'

'What is it about her that she avoids any techno gadgets?'

He shrugged.

Kate pulled a face. 'Do you wonder that's she's so tough!'

'Come on, Kate! You get to thinking why they put up with it. I mean the way Grimstone's been treating them all their lives, why don't they go and complain to the authorities?'

'I asked her.'

'You did?'

'Grimstone is very powerful, highly connected in his local community in London. What if the authorities didn't believe them? Then they'd have to go back home and face him.'

'Shee–it!'

'You really care about them, don't you?'

'Don't you?'

She nodded. 'I think maybe you're all the best friends I ever had.' Kate blinked for what seemed longer than the few moments it really was – she didn't want him to see the stupid tears in her eyes.

Alan nodded. 'I think so too. I just want it to stay like this. I don't ever want it to change.'

Kate hugged his arm.

He said, 'Makes you want to get people like Grimstone back. Teach him a lesson he'll understand.'

'Is this your Irish mother talking?'

'Maybe I got a dose of that from both sides. Dad told me never let a bully get away with it. You do that and it will only get a whole heap worse. I tell you, Kate, if somebody had done to me what Grimstone's been doing to those kids, I'd have found some way to put a stop to it.'

The sun came out from behind Alan's shoulder, making her squint to look at him. 'So what would the brave Alan Duval have done?'

'I don't know – but something!'

'I keep thinking of you, just standing there that day with the swans. I'm beginning to think there's a major streak of stubbornness in you.'

At the summit of the mountains, Mo felt dwarfed by the enormous landscape that stretched away to the horizon on all sides.

There was so much to think about that her thoughts reeled through her mind like the flight of the swallows wheeling overhead. She recalled the moment Mark had explained things to Padraig. A baby abandoned on a church step somewhere in a small town in Australia, like a cruel offering on a cold slab of altar. To an outsider, the church must have looked solid and respectable. Did whoever it was who had abandoned her know that Grimstone was there? Did he or she know exactly what lay concealed beneath his holy veneer? Perhaps he, or she, even knew who Mo really was, knew her real name, the name that had been given to her by her birth mother? It was something Mo had thought about a lot over the years. When parents gave the baby they loved a name, that was when the baby became somebody, a new and unique human being. Kate and Alan knew who they were. They had their names, given to them by parents who brought them into the world and loved them. She knew instinctively, like a self-evident truth, that Maureen was not her real name. It was the name given to her by Bethal and Grimstone, people who did not love her.

Who am I? Mo whispered to the world.

A sudden, overwhelming feeling clutched at her heart as she tried to imagine what it must be like for a mother to bear a child, a daughter, and then abandon it. How could a mother forsake her baby daughter?

Am I truly an orphan?

Could she imagine what such a mother would feel? She tried to, but it felt so awful she couldn't bear the thought.

Am I a witch spawn as Grimstone says I am? Is my mother dead, like Kate's and Alan's? Or is she alive and doesn't care about me?

She had long ago realised that there were advantages

to being nobody. When you are nobody you can pass people by and they don't notice you. Meanwhile you make up for it by noticing more about those who are somebodies.

Mark had always been stronger than she was. Somehow, he had found the strength to fight back. Even his sarcastic humour, his constant self-deprecatory jokes, was his way of fighting back against the hurt. She watched him now unrolling his earphones, getting ready for some solitary listening. Alan was flat on his back in the heather, with his head pillowed by his backpack, chewing on a stalk. Kate was sitting next to him, hunched forward over drawn-up knees, uncapping a bottle of water.

Mo lifted her face to gaze heavenwards at the swallows wheeling. From somewhere nearby came the humming of bees, maybe a nest. Far away, down the slope, a plume of chalk-blue hung in the air, metamorphosing subtly, as if a cloud of butterflies had just taken to the wing. Mo heard a faint sound, a pleasant but unexpected sound. She turned so she was facing the valley of the Suir. She could even smell something now, an unfamiliar scent, not a flower scent but a muskier smell, like the smell of bread baking.

Then she saw the blooming.

It was as clear as an island of lambent green in the middle of a grey ocean, a gigantic circle of fecundity, vast in diameter, around a single focus. The very centre was monumentally clear across the valley. And now, as she opened her mind to it, she sensed a new stirring, as if the very landscape had whispered something into the air, and that awesome message was spiralling and eddying towards her without any sense of wind.

Was she imagining it?

She waited patiently, all senses alert. She sensed it again. She laid herself bare to it this time, throwing open her entire body and mind. It was definitely coming in waves. She felt another wave touch her. It didn't feel like a tangible physical sensation. She didn't know how to describe what she was feeling, other than it was some kind of contact, being-to-being. She felt no premonition of harm. Without hesitation, she slipped off her trainers to feel the ground under her bare feet. She took the bog-oak figurine out of her hip pocket and palpated its familiar shape with the fingers of her right hand. She felt the smoothness of the body, the three knobs of heads, twirling them around and around. She brought it to her lips and kissed it.

She began to sing.

Tentatively, like a glimmer of moonlight, the presence reached out again, eddying like a wave through water, and found her. This time Mo gasped with the intensity of communication, the feeling of oneness.

Turning, in a slow rapture of motion, she looked back at her friends, willing them to join her. But they were too preoccupied to notice. The communication was intended for her alone.

She wondered: *Is it the blooming? Is the blooming reaching out for me?*

She saw the opalescent glimmer sweep past her to reach her friends. Their faces reflected it, as if moonlight were alighting on them, and also washing over their exposed arms and legs. She was sensing communication in some way she had never known it before.

What does it mean?

Kate lifted her head and stared at the tiny doll-like figure thirty yards away, perched, as it seemed, on the very edge of the abyss. Mo's body was erect, forming a perfect shallow curve from her heels to the nape of her neck. Her head was tilted back on the apex of the curve, her dark brown hair standing up in a nimbus around her ears, her arms outstretched to either side of her body, the hands facing forward into the enormous valley. It was her singing that had caught Kate's attention.

Kate heard a voice like the most perfect trill of a thrush or a lark, only deeper, more sibilant and sensual than any thrush or lark Kate had ever heard.

'What in the world!'

Alan's voice sounded in Kate's ear, like a nervous whisper. Mark was also calling out, from somewhere further away, at the edge of her vision, the earphones yanked out of his ears.

Mark said, 'It's Mo. She's singing.'

Kate squealed to Alan, 'I've never heard Mo sing before.'

'Me neither!'

All three friends were struggling excitedly to their feet.

Mo wasn't stuttering at all. There were no recognisable words to her song, but it sounded as if she were expressing words, beautiful words, that belonged to a language softer and gentler than any language Kate had ever heard.

'Oh my God – it's the voice of an angel!'

'What's going on?' Alan's voice was every bit as shaky as the muscles in Kate's legs.

Nobody answered him. Already they were moving, stumbling clumsily, too jittery to run, to reach Mo's side, to join her on the roof of the world.

'Oh, boy!' Alan stared across the valley.

'What is it, Mo?' Kate searched Mo's blank face. She saw the wide, dilated pupils. Instinctively she grabbed Mo's hand.

Kate's body jerked with something that felt like a powerful charge of static electricity. She felt her back arch, her eyes spring wide open, staring with Mo along the perfect line of force, across the green-carpeted landscape of the Suir Valley, to another mountain that rose, soft shouldered and gentle, yet dominating the landscape. Slievenamon glowed in the midday sun, clothed in the lilac, jade and gold of life, the perfect symmetry of her slopes forming the breast that had given it its name, the Mountain of Women.

Kate could only manage a whisper. 'Do you feel it?'

'Yes!' returned Alan's whisper.

She heard a guttural exclamation, perhaps Mark's, as the first wave struck, then eddied about them, enveloping their bodies like the gossamer touch of a million butterfly wings, whispering its presence in their ears, invading their beings.

Come! it whispered.

As the ecstasy of contact ebbed, its retreat made them moan and sigh, their mouths fallen open, willing it to return. They heard Mo's song begin again, heralding a new wave. They couldn't help but hold still, hands discovering hands, trembling fingers closing around each other, then fiercely holding. The new thrill of communication was utterly intoxicating. It overwhelmed their senses, like the sweetest scent magnified a thousand-fold. It rose to a peak in their minds, an ecstasy of total abandonment, swept out into the tips of their fingers and toes, like the whole-body tingling of a dive into ice-cold water.

Come!

Mo's song began again, even as the second wave was still ebbing, so there was no gap between. The next wave rode over the previous, eddying around and through them, breaking and rushing over them, enveloping them with longing. It flowed in their arteries and veins, a tide of enchantment. Their skins erupted into gooseflesh. The hair jerked erect on every head. What could be so dreadful, and yet so wonderful, it demanded such complete possession? There were no further words of communication, only the ravening hunger of the seduction. But even as Mo's song sounded again and again, and as wave after wave swept over them, overwhelming their senses, they knew, at the core of their beings, that it was the mountain, Slievenamon, that was calling them.

Fear of Loss

Alan came rushing through the house, flinging doors wide open, then ran out into the timber yard, calling, 'Grandad!'

He found Padraig in one of the sheds. The old man lifted his eyes from a tally of hardwoods to appraise Alan's tense silhouette in the opening, backlit by the bright sun of late afternoon.

'You look like you ran all the way down the mountain!'

Alan couldn't stop his limbs trembling. He was so breathless he could hardly speak.

'Back into the house with you! You've overheated your engine.' Padraig ignored his attempts to question him, ushering him out of the doorway and back inside the redbrick house, to the foot of the staircase. 'No arguments! A cold shower will do you the power of good!'

Alan stood under the shock of icy water. But even the Niagara Falls would not have slowed his heartbeat. He found clean clothes in his bedroom. He was still yanking a white T-shirt over his head as he ran back downstairs. Padraig was sitting in one of the old Edwardian armchairs of buttoned-back green leather. He was as still as a doll, his arms limp against his thighs.

'I surmise that you've made a discovery?'

'You already knew about the mountain!'

Padraig's eyes seemed to film over. His hoary old head fell. 'Must I lose you, like I lost your mother?'

'Lose me? What are you saying?'

'When you arrived, when I picked you up at Shannon Airport, I saw her in you. Sure you have her in your eyes and your smile.'

'Grandad, I can't stand this! I can't stand not knowing what's going on. You know more. You've always known more than you've been telling me.'

'You think such knowledge will be redeeming?'

Alan was familiar with the sepia photographs on the walls. Stuff to do with his ancestors dating back to the nineteenth century. In a cluster on one wall were pictures of his mother as a girl. He had seen the obvious, but had not questioned it. Now he did so.

'Why aren't there any photographs of Mom and Dad? You haven't a single photograph of me as a kid, of me growing up.'

'I couldn't bear the thought of Geraldine leaving me.'

A fever burned in him, as cruel as it was wild. 'Wasn't that – well, kind of selfish?'

'You don't understand.'

'Well, then! Explain to me.'

Padraig said nothing. He went to an oak cabinet and poured himself a glass of home-distilled poteen. He took a swig of the powerful liquor, which was as clear as spring water, then carried it back to the old leather armchair.

'Please talk to me!'

'You'll never understand anything.'

'Well make me understand. There are things going on – bizarre things – and I've lost the plot. Show me why I've lost it! Hey, Grandad, please?'

'Geraldine was all I had. She grew up here, in this house and these woods. Then, all of a sudden, she was determined to be off.'

Alan hesitated. These were events he knew next to nothing about. He fought against his impatience to know what had happened on the mountain. He had to suppress his overwhelming anxiety, to calm his voice. 'I don't rightly know. Maybe she wanted a change? Maybe she needed to see the world?'

Padraig suddenly took his head between his hands. He rocked, in that anguished posture, and moaned.

'For God's sake!' Alan's mind struggled to grasp what was going on here. 'Grandad, what are you really trying to tell me?'

Padraig shook his head.

'What? You're worrying about me?'

'You're man-sized, but not up here,' he tapped his brow.

'Mentally you're little more than a child. You know nothing.'

Alan shouted. He couldn't stop himself. 'I'll stew in ignorance until you take the goddam trouble to explain what's going on.'

Padraig stopped holding his head. He closed his eyes for several long moments. When he opened them again, he downed what remained of his poteen.

'I hoped, fervently, when you came here, that I was being given a second chance. You were Geraldine come back to forgive me. I consoled myself that you might even be happy here, in time.'

'You're skating around it. You're not really explaining. There's stuff going on I need to understand. All that business about Mark and Mo. And Kate – what happened in Africa. For goodness sake! Don't you think I deserve an explanation?'

'Are your friends more important than what is left of your family?'

'Grandad, I've got to know. I won't rest until I know. You know that, if you know anything at all about me.'

Padraig's eyes widened, as if he were haunted by inner visions. A grey shadow invaded his face.

'Is a father wrong to try to prevent fate? I have learnt that if he is not wrong, he is surely misguided to hope that he can do so. We, who love you, would protect you from that pain. But still you will not be protected.'

'What the heck are you implying? Are you saying you

knew that something terrible was going to happen to Mom?'

'Of course I knew. D'you imagine I didn't try my very best to dissuade her?'

'You knew? And you didn't stop her?' Alan could hardly breathe. His lungs were filling up with something so heavy he couldn't take a real deep breath.

Padraig said nothing.

Alan was close to tears. 'I hate you! I hate you for that. You should have stopped Mom leaving. You knew and you failed to stop her!'

There was a long silence in which he could hear the ticking of the old wall-mounted pendulum clock. Alan really felt like he was drowning. Nothing made sense. Yet he had been there. He had faced the mountain. He had felt the mountain calling. He knew he had not imagined that.

'You failed Mom. I don't even begin to understand why you failed her. I don't care enough to argue with you. If there is anything you can tell me, anything at all, about what's going on? Why Mom and Dad died? Who killed them? Why?'

Padraig's voice was flat, as if all feeling had been wrung from him. 'Don't even think along the lines you're now thinking.'

'You think I could forget that? Forget them?'

Padraig looked like he'd grown old as a century. His voice was dry as sand, his gaze unfocused. 'Alan, sure you're the closest thing to a son I will ever have. You're as fiercely uncompromising as I might have been at your age. I would have cherished you.'

'Grandfather, don't bullshit me!'

'I could no more have stopped her than halt the seasons. And now it's true of you in your turn. I have lost you both.'

'What do you mean? Why are you talking this way?'

But before Padraig could say more, the house was filled with the babble of other voices. Alan's friends had caught him up. A pandemonium of excited voices was flinging questions at the old man in his chair.

Kate had her hands to her face, blurting out, 'It felt as if we were standing on top of the world. And Slievenamon was calling us.'

Padraig spoke, soft as a whisper, 'Well, now!'

Mo's eyes were round and shining. 'It fuh-fuh-fuh-felt like – like a thu-thunderstorm . . . like it was ruh-ruh-raging in me.' She tapped at her breast with the flat of her hand.

Kate hugged Mo. 'Mr O'Brien, every word is the truth. My hair stood on end. I felt like I could just take off the mountain ridge and fly, like an eagle, over the valley.'

'Oh, Muh-Muh-Mr O'Brien, tuh-tuh-tuh-tell us everything about Suh-Suh-Suh-Slievenamon!'

'Oh, yes. You must! You must tell us everything!'

Alan stood trembling, observing how the grey shadow still cloaked Padraig's features as his eyes moved to

FRANK P. RYAN | 99

consider the two excited girls. 'Ah, now, wouldn't we be here for a year and a day.'

'Oh, puh-puh-please!'

'Mr O'Brien, don't torment us!'

'Tuh-tuh-tell us uh-uh-uh-everything!'

'Everything, is it?' A wintry smile lit up the shadows that haunted Padraig's deeply wrinkled face. 'I think, perhaps, that like Alan you should all cool down. Your clothes are one with your skin. Alan will show you to the bathroom. Cool off and get out of those clothes. Find something dry to wear.'

They ran upstairs and, after ten minutes or so, ran back down again. Mark wore a pair of Alan's jeans with the legs turned up. Kate and Mo wore oddments of shorts and T-shirts a quarter of a century out of fashion – they had discovered them in a bedroom that had been kept spruce and clean in homage to a daughter who had never returned home. Padraig could hardly fail to notice but he said not a word. Instead he waved at them all to sit down and join him and eat some sandwiches he had rustled up in the kitchen. There was also a choice of drinks, hot and cold.

'Now,' the old man sat back in his leather armchair, pallid as a marble statue, 'first you must tell me what happened, every last bit of it, if you can manage that while stuffing your mouths!'

Mo, Kate, even Alan, couldn't wait to talk about it. They talked as they were chewing and it took a long time for each to explain what he or she had experienced on the mountain. But Padraig just let them talk and talk until there was nothing more any one of them had left to say.

'And young Mark, what did you make of it?'

Mark shook his head, with an incredulous grin. 'I'm not pretending that nothing happened. But it wasn't like everybody is saying. It couldn't be. Mountains don't call you. Like, "Hello! I'm your big nosy neighbour. I just thought maybe it was time I called in for a chat."'

Kate turned on him, her eyes flashing. 'So what do you think just happened back there?'

'It must have been some kind of mass hysteria.'

'Hysteria?'

'This Irish superstitiousness is getting to us. All that stuff about crystals and power. Mountains don't call you. Come on, Kate! You all know it as well as I do. Mountains are just big lumps of rock.'

'Mark! Shut up!'

Mo whispered to Mark, who was sitting on the couch next to her. 'It was so. It was cuh-cuh-cuh-calling!'

'Calling us to do what?' Kate looked to Mo, ignoring Mark's stare.

Mark's own face turned an angry pink. 'What are you all saying? What? Like we were hit by some pheromone from a million tons of rock?'

Padraig's voice, low and calm, penetrated their argument. 'Ah, now, Slievenamon is more than a lump of rock. She's ancient enough to have seen the first meanderings of the three sisters. She was older than time when your King Henry came upriver, seven centuries ago.'

'Mo, for goodness sake!' Mark appealed to his sister. 'You know as well as I do this is just rubbish.'

Mo shook her head. She refused to meet his eyes.

Kate's voice was insistent. 'Mark, whatever you think about it, you know you can't tell Grimstone about this.'

Mark heaved a sigh, dropping his eyes down to the mobile phone, which he had been fingering in his lap.

Alan said, 'Padraig has been trying to explain things to me ever since I got here. I didn't listen. I didn't want to listen because I didn't want to believe him. It's all somehow linked to the accident that killed Mom and Dad.'

'It was no accident,' Padraig reminded him.

'And Kate's family, maybe they were killed for a reason. And maybe it's even linked to what happened long ago to you guys, Mark and Mo.'

Mark cut in. 'Mr O'Brien, tell Alan he's raving. Stop this, all of you. You're all raving, just like Grimstone.'

Kate cried, 'Stop kidding yourself, Mark. Surely we need to know what's going on! We need to make sense of it all!'

Padraig agreed. 'Of course you must, Kate.'

Mark shouted, 'You're all bonkers!'

'Shut up, Mark!' Alan glared at him. 'Kate is right. If we could find the reason for all we've been through, we could, maybe, find who was responsible. We could even get our own back. Get justice for Mom and Dad.'

'Why don't you go ask the mountain?'

Mo's voice cut through the arguing, her eyes round and pleading, looking to Padraig, 'Puh-puh-puh-please?'

Padraig's face had never lost the grey sheen since Alan had first spoken to him after coming down from the mountain. But his eyes were gentle, turned now to the dark-haired girl dressed in the clothes once worn by his daughter, and deeply touched, it seemed, by the excitement in Mo's elfin face.

'Maybe you all know already that in the Irish Slievenamon means the Mountain of Women. But the mountain also goes by other names, older names, names she had already taken to herself before even the Celts first came to this valley. Those people of long ago saw the richness of the valley of the Suir. They fought battles to win these lands for themselves, each in turn renaming valley and mountain, until, in Celtic times, the valley became Clonmel, the Vale of Honey, and the mountain Slievenamon. Even the three rivers, the Suir, Nore and Barrow, relinquished their older names, the names of a sacred trinity so ancient and powerful that perhaps the Celts were fearful of their true names. But some remembered and whispered the old names in secret places. And they remembered the old names for the mountain herself, and what's more, the knowledge of her portal.'

'Whu-whu-what puh-portal?'

Padraig gazed into Mo's excited eyes. 'The mountain is believed to be a gateway. *Sidhe ár Feimhin*, such was it called. In English it means "the Gate of Feimhin".'

Kate blurted, 'Who was Feimhin?'

'A prince of old – a very terrible prince, if the legends are to be believed.'

'What legends?'

'Legends of grim times, Kate. Battles that scarred the entire landscape of these parts, turning the Vale of Honey into a wasteland.'

'But even if there is a germ of truth to the legends,' Alan asked, 'what has this to do with what's happening to us?'

'Some legends claim that Feimhin merely craved power, others that he was losing everything and his back was to the wall. But whichever is true, he stood on the summit of Slievenamon and there, where the tumulus of stones stills marks the spot, he called for assistance from a power of darkness.'

Mark chortled. 'Hey, come on, kids! If that worked, I'd have done for Grimstone years ago!'

'Mark! Put a sock in it!'

'Young Mark, you should not speak in such terms, even as a joke. *Sidhe ár Feimhin* is not to be mocked. Those who have studied the legends believe that it describes an opening, or portal. Sure enough they've embellished it with fairy tales, peopled with elves and leprechauns. Yet the legends do speak of strange beings that lived in a world very different from ours, a world not dominated by machines but by forces that would appear magical to the likes of us. Magic is despised today, yet in former ages it was seen as natural, the lore of Magi. Yet magic requires knowledge and power which has been lost over the ages.' Padraig spoke softly, but plainly. 'If you would ask my counsel, I would say that *Sidhe ár Feimhin* describes a gateway leading to another world.'

'Grandad, you've got to be kidding!'

Mark snorted. 'Oh, come off it, Alan. Don't you believe in fairy tales?'

'Scepticism is only natural. And sure fairy tales is how most people think of the legends.' Padraig gazed at Mark with the same wan smile he had earlier bestowed on Mo. 'Indeed I wish, with all of my heart and soul, that *Sidhe ár Feimhin* truly did belong to the world of fairy tales. But alas, young Mark, fairy tales do not come with such a terrible burden of responsibility.'

Alan pressed him, 'What do you mean?'

'There's something I am now obliged to show you. Something long guarded from sceptical eyes. A link to that old world of terror and ruin. I would have preferred it to remain lost and forgotten. But I can see that you're special, all four of you, though I cannot even begin to imagine why, or what will come of it.'

Mark cried, 'Mr O'Brien, you should stop this now!'

'Ah, now, young Mark. As I see it, it would appear that the mountain is calling you, like it or not. Moreover, the dangers that threaten you are real enough. Knowledge, be it of the most ancient and forbidden nature, is also a weapon of kinds. And if I can arm you in any way at all, if I can give you some means of protecting yourselves, I will.'

Alan saw the patent honesty in Padraig's worried face. He felt a tiny thrill of fright invade his being.

'The burden would have become yours, Alan, but I would have put it aside for many a year if the choice were mine. But the coming of Grimstone to this town has robbed me of that choice. What Mark and Mo have told me about their adoptive father makes plain that he is not the simple preacher he pretends to be. Moreover, the sigil he adores confirms my worst fears in that respect. And this in turn tells me that it is hardly accidental that you – Mark and Mo – fell into his clutches at such a precious and early age – though the fact he kept you close to him all of your young years, however far from paternal his instincts would have been, is equally revealing. His coming here, to Clonmel, was no accident. Time, therefore, is pressing. Come, then, if your scepticism is to be answered! I'll take you to the place that Grimstone is really searching for, a place of secrets that must be concealed from him at all costs. Then surely your eyes will be opened. But I warrant you'll not thank me for it.'

The Grave of Feimhin

With Padraig's machete hacking through the profusion of nettles and spiky brambles, they made their way up a twisting climb through the dense woodland that coated the foothills of the Comeraghs, finally emerging into a shadowed bower. The surrounding trees were ancient oaks, their barks hoary and fissured from centuries of winters, and mottled with the bright greens and yellows of mosses. To an unknowing eye, it would have hinted at nothing of any special importance. At the centre, gained by more hacking with the machete, a mound appeared, standing no more than a yard above the leaf-strewn floor.

The entrance to the barrow was covered with a great flat stone, itself buried under brambles and soil. Padraig cleared the surface of the stone using the machete. With growing excitement the four friends discovered that, with the cover stone removed, they were gazing into a stone-lined tunnel burrowing into darkness. They switched on the torches, brought at Padraig's insistence, cutting through the gloom of what now appeared to be a narrow, descending shaft, and they followed Padraig's lead into the tunnel on hands and knees. After twenty yards of crawling through dirt and roots, they stumbled through into an octagonal stone-lined chamber, tall enough for everyone, other than Padraig, to stand upright. Here, in the light of their torches, they stared awestruck at a skeleton, as long as Padraig was tall, and laid in final repose upon a bier of solid stone.

'Mind you keep well back. Touch nothing of the mortal remains!'

'Who is it?' Kate couldn't keep a quaver from her voice.

'I'll leave you to decide that for yourselves!'

The fragments of armour, the great bronze helm, filigreed in gold amid the greens and yellows of rimey decay, told them it must be the remains of some warrior prince, laid to rest a very long time ago. The flesh and clothing had rotted away but the skeleton was preserved – the huge skull ivory-white, as if it belonged to somebody more recently buried. The face of the skull was long and lean, with jaws of yellowing teeth that appeared to gather together with a snarl, and with garnets filling the eye-sockets, as if fixing for eternity the rage that had burned in them in life. A cuirass of bronze enveloped the enormous rib cage, decorated and emblazoned with a similar filigree as the helm.

'Look more closely, if you will, at the brow!'

They gathered round, holding the torches closer.

'Holy shit!'

Alan's exclamation was quickly followed by three others.

The blow that killed this fearsome warrior was visible in the great slash that had cut through the helmet and the head within it, from the crown to the roof of his left eye-socket.

'Now mark you his weapon!'

The torches picked out a great sword, with a blade blacker than pitch, which ran diagonally across the lower body and legs. The hilt was still grasped by the skeletal hand within a heavy gauntlet of metal, turned green by the verdigris of time.

'Look!' Mo murmured. She pointed to the hilt.

Mark saw it too and he shivered with fright. Then Alan and Kate, their hearts pounding, stared at the sigil of the triple infinity, embossed in a silvery outline on the hilt of the sword.

'Yes, Mo – the same symbol I recognised in your notebook the day I first met you. So now you know why I realised that your arrival was no accident.'

'Buh-buh-buh-but what does it muh-mean?'

'You're surprised to find this symbol on a sword and not a cross? Things are not always as they appear. I'll wager that what you imagined to be a cross in Grimstone's hand was originally the hilt and cross-piece and a stub of blade of the dagger that was the companion piece to the weapon you now see. Did you not say it came from a barrow such as this one?'

Mark, his voice taut with shock, answered for Mo, 'Grimstone told us he got it from some collector. The collector told him it came from a barrow grave but Grimstone refused to believe it. He pretended it came from Christian times, with some link to the Knights Templar.'

'This collector was almost certainly a grave robber, and one that, if what you suspect is true, your adoptive father killed because he coveted the robber's most precious possession.'

'Mr O'Brien – do you think it came from this same grave?'

'I think not, Kate. This grave has never been looted. My family has watched over it a thousand years – and likely much longer. Our original name was not O'Brien but d'Eiragh. And even the very mountains here still bear the family name, in Comeragh – Cum Eiragh. Which means the fort of Eiragh. And your family too, Kate, was once tied to ours – the name was not always Shaunessy.'

'What do you mean?'

'The Shaunessys and Eiraghs are distantly related.'

Padraig directed the beam of his torch over walls of masoned stone incised with a dense profusion of pictures and scored everywhere with narrow lines, cut across with verticals and diagonals.

'D'you recognise the nature of these?'

Kate's voice was trembling. 'They're runes.'

'Ogham, Kate! An alphabetical script older than runes, though some experts believe they became the basis of Nordic runes. These tell the story of the grave in detail. The Ogham itself is somewhat less than two thousand years old but the grave is a good deal older. I have spent many years studying that history. Indeed, I suspect the Ogham captures what might earlier have been carried down in words, or more likely song.'

'What do they say, Grandad?'

'Tales that must have been retold around many a campfire before the very wonder and terror of them was captured in the stone. But it is this symbol here that will most interest you!'

Padraig ran his fingers over the chiselled outline, first in one place, then repeated here and there, as if it represented such a dark and terrible potency it reproduced itself over the confining six walls.

'Is it the name of the warrior?'

'Indeed not!' The old man's voice fell to a low-pitched murmur. 'Never the name – that curse could not be carved in stone.' He took a breath and calmed himself, allowing his voice to fall to his normal quiet tones. 'These inscriptions are a ward.'

'What's a ward?' Alan asked.

'A protection against evil,' Kate breathed, reaching out to take Alan's hand.

'Kate is right. They ward against a dark force with such

a hunger for domination that none could control their own destiny once under its mantle.'

Mark's voice sounded taut but curious. 'All these stories in the Ogham – they tell of war, don't they, Mr O'Brien?'

'Yes, so they do, Mark. This warrior prince was buried at the close of wars that must have seemed hopeless in those far-off days, wars without end. To stop the slaughter, the wise men of their time made sacrifices. They called upon ancient forces, such as might defeat a warrior prince who wielded such a blade of darkness – a blade, as is written here in the very stone, a hundred times blacker than midnight yet forged neither of iron nor bronze. An iron blade would be long rusted away in this damp air. You can see for yourself that even the bronze of his armour, which would last better than iron, is almost worn away to dust. Yet the sword has survived. Only with help could they defeat this warrior and thus end the chaos. The grave was cut and sealed with warded stone – magic to you, young Mark. But what appears magic today was knowledge in those far-off days.'

Mark's face was ghostly in the torchlight. 'All I can see is an old grave, with pictures and fairy tales on the walls.'

'Ah, now! Must I awaken this thing in order to convince you of something that is staring you in the face?'

There were cries of disagreement from Alan and the two girls. But Mark shook his head, still struggling to believe any of this.

'Stay here a moment and touch nothing. I'll be back.'

Padraig left them and went to the surface, returning in a few minutes with his hands cupped in the shape of a bowl. Under the inspection light, he opened them to reveal a mass of woodlice, ants and centipedes from some rotting tree trunk.

'Ugh!' Kate made a face.

'Now switch off your torches for a moment and watch – you, Mark, in particular.' In the pitch dark, they stared with a prickling awe as they saw how the sigil of the triple infinity glowed, like a silvery malignant eye, in the dark. 'Bear with me a moment longer,' bade Padraig, as he poured the insects in a living trickle over the black blade. There was a sparking, like an electric discharge, on contact, and then a fierce smoky flame. The insects convulsed and burnt.

The four friends jerked back, their nostrils filled with the acrid stench. The torches flared back on, in trembling hands.

'Whuh-whuh-what does it muh-mean, Mr O'Brien?'

'Even today, thousands of years after it was forged, the blade still retains its ancient power. Such is its potency it is still deadly to anything it touches. A formidable weapon. And I'm afraid that you but glimpse its real potential for malice – undimmed by time.'

Alan's eyes narrowed. 'Who was he?'

'I think you have guessed that by now, every one of you!'

'This is Feimhin?'

'The warrior prince himself.'

'But who defeated him? Who killed him?' Kate's finger was pointing to the cloven skull.

'The Ogham tells of a warrior tribe who were not native to Ireland. They talk about little people, no taller than children, but yet the fiercest warriors. Some say they were called to assist another tribe, known as Tuatha De Danaan – the people of Diana – when the de Danaans were being conquered by the newly arriving Celts. More likely it was civil warfare within the Tuatha De Danaan themselves. The name of these ferocious warriors was Fir Bolg. The words, in that old language, are believed to mean something like "Warriors of Destiny".

'According to the legends, it was Feimhin himself who, in his lust for power, first opened the gate on Slievenamon. His call was answered by a force of darkness, perhaps the same force that forged the sword – and Grimstone's broken dagger.

'What followed was chaos, raging throughout the length and breadth of Ireland, and extending far beyond, to Britain, as it is now known, and further still, deep into Europe, and even beyond. Never-ending war, all driven by that unassuageable malice. The slaughter is described as fearsome. Everywhere throughout these lands you find funeral mounds and circles of wood and stone, calling on the gods and goddesses to save the tormented people.

'The wisest of counsels suggested the boldest possible answer. Since the chaos had been imported from another world, through Feimhin's gate, they called for assistance through that same portal. In answer to their call came the Fir Bolg, who had long perfected the arts of warfare in combat against that same dark force in that other world.'

Padraig ran his finger over the Ogham.

'"Here,"' he read, '"the strangers came, in answer to our prayers. They fought through rack and ruin, with indomitable courage."' Padraig's finger ran further along the chiselled lines. '*Fir is Mna* – they fought men and women, side by side, spurning the weapons of local tribes and princes and favouring their own ward-strengthened axes of bronze. Look here at this description. I'll read it so you can see for yourselves – "*Men and women of unearthly countenance . . . Warriors whose very hair turned to flame in battle*". The inscriptions go on to describe them as fearing nothing, not even the darkness that had taken this prince's soul. The terror was finally brought to an end when the Fir Bolg overcame Feimhin's armies and slew the prince himself in the heat of battle, ending the chaos.'

Padraig's eyes fell from the Ogham to turn and look at the cloven helmet and skull of the warrior. 'A blow,' he murmured, 'from the battle-axe of a Fir Bolg.'

Kate murmured, 'What did they mean, describing the Fir Bolg as looking unearthly?'

Padraig shrugged. 'The legends refer to them as strangers, warriors from another world. Perhaps some elements of the stories are fables. People of other races – but from Earth – might have been mistaken for beings from another world. But is it not also possible the storytellers were merely recounting the truth?'

Mark muttered, 'Like Tír na n'Og – the land of eternal youth.'

'Indeed, Mark, the story of fair Niamh, who fell in love with Oisín the hunter and poet and took him to her land of perpetual youth. But even in your English legends, don't you have Avalon?'

Mo was staring at Padraig, her eyes round with a mixture of terror and wonder. In her fright the stammer had worsened. 'Whu-whu-whu-wh . . . what if – if suh-suh-some-buh-body—?'

'If somebody bad were to take up the weapon of Feimhin again?'

Mo nodded.

'Well, now, hasn't the same thought entered my head!' Padraig ruffled her hair, in reassurance, then spoke abruptly to all four of the friends. 'Enough of this talk of wars and ruin. I think we've spent sufficient time in the company of that sword.'

Back at the sawmill, sitting in a daze of wonderment on the grass in the now late-afternoon sunshine, Alan continued to question Padraig. 'Did Mom know about Feimhin's grave?'

'I had no son, nor was I likely to have one since my wife died in giving birth to Geraldine. So I was obliged to pass the knowledge to my daughter.'

Understanding now dawned on Alan. 'That was why Mom ran away? She ran because she was frightened?'

Padraig turned to gaze at their faces, one by one. 'Knowledge of Feimhin's grave, and his black blade, is a great responsibility. Its existence must remain our absolute secret.'

There was a tremor of anguish Alan could not keep from his voice. 'Then why did you show us, Grandad?'

'Are you not being called to the gate? The same gate through which both darkness and the Fir Bolg were summoned long ago?'

Mo spoke softly, 'Buh-buh-but we're not wuh-wuh-warriors!'

Padraig nodded, his face grim.

Kate agreed with Mo. 'We know nothing about those sorts of things. What could we possibly have to offer some . . . some other world?'

Padraig reached out and briefly squeezed her hand. 'You do have something special about you. The killing of your family tells me that. My Geraldine! I have to wonder if what happened is linked with the same burden, and now your involvement. Ah, sure this is an accursed place!'

'What are we to do, Grandad?'

'I will do what little I can to help you. Teach you some things in the short time we have before you leave.'

Leave! Kate's mind reeled just that single word.

'Teach us what?' Mark's incredulity did not stop his asking.

'How to get you past the gate.'

'Get past the gate!' more than one voice shrieked at once.

'Are you not heading for the summit of the mountain that is calling you? *Sidhe ár Feimhin* is surely your destiny.'

'Hey, just let me pack my overnight travel bag, folks. I'm on a little jaunt to the world of fairy tales.'

'Scoff as you will, young Mark. But I wager you will still answer the calling. And you have precious little time to prepare for it. For, if I judge right, Grimstone is back in just twelve days.'

Mark's face paled.

Alan's eyes met those of his grandfather. He understood now the hurt in his expression, his fear of losing him.

'Supposing – let's just say supposing – we did climb to the top of Slievenamon, what are we going to find there?'

'There is a cairn of stones at the very top of the mountain. Legend suggests it marks the portal.'

'But what does that mean?' Alan shook his head in bafflement. 'Are you saying there's no real gateway into this world?'

'If legend is true, and a portal there is, it will hardly take the form of a gate of lintel and wood.'

'But then how the heck do we find it?'

'Hidden within the cairn of stones lies a basin of stone. I know it is there because I have seen it with my own eyes. It seemed an altar of sorts, but to what unearthly power

I could not even hazard a guess. If legend is true, the altar is warded by invocation to that power.'

'What sort of invocation?'

'Drawn in the same Ogham you saw in the barrow.'

Alan shook his head. 'Invocations to what power?'

'Grimstone carries a black cross, which, if I guess right, is the hilt, cross-piece and upper blade of Feimhin's dagger. This has spoken to him of old power, a power lost and buried for millennia, but still clinging to the landscape. Slievenamon is at the heart of it, the mountain itself, and the three rivers that girdle her skirts.'

'Thuh-thuh-thuh . . . thuh-Trídédana?'

'You've a great deal of sense in you, Mo Grimstone. The Trídédana indeed!'

'What does that mean?'

'We know that to the Celts all rivers were sacred. Indeed, rivers were seen as sacred to a great many ancient peoples. Even in Christian teaching, did not John the Baptist wash Jesus in the waters of a river? Do we not baptise using water?'

'Yuh-yuh-you remember what Grimstone said about ruh-rivers.'

'Mark?' Kate turned on him.

Mark smiled wryly, then intoned Grimstone's snarl, '"Three rivers — evocative of the foulest pretence — the stink of a heathen trinity?"'

There was a silence lasting several seconds as they all digested that.

'So,' Padraig rubbed at his brow, 'if I interpret the best course, you should gather the waters of the three rivers – we still call them the three sisters – to mix in the stone basin. Then invoke the Ogham you discover there.'

'But none of us can read Ogham.'

'I'll have to teach you what I can.'

'In just twelve days?'

'It's all the time you have. And we must also equip you with a weapon.'

'What weapon?'

'One appropriately warded with force. I doubt you will get safely through the gate without it.'

Alan shook his head. 'Aw, come on, you guys! This is getting crazy!'

Mark laughed softly in Alan's ear. 'What have I been telling you? Welcome to cloud cuckoo land!'

The Spear of Lug

When, at the crack of dawn, Padraig emerged from his front door, Mark was already up and waiting for him. Mark sat in the fragrant grass by the side of the dairy, leaning against the pear tree, which was fruiting tiny, stone-hard fruit, meanwhile watching Padraig stride up the short curl of gravel path in his direction, then halt mid-stride when crossing the yard in the direction of the timber sheds. Noticing Mark, he came over to see what he was doing there so early.

'Well?'

'Mr O'Brien, I want to help you.'

Silent for a second or two, Padraig peered at the young Londoner as he swiped at grass heads with a stick.

'How do you propose to help?'

'I've a pretty good memory for languages – foreign words.'

'You mean you want me to teach you Ogham?'

'I'm not pretending to believe everything you've been telling us. But one thing I do know now is that we're down to eleven days. Then Grimstone will be back. When he comes back he'll take me and Mo away from here for good. I – I don't want that to happen.'

Padraig swivelled his head round, as if ready to walk away.

'Mr O'Brien – I'm telling you the truth.'

Padraig hesitated, gazing down at Mark, eye-to-eye.

'Please, Mr O'Brien! Mo is really frightened.' Mark pressed his lips tightly together. 'I don't want to appear vain, but I really don't believe any of the others could learn enough Ogham in that time.'

'But you reckon you could?'

'I could learn a little – maybe enough to make a difference.'

'Why would you offer to become sorcerer's apprentice when you doubt the very art of sorcery?'

Mark nodded. 'I know how it must look. I can't pretend to believe everything you've told us. But I saw the sigil on the sword. I saw it glow in the dark. I saw the insects fry on the blade. I don't think Grimstone's cross is a cross at all. I think you're right – it's what's left of a dagger.' Mark scrambled to his feet so he wouldn't have to squint in the low morning sunshine when looking into Padraig's face. 'I don't really know what it is, or what Grimstone is up to, but it frightens me too. I can't bear the thought of going back to live in that house.'

Padraig put his hand on Mark's left shoulder.

'I know you've done your best to protect your sister.'

'For all the good it did her!'

'And you believe you can learn some Ogham in eleven days?'

'I'll work really hard at it.'

'Arrah, this will be blacksmithing in a hot forge. Devilish hard work – harder than you could possibly imagine.'

'I don't care how hard it will be.'

'Then we are agreed!'

Padraig surprised him by spitting into the palm of his right hand, like a tinker at a horse fair. He extended his hand. Mark hesitated, then did likewise. His hand was dwarfed by the callused and horny grasp of Padraig's.

Later that same morning, when Alan heard that Mark had volunteered to assist his grandfather in the little-used smithy behind the house, he couldn't hide his astonishment. He couldn't stop talking about it to Kate and Mo, when they gathered, as usual, over the table in the dairy.

Mo said, 'Muh-Muh-Mark is duh-desperate.'

'Heck, I don't know! I just don't know what to make of Mark any more.'

What was he supposed to think? Just when he was beginning to admit to himself that the sceptical Mark had probably been right all along, Mark did the very opposite to what you would expect, going to work for Padraig like some willing convert to his grandfather's superstitions. Since yesterday's trip to the mountains, Alan had had time to sleep on it, and today it seemed that the strange calling on the top of the mountains simply defied all common sense.

'We've got to look for normal, rational, explanations for all of this.'

Kate shook her head. 'Don't you start pretending that yesterday didn't happen.'

'C'mon, Kate! You can believe it's like Slievenamon calling?'

'You have an alternative explanation?'

Oh man!

Where was the sceptical Mark when you needed him? 'Oh, come on guys! How the hell are we supposed to buy what's going on? You know as well as I do it's crazy. You can't communicate with a mountain.'

This just led to furious glares from the girls.

But his natural scepticism continued to haunt Alan and he couldn't help going over things, again and again, in his mind.

Wasn't it more than enough that they were no longer orphans struggling to carry on alone? They were friends, with common experiences, who wanted to support one another. That was good enough for him, without the contagious blarney that had taken hold of them on the mountain. He tried again with the girls. 'Hey, we have a lot of hurt in common. We've got to recognise that that could play tricks with our feelings, like some kind of common emotional charge.'

They shook their heads.

'Can't we just go back to having fun?'

'Oh, Alan!'

But he really meant it. The way he saw it, something really nice had blossomed, easy and natural as cherry blossom. His rational mind ached to find a way of getting back to that.

Over the days that followed he took to driving around the tracks in the woods, sitting on his own in the bench seat of the old flatbed truck Padraig used to deliver logs. He'd pull in to a halt in the middle of the track, or in a tree-framed glade, looking out the windshield into the summery sky, watching the clouds roll over, as if the answer lay there. Clouds and sky and trees. And mountains – one mountain in particular!

Oh, boy!

Here in Clonmel, even in the depths of the woods, you couldn't escape the brooding shadow of Slievenamon!

The townspeople, now that his despair was lifting, seemed like friendly, decent people. They talked a little different, with a lilt to their words, but essentially they came across as the same kind of commonsense people he had grown up with. That approach had been drummed deep into his way of looking at the world. Now, suddenly, right in the middle of things getting right for him, a big hole had appeared in his world. Nothing added up any more.

It was driving him crazy.

He was just sitting there in a daydream, the truck's cab throbbing to the rhythm of the diesel engine, when he was aware that somebody was rapping for his attention on the doorframe. He jerked with surprise, then saw that it was Kate.

'Alan! You have to turn this thing around and go back to the mill. Your grandfather has something to show us.'

Alan groaned. He threw open the passenger door, which was missing a handle on the outside, so Kate could join him in the cab. He performed a six- or seven-point turn in the narrow confines of the tree-hemmed track, and headed back.

Kate had to hold firm to the dash, grinning, as the vehicle rocked and jerked through the manoeuvre. 'Where did you learn to drive a thing like this?'

He shook his head, little inclined to explain that his dad had taught him to drive, off-road, for his fourteenth birthday.

'Alan, will you stop moping like this?'

'Like what?'

'Like you're out of your mind with jealousy, because Mark is working in the forge with Padraig?'

It hadn't for a moment occurred to him that that was what the girls were thinking. And now she said it, it only made things worse. He refused to speak another word over the mile or so of weaving and winding, until they broke free of cover at the edge of the mill yard to find Padraig sitting with Mo and Mark on the knoll by the dairy. Across Padraig's knees was a strange metal object, about three and a half feet in length, and heavy, like a shallow S-shape. It certainly wasn't made of steel. It had a greenish metallic sheen, like old bronze, but was cut with patterns and arabesques that flashed and glimmered with the slightest movement.

Even the sceptical Alan couldn't deny his curiosity. 'What the blazes is that, Grandad?'

'Well now!' Padraig's lips crinkled into a wry smile. 'Will you take a look at the weapon that killed Prince Feimhin!'

'I don't understand!'

'I was impetuous, foolishly arrogant. Not a lot older than you and young Mark here. My father brought me to the grave and explained it, much as I explained it to you. But there was a single difference. This battle-axe adorned the lintel, just inside the entrance, as if to ward it. Though hoary, with three thousand years of patina, yet it had resisted decay – much as you saw with Feimhin's blade.'

Alan stared at the weapon, which was about three-quarters the length of a long bow, with a central hilt between two heavy blades, curved like opposing scimitars.

'What are you saying – this is what killed Prince Feimhin?'

'Cleaved right the way through helm and head! Sure didn't I hold it square against that terrible wound to confirm my suspicions, soon after I had first cleaned and oiled it? Everything fitted exactly, like the pieces of a jigsaw. This is certainly the weapon.'

Padraig took a firm grip of the central stock of the battle-axe with his right hand, allowing it to twist and turn with a balanced flexion of his wrist. The bright-cut patterns decorating the cutting edges glittered. Alan realised that the patterns were not mere embroidery. They appeared to be invocations, but drawn in a very different script from the Ogham they had seen in the burial chamber.

'It doesn't look like any battle-axe I've ever seen.'

'Of course you've seen many ancient battle-axes!' The old man laughed at his expense. 'But you're right – there's none to my own mind that is remotely like it. From the shape of it, I believe it's intended both for close quarter hand-to-hand combat and most particularly for casting.'

'You mean, like throwing?'

'Indeed!'

'Can I hold it?'

'You may – but be prepared! It's quite a weight.'

Padraig laid the axe across the palms of his outstretched hands so Alan could take it in both hands by the central stock.

'Careful now!'

'Oh, baby!' Heavy was an understatement. Alan found that he was pressed just to hold it steady in his hands.

'Study its geometry carefully, its curves and patterns. As you'll discover, it's not flat, but subtly curved in three dimensions. The work of a master craftsman – truly a fearsome weapon!'

Alan felt a curious thrill just to hold it. 'You're saying that this belonged to a Fir Bolg warrior?'

'I would assume that you're holding the weapon of a warrior prince – a leader of that race in his own right!'

'Man! This is really what killed Prince Feimhin?'

'I'm certain of it. Haven't I studied that axe for most of my life? But even in all that time I've glimpsed no more than a hint of its potential. I'm going to attempt a demonstration. See – I've set up the target yonder.'

Padraig nodded to the stump of a tree about forty yards away, close to where the track took off into the woods. It was perhaps a foot in diameter and stood about six feet out of the earth.

'I'll attempt a single throw. No more! I've learnt from experience that use of the weapon draws deeply on the thrower, in body and spirit. It's my guess that the inscriptions you see on the cutting edges of the blades were meant to be invoked in the act of throwing. I cannot read a single character of these but I'll make do with a mantra of my own. In the meantime you should all stand well clear.'

They drew back and watched.

Padraig closed his eyes, rocking slightly on his feet as he searched for balance in his grip about the stock. Opening his eyes again, his gaze focused on the distant tree trunk. His right arm sprang back in a curve, muscles standing out like hawsers. In that same movement, his head inclined so that his line of sight was one with the target, and then, as a low-pitched growl of song burst from his lips, the weapon leapt from the twisting curl of his wrist.

The battle-axe whirled, making a low humming noise, as if in reply to the invocation of Padraig's chant, while the four friends watched in astonishment. When the axe struck the tree trunk, the dense wood shattered, as if struck by an explosive missile. But still the humming and whirling continued. Only the pitch changed, signalling what appeared to be an impossible change of direction, as the spinning blade wheeled around in an arc, heading back to be grasped, as if in a consummation of purpose, by Padraig's upraised hand.

With gasps of awe, the four friends gathered around Padraig, witnessing the discharge of spiritual tension that exhausted him as he slowly fell to his knees and, with a reverential right hand, laid the battle-axe on the ground.

That night Alan woke from sleep with the memory of Mo's sweet song to the mountain like a caress in his mind. He sensed what was coming.

He murmured, 'No!' But it was a token resistance.

The wave came, more gentle than before, a slow rise over many minutes, washing over his skin like a mist of kisses, as though this time the seduction was meant for him alone. His mind opened out onto the vast panorama that bridged the valley, until the vision of the mountain filled all of his senses. He felt its breath touch the membranes of his eyes. He tasted the exultation of its longing on his tongue. His body unfolded to the ecstasy of the calling, embracing every delicious mote as it flowed, in streams and rivulets of abandonment, through the inner spaces of his being.

Day after day, blue smoke rose from the soot-stained steel chimney over the corrugated iron roof of the old forge. Here, in the summer's heat, the pulse of the hammer rang out, steel-ringing and clear, disturbing the blackbirds, robins, blue tits and sparrows, and causing them to shriek outrage at the invasion of tranquillity in the broken walls, hedges and hinterland of trees that framed the mill yard. And meanwhile, the days passed by in a blur of enchantment.

Indeed how else could they think of it but as enchantment, days and nights that were woven with spells of seduction, a calling every bit as strange and inexplicable as the caterpillar entombed in its cocoon of magic, from which the magnificent new being, the moth or butterfly, would ultimately appear? An enchantment in which the last vestiges of rational resistance, the last clinging to orderly commonsense, were abandoned to the waves of calling, no matter that, in their more lucid moments, the four friends sensed the anguish of having to say farewell to the world they had been born into, with its comforting bedrock of reason.

It was frightening to accept that there was no logical

explanation for what was happening to them. That there was no way of dealing with it other than to embrace it.

And yet it seemed curiously unsurprising to discover that, night after night, all four friends were now sharing common dreams – dreams of Slievenamon, and its age-old history, of the brutal conflicts that ebbed and flowed around its breast of stone. Dreams of battles in which a prince with blazing eyes laid siege and broke through wooden forts atop mounds of earth, to end in slaughter. Dreams about the eternal movement and murmuring of the three rivers, the Suir, the Nore and Barrow, which flowed about the mountain's skirts. And dreams about the peoples who lived about their shores and adored them before the coming of the Celts. Whispers, sometimes, of the names of people, like the Tuatha De Danaan – and others, the strangest visitors of all, beings that came as lights, or masks of fire, who brushed their minds like Lords of Magic, as though to promise truths and wonders beyond human logic and comprehension.

If, in their waking moments, they knew that such things made no sense, that what was happening to them couldn't possibly make any sense, it no longer mattered. They had moved beyond caring whether things made sense any more.

One morning Mo followed her brother as he entered the forge at first light. She stood just within the open door, and watched, in fascination, as Padraig kindled a battered cob pipe from a piece of red glowing iron, humming some lines in the old language, then dowsed the fierce metal in water, so it hissed and spluttered, with his smoky blue eyes sparkling.

'Wh-whu-what are yuh-yuh-you doing, Mr O'Brien?'

'Aha – it's you, Mo. Come looking for the meaning of dreams?'

Mo's eyes widened. 'Do yuh-yuh-you know the uh-answers?'

'Hasn't young Mark here been asking me the same questions? My answer to you, as to himself, is that you're sharing the memories of the mountain.'

'Buh-buh-buh-buh—' Mo shook her head in frustration.

'But mountains don't have memories? Is that what you wish to say?'

She nodded.

Padraig stopped working and arched his tall body back beyond his centre of gravity, as if to ease a nagging ache in his spine. His chest above the broad belt holding his trousers was only partially covered by a scarred leather waistcoat. He looked over his shoulder to where Mark was stirring a bowl full of engine oil. 'If your brother is determined to make himself useful, he'd do better to work those bellows.'

Mark's face was already awash with sweat from the heat. He was stripped to the waist, and covered in streaks and smudges of soot. He winked at Mo as he started to pump the big wooden paddle.

Mo turned back to Padraig. 'Wuh-wuh-wuh-will you explain . . . how muh-muh-mountains have memories?'

Padraig withdrew the red-glowing bar of iron from the furnace and, in a single sure swivel, dropped it on the anvil. He started to hammer it, talking disjointedly in between blows and the crackling showers of sparks. 'The entire countryside is alive with memories: mountains, woods – if they are old woods – and rivers too. But these are not memories such as you might imagine them, memories seen through human eyes and preserved in the language of human tongues.'

Mark wiped sweat from his brow with his discarded T-shirt. He had stopped pumping while the metal was out of the furnace. Mo knew he was listening, while pretending his concentration was elsewhere.

Padraig brought the metal back into the coals. Mark started pumping again. Mo could see her brother's sweat dripping onto the flagstones.

'So whu-whu-what kind of muh-muh-muh-memories are they?'

'Harder, Mark!' Padraig shifted the iron in the furnace to find a hotter position before glancing over his shoulder at Mo. 'You wouldn't be playing with me, thinking me simple as mutton?'

Mark's ears followed the conversation, hearing Mo dissolve into a rare fit of giggling. He grinned to himself. They enjoyed bantering with Padraig, now that they were no longer afraid of him.

'You still huh-huh-huh-haven't explained.'

'Do you omadawns imagine you will simply go up there and take a stroll through Feimhin's gate?'

Mark's ears bristled to full alertness.

'Whu-whu-what are you trying tuh-tuh-to tell me?'

'I'm growing a bit tired of your games. We're gabbing too much. The furnace is cooling. Mark Grimstone, put your lily-white English back into it!'

Mark worked like a fury until the entire smithy was bathed in a fierce white glow from the furnace. He wanted Padraig to be impressed enough to continue to talk. The metal came out of the coals again for another thunderous racket of spark-haloed hammering on the hard grey steel of the anvil, then back into the water again.

More pumping.

Padraig paused, waiting for the reheating. 'Isn't it obvious that such a portal will be fiercely protected – and thus dangerous?'

Mo decided to risk irritating Padraig with another question after a new hissing and spluttering in the steaming pit of water.

'I duh-duh-don't understand.'

'Sure you, who can sense the forces of mountain and river, should know the answers better than anybody. The gate will be warded by some form of guardian – a dangerous one that will already be aware that you are coming.'

*

As Mo ran from the forge, looking for Alan and Kate, Mark stared in her wake, his own heart beating like a drum inside what felt like a hollow rib cage. He wanted to join Mo in talking to Alan and Kate, but he was obliged to stay and keep working the bellows. There were times each day when the old man explained the strange spellings and grammar, or chanted for his education the common invocations that had been found in examples of Ogham, and sometimes Mark imagined Padraig's throat encircled by a golden torc, like he recalled from Celts he had seen in the history books. He imagined a circle of believers all gathered around a sacrifice, of an animal or maybe even a human, with the druid invoking the old powers.

Right now, as Padraig put the hot metal through another cycle of annealing, Mark expressed his curiosity about the weapon.

'Why don't you make an axe, like the Fir Bolg battle-axe?'

'Such a weapon is beyond my skill. My aim is to construct a spear. Even then it should be cast with a head of bronze. Bronze would carry the Ogham invocations better. But bronze working is a skill largely forgotten. Iron is easier because it is more malleable with the heat. We must have faith that a spear of tempered iron, spell-warded, will be enough to protect you. I take comfort from the knowledge that a blade of warded iron was woven for the great king, Lug, remembered in legend as Lug the Longhand for his fierce strike with the spear.'

It was all Mark could do to stop himself grinning, much as Mo had earlier. It was all so fantastic.

Over lunch in the sunlit grass, Padraig regaled them with the tale of the boy hero, Lug, whose father, Cian, was a prince of the Tuatha De Danaan and whose mother, Ethniu, was the beautiful daughter of the one-eyed monster, Balor.

'Hopefully,' Mark whispered to Mo, 'Ethniu took after her mother.'

Mo pinched Mark's blackened arm, wanting just to listen to another of Padraig's wonderful tales. Mark merely grinned, amused to find himself set apart from the others, like a reproach. Surprise, surprise – of the triplets, only Lug survived! And surprise, surprise, and surprise again, it all led to a great battle in which Lug wounded the monster, Balor, with a single cast of his magic-warded spear!

The prophecies predicted that Lug would kill his monstrous grandfather and so Balor imprisoned Ethniu in a tower of crystal. But with the help of the druidess, Birog, Cian broke through the seals and seduced Ethniu and she gave birth to triplets that Balor tried to drown in the Atlantic Ocean.

Mark clapped with the others at the end. Padraig was a pretty good spinner of yarns, with princesses as ambitious and lecherous as the worst of the men. 'No problems,' Mark intoned seriously, 'boys and girls. If we encounter Balor, we'll know what to do.'

'Your mocking tongue has not abandoned you, Mark Grimstone. But let me warn you not to confuse the romance of storytelling with the real danger you will face soon – or the power of real magic.'

Kate squealed, 'Real magic?'

'Perhaps,' added Padraig, 'young Mark should reflect on the fact that, if my thinking is correct, his adoptive father has kept him and Mo close so they would lead him, ultimately, to this very situation.'

Mark was silent after that. Had the old man, in a single sentence, explained the puzzle of Grimstone's behaviour – explained, indeed, why Grimstone and Bethal had kept them alive, while appearing to hate them? Mark was deeply thoughtful all the way back to the forge. Then he called out to Padraig above the hammering, 'So that's what we're forging – the Ogham-warded Spear of Lug?'

Padraig nodded, the wry smile wrinkling his lips. 'Yes – or as best my ageing memory and arthritic hands can fashion her!'

'That sounds like quite a challenge!'

'Sure there's a devilment in you, Mark Grimstone, that would make a mischief out of virtue!'

Mark had to look away again, to hide his ear-to-ear grin, working the big paddle for all he was worth. 'I don't imagine, Mr O'Brien, that you believe in princesses in crystal towers any more than I do.'

'Take care that sarcasm does not lead you into confusing truth with fact.'

'Surely they're the same?'

Padraig lifted the fierce red-glowing blade from the furnace and inserted the point into the jaws of a vice. Then, with enormous grippers, he began to add the spiral twist that would run lengthwise from tip to stock.

'Sometimes,' he panted, wiping sweat from his brow with his forearm, 'a very great truth, yes even a very terrible truth, can become embellished in the telling. When you were very young how did your adoptive parents talk of your biological mother and father? Did they say they had gone away?'

'Nothing so sweet.'

Padraig loosened the blade from the vice and rammed it back into the furnace, speaking all the while without losing his concentration on the task, or even glancing in Mark's direction. 'I have no doubt they were unkind. But even if they had told you your parents were hymning with the angels, do you think that sugar coating would have hidden the painful truth from your heart?'

Mark was silent through some more pumping and reworking of the metal.

'I'm doing my best to understand, Mr O'Brien. But if there really is something, some important lesson, hidden away in the fairy tales and legends, I just don't see it.'

Padraig continued to extend the spiral for a while in silence, dousing the metal in the oil-sheened water, then started the cycle of reheating all over again. Only then did he pause to look assessingly at Mark.

'Take comfort from scepticism, lad, but don't let it rule you. If it's real truth you're after, put aside your gadgets and look into your heart.'

Day after day they worked on the spear. Mark learnt some of the tricks of forging iron, in between studying Ogham and its common inscriptions. To his surprise, he discovered that Irish was a very ancient language, one of the most ancient languages on Earth, and little altered over thousands of years. It had no *th* diphthong, and no letters *v* or *w* or *y*, so it manufactured the sounds out of pairs of letters, or dots on top of the most unlikely letters, like *b* and *d*. An *h* after a consonant was the same as a dot over it. This was why the Sidhe, of *Sidhe ár Feimhin*, was pronounced Shee – because the *dh* was pronounced like a *y*. The v sound in Slievenamon was really spelled as *bh*. This was apt to confuse anybody, even when they were skilled at reading Ogham. There was no answer other than to work like hell at it. So it was that the first Ogham words he learnt to spell and inscribe for himself, over the edges of a square tile of blue slate, were the words *Sidhe ár Feimhin*.

He took home the handful of battered old books Padraig lent him and he hammered their rules and coded message deep into his brain, even when it involved staying up half the night. And day after day he found it worth his while learning the rules of this new game he was playing. Knowledge was power, as some wise old wrinkly had once said. And so, with Padraig's help, and the monotonous details he discovered, Mark felt closer to understanding the old legends and superstitions. And boy was there a bonus!

The way he saw it, it was a matter of logic. If there really was some magical wormhole on top of the mountain, and if Ogham was the key, he'd be the one holding the answers.

The Three Sisters

So it was that sensuous July metamorphosed into early August, a time of tottering sandcastles and incoming waves of change – eleven days, to be precise, in which the four friends were summoned again and again by the mountain, their hearts and minds seduced by enchantment until they had no more control over their destiny than the swallows that blacked out the telegraph lines along the Marlfied Road. And then, all of a sudden, the waiting was over. It was that beautiful sunny morning in mid-August when Alan had kissed Kate for the very first time. They were cycling away from the Doctor's House, heading over the second of the stone bridges with the Comeraghs directly ahead of them, riding into the sunrise in silence. And his heart was still racing from the excitement of the kiss even as he stood on the pedals to push against the upslope of the approach lane, rattling and swaying through the green-painted gateposts, past the blacksmith's forge, with its smoke-blackened tin roof, heading for the red-brick garages, still retaining the old wooden horseboxes. Standing by the gates was the flatbed truck, its hinged splats hand-painted in camouflage shades of brown and pea-green. Now, at the sight of it, the real implications of what they were planning was at once exhilarating and frightening.

Mo was waving to them from the open door of the dairy.

Kate abandoned her bike and ran to hug her friend. Mo's face was dimpled with a nervous smile. She murmured, 'Guh-Guh-Guh . . . Guh-Guh-Grimstone wuh-wuh-will be buh-back tomorrow.'

'Oh, Mo, I'm a complete bundle of nerves.'

'I'm muh-more tuh-terrified of whu-whu-whu-what will huh-happen if we don't escape!'

Kate's heart missed a beat with Mo's choice of the word: *Escape!*

Leaning against the pear tree, Mark welcomed their arrival with a cheeky smile. How jealous Mark would be if he knew about the kiss! Alan turned away from the glimpse of tousled fair hair, as if embarrassed by it, then joined Kate and Mo in entering the den to gather up precious possessions.

Mo was the first to come back out, her backpack in place, and clutching the bog-oak figurine and her precious notebook. She looped the figurine round her neck on a shoelace but she kept the notebook in her hand. Making a final tour of the den, she inspected her altars of skulls, starfish and sea urchin shapes, her piles of feathers and gemstones – a treasure trove that had grown into a continuous sweep around all four walls.

'Jeepers!' murmured Kate, overcome with the excitement. 'I hope you lot remembered to bring some money.'

Mark, who was still leaning against the tree, remarked, 'Hey – you think the Irish Euro will be legal tender where we're going?'

'I don't care,' laughed Kate. 'I know that it's legal here. So let's all empty what we've got onto the grass and count it.'

Dutifully they sat in a circle and emptied their pockets. Kate was impressed to find that they had gathered more than thirty Euros between them. She gazed at the pile of money with awe before Alan gathered it up and stuffed it into the pocket of his jeans. There was a moment of silence in which all four looked exceedingly nervous yet impatient to be off.

Mo broke the tension with a giggle.

Kate and Mark slung their backpacks over their T-shirts. Wordlessly, they all came together for a team hug.

Alan hauled out three battered-looking plastic drums, opaque and weightless, and lifted them onto the bed of the truck. Mark took pictures with his camera phone. Mo twirled in a circle that took in the entire sawmill yard, holding aloft her triple-headed talisman. Finally, Alan loaded the Spear of Lug onto the truck, placing it carefully along one of the long sides and hiding it under a layer of logs. His preparations complete, he brought out a small, flat silver flask embossed with the American bald eagle that had belonged to his father. He filled the cap with the throat-burning poteen he had lifted from his grandfather's stash behind the kitchen.

'Girls first!' He passed the capful to Kate.

The two girls coughed after mere sips of the fiery liquid, then passed it on to Mark who threw a capful back in one swallow, screwing up his eyes and gagging, then farted loudly and solemnly, like a drum roll.

'Slievenamon – my bum salutes you!'

The other three chorused, in unison – 'To Slievenamon!'

Mark donned a leather Parka over his T-shirt while Alan slipped into the faded brown all-weather denim jacket that had been his last present from his parents. Like Kate, Mo wore a pullover with her T-shirt and jeans. Alan left the others to put their packs on board the truck while he headed back to the main house. It was the moment he dreaded. Padraig was sitting in the leather armchair, in the room with the photographs of Mom growing up. Alan felt hopelessly inadequate, holding out his hand as if to formally shake Padraig's.

As his grandfather climbed stiffly to his feet, Alan felt himself tremble with emotion. He just threw his arms around the tall figure and hugged him.

When he had recovered his voice, he spoke huskily. 'I'm really sorry, Grandad, but you know I've got to do this.'

Padraig was stiffly silent.

'I have to do it – for Mom and Dad. If these people, these unknown forces, had anything to do with their deaths—!'

'Sure I'd feel exactly the same as you do if I were in your place!' Padraig took a step back and took a firm grip of Alan's shoulders.

'That nutcase, Grimstone – you know he'll be back tomorrow. Things could get pretty mean when he finds Mark and Mo gone.'

'I'm capable of taking care of myself.'

'You know he has spies here in the town. Maybe we should leave the truck and just take the bikes – make it look like another beach trip?'

'The truck it must be. You cannot arrive at the mountain already exhausted. Conserve your strength for what will face you there.'

Alan nodded.

'So long then, Grandad!'

'You take care. I've already lost too many of those I love. I couldn't bear it if I lost you too!'

When Padraig came out to wish the others farewell, Kate kissed him on his white-stubbled cheek. Mo just stood in front of him and trembled. She pressed her notebook into his hand.

'Ah, you know I cannot accept it, Mo. It's too precious to you!'

But Mo just hugged him once and then spun away, running madly towards the truck.

Mark also stood there a moment, overcome with emotion, and then, awkwardly, he reached out and shook Padraig's callused hand before hurrying after his sister.

Padraig gazed after them all with his eyes liquidly glistening.

Mark helped Mo to clamber into the back of the truck, then joined her among the logs. Alan raised the flatbed sides and fixed them into position before yanking himself up into the cab. He couldn't help but smile at Kate's excited face as he reached across the bench seat to throw open the passenger door for her. Then Kate suddenly howled with laughter, scratching at the boyish stubble that prickled Alan's cheeks.

'I bet you've forgotten to bring a razor!'

'Damn!'

That provoked a round of laughter.

'All ready?' He called back through the broken window into the bed.

'Aye, aye, Cap'n!'

Alan's eyes met Mark's in the rear-view mirror.

The sound of the revving engine, Mark and Mo high-fiving in the back, the stench of diesel – suddenly they were off, the logs and passengers alike bouncing about on the bare metal floor as the truck lurched and swayed down the slope of the rutted track.

Alan slowed as he approached the gates. He squeezed

his head and right arm out through the open window and gave a final wave to the solitary figure in the yard, continuing to watch Padraig in the side mirror until he disappeared as they passed out through the gate posts. He thought: *Take care of yourself. Don't get yourself hurt. Be safe until I return.*

They trundled down Irishtown, where the houses hugged one another in pastel-washed single-storeyed terraces, until the stony bulk of the West Gate straddled the road. They cheered as they squeezed through the medieval walls and into broad O'Connell Street, then the Narrow Street, past the Main Guard and by the Old Bridge. Although Slievenamon was still twenty miles away, it towered over the graveyard where Alan's Irish grandmother was buried.

They made their first stop at a filling station on the Carrick Road. Here, just about the only place that was open this early on a Sunday morning, they topped up the diesel and bought some cola, potato crisps and chocolate. They departed the town boundary, trundling along the tree-lined banks of the River Suir. As if knowingly approving, the river coursed by them, mile after mile of broad slow-moving current. It was a chilling reminder that at least once a year somebody would drown in its waters: a careless child, or even an experienced swimmer, underestimating its flows and currents, so it seemed that the ancient sacrifices continued to this very day in homage to its darkling majesty.

Alan pulled the truck to a creaking halt on the riverbank about half a mile after Carrick, where young willows dangled their drooping leaves over the water. It seemed as good a place as any to fill the first of the plastic drums with water from the Suir.

After helping Mo through a gap in the hawthorn hedge, Alan followed her down the bank into the shadows of the trees, watching as she pressed the neck of the container below the surface, Mo turned for a moment and looked fearfully over her shoulder. He saw the expression on her face, the prickling of worry in the dark pools of her eyes. For a moment, as he leaned down to pull her back, he thought he saw a shadow at the periphery of his vision, as if a darker mass was congealing out of the shade of the trees.

Then as they reached the hedge, an instinct prompted them both to look back. A figure was silhouetted against the bright reflecting water. Mo left Alan with the container as she tore through the hedge, calling out a warning to the others. A creeping horror prickled Alan's skin as he paused to take a second look. The figure really was there, shrouded by a black hood and cloak. The figure seemed to reach out as if to close the distance between them. Alan had to suppress the instinct to abandon the container in his panic to run back to the truck.

Kate murmured, 'What was that?'

'I don't know!'

With a clattering roar of the cantankerous old engine

and trailing clouds of smoke, Alan accelerated along the Carrick road, only reaching out to take Kate's hand when they had put a mile or more of distance between them and the stopping point. Her hand felt cold, the fingers stiff and crabby with fear.

After they had travelled a few miles further, Mark tried to cheer Mo up, telling her jokes in his Homer Simpson voice. Mark was so clever with his jokes and his voices that Mo, although not exactly laughing, appeared to take comfort from his attempts.

All four talked to each other through the missing rear cabin window.

'Duh-duh-do you think that Puh-Padraig is really a duh-druid?' Mo asked as the truck took a left turn and headed north.

Alan shook his head. 'I don't rightly know.'

'I muh-muh-mean, he saw it all from the buh-beginning. Buh-buh-before any of us ruh-realised . . .'

'Yeah, Mo! I wish now I'd talked a lot more with Grandad.'

Kate screwed her head around so she could talk to Mo directly. 'Wasn't it mind-blowing when we all started dreaming the same dreams!'

Alan rubbed at some scratches he had picked up from going through the hawthorns, meanwhile wondering if Mo was right, and that maybe his grandad really was a druid. If so, a druid's grandson was driving this truck, illegally as it happened, since Alan was well under the official licence age. Mark suddenly cut through Alan's thoughts, pointing into the air behind them with a trembling hand. He cried out, 'The watcher! The watcher!'

Kate paled and she clutched at Alan's hand.

They passed through minor roads that were so overhung with trees that they were effectively driving through tunnels. The sky that had been so limpid earlier had given way to gathering clouds and, although they would sometimes emerge from shade into sparkling sunshine, it was never long before the shadows swallowed them up again. Alan knew some of the byways from helping his grandfather to deliver loads, but he quickly lost track of the narrow and winding lanes, which, at times, were no more than single-track shortcuts. Kate did her best to follow the route on her crumpled map. An hour or more passed, weaving through flat farmland with scattered, grey-walled cottages surrounded by fields of crops. Then a shout from Kate announced that they had arrived at the second of the sisters. More eerie than the Suir, they had arrived at the Nore close to its headwaters, where it was little more than a stream below gentle rapids, with white spray flecking the currents over glistening black rocks.

This time it was Kate's turn to fetch the water.

'You go with her, Mark,' Alan called up to him.

But Mark had already climbed onto the roof of the cab, holding up the harmonica, ready like some kind of warning siren, and shading his eyes from a sudden appearance of the sun.

Alan snorted with irritation.

He had to squeeze past Mo, her hands holding apart the barbed wire at the top of the slope, so he could run after Kate, who was thirty yards ahead, lugging the second of the plastic drums down a slope of tussocky grasses and birch saplings. By the time he got to her, Kate had already jammed the neck into the stream. It took longer to fill in this shallow water, and the Nore hissed softly, as if warning them to be quick. Alan found himself darting fearful glances back over his shoulder into every shadow under the small trees.

The shadow loomed over them as the sun clouded over. He sensed it like a cold shroud spreading over the landscape, licking about them, discovering them, making the hairs on the back of his neck stand up as he pressed his lips into a taut line, willing Kate to hurry.

Clammy tentacles wrapped themselves around his legs, as if inhibiting all possibility of escape, as Kate's hand reached up with the container. He yanked it from her hand and together they ran. Lungs bursting, they reached the barbed wire at the top of the slope, struggling between the strands of wire that Mo was again holding apart for them. Suddenly the harmonica began to scream out a warning. Neither Alan nor Kate could bear to look back behind them. Mo was stammering incoherently as, bleeding from multiple tiny scratches, they dragged themselves through the wire, hauling the water onto the back of the truck, then diving into the cab, with its ticking-over engine, and tearing off with the pedal to the floor.

They were all jittery and needed a break. Somewhere along the open farmland between Kilkenny and Carlow Alan pulled the truck off the road onto a grassy track that led down into a disused quarry. Here, screened from the world in a bowl of shadow, they talked in hushed voices and shared out the crisps and chocolate and the first of the two bottles of cola. Over the rim of the quarry, the mid-afternoon sun hid behind gathering clouds. Mo held on tight to the talisman dangling on the shoelace around her throat.

'Padraig did warn us that the gate would be warded!' Kate muttered quietly.

'He did,' Alan nodded, 'but I don't think any of us imagined it would be as scary as this.'

As they hurried on again towards the last of the sisters – the Barrow in its upper waters between Carlow and Athy – they knew the watcher was stalking them. The quiet lanes felt creepy as they hurried through them.

In the deepening shadows of late afternoon, Alan pulled to a halt over a slope of marshy ground, where the road and river parted, making them fearful of the distance between them. No one hurried to volunteer.

'Looks like it's you and me, Mark!' Alan confronted Mark, with a challenging look in his eyes.

Mark snatched the third container from the back of the truck and started down the slope. Kate wanted to go with him but Alan said no. 'Stay in the cab. Make sure the engine is running. And Mo, you just sit tight in the back. We may have to get out of here in a hurry!' Then, with a sigh of exasperation, he shouted to Mark to hold on so he could catch up with him. But Mark continued on his own.

'Don't be a dork! I'm coming!' Alan hopped up into the back of the truck and he grabbed the spear and vaulted back to the ground.

But the fair-haired youth was already well down the slope, in a loping stride, so Alan had to break into a sprint to catch up with him, using the long wooden shaft of the spear as a prop against the boggy ground. The slope soon levelled onto a flat plain of clinging mud, with fouled rushes and giant weeds. Mark had to pick his way carefully now, doing his best to keep to the firmer humps of ground, using the empty container in places to stop himself slipping into the mud. Following behind Mark into the dense shrub of pussy willow and overgrown oaks by the riverbank, Alan was startled by the silence. Other than the merest whispering of the water over slippery stones, there was none of the chatter of nature. And then, deep in the shadows, as Mark slithered down the bank to force the neck of the container into the matt-black water, Alan saw in the foliage above him an empty nest that had once been home to a family of wagtails.

The broken bowl of the nest was littered with feathers. He saw other clusters of feathers still attached to some fragments of wing and splinters of bone, scattered about the ground close to his feet. There were tiny flecks of bloodied flesh round the bones. Panic rose in his chest. His lungs felt waterlogged. His eyes lifted to the shadows between the trees. The hooded figure was only yards away and stiller than the stones. Its eyes had the unblinking glare of a pike.

He called out hoarsely, 'Mark! Don't look up. Just pass me the container and let's get the hell out of here!'

The embankment was much harder to climb up than it had been to slither down. There was no time to place their feet and they sank to their ankles in the clinging mud. Unburdened by the container, Mark moved faster than Alan, who saw him extend his lead on him, already a third of the way up the field, while, breathless with effort, and jabbing at the foul ground with the shaft of the spear, he struggled to follow.

'Go on! Warn the others!' he shouted after him. 'I'll see if I can delay it with the spear.'

He had arrived to about mid-slope. From what seemed a long way above him he could hear the high-pitched exhortations of Kate and Mo. He felt the mantle of suffocating darkness close about him. He could run no further. He stopped and wheeled about him. The eyes were so close he saw the wavering discs of quicksilver that were the irises, the imperfect pupils, black without reflection, opening on a void. His heart seemed to stop and he felt his legs buckle under him. In moments the darkness was lapping about him.

'Jesus – come on!' Mark shouted from far above him.

He had almost given up hope when he heard Mo's song. She had left the truck and was standing at the top of the slope, her eyes clenched shut, the talisman raised above her head. Her song was sweet and repetitive, like a mysterious incantation. The monstrous presence seemed to recoil a little, the pike eyes wavering as if they had lost some of their substance.

He heard Mark's voice roaring, 'Now run, you idiot! *Run!*'

In that strange suspension of time and distance, the slope, with its boggy ground, became a treadmill of pounding heart and rasping breath. A mist invaded his eyes. His feet sank into the boggy ground, only tearing themselves free in wild yanks of desperation, and his flailing legs were clockwork extensions of his terror. Yet, though it harried and closed on him, the foul mantle appeared to hold back from attacking him, as if the presence of the tiny singing figure at the top of the slope was having some effect. Alan was grabbed by Mark on one side and by Kate on the other, as they hauled him, and the container, over the top of the field and onto the dirt road.

Oh, man!

He couldn't believe he was safely back at the wheel of the truck, with Kate screeching and Mark and Mo on their feet in the back, hammering with their fists on the roof of the cab, as he shoved his foot to the floor.

'Nassty – nassssssty! We hates ol' fish-eyes – yes, my preciousss. Nassty ol' fissh-eyes, yesss!' Mark's Gollum voice.

His mind still in a daze, Alan crashed through the gears. He hardly registered the remainder of the journey, although it must have lasted an hour, along the main road southwest from Carlow, through the open streets of Kilkenny, past the ruins of the ancient castle, before, with the truck rumbling noisily in low gear as he turned right off the main Kilkenny to Clonmel road, he heard Kate's relieved voice exclaim, 'We're here!'

He saw the sign for Nine Mile House and soon the final village, Kilcash, with its fading baskets of flowers outside the post office.

Through Feimhin's Gate

Suh-suh-suh-Slievenamon!' Mo looked up at it with round eyes.

Alan took them as close to the slope as the small lane would allow, then killed the engine, enabling them to alight from the truck and stand gazing close-up at the mountain that had called them, swathed as it now appeared in the heather of high summer. From this close it looked different, flatter, the peak invisible, including its cairn of stones. The boys took a drum of water each and the girls one between them and then they began the long slow climb through the brambles and ragged trees on the lower slopes. Taking the lead, Alan balanced the drum of water in his left hand and the Spear of Lug in his right.

Moment by moment, the sky appeared to grow more heavily overcast. Every instinct bade them hurry. It wasn't long before the weight of the drums tired their arms. But they refused to rest, or even to slow down, even when the narrow handles of the containers cut impressions into the flesh of their hands, forcing them to keep changing arms, no matter that their muscles soon began to cry out for a rest, even for a little while. So it continued, ever upwards, under the black race of cloud and a sky that increasingly lowered down upon them. A charge of static electricity lifted the hair of their heads as, too exhausted to cheer, they crested the summit. Clonmel, within the crumbling remnants of its ancient walls, was visible in the hazy distance, its outline ghostly amid the smoky plumes of its chimneys.

Here they allowed themselves a minute or so to recover.

They had run out of cola so they refreshed themselves with the water from the high Barrow – it had looked like the cleanest of the three they had gathered.

Change was in the world about them, a galvanising excitement that tingled on their skins, a pins-and-needles prickling that invaded their bodies from the charge of the mountain. Suddenly Alan's heart was pumping madly, a cry rising to his lips. But Kate beat him to it. She shrieked so hard it hurt Alan's ears, pointing ahead with a trembling hand.

Wheeling, they all saw the place where she was pointing. Kate and Mo were already running towards it, carrying their drum between them – the place every one of them had seen so many times in their dreams, a collection of dark grey boulders shaped like a table that was now no more than a hundred yards distant. But even as Alan shared their excitement, his instincts caused him to glance over his shoulder, towards the west, where a growing darkness was blanking out the light. Mark, Kate and Mo had dropped their burdens and were already exploring the stones by the time he turned round again.

In a flushed but silent awe, they darted about the ancient tumulus, peering into clefts and touching the rough, lichen-encrusted surfaces. Then Mark's voice was raised a pitch, looking at Kate who was shrieking, ear-piercingly, again. 'What is it, Kate? What are you raving about?'

'Look there – *there*!' She waved to what appeared to be a stony ledge about four feet above the ground, and half hidden in the jumble of stones.

Alan saw what she meant.

'Everybody – keep clear a moment!'

He placed the spear on the ledge and climbed up after it, then started to clear the rubble off the top.

'Hey – there's a second level, under this rubbish!'

Mark hauled himself up to join him.

'You see what I mean? Under this big flat stone?'

Mark nodded. With their eyes bulging and the veins and muscles in their necks standing out, they tugged and levered at the big stone. It took every ounce of their combined strength, their muscles straining and the blood squeezed from their fingertips. At last, they felt it begin to slide.

'Watch out, girls!' Alan cried as, with a grinding rumble,

the rock moved far enough for the two boys to get their hands fully beneath it, then tilt it over the edge and send it crashing into the surrounding heather.

Both raised their fists and hollered and the girls cheered.

'What is it?'

The girls climbed up onto the ledge to join Alan and Mark in peering at the flat table of stone that had been exposed, at about waist level. They brushed away the dust over a circular basin cut deep into the table, perhaps two feet in diameter – a font, as it now appeared, that formed a perfect half sphere. As Alan wiped his fingers over the rim, they could all see, deeply inscribed into the blue-grey lip of the basin, the lines and angles chasing the rim – words of power, clusters of them, running over and into the bowl.

'It's Ogham!' Mark exclaimed.

'Ooh!' Kate murmured. 'But what does it mean?'

It was Mark who answered Kate, Mark whose voice had suddenly become knowing. 'Remember what Padraig said. He told us we'd find the basin here. If Padraig is right, it's . . . Oh, bloody hell! This is it. This is the gateway he talked about – *Sidhe ár Feimhin.*'

All four stared at the font in wonder.

Alan put his right arm around Kate's shoulders. He felt Mo clasp hold of his free hand, trembling with nervousness. 'Thuh-thuh-thuh-the guh-gateway!'

'Read it, Mark!'

'I'm doing my best. But I can hardly make anything out, it's become so dark.'

They had been so wrapped up in their excitement that none of them had been aware of the enveloping darkness. Clonmel was no longer visible in the west. Mark moaned aloud, 'How am I supposed to make out the words!'

Then, from out of the gloom, they heard a strange sound: *'Duvaaalll!'*

'Holy Mother of God!' Kate's left hand clutched at Alan's T-shirt.

'C'mon you guys!'

Mark passed up the first of the drums, so Alan could empty it into the font. There was a gurgling of splashing water, together with the hollow crunching sound of a plastic container when it emptied too quickly and sucked in the sides. A faint pink glow was coming out of the font. Mo's face, closer to the water, was highlighted by it, like a ghostly reflection.

'C'mon, everybody,' Kate addressed them urgently, 'take off your shoes!'

'Whatever for?' Mark's voice sounded discordantly calm.

'Remember the way Mo did it on the Comeraghs. Do it, quickly!'

Alan set the example, sitting down on the ledge between Mo and Kate, tearing off his trainers. 'Tie the laces round your neck, so you won't lose them. But let's get our bare feet planted on the ledge.'

Suddenly the air felt dank in their lungs, as if the individual molecules were turning chill. Hurriedly, they ripped off their trainers. Kate sprang up onto the ledge.

'The second drum – come on, boys!' Kate's voice sounded out, quavering but still authoritative from above them.

Alan and Mark jumped back down to the ground, scrambling about in their bare feet, barely able to make out the containers in the gloom. Alan's limbs felt leaden as if he were floundering under water. Then he heard it again, that same horrible rasping voice, coming out of the enveloping gloom.

'Duvaaalll!'

Kate was shrieking, 'Oh, God – be quick!'

Alan and Mark groaned as they heaved burdens that seemed to have grown heavier than ever up onto the ledge, then scrambled up themselves. Kate was already adding the second river to the mix in the font. They saw the splash of light, like a cataract of glowing silver invading the darkness, a spiral of vapour rising and illuminating all of their faces.

'Just one more!' Kate's face seemed mask-like, her mouth closed tight, as if suppressing a scream.

Alan passed her the heavy bulk of the last container. It was the water from the River Suir. He helped her drop it onto its side, seeing the cap come off in Kate's hands. Her eyes were liquid reflections of the furnace that fumed and spiralled within the black outline of the stone. Her hands became one with the cataract of silvery light. Alan hugged her shoulders to steady her as she tipped the drum into the basin.

A rush of foul air enveloped them, cut through by the

sound of Mo chanting. Green cataracts of putrefying luminescence were approaching from the direction they had heard the rasping of Alan's name. A shape was coalescing out of the gathering darkness, a cowled head.

Alan shouted, 'Hold onto each other!'

They formed a tight circle about the white-glowing font. No more than thirty yards away a growing malignancy spat green fire. Mark was violently shaking his head:

'I don't believe it – it's impossible – I don't believe it!'

The monstrous presence was gathering substance and strength. The sanctuary of the stone font would not save them.

Mo's face lifted heavenwards as she uttered a rapid litany of incantation. A shower of brilliant sparks swirled from the moiling surface of the font, defying the darkness that was suffocating the light. Alan saw eyes appear within the cowl. He saw how the eyes changed from moment to moment, the silvery blue-green of rancid flesh, the rose of butchery, then a mad altercation, like a corrupted rainbow. The power of its malice was invading their minds.

'I cuh-cuh-cuh-can't stop it! I cuh-cuh-cuh-cuh . . .' Mo wailed.

'Come on, Mark! You've got to read the Ogham!'

Mark stared at the glowing font. Now, in the bright light from the spiralling water, the letters stood out, as if aglow with some inner illumination.

'I can't make myself think. I can't remember anything.'

Kate shouted, 'Will you just try, you idiot! Remember what you've been learning from Padraig.'

'Now I'm here, everything looks different.'

'Holy Mary and Joseph!'

Mark ran a shaky finger around the circle of inscriptions. He read it slowly, making it out letter by letter, and word by word, in the ancient Irish and then, as best he could, translated it into English:

Ye . . . Ye who would pass . . . pass through Feimhin's gate . . .

'Whuh-whuh-whuh-what?'

'Stop it, Mo! You're winding me up.'

Alan hissed, 'Get on with it, Mark!'

'Don't you think I'm racking my brains to understand the rest of it? You have a go for yourself, if you think you can do any better. It's your name that thing is calling. It's you it's after.'

Mark's words terrified Alan. He couldn't help but glance towards the looming evil. Was it his imagination . . . or were the eyes gathering strength?

'Just try – you're the only one who can!'

Mark focused on the Ogham blazing over the edge of the font. The water spun in an increasing vortex, now turquoise, now the old gold of the Celtic torcs about the throats of those ancient shamans.

'Duvaaalll!'

The voice sounded from so very close. It seethed, driven

by a loathing so dreadful it vibrated in the rocks under Mark's feet.

Mo sobbed out loud.

Alan grabbed the spear from the ledge. Although his legs were trembling with fright, he forced himself to climb up onto the table of stone that contained the basin. Now, with one foot on either side of the whirlpool of light, he held the Spear of Lug aloft, the spiral of the lance head glittering in the cataract of ascending light. He shouted his defiance into the air.

'Come on then! I'm not afraid of you!'

Brave words, they scarcely hid his terror.

The eyes turned their full glare on his defiant figure. The upraised spear goaded the monster into a mounting rage. Alan wilted under the force of its malevolence, yet he held his ground while those eyes came ever nearer. The stench made him want to be sick. Open jaws were now visible below the eyes, glistening fangs protruding from a hideous maw. He could feel its rank breath on his face and in his hair.

He held his nerve until the maw was about to enclose him, the eyes black pits in whirling pools of blood, and then, dipping the blade in the foaming waters, he hurled the spear with all of his might into the monster's right eye.

It burrowed deep into that baleful face. With a roar of fury that shook the ground, the monster shrank back into its own vortex.

But it wasn't over. The presence merely drew back, incandescent with rage, in anticipation of a new charge.

'Bloody hell!' Mark's voice was croaky with horror. 'Alan – this is it, the best I can do:

> *Ye who would pass through Feimhin's gate*
> *Invoke her name . . .*'

'Whose name?'

'I don't know.'

Alan's mind raced. One of the three rivers? He shouted all three names, 'Suir – Nore – Barrow!' But nothing happened.

What name?

In desperation, he stared at the circle of Ogham at his feet. He knew from the moans of his friends that the monster was no longer retreating. The new charge was beginning. In despair he gazed deep into the spuming cauldron where the waters of the three sisters had been brought to consummation. His mind reeled with the terrible visions that were growing there. He saw a battlefield from long ago, over which a thunderous sky lowered. An armoured warrior lay mortally wounded amid the flames and blood-soaked ground, his final act of defiance to raise his bloodied arm with its broken sword into that terrible sky. The warrior's mouth was twisting into a desperate cry, a name anguished and broken:

'*Mó-rí-gán!*'

The monster roared, its maw an abyss of crimson between the slavering tors that were its fangs.

Alan sensed a faint sound of the warrior's cry rising, spiralling and receding into the maelstrom overhead, where something distant and black held utterly still. The name was familiar, but he didn't remember why. If only he could focus on what it meant . . . He recalled his grandfather's words, 'I will do what little I can to help you.' But what, in all he had learnt from Padraig, might help him now?

The dying warrior reminded him of Padraig's stories. Was it something he remembered from one of legends, of Niamh and Oisín, or Balor and the imprisoned Ethniu, or the triple goddess, the terrible Trídédana?

Alan gasped.

Mórígán!

He remembered it now from several of the yarns his grandfather had told them – *Mórígán*, raven of the battlefield – goddess of death!

The impulse to incant her name became overwhelming. Alan had no more conscious control over his own diminished figure standing astride the cauldron where he felt the spiralling motes of sacred light from the font invade his flesh and glow fiercely within his very being.

The monster was closing.

With his face grotesque with urgency, Alan hurled the name into the darkening sky:

'MÓ-RÍ-GÁÁÁN!'

The cry rose from his lips, his gaze following it to where a pinpoint of black was suddenly expanding. He gaped as the pinpoint expanded and took form, proliferating until it became a gigantic triangle of black, at the fore the cruel chisel of a beak the size of a mountain in a skull with cavernous pits for eyes. Swelling to either side of the triangle, he could see the slow beating of leviathan wings. In mere moments the shadow of an almighty raven grew so vast that it circumscribed the heavens. In the protective shadow of its wings, utter darkness fell over the four friends. Outside the darkness, their tormentor snarled and lunged, but it was to no effect.

Voices were calling Alan, alien voices, speaking to him in tongues he did not recognise. In his mind he worried about his friends, but his lips were unable to articulate the words. Somehow he sensed, without understanding how, that he was passing through the gate.

A force was invading his being. He felt an almighty shock of dizziness, a disorientating sense of change. His consciousness was probed by some vast and impersonal matrix. It amazed him that he was still able to think. *I want to know if my parents really were murdered. I want to know if this suffering will make me understand why they were murdered.* There was a rage of confusion in which his limbs felt as if they were being torn from their sockets. His body was in the grip of agony so bad it went beyond anything he recognised as pain. *I so want to punish them – I want to get them back – whoever was responsible.* He no longer had physical substance. He was diminished to nothingness. The loneliness was worse than the agony. It was unbearable, as if he were a single mote utterly lost in a universe of starlight.

PART II

The First Power

The Stone Circle

Kate's head reeled with dizziness. For several minutes she hardly dared to move. She just lay there, struggling to open one eye to see. Clumsily, through a mixture of pain and giddiness, she peered again with both eyes: *Snow!*

How was it possible that she was lying out in the open, in – she widened her eyes for an instant – a blizzard?

Coughing to clear her throat, she blinked, and looked again at a landscape of black rock and snow.

Well, if she wasn't dreaming, this was insanity. All of her common sense denied the possibility of her being here. Yet around her she could hear cries and moans that suggested her friends were experiencing similar difficulties. Somehow they really had arrived in this place, wherever this place happened to be. Slumping back into the snow, she just had to acknowledge that there wasn't going to be any rational explanation.

'Kate?' she heard a nearby voice call out.

'Alan? Is that you?'

'No!' Mark wheezed. 'It's me!'

Mark's voice had been so husky she hadn't been able to tell his English accent from Alan's American. But turning her head, she saw him now, a hunched-up figure moving towards her through the blustering snow. She asked him, 'Where on earth are we?'

'I wish I knew.'

She sat up too quickly and the dizziness swooped down on her like a punishment.

Mark leaned for a moment against a huge black stone soaring vertically out of the ground. He flopped down and started to pull his trainers over his feet. Kate blinked with the memory of taking off her own trainers. Suddenly Mark's example seemed a very good idea. As she bent down to follow suit, she noticed that drops of blood were seeping out of her nose and splattering in small red circles in the snow. Fright made her gasp. She tried to calm herself down with deep breaths. Then she pulled on her trainers, knotted the laces. She only wished she had socks as well, but socks under trainers had not been fashionable this summer. While she sat upright again, feeling was returning to the skin of her face. She registered the icy-cold touch, the brittle feel of the snow crystals against her skin, the flapping of her disordered clothing in the wind.

'Alan?'

'Alan is out of it.'

'What do you mean?'

'Stunned, I think.'

'Help me up, Mark. I want to see him.'

'Whoa there!' Mark took her arm and they both tottered for several moments. 'There's nothing you can do. No injuries that I could see. But his forehead is hot. I put my hand on it and it felt like it was burning.'

She let go of Mark's leather-jacketed arm and followed him to where Alan was lying unconscious in the snow. Mo was sitting next to him, looking bewildered. Kate felt overwhelmed by panic. Kneeling down in front of Alan, she put her hand on his brow, under the brown fringe of hair. Mark was right. His forehead felt as if it were on fire.

'Whuh-whuh-what is it, Kuh-Kuh-Kate?'

'I don't know. I can't see any kind of crack to the head that might have knocked him out.'

'Muh-muh-muh-maybe it was buh-buh-bringing us here. He tuh-tuh-took it all on himself.'

Kate looked into Mo's eyes. 'Help me wake him up!' She leaned over him, rubbing a handful of snow over his face.

'Uh-uh-uh . . . I've tried!'

'What are we going to do?'

Mark had his mobile switched on. 'Nothing – no signal!'

Kate knelt upright. She tried her own. She got the same blank screen. 'What's going on?'

'Maybe we're nowhere on Earth at all.'

'What?'

'You asked me, earlier, where on earth this could be. If Padraig is right—'

'Oh, button it, Mark!' Kate turned away from him and put her hand onto Mo's shoulder, giving it a gentle squeeze.

Mo clenched her eyes shut, as if to control some inner demon. 'Muh-muh-muh-maybe . . . muh-maybe Mark's right.'

'Oh, holy blessed mother!'

Mark looked at the two girls. 'Look around you! Do you imagine that Clonmel is just over the horizon?'

Kate saw that she was kneeling in a circle of stones, like a smaller version of Stonehenge in England.

Mark whistled. 'And here was I thinking we'd been chosen for some great adventure. Now I think we're the offerings for some weird sacrifice!'

'Stop it, Mark!'

Kate felt Alan's brow again. She noticed something Mark hadn't. The heat was coming from one small area, right at the centre – from the triangular birthmark he called his 'stork bite'. Poor Alan! That was why he grew his fringe over his forehead.

But why should a birthmark get heated up?

'We all know this is bananas.' Mark patted at his pocket, establishing the presence of his harmonica. 'Maybe it's another of those shared dreams. Any moment now we're all going to wake up!'

Gasping with a new explosion of dizziness in her head, Kate made a more careful appraisal of her surroundings. There was a residual sensation of . . . of what? The impression of change, of incredible dislocation. The experience had seemed dreamlike all right, but there was nothing imaginary about this place.

'Oh . . . Oh . . . oh man!'

That was Alan's voice! Kate's heart leaped to recognise the American accent, in spite of the fact he was moaning. Oh, why couldn't her heart come down out of the debilitating sense of panic? Her hands flew to her mouth, grateful to Mo, who was brushing more snow against his fevered brow.

'Kuh-Kuh-Kuh-Kate . . . huh-huh-help me!'

Between them they fastened the front of Alan's jacket, then lifted his head out of the freezing snow and laid it on Kate's lap. Mo lifted one foot after the other and put on his trainers.

Alan's eyes were open, but staring in bewilderment about him. His gaze faltered on the huge shadows of the surrounding mountains.

Mark patted Kate's shoulder. 'Listen! You stay here with Alan and Mo. I'm going to look around.'

She shivered and kept rubbing snow over Alan's heated brow until Mark came stumbling back from the edge of the circle. 'Look what I found!' He held the Spear of Lug aloft, its former bright steel blade now blue-black, as if scorched beyond anything that Padraig's forge could have achieved.

'Maybe Alan could use it for support.'

'We're going to have to get out of here as fast as we can. We're halfway up a mountain and there isn't any shelter. I don't know how many hours of light are left, but we can't stay here overnight.'

'What are we going to do?' Kate did her best to keep a wail of fear out of her voice.

Mark exhaled. 'If I'd known the destination of this mystery tour, I'd have packed my sleigh and huskies. I'm just praying Alan brought the poteen.'

Alan whispered, 'Help me!'

Mark rammed the shaft of the spear deep into the snow next to Kate and fell to his knees, searching Alan's pockets. He pulled out the silver flask, with the bald eagle embossed onto the front face. 'Thank you, Padraig!' He glugged a mouthful, winced, then screwed the cap back on and passed it to Kate. 'Might be worth giving Alan a sip?'

It was a difficult task for Kate, with her numb fingers, to get the cap untwisted. Her arms trembled and she spilled some of it over Alan's face as she brought the flask to his lips, causing him to cough and retch.

'For God's sake – don't spill it!'

'Luh-luh-let me huh-huh-help you.' Mo supported Alan's face, encouraging Kate to give Alan a second sip.

Alan came to with the sensation of burning in his throat. He coughed and jerked his face away. He realised with shock that he was lying in snow with his face in Kate's lap.

'Where are we?' he asked her groggily.

'We're halfway up a mountain.'

'Yeah – in deepest Antarctica,' somebody added. It took him a moment or two to register that it was Mark's voice. Mark was standing back a pace and looking all around him.

Alan pushed the flask away, attempting to climb to his feet. 'Oh, brother!'

Kate motioned to Mark, who accepted Alan's silver flask and stuffed it into his coat pocket. Between them they helped Alan onto his tottering feet.

Alan muttered, 'Feels like my head is on fire.'

Kate pressed the spear into his right hand, so he could lean on it.

'God almighty!' A howl of wind lashed his face. 'Feels like I've got a piece of hot shrapnel buried in my skull.'

Every shriek of wind whistled through the fibres of Kate's pullover, as if somebody was scourging her with fishhooks. 'Mark! Give us a bit more of a hand!' she called.

Alan put his left arm around Mark's shoulder and, leaning on the spear with the other, he staggered forward on unsteady feet, forcing down nausea and ignoring the wrenching pain and debilitating giddiness. Then, lurching around a huge stone poking out of the snow, he looked around himself in astonishment. Huge slabs of rock jutted out of the snow like the snarling teeth of some monster at bay. He realised what the others knew already, that they were standing in a stone circle that looked as old as the mountains.

The skin of his face felt as stiff as a mask. Breathing

steam into the air, he took in the darkening sky, the wrack of clouds wheeling above, and the light rising from the white ground as if a black sun reigned in this blasted world, and darkness instead of light was falling on the earth. He recalled what Kate had told him: *We're up a mountain.*

He tried to consider that fact calmly, though his heart hammered beyond logical consideration. Peering upwards, he could see ridges jutting into the sky for thousands of feet.

Mark spoke quietly into his ear. 'We're not going to survive here. We've got to make it down the mountain. Find shelter.'

Now, looking down into that terrifying panorama, a prickling erupted over Alan's face that would have been sweat in temperatures above zero. Squinting down the slope, he estimated ten miles of snow and ice with hidden crevasses before they reached more level ground.

'No way we're going to make it down in the state we're in.'

'We don't have much of a choice,' retorted Mark.

Moaning, Kate pulled up the neck of her sweater so it was higher and tighter round her throat. 'Mark's right. We can't stay here. We're going to freeze to death if we do.'

Alan wiped snow out of his eyelids. 'I've got to think. We all need to think about this. We were called here, remember!'

'Yeah,' added Mark. 'By the Snow Queen!'

Alan looked around himself all over again. The fact was they were here, so they had to make the best of it. Even within the few minutes he had been staring down the valley, the wind had reared into a new crescendo of howling. Down a scree of ragged boulders and shale, and between those towering black ridges, a torrent of wind and snow fomented and roared, accelerating madly over the flatter ground,. He shivered. 'We were brought here for a reason. We've got to trust our feelings about the calling. We've got to try to figure this out.'

Kate shouted above the howl of the wind. 'What was that name you called out on Slievenamon? Why don't you try it again?'

Alan said, 'Mórígán – she's the Celtic goddess of death!'

They all shouted it out into the blizzard. They called on the goddess again and again. But there was no response. And soon they were too cold and exhausted to shout any more. Mo's body was trembling, her face icy with tears.

Mark put his arm around his sister, 'I once read that freezing to death isn't such a bad way to go. You get so cold you don't feel anything.'

'Get stuffed, Mark!'

'We're getting nowhere,' Alan sighed. 'Let's try building a shelter. Use one of the stones as one wall and build a half-circle around it. Maybe we could do it like the Inuit. Use hard-packed snow like building blocks.'

'Yeah!' Mark countered. 'And we can dig a hole in the snow and use the spear to catch seals.'

Alan soon found how impossible it was to make an igloo in such conditions. Decidedly groggy after just a few minutes of attempting to cut one or two snow bricks, he rested back against the ungiving stone and put his left arm around Kate. He held Kate tight against him, so his face was pressed into the auburn pillow of her hair.

Mo wandered away from the others until she stood in the dead centre of the stone circle with her legs buried to mid-calves in snow. Here she gazed up into the lowering sky. A spindrift of snowflakes appeared to spiral gently downward. The steam of her breath blew about her. She felt it freezing on the skin of her face, congealing as ice. But now she thought about it, even that was telling her something. Her breath was not ripped away by the howling wind, not while she still stood here at the heart of the circle.

Mo frowned.

'Muh-Muh-Mark!' She called out to him.

Mark came and flopped down in the snow next to her, where he just couldn't resist taking the harmonica out of his pocket and clowning about with playing a few half-hearted blues riffs.

'Shush, you lot!' Kate rushed out of Alan's embrace to join Mark and Mo in the centre of the circle. 'I thought I heard something!'

Alan came and joined them.

'Shush, I said!'

They all stared at Kate.

'Stop fooling around and listen!'

They held their breaths but all they heard was the howling of the wind.

Kate shook her head. 'Mark – do it again. Play something.'

'I've been trying to remember what the band played on the *Titanic*.' But then, looking at their faces, Mark shrugged and said, 'I have a better idea. Mo – why don't you give us one of your songs.'

'Shuh-shuh-shuh-shut up, Mark!'

'No – no! Mark's right!' Kate said, recalling what had happened on the roof of the Comeraghs. 'Oh, come on, Mo – please try it.'

Mo looked around at their expectant faces. Suddenly they all began to encourage her. 'Go on, Mo! Just one song!'

Suddenly, tremblingly, Mo began to sing. They all listened, with their hearts faltering, to the same angel voice they had heard calling out to the mountain. It was such a beautiful voice, the most magical sound imaginable in that place of desolation.

> *A mother came while stars were paling*
> *Wailing round a lonely stream*
> *Thus she cried, while tears were falling*
> *Calling on the Fairy King . . .*

Mo stopped singing, embarrassed to tears. 'I – I duh-duh-don't recall – duh-duh-don't know—'

Mark shrugged, then hugged her to him. 'Mo imagines that her real mother sang it to her, when she was a baby.'

'I – I – I . . .'

Kate whispered, 'Oh, Mo – *Mo!*'

Alan muttered, 'Knock it off, you guys! Listen. Can't you hear it? Kate was right. There's something – like an answering sound. I don't rightly know what . . . maybe just an echo.'

Kate agreed with him. 'I know I heard it too. It's as if the stones were singing in chorus.'

'Oh, for goodness sake!' exclaimed Mark. 'First it's mountains calling, and now it's the stones singing!'

'C'mon, everybody,' Alan called out, 'let's form a circle.'

'Hold hands, you mean,' said Kate, getting the idea.

They linked arms. Alan took Mo's right hand while Kate held her other. Mark shook his head but he joined them anyway. 'Now, sing it again, Mo,' Alan bade her. 'Give us just one more verse.'

'Oh, please do it, Mo!' Kate also encouraged.

Mo sang again, in that lovely, unearthly voice:

> *Why with spells, my child caressing*
> *Courting him with fairy joy*
> *Why destroy a mother's blessing*
> *Wherefore steal my baby boy?*

This time there could be no doubt about it. The stones were echoing every note. But the music did not end as

Mo stopped singing. The stones began to syncopate around her theme, as if a gigantic natural organ were taking up the melody, wheeling and spiralling around it, at once both eerie and delightful. Whether it really was the numbing effects of the cold, or the mesmerising effects of the music, or both, their fears were beguiled away. They sat, holding hands in the snow, entranced.

As they drifted into sleep, they were only vaguely aware that darkness was falling about them. None heard the slouching presence that approached the circle from the enveloping night, or felt the gnarled fingers that probed their limbs and faces, any more than they sensed their bodies falling, tumbling head over heel, heedless and lost.

Granny Dew

Kate woke to discover a figure standing over her, peering at her with the help of a firebrand. Beyond the limited range of the light her surroundings appeared to be black as pitch. She squinted her eyes and tried to peer around her.

Where am I?

There was no snow. So she had to be indoors, somehow. She couldn't hear anything of the blizzard, not even in the distance. She had to be well out of the weather. She remembered Mo's plaintive song in the circle. Was it possible that Mo's song had caused something to happen to them?

Am I on my own?

A sudden flash of memory, of hiding in the pit at the Mission, filled her with panic. She jerked her head around, saw a body to one side of her, the long-jeaned legs that had to be Alan's.

Oh, thank God! Thank heaven I'm not on my own!

She heard noises to the other side of her. It had to be Mo and Mark. They were all here. Wherever *here* was. It seemed they had jumped out of the frying pan into the fire. Her senses, now the panic had subsided a little, still reeled with an overwhelming claustrophobia. Her hair felt dirty and bedraggled, as if matted with dust and cobwebs. It was all so horribly unfair she wanted to scream, to shriek at this figure that was frightening the life out of her. But a deeper caution kept her still, froze her so she merely watched and waited, doing her best to make sense out of the situation. She was lying on something soft and springy. She felt at it with her fingers. Something natural, like moss. A thick bed of that mossy material separated her from the cold dirt of the floor.

'Who . . . who are you?'

There was no answer, other than a low-pitched growling.

But the figure was already moving away from her, allowing her to work out the rough size of whoever – or whatever – it was that was holding the firebrand. Kate guessed that the stranger was smaller than herself, no more than five feet or so, and amazingly compact.

Suddenly there was a low-pitched snarl.

Fright made Kate try to jump up. But the same fright made her muscles turn to jelly. Darkness yawned about her as the figure moved away, leaving her bathed in sweat.

'Alan – Mark – Mo? Are any of you awake?'

There was a chorus of jittery whispers that told her they were all awake.

Suddenly they all heard that low-pitched growl again: 'Arrrhhhggh – Duuuvaaallll!'

Kate heard that clearly. The figure had called out Alan's name in a voice as dry as desert bones, yet so deeply pitched it demanded complete attention.

'Shee–it!'

She could just about make out Alan's face directly underneath the firebrand. The figure was holding the flame so close to his face he was clenching his eyes shut.

Mark called out, 'We need some light of our own.'

There was a momentary silence as each realised that in their preparations for the adventure not one of them had brought a lighter, or even a box of matches. Kate could see how Alan was averting his face from the flickering flames. Then suddenly, strangely, the light mellowed. A greenish tinge settled over it so that Alan could open his eyes again, bravely she thought, to look up at the figure that was standing over him, peering down at him, and growling his name, like a summons.

'Who are you? How do you know my name?'

There was a muttering – it sounded like a grumbling – in that same gravelly tone, as the figure poked at him with one index finger, armed with a talon of nail that projected from an incredibly filthy hand. Kate saw how the hand itself glowed with greenish phosphorescence.

'Great!' Mark muttered. 'It's the ultimate bag lady.'

Kate couldn't help a nervous laugh.

But Alan wasn't laughing. He was moaning as the grimy nail scratched over his brow. The figure seemed to be interested in the birthmark that had been burning hot when they were back in the stone circle. Kate winced in sympathy. Alan grabbed the probing hand and he turned his face away from the insistent prodding and probing. But he couldn't stop himself from groaning as the figure's hands, which seemed far too large for the figure's small size, closed around his brow and appeared to squeeze right through to his brain.

Mark hissed, 'Where's the spear?'

Kate couldn't believe what Mark was thinking. 'Forget about the spear!'

'Do you have a better idea?'

'Listen!' Kate's whisper sounded husky, even to her own ears. 'Let's all switch on our mobiles. I bet the screens will throw some light.' She scrambled around in the moss, eventually finding her backpack. Her fingers located the mobile phone. But they trembled as she tried to find the on-switch in the dark. Suddenly her screen lit up, followed by Mark's. The effect was dramatic, the darkness suddenly illuminated as if by two beacons, and they could see they were in an enormous cave. It had to be somewhere deep in the mountains. The creature shrieked. In the snarling twist, as it wheeled away from them, motes of dust swirled and sparkled, as if set alight by its passage. There was a smell, like burning hair. And in that moment, as the light from the screens fell onto the figure, Kate glimpsed an impossible face . . .

A woman's face – the most incredible old crone.

The after-image of that face haunted Kate's imagination: skin of a brindled brown over silvery grey, with a thick, bedraggled mane of frosty white hair that tumbled down over the filthiest collection of rags that had ever passed for clothes. Her build was squat and powerful, with heavy eyebrows and a broad, widening nose that dominated the dewlaps of her pendulous cheeks, giving her face, momentarily perplexed by the light from the phones, a curiously turtle-like look. Even after she had gone, Kate could still smell her, like the organic compost at the bottom of her uncle's vegetable garden: the smell she recalled from taking a handful of mulched soil to her nose.

Mark was on his feet. 'Hah! We've got the witch! Keep your screen turned on her! Don't let her escape!'

But suddenly Kate's breath caught as another presence appeared out of the gloom of the cave. It appeared to beckon towards Mark in particular, a grim shadow cowled within darkness.

'Nuh-nuh-no!' Mo's voice rose to a cry. 'Tuh-tuh-turn thuh-them off! Thuh-thuh-thuh-they're huh-hurting her.'

Mark was dumbstruck, just staring at the shadow.

Kate switched off her mobile. She called to Mark to do the same. 'Mo's right. Turn off your screen.'

Mark's mouth opened wide with fright. The shadow was growing. It appeared to be taking substance in the ethereal green light from the screens. Mark's eyes were wide and staring.

Alan threw himself over. He grabbed the mobile from Mark's paralysed hand and doused the light. Immediately gloom enveloped them again. Kate heard Mo shuffle across the moss to throw her arms about her brother. She heard Mo's panting breath as she rubbed at Mark's goose-pimply arms to get some warmth back into him.

Within minutes, a friendlier light began to glow, no more than ten feet away. Alan watched this happen with his heart in his mouth and his breath still panting. The shadow that had threatened Mark was still there, somewhere in the dark. He sensed it rather than saw it. But the focus of the light was back on the gnarly old woman, who was squatting on the cave floor in front of a fire. The flames roared, illuminating a black pot that sat in the middle of the flames. The old woman used her fingers to stir some unpleasant-looking ingredients into a stew that was bubbling noisily in the pot.

Alan watched her in growing amazement.

She snarled what sounded like a curse, waving a casual hand to the darkness, as if warning the shadow to shrink away, then returned to her preoccupation with her cooking, grumbling incessantly. In the glow of the fire, her matted white hair cascaded about her triangular figure onto the surrounding dirt.

Abruptly, she veered towards them with an expression

more determined than earlier, as if a restless energy seethed just under the heavily lined brow, and at the same time Alan saw her eyes clearly for the first time. They had neither white nor iris, but were all black, liquidly glistening, and as fierce as an eagle's. His gaze fell from her eyes to the voluminous rags of her dress, which shifted and moved like something quick and horribly alive, and in which minuscule diamonds of light seemed to gambol and reflect the firelight. His heart hammered against the cage of his chest as he realised the true nature of her dress. It was woven from cobwebs. The diamond lights that scrabbled and sparkled in its dark, lacy depths were the eyes of the spiders that were actively spinning it.

She appeared to be singing to herself, with her head down and her chin lost in the folds of her neck and upper chest.

Her song crooned like a hymn in some age-old cathedral of shadow, closer to the grinding of pebbles than any sound that could come out of a human throat. It seemed to be directed at Alan in particular, in the strangest, most guttural language he had ever heard. And in her ruminations, he seemed to catch the same word, 'Quuuruuunnn', again and again.

Qurun . . .?

He sensed that the word was important, although he had no idea what it meant.

With a sudden pounce, she was upon him. She took hold of his face with one grimy hand, forcing the index finger of the other into his throat, the exploring probe wriggling ever deeper. He tasted the dirt of ages on that grimy finger. He choked, unable to breathe. He saw that her nose was running, heard her breath crackling with rheumy phlegm. Abruptly, with a powerful flick of her wrist, she twisted his head back on his neck, ignoring his moan of discomfort, and stared intently into his eyes.

Gagging, sweating with horror, his gaze was drawn into the black eyes, unable to resist her probing of his mind. In what seemed mere moments, she cackled loudly, then crooned in triumph.

'Duuuvaaalll – paaaiiinnn!'

That mind-boggling word, 'pain', hung in the air between them, like the throaty growl of a tigress.

Once more, she reached deep into his throat with her finger. Nausea rose in him, causing his back to arch off the floor of the cave. He thought it would drive him crazy, but then gradually it subsided. Then he felt her search his pockets. She held his mobile phone in her hands, staring at it with a look of fury.

'Hey . . . it's just a phone!'

Wheeling about again, she headed away towards the fire, whipping up clouds of dust with the wide hem of her skirts.

He inhaled the excrement of insects and spiders from the billowing dust.

Without warning, she turned upon him once again, her heavy head jutting forward, the grimy finger poking aggressively into his face. 'Duvaaaal aaassskkks – yeeesss! Duvaaaal seeessss – noooo!'

What was that supposed to mean?

His head jerked away from that finger, while he continued to search for some meaning in the depths of those black eyes.

The finger, the eyes too, motioned to one side; he interpreted this as an indication of outside. He heard a rattling sound from deep in her chest, a warning, as if the meaning was in the sound.

'Cha-teh-teh-teh-teh-teh!'

The grotesque finger was making darting signs at his heart.

'What are you trying to tell me?'

'Cha-teh-teh-teh-teh-teh!'

'I'm in some kind of danger?'

'Daaannngggerrr!' Her growl deepened, as if it rose out of the very bowels of the earth.

'What danger?'

Her eyes sprang wide open, the darkness in them glittering. Then she reached out and her finger appeared to brush against his mind. Peace overcame him. It was a wonderful feeling. He guessed, judging by the cries and sighs surrounding him, that she was doing something very similar for his friends. Alan was relieved to drift into a deep and restful sleep.

When Alan woke, feeling refreshed, the old woman was approaching him with a rolling movement on her widely spaced legs, her head thrown back and her tongue, as green as mould, poking out between grimy stumps of teeth. She was carrying the pot of foul-smelling gruel she had been stewing earlier, dumping it onto the dirt in front of him. She dipped a filthy clay bowl into it and brought it to his mouth.

'SSSlllluuuurrrrpppptltltl!'

She made spittle-flecked sounds, while flicking her tongue over her lips, all the while studying him with her eagle eyes. Doing his best to overcome his revulsion, he brought his lips to the edge of the cup.

He gagged with nausea.

'Uuuummmsssslllluuurrrpppp!'

Her tongue licked over her teeth.

'Uuummmhhh!'

She forced the cup to his mouth once more, making more of those lip-smacking sounds, intermixed with growls. He tried again but it only ended with retching and coughing. He jerked his head away.

Her black eyes blinked, a single contemplative blink, then held him in a belligerent confrontation, with her finger reaching towards his mouth.

'No!' He gritted his teeth.

'Aaaarrgghhh!'

She whirled away in a fury, vanishing with what appeared impossible speed from the circle of firelight, but he could hear the echoes of her grumbles chasing one another along what sounded like a maze of tunnels.

'What in hell's going on?'

Alan turned his bewildered face to his friends, made visible by a sudden brightening of the fire. The vault of the cave was high, much higher than he would have imagined. In other circumstances he would have thought it awesomely beautiful. But he knew they were not alone. The shadow thing had to be somewhere nearby. And there were sounds in the dark beyond the reaches of firelight: faint hisses, sighs, cracklings, the dripping of water, the suggestions of whispers. He thought he glimpsed other shapes out of the corners of his eyes, sinewy movements that seemed to glissade along walls or floor or ceiling, independent of gravity or the laws of nature. Then suddenly he could smell the fact she was back even before he could see her. She was standing over Mark, whose leather jacket she had somehow spirited into her grimy hands. To the accompaniment of low-pitched garglings and burblings, her fingers were reaching into the pockets.

'Stop that! Leave my things alone!'

'Huummmmphhh!'

She inspected the harmonica, then tossed it into the dirt. Mark scrabbled over on hands and knees to get it back. She discovered Alan's silver flask, still half full of Padraig's poteen. Sniffing at the screw-top, she discarded the cap and held the flask to her nose. She tasted the contents, her tongue lapping around the neck.

Her eyes bulged out of her face.

'Bag lady likes poteen!'

Alan ignored Mark, staring in nervous fascination.

With a growl of satisfaction the old woman inverted the small flask over her broad, fissured lips, her tongue making lapping sounds as she swallowed the contents in a single draught. She trumped a loud, long resonant fart.

'Ooh – gross!' came a chorus of exclamations.

Alan murmured, 'I think she's been taking lessons from you, Mark!'

The old woman gazed at the now empty flask. She secreted it away in some pocket of her dress. Then she came to Alan and held out her hand, growling.

'What does she want?'

Kate urged him, 'Give her your phone!'

'Why should I?'

'The phones don't work here anyway. And they frighten her.' Kate searched for her own mobile, finally holding it out at arm's length. 'You too, Mark. It's lying right next to you, where Alan left it.'

Mark complained, 'It still has my music in it!'

Alan muttered, 'That's the only goddam blessing.'

With a croak, the old woman snatched the three phones from their hands and stuffed them into a pocket of her dress before shuffling back to squat by the fire. She retrieved the silver flask from another pocket and coddled the gleaming silver, her finger chasing the embossed outline of the eagle that decorated the front surface, turning it over and over mere inches from her eyes. She began to sway and croon over the dancing flames, then, calmly, as if it were nothing unusual, she leaned forward and pressed the flask into the fire.

The flames erupted much higher, spitting and flaring in what was now a crackling furnace. Though her back was half turned to him, Alan could see that she had no fear of being burnt, pressing her cupped hands deep into the flames. She was crooning happily, her body swaying from side to side, as she performed a series of moulding caresses with her hands.

In amazement, he watched her lift something out of the fire. What had been the flask was now shiny and molten, in the process of being coaxed and transformed in her hands, its elements woven with the elements of fire, with added ingredients of charcoal and sand – and even her own spit – until it appeared to move within her fingers, as if imbued with life.

There was a chorus of gasps from the watching faces. Kate put her arm around Alan's shoulder.

A tiny bald eagle, as bright as the sun, beat its wings within the cradle of her splayed fingers. It rose several feet into the air, the brilliance of its fluttering wings reflected in the dark eyes that beheld it.

Catching his breath, Alan watched the eagle settle back with a gentle grace within the cage of her fingers. Then she closed her hands over it, reforging its elements to become a goblet, whorled with blue and silver; and, finally, with a circular friction of her finger that set up a melody of harmonics, she finished the bowl with a perfectly lipped edge.

'Muh-muh-muh-magic!' Mo whispered.

Immersed in her act of creation, she warbled from deep within her chest before applying a final smoothing gloss by licking the goblet inside and out with her tongue. Then she held it aloft, revelling in the rainbow sparkle of its luminescence, a sudden brilliant glow that eddied and coruscated over the walls and ceiling of her cave.

Alan's voice was guttural with shock. 'Who – or what – are you?'

In her sudden glower, in her croon of triumph, they all heard what sounded like a name: 'Graaannneee Dewwww.'

'Granny Dew – is that what we call you?'

'Duuuvaaalll!' She was mocking him again in that gravelly voice, while polishing the goblet on the murky folds of her dress. 'A biiirrrddd siiingggsss.'

Against the mockery of her reply, he felt foolish and ignorant, but he was determined to find out more. 'What kind of a place is this, Granny Dew? Where are we?'

A crinkle of amusement lifted the corners of her eyes at his use of her name. She thrust the goblet deep into the simmering pot, removed it now brimming with the oily liquid, and then, in a whirl of uninterrupted movement, she brought it purposefully against his lips. This time he found himself unable to refuse it. He drank the lot in a series of gulps, ignoring the nausea. The potion had a wilder, deeper taste than leaves or roots, or even herbs – a taste of fungi, with gristly bits, which seemed to creep and crawl in his mouth in a way he just didn't want to think about. The gruel tingled on his tongue. It slithered down his throat, expanding to fill every corner and hollow in his gut.

Alan felt weak and light-headed as he watched, without hope of understanding, the old woman return to the fire and refill the goblet. He was unable to drag his eyes away as she brought the goblet to Kate and Mark in turn, all the while cackling with glee as she invited them to drink the gruel from a vessel born out of magic.

Strange Comforting

Mo had always been able to sense an aura about people, one of those qualities that Grimstone loathed about her. And now, in the cave, she sensed that there was a very powerful aura about the old woman, if she was human at all, that reminded Mo of the experiment with magnets that her teacher had conducted in science classes at school. The teacher had put the pole of a magnet under a piece of paper and sprinkled iron filings on top of the paper. When she tapped the paper with her finger the iron filings had lined up along the lines of magnetic force, all around the focus of the pole of the magnet underneath. The old woman's aura was something like that; it was as if she was the focus of immense lines of force – lines of power. So it was, dry-mouthed with nervousness, that Mo watched as her three friends were lulled into sleep by the gruel. Only then did Granny Dew extract the mobile phones she had secreted away in the folds of her dress, and study them once again in the firelight. How closely she pored over the phones, showing the same fascination she had shown earlier with the silver flask, sniffing at each phone individually and peering closely into the face of its owner, all the while whispering in those strange, growly cadences.

Mo wished, desperately, that she knew what was going on. She'd felt decidedly strange since crossing into this world and now that sense of strangeness grew as Granny Dew finally turned her attentions to her.

In Mo's case there was no phone to be examined. Instead the old woman did something entirely unexpected, coming across to pick Mo up into her arms and carry her over to the fireside. Here, ignoring the goblet, she scooped a bare hand deep into the pot and carried the gruel to Mo in this personal cradle, crooning softly as she pressed it to her lips. Mo didn't dare to resist. She gulped down the earthy liquid until only an oily sheen of wetness was left on those grimy fingers. No more did she resist when Granny Dew laid her head against her cobwebby breast, crooning softly.

Mo had often wondered if her real mother, her biological mother, had ever held her to her breast.

She would have had plenty of opportunity to do so since she hadn't abandoned Mo until she was eleven months old. According to Grimstone, the date 31 October had been scrawled in felt-tip pen on the skin of her arm, so that he never tired of informing her that All Hallow's Eve, or more likely the more paganish Halloween, was her birthday.

Whoever had abandoned her, whether it had been her real mother or someone else, they hadn't even taken the trouble to wash her clean. Mo knew this too because Bethal frequently reminded her of it. Bethal took a delight in pointing out that a mother who couldn't even be bothered to wash her baby was hardly the sort to caress her, or croon over her. Not that there was any doubt in Bethal's mind as to the reason why. Bethal would haul her up in front of the mirror and show her why she had been unloved from the very moment of her birth. There was no loving, or caressing, the product of sin. But now, curled up against that strange cobwebby breast, Mo felt strangely comforted by Granny Dew.

Lifting up her gaze, Mo looked deep into those all-black pupils. What she sensed there caused tears to gather in her own eyes, so she was forced to blink them away, but all the while she just wanted this feeling to go on and on and never stop. She closed her eyes as Granny Dew stroked the skin of her face, brushing back the fallen fringe of her hair, crooning softly and occasionally singing a word or a phrase in a language so guttural that Mo could not imagine what it meant . . .

'Meeerrrraaa . . .

Arrrrrryynnnn . . . Arrrrrryynnnn

Aaaarrrrrggggghhhh!'

Alan woke from his daze to a sharp crack on his shins. He saw that the fire was down to its embers and that his friends were being woken up in similar fashion. There was no longer any mystery about the whereabouts of the spear. Granny Dew held it in her right hand, while in her left she gripped a firebrand, with flames at least a foot high. All four climbed shakily to their feet, those who did so too slowly receiving a second rap on the shins from the spear shaft, before they were assembled, looking bewildered and brushing moss from their clothes.

Granny Dew brought the spear round in a wide arc and then pointed forward, in an unmistakable gesture.

'Cha-teh-teh-teh-teh-teh!'

She led them out of the chamber, down a steep descent, step by step into a winding tunnel. At times she seemed to force a way through solid rock that creaked and groaned in protest at their passage. Alan's ears caught the murmuring of water deep underground, and his nostrils sniffed the mustiness of rot and damp, and, as they bored deeper, the stink of sulphur. Yet all the while the solid rock appeared to open up before that strange squat figure, trailing her cataract of frosted hair in the storm of her progress as she scurried through her protesting underworld, rapping out her purpose with the spear.

They rested from time to time, although it seemed to Alan that it was more for their benefit than their guide's aged bones. He heard echoes, as if her snarls were being answered by forces within the mountain. At other times her shadow, cast by the firebrand, would expand to gigantic proportions and her cackle, reverberating about the massive walls, would rumble in her wake like thunder.

It was easy to lose track of time and distance. But he gauged they must have travelled deep into the roots of the mountains. Here at the centre of the labyrinth of caves the old woman led them into a chamber whose walls glittered with reflections, like a chamber of mirrors. Suddenly the light of her firebrand flared and every mouth dropped open. The sight simply took their breath away.

The walls, floor and ceiling were carved out of crystals of every colour and shade. Even Mo, despite her fascination with crystals, could not even begin to name them, since there was such a proliferation of shapes, textures and hues. High above them, stalactites as fine as straw trailed down from the ceiling, their surfaces dazzling with glints and sparkles, as if they were studded with diamonds. But the old woman ignored the beauty that surrounded them, pausing to squat on the crystal floor before a lake of sulphurous lava.

They abandoned their whispering to watch her reach into the depths of those spidery rags and find the goblet. Once again, in the creative weave of her hands, the vessel metamorphosed into the glowing eagle.

'Aw, man!' Alan sighed in a mixture of bewilderment and awe, watching it rise up out of its living cage to spiral for a moment before making a fluttering descent into the spitting lava. With her left hand, Granny Dew reached back into the folds of her dress, bringing out Alan's mobile phone. All of their gazes followed the descent of the old woman's left hand into the yellow-spuming furnace. Still holding the phone immersed in the lava, with her right hand she beckoned to Alan, demanding that he should come over to join her. Alan backed away with all of the others.

'Duuuvaaalll – paaahhh!' She grabbed hold of his reluctant right hand, prying open his fingers and then dashing them into the sulphur.

Clenching his teeth in anticipation of scorching heat, he was startled instead to encounter an icy cold. He yanked his hand out again and gazed at his clenched fist. Red light spilled out in rays and darts from between his fingers. When he opened them there was an oval ruby as large as a bantam's egg in his palm. Granny Dew was nodding her head and growling incantations.

'Quuurrruuunnn!'

He stared at the glowing gemstone, the light of which cast shapes and gyrations into the air about it, fathomless creations that melded and writhed in his vision as if forever on the point of producing something even more wonderful. Granny Dew reached deep into her voluminous dress and retrieved the two remaining mobile phones. With sudden snatches, she took, in turn, Kate's hand and then Mark's, pressing their mobiles back into each reluctant grasp. Each hand, with its mobile, was dashed into the sulphurous yellow furnace to emerge holding a glowing egg-shaped crystal. Kate's had a soft green matrix speckled with shifting autumnal shades of gold, while Mark's was black as obsidian in which tiny arabesques of silver appeared to glisten and pulsate.

For Mo there was none.

Standing back, Mo watched as each of her friends in turn drew his or her crystal from the glowing furnace. She could only wonder at the shock it seemed to induce in its new owner, observing how her friends' eyes glazed over as they came into contact with their crystals amid Granny Dew's incantations. Alan's eyes were already closed as the old woman, consumed by a new purpose, took the ruby egg from his grasp. She inspected the stork mark on his brow, scratching at it with the long fingernail, until she was rewarded by a trickle of blood.

Mo was terrified of what might happen. She grabbed at the wrist of the old woman. 'Nuh-nuh-nuh-no! Puh-puh-please!'

The left hand of Granny Dew caressed Mo's brow, as if reassuring her, while she closed her eyes and cackled some hymnal cadences, hatching some strange new magic within herself.

Mo sensed that she was the sole enraptured audience as, by the same mysterious force of will, Granny Dew transformed the ruby into a repository of her own energy. She saw how the features of Granny Dew's face, grotesquely distorted by the rays and spangles of light that burst through the cradle of her enfolded clasp, turned colder and greyer as the ruby increased in power. The light grew even more brilliantly incandescent, illuminating the bones of those gnarled fingers. Mo couldn't drag her eyes away from this new vision. Suddenly, the old woman pressed the ruby against Alan's bleeding brow.

He came out of his trance with a scream.

Mo took hold of Alan's hand. At the touch, she felt an immense wave of power coursing through him. But Granny Dew pulled their hands apart. She shook her head, gazing down into Mo's eyes with a glare of caution before returning her attention to Alan.

'Duuuvaaalll aaassskkks! Duuuvaaalll sees!'

Mo pleaded. 'Puh-puh-puh-please . . . Yuh-yuh-you muh-muh-must suh-suh-suh-stop.'

But the old woman paid her no heed. She wheeled away, satisfied that her work was now done. Growling, she woke the others out of their trances with prods and taps of the spear shaft, like a schoolteacher exasperated by a class of stupid pupils. Her power and strength were ferocious and they gave up any pretence of fighting back. The four friends could only follow her onrushing figure for what appeared to be miles through the groaning walls of stone until they arrived at a new cave, close enough to the surface for them to feel the biting cold. With an impatient wheeze she tapped her knobbly index finger against Kate's and Mark's hands, each still grasping the crystal eggs, then pointed to Alan's still-bleeding brow in which the ruby crystal was implanted.

They stared back at her in fright.

With a shake of her head, Granny Dew hammered the base of the spear against the floor of the cave. It provoked an explosion of sound, deep under foot, as if a peal of thunder was passing through the very grains of the rock.

Still muttering her impatience she tapped around the floor and walls, eliciting a flurry of spidery movement – and shrieks from the four friends. From the floor, walls and ceiling, the cave was invaded by armies of spiders. Myriad spinnerets wove cloaks about them, made from the same cobwebby material as the old woman's dress, the living edges expanding rapidly over their heads until each of them was cloaked from head to feet in a mantle of living lace. Mo, Kate and Mark all found themselves staring at each other from holes they had poked through for their startled eyes. Even Alan shuddered, although he already felt warmed by his own body heat inside the creepy mantle. He established that he could at least breathe through it. Reaching up with shaky hands, he copied the others by poking two slits for his eyes to peer out of.

Within minutes, they found themselves outside in the bitter cold, the driving snow settling over their thick new coverings. As if with a will of their own, their legs began to shuffle forward, so they formed a small file, trudging like clockwork mannequins down from the mountain.

Alan even thought he heard a tick-tock in his head that beat time with his legs.

*

Mark was the first to rouse from the automatic trudging, many hours later. He was still heading downslope through the blizzard. Seeing no one ahead of him, he felt a momentary stab of panic. But he was not alone. A glance behind confirmed that the others were following on behind him in what appeared to be an animated stupor, so camouflaged with snow it was as if minuscule fragments of the landscape were on the move.

Snow gusted about him. It blew into his eyes. Even where the snow could not penetrate, the cold did, searing his nostrils and his gaping, breathless mouth. The cold, the anguish of it, penetrated his skin and stiffened his muscles underneath. But it no longer troubled him. Anger – rage – was the force that drove him on. He had learnt the lesson of rage long ago, when it had enabled him to survive life in the Grimstone-and-Bethel household. And now he took refuge in his rage. His exhausted legs drew strength from it to make another step, another ten, a hundred yards. A series of hundred-yard intervals and – as Alan might have declared, 'Hey, man!' – it was another mile.

Had he dreamed that stuff back there in the cave?

No, he didn't think so, tightening his fist about the jet-black crystal. Boy, did it feel hard and heavy, yet coursed with some weird inner power. He squeezed it and identified with it, enduring the continuing shock of what felt like static electricity. The bag lady had also given them something in the gruel. The gruel had given them the strength to make this journey. But here in the snow it was he and not Alan who was the leader. It was he who had decided there could be no resting. Because he knew, absolutely, that if they stopped for a rest they would fold over and die.

Under the spider's web mantle he also patted the shape of the harmonica in his coat pocket, recalling how he had first acquired it.

It had been six years ago, when he was nine years old. A bad time at home. It had been some tramp, a man with straggly fair hair like his own, and about the right age to be his father, who had bumped into him in the rain-washed street. The tramp had pushed the harmonica into his hands. It had been early evening, in winter, and Mark remembered the tramp's face, illuminated by the harsh yellow glare of the street light, with absolute clarity. He remembered the haunted look in his eyes – that had impressed him, and the fact he hadn't asked for money. In fact he never said a word. Mark remembered how Grimstone had reacted to finding the harmonica in his possession, squeezing the story out of him with a terrible beating. Mark had derived a perverse, if painful, pleasure from the look in Grimstone's eyes when he had described the tramp.

Grimstone had broken Mark's wrist, twisting his arm just to tear the harmonica from him. The broken wrist had made it all the more awkward for him when, with Mo standing guard, he had climbed out of the bedroom window before dawn and sneaked out to the dustbin to reclaim the harmonica. He had taken great care to keep it hidden from Arseless ever since, coming to see it as his most precious possession, taking care to practise playing it only when he was far away from the house.

That memory – the sweetness of it – kept him going for another mile. But his tired legs needed new things to be angry about, new hungers . . .

Hunger – that felt like the right word for it. But he wasn't really thinking about food. He was beyond any hunger for food.

Tick-tock . . . tick-tock. The clock in his head beat time with his legs.

Tick-tock. Tick-tock.

Suddenly he pitched headlong into snow, deep snow, as if he were falling into a cloud of bitter, threatening cold within a paranoid dream. Still he dragged himself up, sitting first, resting on his arms, then pushing himself onto his haunches before climbing back onto his legs.

The thing is, it's up to me. I'm the leader! Got to do it . . . no slacking. Just got to keep moving!

He shook his head, within the cowl of webs. Blinked his eyes.

That bloody never-ending snow!

There was too much of it. He hated the bastard, the way it just kept shitting down on him out of the sky. He hated the way it stuck to him, sucking the heat from his head and shoulders even through the spider's web mantle. He felt it strike back at him in a series of heavy, solid blows. His eyes swivelled upward, to glimpse green patches where the big clumps of snow were falling from.

Green!

He looked up again. Saw pine needles.

I made it . . . I made it to the trees!

He tried to laugh but ended up tottering for support against a branch. His contact shook the tree, shaking more snow down on his head.

Don't stop, stupid! Get a move on . . .

Tick-tock . . .

A mistake, that. Should never have stopped. His legs were a lot more wobbly now. Yet still he discovered the rage to keep on trudging, the air wheezing out of his open mouth like exhausted bellows, his breath freezing to a mask of ice in the cobwebs over his cheeks and chin.

Blinking again . . . his eyes trying to make sense of what he was looking at . . . It seemed that he had wandered into the sea.

No, not the sea . . .

What it is, stupid, is just more snow! A whole flat field of it!

He peered again.

No – not snow. More like the sea and the snow have become one . . .

As in the slow motion of a never-ending dream, he trudged on, his feet numbed with cold so he couldn't feel them hit the ground beneath him. It really was a disorientating feeling. He was gliding over a still sea in which dark shapes were floating, yet perfectly motionless.

Boats. Wooden boats . . .

A fleet of wooden boats was floating on this sea of ice in this world of perfect stillness. They wheeled and spiralled about him.

And then his heart thudded with alarm as a strange face appeared above him, a ludicrously impossible face. The face was on top of a huge shaggy body and it was peering down at him.

A Village, Ice-Bound

Alan, who had insisted on taking last place in the trek down the mountain, could see tall figures, dressed in thick-furred animal hides sewn with leather thongs. He tried to talk but no sound emerged from his frozen lips and tongue. 'People who could help us,' he insisted mentally, his legs still propelling him forward, in stumbles and staggers.

Now he was among them he saw that they were bigger and more fearsome-looking than anyone he had laid eyes on before. Their heavy-set faces were moving in and out of his spiralling vision. A man abandoned his repair of fishing nets to walk alongside him, looking him up and down as if he were some exotic animal. The man's face was tawny, his dark brown eyes thickly padded against the cold. His skin looked strangely leathery.

More and more people were arriving to look at him. They were coming out of boats built out of stout cedar planks, with decks and timbers peeping out from under their burdens of snow.

Alan followed on after the others, leaning on the shaft of the Spear of Lug, unable to feel his legs moving under him. Then another stranger was walking backwards in front of him, a man so tall he would have dwarfed Padraig, but far burlier, built like a heavyweight wrestler. He wore a wide-brimmed hat, indigo in colour, like a Pilgrim's hat with a downturned brim. Underneath the hat his face was a gingery brown in colour, with a fawn moustache filling his upper lip and curling down at the sides of his mouth. Reddish whiskers covered his cheeks, from his chin to the brim of his hat, and there were dark circles around his chestnut-brown eyes and over his broad flat nose. His neck was as thick as a grown man's thigh, widening to massive arms and shoulders, while his chest was as stout as . . . as a bear's, Alan now thought with growing alarm. It was this bear-like man who finally stopped Alan walking. He yanked the spear out of his hand and threw it to one side, where it became the centre of attention for the excited children. Grasping Alan solidly by his mantle-capped shoulders, the burly man brought the automatic walking to a halt, then stared into Alan's web-shrouded face. Sharp fingernails poked through the icy mask, tearing it away from his mouth and nostrils.

Alan's breath caught in his throat.

Except for his nose and lips, the man's face was covered with fur. Even the enormous hand, tearing the cobwebs from Alan's face, was covered with that same gingery-brown fur, other than the leathery pads of the fingers. His broad dark lips were moving, calling out in some guttural language. Alan, with his heart pounding, caught a single word: 'Hul-o-ima!'

His voice was deep as a bellow.

'Hul-o-ima! Hul-o-ima!'

The cry was taken up by the others milling around them, the children too. Alan gazed in astonishment at the bear-like resemblance of their faces, with many shades of brown, grey and creamy yellow, and burly bodies dressed in the same leather-sewn furs. Soon, the air was filled with strange hisses and growls, the champing of teeth, and a high-pitched whining from the little ones. The whole village milled around the four exhausted friends, the villagers' breath clouding the air and their fur-booted feet shifting and stamping on the ice.

When Alan poked his hand out through the mantle of cobwebs, its hairless appearance stunned them into silence. He tore away the remainder of the cobwebby mantle and tried to speak to them, but still his lips and tongue were too frozen to let the words come.

Kate seemed to be equally dumbstruck. She had also torn away the cowl and was holding onto Alan's arm, unable to speak but clearly astonished by everything she was seeing in the ice-bound village.

Kate gave up her attempt to communicate. She was

bewildered and utterly exhausted. But there was no time to wonder what any of this might mean. A bear-man picked her up and threw her over his shoulder, carrying her as if she were a sack of potatoes. The others were all being carried or assisted in one way or another, until they arrived at a central area, where the boats were clustered about the central focus of a massive ship, a great galleon, with timbers of black and fissured oak soaring above the smaller boats.

Another face was blocking out her vision. This man had grey fur, the colour of slate, and narrow weasel-like features, with eyes that were black. He poked at her face with black-clawed fingers before discarding her to examine the others. In that fleeting contact, Kate shrank from the cruelty she sensed in those eyes, which were now scrutinising Alan.

The thin man gesticulated at Alan's brow and he growled and snarled at the other villagers.

Then, abruptly, another of the villagers confronted the thin man. This new man was the oldest of all, almost as tall as the gingery-haired giant, but leaner and bent, with silvery hair in a wrinkled and weathered face. His lips, like his broad flat nose, were matt-black, in striking contrast to the silvery fur over the rest of his face, and his left eye was blind. Kate noticed that he also hobbled on his left leg as he put himself between Alan and the thin man, before stooping to examine Alan's brow with his good eye.

At a signal from the old man, the villagers herded the four friends up a gangway, through a leather-hung door, and into the gloom of one of the boats. Kate could smell fish and something else – a heavy animal odour. It was much warmer here, out of the biting wind, although there was no sign of a fire. She winced with stiffness as they deposited her onto some hide-covered planks. Her senses swam in the heady mixture of smells and she squeezed her eyes shut for a short while to clear her mind. When she opened them again all of the bear people had departed except for the limping old man.

'Al-ah mika chak-ko?' He spoke in a growl, but low-pitched, as if in a passion. Kate stared up into his silvery-grey eye, wishing she knew what the words meant.

There were other words spoken with that same passion, words she could not understand, though she heard that key expression again, 'Hul-o-ima!' That same word went round and round in her head as she fell into an exhausted sleep under a blanket sewn from seal skins – that and the old man's silvery eye peering down at her, his low, growling voice with its unanswerable questions, his limping movements in the murky interior.

When Alan woke it was daybreak, judging from the wintry light diffusing into the room through chinks and gaps. He discovered that he had slept curled up in the hide of a walrus. A gangling youth was moving around in the murky light between the sleeping shapes of his friends.

The youth had the same gingery-brown face as the giant from yesterday, though he was smaller, relatively speaking – he was still half a foot taller than Alan – and with a lighter halo around his mouth. Alan looked all around for the spear, but there was no sign of it. The gangly youth handed him a bowl of soup in which there were chunks of fish mixed with roots and red berries. Alan's stomach was so growling with hunger he could hardly contain his impatience, lifting the bowl to his mouth and taking a sup. The shock of it almost made him vomit. The soup was icy cold and the fish, vegetable and berries were raw. He dropped the bowl with a clatter.

The youth stared at him, then rushed back out through the leather door, letting in a blast of freezing air.

Alan swilled his saliva around in his mouth to get rid of the taste of raw fish, then pulled the walrus hide around his shivering body and began calling out to the others to see who else was awake.

Mark was the first to call back. Alan told him about the uncooked food.

'Fishier and fishier!' Mark cackled.

Alan swallowed, realising that Mark's voice had recovered from the cold. He tested his own. 'You thinking what I'm thinking?'

'Cool eating if you're a – growl, growl – bear?'

'Oh, man!'

'Man is hardly the word!'

'Those faces! Did you see the claws on their fingers?'

There was a murmuring from the two girls. Kate's voice sounded plaintive. 'Oh, will you two stop trying to frighten us!'

Mark chuckled. 'We'd better hope they're of the teddy variety – and not the grizzly.'

'Put a sock in it, Mark.'

Mark opened his eyes wide. 'Come along now – no cause for panic, folks. They're just fattening us up for dinner!'

Alan threw a trainer at Mark. 'Oh, don't listen to him! Are they running around on four paws? Are they roaring and snarling, showing their fangs?'

'Alan's right,' Kate shuffled over to sit next to Mo, 'they're fisher people. We saw the nets and boats.'

'Grrrooowwwlll!' Mark fell back on his bunk, collapsing into laughter.

'Okay, Mark,' said Alan. 'You can joke as much as you like. But think about it. The old guy put us up on his boat. He gave us these rugs to keep us warm. They're civilised, no matter how different they look.'

Kate said, 'Maybe they just don't cook their fish.'

Mark chortled. 'What bears do?'

'Hey, maybe you're right, Kate.' Alan laughed aloud with relief. 'That's got to be the explanation. They eat it raw.'

'Luh-luh-like suh-sushi!'

Kate nodded. 'That's right. And think about it. It isn't always the best thing to cook food. We know that cooking vegetables kills off the vitamins.'

Alan tried to stay cheerful. 'Well I don't know about

you, but I'm starving. What do you say we go out there and tell them we cook our food?'

'That's an excellent idea,' muttered Kate. 'We need to find some way of communicating with them.'

'I think I know a way of capturing their attention.' Mark grinned, twirling the harmonica he had drawn from his pocket.

Alan picked up the discarded soup bowl, which was still about a third full, and he stared at it while Mark played around with a bluesy tune. Within a minute, the lame old man was standing in the open doorway, staring at Mark, with the gangling youth equally curious, hanging back behind him. Alan held out the bowl, doing his best to convey in sign language the lighting of a fire under it. The old man watched him bemusedly for several seconds. Then he growled an instruction to the youth, who disappeared into the cold. Meanwhile the old man took Alan gently but firmly by the arm and brought him closer to the bright daylight streaming in through the open door.

Alan called back to the others, 'It's okay. He's just fascinated with my birthmark.'

'So what's the big fascination?'

It was Kate who answered. 'Granny Dew did something to it – to you, Alan. You have a ruby triangle in its place.'

'You're kidding me?'

Mark cut in. 'She isn't kidding. You have a crystal in your head where the birthmark used to be.'

Alan lifted a finger to touch his brow, jerking it away

as he felt some kind of electric shock. It left him feeling sick in his stomach.

'We were all given something by Granny Dew.' Kate held up the gold-speckled green crystal she had brought down from the mountain.

'All except muh-muh-me,' Mo grumbled.

When the old man let him go, Alan hurried back to his bunk and sat there in silence for several moments. Then he reached up, more gingerly this time, to touch his brow – and jerked his hand away with that same sensation of shock.

'Shee–it!'

Kate reflected, 'Granny Dew – do you remember how she reacted when we switched on the screens! She did something to them. She changed them.'

Mark widened his eyes. 'Maybe she changed us too?'

Mo nodded.

Alan muttered, 'Who the hell was she?'

Mo shook her head, her expression deeply thoughtful.

'What is it, Mo?'

'The Eh-Eh-Eh-Earth Muh-Mother.'

Mark gave Mo a hug while roaring with laughter. 'Oh, Mo – are you seriously suggesting that we've just met the Earth Mother?'

Kate whispered, 'The Earth Mother?'

Alan shook his head. 'But this is hardly Earth!'

While discussion continued, the gangling youth returned, bringing a piece of wood, like a box-lid, in which there was a flat layer of soft clay, together with a narrow stick. He pressed them both into Alan's hands. It was obvious they hadn't understood Alan's earlier gesticulations about cooking food. Alan spent several moments just thinking about it before sketching something simple, using the stick on the soft clay. When he was finished, the gangling youth took the clay from him and looked at his sketch of a fish in a pan over the image of flames. His face wrinkled with disgust before he departed through the doorway.

'What's happening?' Kate asked, coming over to sit by Alan.

'I think he got the message. But he didn't seem to like it.'

'Let's hope we haven't given him the idea of cooking us,' whispered Mark.

'Oh, button it, Mark! If you can't say something useful, go play your harmonica.' He threw the walrus hide over his and Kate's shoulders, then hugged her shivering body.

About half an hour later Alan sniffed the air, then left Kate, still wrapped in the walrus hide, so he could poke his head out onto the deck. 'You guys get a whiff of that?'

'Fish cooking!'

Alan laughed in triumph. 'C'mon, Kate! Let's go see if we can attract the cook's attention.'

'Do come back and let us know,' Mark's voice followed them through the flapping doorway, 'if it means food for us – or for them!'

With warm hides pulled tight around their shoulders, Alan and Kate followed the smell of cooking back along the deck until they came to a wider platform at the stern, where the youth was grilling a whole salmon over a brazier of burning charcoal. The brazier stood on a wide flat stone, to keep it clear of the deck. They watched as the youth sprinkled herb-scented oil and fresh berries over the salmon's silvery length before turning it over to cook it through. Nearby, a second pot bubbled over another brazier, full of fish soup. The youth grinned back over his shoulder, to where Alan and Kate were watching him, making no secret of the fact they were so hungry that they couldn't help but make appreciative noises, hunkered under their furs, their teeth chattering.

Kate winced. 'I'm so famished I can't bear the sight and the smell of it. I'm going to have to head back!'

She made a prayer sign with her hands, as if imploring the cook to get a move on, before dashing back to the warmth of the cabin. Meanwhile, Alan stayed behind and watched the youth, noticing the jerky awkwardness of his limbs. Alan couldn't figure whether he was naturally awkward or just nervous. But there was no mistaking the intelligence he saw in those large brown eyes.

He pointed to himself and said, 'Alan'. Then he pointed at the youth, in an obvious appeal for him to supply his name.

But the youth ignored him, ladling soup out of the pot into a jug. He handed Alan the steaming jug, together with four wooden bowls, then signalled for Alan to lead the way back to his friends, with the youth following on with the fish on a platter.

Their arrival was greeted with cries of delight from hungry mouths. All four were too impatient to wait for the food to cool down, burning their fingers and throats, and hardly caring. They were still devouring the soup and fish when they heard footsteps approaching the leather door. The cook was back, carrying the large flat stone, which he placed in a clear area on the floor between the bunks. Grinning at Kate, he imitated her expression minutes earlier on the deck, when she'd been shivering and rubbing at the gooseflesh on her arms. He was a pretty good mimic and had them all laughing.

Then he left them to go fetch the brazier, in which charcoal was still burning. Setting it down on the flat stone, he made another journey to bring in fresh charcoal, blowing it aglow with long gentle puffs, then fetching a large basin and an earthenware jug of water, placing the basin on the brazier and pouring the water into it.

He made a sign, as if washing his face.

Kate, still somewhat puffy-eyed from sleep, nodded her thanks, taking first turn before the bowl, washing her face and neck in the still-cold water, then drying herself with a fleecy sealskin.

The youth averted his eyes, as if to save her embarrassment, but grinning all the while.

From a pocket deep in his furs, he produced a small

wooden flask, which he handed to Alan, making rubbing movements over his arms. Alan removed the stopper and sniffed at what proved to be scented oil. Ignoring the cold, he stripped to the waist and washed his face, neck, arms and chest, then nodded his thanks to the youth as he made a show of rubbing the oil into his aching shoulders and upper arms.

As he was leaving, the youth tapped his chest as he cried out a single word, 'Tur-key-a', before the leather door banged shut behind him.

Kate clapped her hands. 'He's just told us his name – Turkeya!'

That started a commotion of excited voices.

'Hey, I don't know if I'm just imagining it, but the oil really seems to be helping these aching muscles.'

Suddenly they were all fighting to try it. The girls insisted that Alan and Mark should leave them on their own so they could undress and have a proper wash and rub the oil into their aching muscles. While they were still arguing about who was to go next, Turkeya came back, carrying a bundle of fur-lined surcoats. They were made out of sealskin, woven of the same hand-stitched skins as his own clothing, with the outer leather oiled to make them windproof. Holding them up for size caused a great deal of hilarity, with the girls pretending to model and the boys throwing items of clothing from one to the other. The fisher people were so tall that these clothes had to be made for their children, but they were plenty big enough for the friends, even for Alan, reaching halfway down their calves. The boys carried their surcoats outside to try them on, leaving the two girls to a modicum of privacy. The cold, out of doors, was so severe that even Mark, who was so vain about his leather jacket, was glad enough to don the extra layer of protection. But the hilarity stopped when they heard heavy echoing footsteps approaching and they knew it was the old man, whose gait was unmistakable, his lame leg clumping up the bare wooden planks of the gangway leading up to the deck.

As they followed the old man back into the cabin, where the two girls were now fully washed, oiled and dressed in their own surcoats, Alan murmured thoughtfully to Mark, 'I don't know what you think, but my guess is that this guy could be the shaman.'

Turkeya followed the shaman into the cabin. The old man was tall enough to have to bend his head in order to fit under the ceiling and his good eye glanced around at all four friends, as if checking their choices of coats. In particular he looked Alan up and down, pleased that Alan had copied the fisher people in belting his coat with a strip of leather. Turkeya made a comment that brought the hint of a smile to the shaman's wrinkled face and the shaman spoke in that same guttural voice to his assistant, who disappeared again, returning with his arms full of fur-lined boots. The largest of these – Alan suspected they were the property of the youth himself – fitted him for calf length, though they were a little too big for his feet.

Judging that they were now sufficiently protected against the weather, Turkeya led them out through the leather doorway onto the deck and down some planks onto the ice-field. The sky was the mauve of a healing bruise and the temperature well below freezing. They appreciated the fur clothing in a wind that was so cold that none of them could open their eyes wider than slits. Virgin snow squealed underfoot as they tried out their new boots.

As Turkeya showed them around, Alan saw that the village was made up of about a hundred sturdy boats, each boat very likely housing a family, and about thirty feet long, with a single mast for an oblong leather sail. The living quarters were struck from the same adzed cedar as the keels, although many of them were painted with bright colours, such as reds, yellows and greens. The entire fleet was becalmed in a frozen lake that, in less wintry times, must feed into a river. At the heart of the village was the galleon he had seen on his arrival. The great ship, triple-masted and built of oak, was more impressive when viewed from close-to. Although his head throbbed with cold, Alan couldn't help but whistle with admiration as his eyes roamed the majestic structure of the galleon which towered over the simple fishing boats like a medieval cathedral amid the ramshackle streets of its builders.

Mage Lord

Alan's queasiness returned and forced him to head back to the shaman's boat, leaving the others to explore the village. With a splitting headache, and feeling lonely and confused, he was unable to come to terms with what was happening to him in this bizarre world. He missed his grandfather, Padraig, and he wondered what had become of him now that Grimstone was back in Clonmel and looking for Mark and Mo. The fact was that he missed it all – the sawmill, the freedom to go rambling in the woods, or go fishing in the river – a lot more than he would ever have imagined he would. Only now, with all this distance between them, did he fully appreciate how caring Padraig had been.

I'm really sorry, Grandad! I took it out on you, and now I wish I hadn't.

That something really was happening within himself, he could no longer doubt. Waves of altered sensation flooded his senses, as if the ruby in his brow was somehow invading him, interfering with his body and mind. And now, feeling overwhelmingly nauseous, the last thing he wanted was confrontation or aggravation, so it was with trepidation that he found the shaman waiting on the deck of his boat, seemingly for Alan's return. He tried to shuffle past him, but the old man gripped his shoulders and stared at him with the same passion as earlier. The same depth of emotion contorted his face, and he spoke to Alan in that same tense, guttural tone of voice. But Alan could no more understand him now than earlier.

'Chahko kloshe!'

The shaman opened his black-palmed hands, indicating Alan's brow, as if in admonition that Alan should understand.

'Kah mika chahko?' He swung his long bewhiskered head from side to side, groaning aloud. 'Hyas Dia-ub!' All of a sudden his expression became so urgent, so full of animation, it only worsened Alan's headache.

The shaman pointed to Alan's brow, then made a kind of fluting sign with his fingers over his lips. As Alan tentatively reached up to touch his birthmark, he felt how hot it was to the touch.

Aw, Jeez – I'm burning up – my whole body is burning up with some kind of a fever!

For several seconds he felt a jitteriness invade his limbs, so debilitating it forced him to sit down on the bunk where he had spent the night. Suddenly, the crystal in his brow throbbed, and he felt a tremendous shockwave course through him, as if the thing had connected up with his heartbeat, and the combined pulse of energy went out to every nerve in his body. He hands fell onto his lap and he just stared down in bewilderment at his trembling fingers.

The shaman put his arm around Alan's shoulder and helped him back onto his feet, leading him to the basin he had earlier washed in. The old man pointed to the water in the basin, in which Alan saw his reflection. He lifted the lock of hair that had fallen down from his forehead and saw that his birthmark was no longer an inverted triangle of faintly pink skin, but a bright ruby triangle, each of its sides sharply demarcated and about an inch in length, the whole glowing eerily in the gloom of the interior. When, very carefully, he brushed his finger over it, it felt as flat and smooth as the ruby crystal the old woman had taken from the sulphurous lava.

Suddenly, he jerked his whole body back in alarm.

No – it can't be!

He bent down and peered again. But his initial impression was not mistaken. In the depths of the ruby crystal he saw movement. Flickering patterns were coming alive within it, strange flows of light and arabesques of colour glowed deep in the matrix of the crystal, changing, metamorphosing, from moment to moment. The patterns were pulsating in time with his heartbeat. A wave of gooseflesh swept over him. He tottered back. He had to be assisted to sit down on one of the bunks where he put his face in his hands.

Oh, heck – what's happening to me?

The shaman left him for several minutes, then returned with what appeared to be a thin flake of blue crystal, perhaps three inches wide and an irregular oval in shape. The old man held the crystal in the palm of his left hand, then extended his right hand over it with the fingers splayed. His face tensed in concentration. Alan watched how five claws extended from the black pads of old man's fingers. With a throaty incantation the shaman picked up the blue crystal by its edges, using only the tips of the claws. It was as if he had to avoid any flesh contact with the blue crystal. Then he held it about an inch away from Alan's throbbing brow. Alan felt the shock of communication, then a strange intoxicating feeling, as if all his tensions and fears were draining away from him. The shaman rocked his upper body slightly from side to side, incanting words that sounded like a prayer, still holding the blue crystal close to Alan's brow. Suddenly, unbelievably, Alan realised that he was hearing the old man's thoughts aloud.

The shaman was telling him his name: *Kemtuk Lapeep*.

Without having to think about it, Alan knew what it meant. In the language of the fisher people it meant 'Kemtuk the lame'.

Alan was bewildered by the strangeness of it; he hadn't a clue how this was happening, or what it meant.

Kemtuk Lapeep drew back his hand, holding the blue crystal. He gestured, a half-shrug of the shoulders, as if to suggest that crystal-to-crystal contact was no longer necessary.

Alan thought about what the shaman was trying to tell him, that maybe his own ruby crystal was making possible this communication, and he wondered if he was being invited to figure a way of testing it out for himself. What was there to lose? He shrugged, brought to mind some simple words of greeting in English. He heard himself murmur, 'Nah sikhs, Kemtuk Lapeep!'

Greetings to you, Kemtuk the Lame!

Somehow, marvellously, he had actually spoken in the alien language of the fisher folk, while realising what he was saying in his own mind. Meanwhile he couldn't help but notice the mixture of relief and delight that came over the old man's face.

It took several more hours of trial and experiment before they were able to communicate meaningfully in this bizarre manner. Meanwhile Alan learnt some useful facts about Kemtuk and the fisher people. The old man was a great deal more than just a medicine man to his village. He was the 'lore master' – a term that meant something like spiritual leader – of a people widely scattered about the entire northeastern shoreline of a great continent, known as Monisle. There was a hint or two, cautiously touched upon, that the shaman had other knowledge, secret lore that was passed down from such a spiritual leader to a chosen apprentice. Turkeya was his apprentice. Turkeya was also the son of the tribal chief, Siam, the barrel-chested giant Alan had encountered on his arrival. When Kemtuk, with a laugh, first spoke Siam's name, Alan saw the image of a roaring grizzly bear. Alan also learnt that the chief was married to a noblewoman called Kehloke, and that Turkeya had a younger sister, who was called Loloba.

'We look very different, your people and mine.' Alan shook his head, still dizzy and headachy, but also hesitant to say the obvious for fear of offending the old man.

They were standing together on the deck of the shaman's boat, looking down at the fleet of other boats and Kemtuk's people. At Alan's comment, the old man grunted, lifting his gaze beyond the ice-bound lake to the snow-covered peaks that encircled it. In the shaman's mind Alan heard the name the Whitestar Mountains – giving rise to the headwaters of the Snowmelt River. In the old man's mind Alan sensed awe, in relation to both mountains and river, awe and perhaps a religious sense of reverence such that Kemtuk's functioning eye refused to meet Alan's eyes directly. 'Yes, we are different. We are Tilikum Olhyiu, the Children of the Sea. You, if you will take no offence, are naked-skins, children of monkeys who burn good flesh with fire until it is unfit even for the vultures.'

Alan shook his head. He wasn't offended. But the communication appeared to be helping him in some way.

He was feeling less jittery, less nauseous, and suddenly intrigued with a startling idea. 'In this world, this land, there are different kinds of people?'

At this Kemtuk roared with laughter, showing a mouth missing a few teeth, and all those remaining being much larger than Alan's own. 'Of course there are many different peoples. In the great cities, such as Isscan, by the confluence of the great rivers, and in Carfon, by the Eastern Ocean, you would find naked-skins like yourself.' Suddenly the shaman wheeled and the distant look was gone from his eye. 'There will be time enough later for idle chatter. But today we have precious little time. You must tell me how is it that you, bearer of the soul eye, have come amongst us?'

Assuming the shaman must be referring to the ruby triangle in his brow, he could only shrug his shoulders and drop his head. It was an effort to keep panic out of his voice. 'I wish I could explain it to you. But how can I explain what I don't even begin to understand myself?'

'Yet, even if you do not understand the greater purpose, you might tell me in such simple terms as you remember.'

Alan nodded. It sounded reasonable. And so he attempted to explain their being summoned here from another world, the circle of stones in the blizzard, how their lives were saved by the strange cave creature who resembled an old woman, and who called herself Granny Dew.

On hearing the description of the old woman, the

shaman's grey eye grew round and he fell onto one knee before Alan, muttering incantations. 'It is as I hardly dared to hope. Even when I first saw the soul eye in your brow, I could not credit what it truly meant.'

Alan just stood there, bewildered.

But Kemtuk persisted, his hands once again gripping Alan's shoulders. 'Even the simplest child among us would see in the mark that you are the one we have so long awaited – the heralded one who would come out of the snowy wilderness. And now I hear your story! Only a great Mage would carry such a mark of power.'

Alan pulled himself free. 'I'm not a Mage, whatever that might be. I'm just a kid – an orphan.'

The shaman stood erect, his head towering above Alan's. 'If I judge correctly, you neither understand your purpose nor have you learnt how to use your power. But in you I sense the seed of destiny. In time you will become a Lord amongst Mages, Alan Duval.'

Alan shook his head. 'Hey – there's so much I don't have a clue about. Maybe you can help me to understand all this – the real reason my friends and I were brought here, to this world.'

'In time, perhaps, we may search for answers. But this is not the time for explanations. We must make haste. Ignorant though you seem of your purpose, I have to warn you that our situation here is desperate. Since the fall of Ossierel, we, the proud Olhyiu, have been in thrall to the accursed Storm Wolves. The Children of the Sea are forbidden to cast their nets in the Eastern Ocean. We must fish only in this accursed wasteland of ice and snow, and the cream of our harvest fattens the bellies of the traitors in Isscan. Shamans such as I are forbidden to practise our art, even to succour the sick.'

'Then you've already broken these laws in helping us?'

'Your arrival here is welcome but also extremely dangerous. There is one amongst us, a hunter called Snakoil Kawkaw – rightly named, for he is the deceiving crow. Our chief, Siam, will hear no ill of him because he is his maternal cousin. But Kawkaw will attempt to use you for his own purposes.'

'I don't understand.'

'Our chief, Siam, might insist that Kawkaw would not betray his own people to our enemies. But I fear that he will. And if such were to happen, the situation would become perilous.'

Alan rubbed at his brow. What had the old woman really done to him with this strange ruby crystal that it should cause such a reaction? 'I just can't take this in. I don't understand anything of what you're saying.'

'There will be time for talking later. For the moment we must make ready to flee.'

'But how can we? Your boats are trapped in ice.'

'Mage Lord – we must find a way.' Kemtuk dropped his face to look down into Alan's, with a desperate expression. 'The Storm Wolves are no more than a day's travel from this place. If they find you here, they will kill you. I must call together a council that will persuade my people to action.' So saying, the shaman hurried from the boat.

Alan clenched his fists in frustration. He was still nauseous and bewildered at what was happening to him. He could feel his own pulse, quickened by anxiety, in the triangle in his brow. All the same, he knew he had to go find the others. Warn them about what was going on. *But how – how the heck am I going to explain any of this to them?*

A Council of Life and Death

Haltingly, at times with his hands running through his hair in frustration, Alan did his best to explain what he had learnt from the shaman. The friends were standing out on deck, so scared that they were scarcely aware of the bitter wind that numbed every inch of their exposed skin.

'Oh, Alan!' Kate put her arms around him, squeezing him tight.

'Oh, Alan, my foot!' Mark was less comforting. 'You Americans have just the term for it – *bullshit*!'

'Mark,' said Kate, 'I'm warning you!'

'Hey, Kate, it's okay. Mark's right. I can see how that's exactly how it must sound. All I can tell you guys is exactly what I saw and heard, just as it happened.'

Even as Mark's face creased with disbelief, a bell began to peal out over the ice-bound lake, and the boat people began to gather, putting down whatever they were doing and streaming towards the galleon. Kate clasped Alan's hand. She didn't need to tell him how frightened she was.

Mo was equally shocked, and puzzled. 'Thu-thu-this . . .?' She pointed at the triangle in Alan's brow.

'The soul eye, the shaman called it.'

Kate spoke for herself and Mo. 'You really can understand what people are saying through it?'

Alan shrugged. 'I'm just doing my best to explain what I saw and heard. I'm not sure I believe it myself.' He hesitated, hardly daring to tell them what he now suspected. 'I . . . well, I think that sometimes I can read some of what people are thinking – what's in their minds.'

The three others stared at him dumbstruck. Then Kate grew excited. 'It must be terrifying.'

'You're right – it is.'

'But if it's true – I mean, think about it! Do you think Granny Dew might have put some similar kind of magic into our crystals?'

'Who knows? Maybe it's possible.'

Kate looked down at the egg-shaped crystal given to her by Granny Dew. She pored over its subtle shades of green, and the complex whorls and patterns within the green which were constantly metamorphosing, like the whirling of autumn leaves in the wind. Mo suddenly grew tearful and Kate understood, putting her arm around her shoulders. 'We were all given crystals, except for Mo. Poor Mo – why was she left out?'

Alan could only shrug. 'I haven't a clue. I guess, maybe, because she didn't have a mobile.'

'That hardly seems fair.'

'I'm not sure fairness counts for much here.' But then he sighed and his voice dropped to a whisper. 'Who knows, it might be more of a blessing to have no crystal!'

But there was no time for further discussion. Several Olhyiu arrived to herd the four friends down onto the ice, leading them to where the great ship was becalmed. They escorted them up the gangway that led to the centre deck of the galleon, which extended to at least a hundred and fifty feet in length and forty feet in breadth, with balustraded sides over all the different levels of the decks, and overhead a complicated maze of snow-grimed rigging. There were huge raised sections of deck at the fore and aft, with a stretch of mid-section in between. It was towards the rear raised section they were now being herded, passing under a massive carved arch, from the apex of which hung a brass bell that was still faintly vibrating from the summoning. Two heavy doors were thrown open onto a broad staircase and they descended under a circular carving of a whale leaping out of the ocean over two crossed harpoons; given what Kemtuk had told him, Alan assumed this symbolised the Children of the Sea and their former freedom to fish the oceans.

But now that Alan was up close enough to witness the complexity of the galleon's art and engineering, he couldn't help but wonder how these unsophisticated people could possibly have built it.

Where the other boats, like Kemtuk's, were simple and functional, masted for a single leather sail, this giant stirred feelings of wonder and awe in him. It was piloted by a great wheel and driven by a complexity of rigging that must have demanded great navigational skill. Every square foot of the superstructure was exquisitely carved, as if by master craftsmen. Exotic birds and butterflies preened and fluttered their wings. Shoals of fish darted through a labyrinth of coral and seaweed. Other panels depicted what appeared to be mythological creatures of the land, sea and air, at play amid forests, against a vista of mountains and sky, yet all captured with an artistry that seemed out of keeping with the simple fisher folk and their other boats.

He knew from Kemtuk that they called it the 'Temple Ship', a good name for a cathedral dedicated to Akoli, the Creator, which also appeared to be their word for the sperm whale.

At the bottom of the staircase they were led into a great chamber with a low ceiling. The room was so dark it needed the additional illumination of oil lamps, which reflected now in the eyes of many faces. The whole village appeared to be here, and now the arrival of the four strangers among them threw the Olhyiu into an excited murmuring. There was a strong odour of sweaty bodies.

The Olhyiu were sitting cross-legged on the bare planks of the floor. The crowding was so dense that those in the nearest row could have reached out and touched them.

Alan noticed that the older men and women, presumably the elders of the tribe, were gathered closer to the front. The walls, between murals, were festooned with carved oars, ornamental maces and clubs. As his eyes grew more accustomed to the gloom, he saw that the murals depicted the history of the Olhyiu. Whale hunts he recognised from boats similar to those around the frozen lake. He could see that in better times their lives had depended on the whale: for the oil that burned in their lamps, for meat, even for the brackets that supported the oil lamps, which were constructed from its bones. But he also picked up something more: the sense that the whale was revered as well as hunted. One of the murals showed a community on its knees, praying by the carcass of a sperm whale in what appeared to be a vigil of atonement.

The council waited until the excitement settled. Now the four friends were made to turn around and face a long table, on the other side of which a committee of three men and a woman were settling into place. Alan recognised their leader as the thick-set ginger-haired giant with the dense brown side-whiskers. This had to be Siam, chief of the tribe, and Turkeya's father.

With shock, Alan saw that Siam was carrying the Spear of Lug, which he placed on the table in front of him.

The shaman, Kemtuk, was seated to Siam's left. Further to the left was the weasel-faced man with the cruel eyes. To Siam's right was a tall and elegant woman with snowy white hair framing an ivory-coloured face. Her regal head, above a slender neck, was tattooed in whorls and lines of slate and silver, drawing Alan's attention to her lustrous jade-green eyes. She had to be Siam's wife, co-leader of the Olhyiu. Behind the table, and running almost the length of the wall, was an enormous lance. The blade, of pitted black steel, was four feet long, and the heavy weathered shaft twice that. Attached to the neck with twisted leather thongs were two huge floats, made out of inflated seal skins.

A whaling harpoon!

It made Alan see the chief in a different light: the huge man balancing barefoot in the prow of a seagoing canoe, pitching and tossed by the elements, the massive blade hefted in both his hands. The fierce courage.

There was a sudden powerful pulse in the triangle on his brow. It caused Alan to look at the thin man, Snakoil Kawkaw, who was staring at him with undisguised hatred in his coal-black eyes.

Siam brought the proceedings to order. Raising his voice above the shuffling and coughing, he addressed Alan in a deep growl. 'I am assured that you understand these words I speak to you. Then understand this, huloima. It is unprecedented for strangers to be allowed entry into the Temple Ship. For this honour you may thank the sage of this tribe, Kemtuk Lapeep.'

The big man paused, as if awaiting Alan's reaction.

Alan paused, realising that the word *huloima* meant more than just strangers – it was something more akin to 'aliens'. He needed to allay their suspicions. He said, 'I would like to ask a favour. My companions do not speak your language. Will you let me explain to them what is happening?'

'So be it.'

Alan noticed that the shaman nodded, as if to acknowledge Siam's response to be reasonable.

The chief continued. 'The Tilikum Olhyiu are gravely alarmed. For strangers to arrive amongst us in such times – are these not days of the gravest peril? We demand that you give an account of yourself and your arrival amongst us.'

While Alan translated this for the benefit of his friends, his alien language provoked a rising hubbub from the Olhyiu. Kemtuk called out to the people to be silent and to allow the strangers to speak among themselves. He put a wide-eyed urgency into his gaze as it fell upon Alan, whose heart shrank at the look, though he couldn't bring himself to explain it to his friends. He realised now that this was a court that would decide if they lived or died. He took a deep breath, to allow his thoughts to calm down, and then he summarised the events that had brought them here. He described how the four friends had come together, whether by fate or accident, in a small town in another world. He described the mountain, Slievenamon, and its calling, and the common dreams that had brought them here, to a destiny they themselves did not understand.

There was a renewed outbreak of murmuring, with several cries of derision.

The chief silenced his people again with a blow of his huge open hand on the table. 'Huloima, you speak of ominous and disquieting things. I am a simple fisherman. Who, I ask myself, would wish to come here to these starveling lands? Strangers, you say, with no given purpose? Such an arrival might herald mischief. We have no food to spare. Our children run wild in the woods, scratching for pine nuts to fill the emptiness in their bellies. I demand that you stop this lying and confess the truth. What is the real reason you have come here amongst us?'

Alan had to control his rising sense of unease, remembering the words of caution from the shaman. 'You're right. We are strangers here. We didn't ask to come to this world. We appear to have been chosen by others – other forces – whether we like it or not.'

When he gave his friends a summary of this, Mark was the one who most vehemently shook his head. 'For God's sake! Tell them some yarn they're likely to believe.'

Siam spoke again, his growl deepening. 'You speak of a destiny that remains a mystery to you, and yet there is much that implies a hidden purpose to your coming here among us. How then did you survive in the wilderness? What was the nature of those strange coverings of spider's web you wore when first you arrived amongst us?'

Hoisting the Spear of Lug off the table, Siam held it aloft, so all could behold it. Alan could see the Ogham inscriptions in the spiral of blue-black spearhead glowing brightly, as if they had taken on a power of their own.

'All can see this is no ordinary weapon. What sinister magic governs the blade you have brought among us?'

Alan explained how his grandfather had forged the spear, and told of their arrival into the world and how they had found themselves within the cave receiving the attentions of the strange old woman. Siam stiffened, as if apprehensive.

It was Kemtuk, quietly spoken, who continued the interrogation. 'What was the nature of this old woman, who took it upon herself to save the lives of strangers?'

'I don't know who or what she was. But when she spoke her name it sounded like "Granny Dew". Yet I can't pretend to understand the things she did. In our world we have a word for what she did – we call it "magic". Magic is a thing that can be seen and felt and yet cannot be explained.'

From behind him Alan heard more raucous shouts. When he turned to look at them, he saw people shaking their fists. As the uproar deepened, he turned once more to address the four leaders behind the table.

'Everything I have told you is the truth. My friends and I owe our lives to this old woman, though I don't know who or what she represents to you.'

It seemed to be the moment that Snakoil Kawkaw had been waiting for. Rising to his feet, he had to bow his head to accommodate his height in the low-ceilinged chamber, a claw-like hand extended towards Alan's face. 'Now we know the extent of this treachery. Not only does he bring danger of reprisal against us from the Storm Wolves, but he profanes the faith of the people.' With a lightning move, Kawkaw drew a long-bladed dagger from his side and he made a sudden lunge towards Alan, but was restrained by the powerful arm of the chief.

It took all of the authority of Kemtuk to impose calm upon the murmuring and gesticulating crowd.

The shaman held up his right hand and there was a quiet gravity in his words. 'The Olhyiu know better than to listen to the words of a thieving crow. Do we not hear in the very innocence of this Mage Lord's words that here before us is the heralded one of the prophecy? Yes, I call him Mage Lord, for such all my senses proclaim him to be. All know of the blasphemy of the High Architect, Ussha De Danaan. Yet though many now revile her, the knowledgeable few have suspected wisdom and purpose in her abandoning Ossierel to rape and plunder. Did she not cast the prophecy in her dying breath, an omen so profound as to make the earth tremble! So the true believers amongst us, those who know and revere the De Danaan lineage, have refused to believe her capable of cowardice. And that faith has kept a single hope alive. The heralded one, a child who would come out of the snow, will save us. This youth, Alan Duval, and his friends, have surely come from an alien world to redeem Monisle from persecution.'

The shouts quickly settled to a murmuring as the Olhyiu people discussed among themselves what Kemtuk had told them.

Taking to his feet once more, Siam pounded the table, this time with what looked like a sledgehammer fist. His eyes stared directly into Alan's. 'What do you have to say to this?'

Alan shrugged. 'I don't understand this soul eye, as the shaman calls it.'

'Hah!' Siam raised his voice to a roar, addressing the entire gathering of his people. 'Then we are left to decide for ourselves. Only one of our senior councillors is right, the other wrong. Which is it to be – the shaman, Kemtuk Lapeep, or the hunter and tracker, Snakoil Kawkaw? We must take care in arriving at a common view, for many lives hang in the balance.'

'Would it not be reasonable,' spoke the elegant woman to Siam's right, 'to ask this visitor for evidence of the strange and worrisome events he describes?'

In the whisperings from behind him, Alan now caught her name: Kehloke. He read the meaning as 'swan-like'.

'What proof can lies and treachery offer!' scoffed Kawkaw.

Kemtuk demanded, 'Did he not learn to use the soul eye to speak our language in the few hours he spent in my company?'

'What spy would not acquire some use of our language before coming amongst his enemies? Is it not evidence of the most perfidious planning? Have a care, Kemtuk Lapeep, that you do not find yourself tainted. For we have seen how readily you profane the old ways in bringing these huloima within the hallowed walls – these same huloima you have so assiduously attended in your boat!'

A roar erupted in the crowds behind Alan. One of the Olhyiu broke through the guards and Alan felt a burly arm grab him around his neck. Kemtuk, with a look of fury, dashed forward to free him, before bringing them back to order. 'Are we so broken on the yoke of the Storm Wolves that we cannot see the truth? All this time our people have been hungry and humiliated in this desert of snow and ice. Have we not prayed for redemption?'

'Redemption!' roared Kawkaw. 'These are no redeemers. Did not the prophecy give us the name of this so-called redeemer? That name was Mira, the one of the light. None among these strangers bears that name.'

The shaman spoke quietly, but firmly. 'Does this boy, Alan Duval, not bear the soul eye of the Trídédana upon his brow? Have you not all felt a force of change during his stay among us? Are you so consumed with fear you do not recognise the time of your deliverance?'

But Kemtuk's wisdom was no proof against the anger and terror that was growing in the people now milling around Alan.

With a clatter, the great harpoon fell from the wall. The multitude was stunned into silence. Siam sprang to his feet, his head and shoulders bowed to stand under the low ceiling. With sweeps of his brawny arms, he compelled his advisers on his left and right to sit down. Then, in the palpitating silence that followed he addressed himself to Alan alone.

'You come out of the wilderness, cowled in spider's web. Your speech is strange to our ears. Your skin is for the most part hairless, like the flesh-spoilers of Isscan and Carfon, people who are no friends of the Olhyiu. Your bearing is humble but your words belie it. Snakoil Kawkaw is right, for the name of the redeemer is foretold to be Mira, the one from whose countenance the sun will shine. So, at pain of your lives, I demand of you for the last time – where have you come from? Why are you among us? Do you not realise the dangers that oppress the Olhyiu from all sides? Yet if only the words of the shaman be true! Prove it, then! Prove that what you say is true or we will be obliged to kill you before the accursed Storm Wolves descend upon us.'

Alan's heart quailed. 'I know nothing about anyone called Mira, any more than I know of these Storm Wolves, or the suffering they have caused your people. But using this triangle – what Kemtuk calls the soul eye – I can sense the thoughts hidden in the minds of others. While you have been debating what to do with me, I have been sensing the mind of this man, Snakoil Kawkaw. What I have observed there is selfishness and greed, and a willingness to betray his people for profit.'

'Serpent-tongued hogsturd!' Kawkaw broke free of the grasp of the chief and hurled himself towards Alan.

But he never reached him. A sudden flare of anger from Alan's own mind flashed from his brow, a flare of light, like a bolt of sheet lightning that lit up the entire room. Kawkaw was arrested in shock, his claws no more than inches from Alan's eyes.

There was a new pandemonium of voices, not least among Alan's friends, as the doors to the chamber burst open and Turkeya entered, carrying a wooden container in his arms, and nodding in the direction of Kemtuk Lapeep. Turkeya hurried to his father's side and he emptied the container over the table top in front of Siam. 'Father, while you have been debating here, I have been searching the boat of Snakoil Kawkaw. I did so at the insistence of the shaman, who has long had his suspicions of Kawkaw. The hunter's treachery was well hidden, but I discovered this under the floor of his sleeping quarters. You'll find all the evidence you need here. Here are the folded notes he has been exchanging with our enemies, the Storm Wolves. He sends them messages by night attached to crow's feet. But his treachery runs deeper than that. There is a price he intends to demand for his cooperation with our enemies. Something he covets even more than gold and silver. That price is your wife, and my mother, Kehloke.'

'Hold him!' Siam growled, his voice little above a whisper. Meanwhile his eyes narrowed to glittering slits as he pored over the evidence. 'If this is true, I will deal with Kawkaw myself.'

Kemtuk whispered into Siam's ear, 'Is it not true that Kawkaw wanted Kehloke for his own? Was he not jealous that she chose you?'

With a sudden roar, Siam leapt to his feet, his eyes ablaze with rage. 'Lay him in the circle so all can see.' Several burly men tore away Kawkaw's clothes and splayed the man's limbs while the chief hefted the Spear of Lug.

'No!' Kawkaw snarled.

'You would have had us murdered and taken Kehloke as your slave. Now I shall first make you into a woman before I cut your heart out.'

Kemtuk spoke to the traitor as the wild-eyed chief stripped to the waist. 'At least confess your crimes and give us the information that might yet save some lives.'

'Fools!' shrieked Kawkaw. 'How I relished making plans for you! And as for you, Siam the Stupid, what frolic I would have had not only with your jumped-up trollop of a wife, but even better still, with your pretty daughter. I relive my fantasy in every exquisite moment.'

'We shall see how pain cleanses such filth from your mind!'

Kawkaw laughed through contorted lips. 'It may be my turn to be tormented today – but it will be your turn tomorrow. And the Storm Wolves are your masters in that art.'

Siam struck the man in the mouth with the haft of the spear, silencing his mocking tongue. Then, in fury, he lifted the Ogham-warded blade to shoulder high, as if to plunge it into Kawkaw's heart.

'Wait!' Alan raised his hand to restrain the chief, and then squatted by the trembling Kawkaw. 'How much time do we have?' he pressed him.

Kawkaw bared his bloody teeth, his eyes glaring a hateful defiance. 'I cannot be certain,' he said, spitting blood through gritted teeth. 'I only sent a message before this council meeting. I saw no reason to press for urgency. You have days, perhaps a week.'

'He's lying.' Alan gazed away from Kawkaw, towards the chief. 'We have no more than a day.'

The shaman put a comforting hand on the chief's shoulder. 'It was not for wisdom but for your courage that Kehloke chose you. Now your people have need of that strength. Heed my counsel. Keep the traitor alive while ever he is useful to us. He might still prove a source of further information in the difficult hours to come. In the meantime, lead us away from this place of hunger. Make haste, proud Siam. Though our path may be one of danger, yet it is not our lives that matter. There are those amongst us whose safety overrides our own. We will assist their escape to Carfon, these chosen ones from another world.'

A Sense of Grief

Mo woke from sleep, listening to the noises all around her. The river nearby never stopped crackling and sighing. Yesterday, she, Mark and Kate had stood on its snow-covered bank and marvelled at the central melt, where the water was too fast and too deep to freeze even this close to the huge glacier-wrapped mountains. But there were other noises too, the sounds of objects being hauled and dragged over the ice-bound lake, the whispers of voices, the cries and whimpers of children that told her that the whole village was in a fever of movement. And now, with daybreak, she saw that all the other bunks were empty. She guessed that Alan was out there, helping the shaman with getting ready to flee. But where were Kate and Mark?

Mo dressed hurriedly, using the last change of underwear from her backpack, and covering her normal clothes with the coat and boots provided by Turkeya. When she emerged onto the deck, Kate was standing at the high-point of the prow, looking up into the sky with an expression of amazement.

'Huh-huh-hi, Kuh-Kate!' she murmured, padding forward to stand beside her. Kate smiled, still staring up into the sky.

'Will you take a good look around you. Can't you just feel it, Mo? There's magic in the air!'

Mo wasn't sure she felt anything other than the freezing cold.

'We're all changing, aren't we?'

Mo stared up at Kate's face, her green eyes. *Changing?* Yes – she believed that the others were changing. They were all changing and she wasn't. But Kate just laughed, spinning her body around, her auburn hair blowing in the wind. 'You can almost taste it.' She put her arm around Mo's shoulders and threw the other hand into the air. 'Will you look up there – can you credit that sky?'

Mo threw her head right back to gaze up with Kate at the thunderheads that were invading from the north, squeezing the air like gigantic pincers. The air whistled and tossed, making her eyes hurt. It was as if the elements were one with the hustle and bustle of the fishing village. She sniffed: she could smell burning. Suddenly she heard Alan call out hoarsely:

'Kemtuk!'

A prickle of gooseflesh crept over Mo's skin as she realised that she must have heard Alan call the shaman through the triangle. Leaving the boat, Mo ran in the direction of the call until she came across Alan standing out on the ice. He was looking up at the shaman, who was standing high on the middle deck of the Temple Ship. A low morning light bathed the tall figure in a silvery glow. His blind eye glittered like a pearl in a face that was a mask of concentration. Mo desperately wanted to talk to Alan but he looked as preoccupied as ever. Just now, watching that strange communication between him and the old man, Mo felt a new flicker of worry clutch at her stomach.

Mo's hand moved to the talisman hanging on the lace around her throat. Was Alan changing so much they could lose him entirely?

Instinctively she squeezed the bog-oak figurine.

She wandered away from Alan to watch the bands of men hurrying back from the pinewoods, dragging piles of brushwood on makeshift sleds fashioned out of sail leather. Others were heaping the brushwood along the ice around the Temple Ship. She watched them drenching the piles with lamp oil. Suddenly she flinched, her feelings flooded by a sense of longing. It was so overwhelming she reeled in confusion for several moments before she could lift her head again and focus on what the Olhyiu were doing. The oil-soaked brushwood was being laid out in a broad path linking the boats to the river and beyond its banks out along the frozen stream as far as the central melt. It looked desperate – the attempts of frightened people trying to soften the ice enough to create a passage.

Picking out the lonely figure of Mark, Mo contemplated her brother, who was standing in silence in front of the Temple Ship, gazing up at it with that same look of amazement Kate had bestowed on the gathering storm clouds. Hurrying towards him, she put her hand on his arm.

He blinked with her sudden arrival, as if she had startled him out of a daydream. 'Hi, tiddler!' He raddled her hair. He hadn't called her that for years. 'Did you just feel something really weird?'

Mo gazed up at him, nodding.

How deep in thought he appeared to be! He shook his head, as if struggling to put his feelings into words. 'Something like . . . I don't really know how to describe it.'

'Like a guh-guh-great suh-suh-sadness?'

Mark frowned at her. 'Yes, Mo, you're right. It does feel sort of like sadness. But what does it mean? Where can it be coming from?'

Mo shook her head.

'Weird things are happening, Mo. Don't you feel like you're changing?'

It was exactly what Kate had said to her just minutes earlier. Mo blinked rapidly, not knowing what to answer.

Mark laughed, but it was a laugh of bewilderment. 'What on earth is really going on? What's happening to us?'

Mo shook her head. 'I duh-duh-don't know.'

'Let me show you something!' He dropped down onto his haunches and held out his left fist. 'Look at that!' He threw his fist wide open.

Mo stared at Mark's egg-shaped crystal, the light-devouring black in which tiny petals of silver flickered and metamorphosed. With a start, she realised that the flickering patterns inside the crystal were pulsating.

'It's buh-buh-beating!'

'Yes it is, Mo. Beating in time with my heartbeat. But let me show you something even stranger.' He slipped the crystal egg into his pocket and opened his hand for her to inspect it.

Mo saw the dark colour and movement in the skin of Mark's palm. It just wasn't possible, but the longer she looked, the more certain she was that she saw the same pulsating matrix in his palm, as if the crystal had transferred something of itself into Mark's flesh.

'Whuh-whuh-what does it muh-mean?'

'All I know is I slept with the crystal in my fist. So did Kate. When I woke up, I could feel it happening. Bloody hell, Mo! I could actually feel it – as if it was somehow melting into me. Insane, or what?' He laughed, shaking his head. 'Then, a few minutes ago, I felt that . . .'

'Suh-suh-sadness!'

'Sadness – yes! I felt it and at the same time my mind was filled with the image of the ship.' Mark stretched his back to stand erect again and both their eyes swivelled up to stare at the ship. 'God, I can't help thinking about it, Mo. I know it sounds insane, but I'd say the feeling was coming from up there, from the ship itself.'

'Buh-buh-buh-but how?'

'They're planning on leaving her behind, Mo. The poor old thing, she's too damaged to sail. There's no time to repair her. I'm not sure they even know *how* to repair her. That's why they're putting the brushwood around her. They're going to burn her timbers to melt the ice.'

Mo felt it again – that overwhelming clutch of anxiety.

Mark ran a hand, red with cold, through his fair hair. 'I only wish there was something we could do to stop it happening. But the superstructure is damaged. The timbers are completely rotted away in places. I had a good look over her at first light. There are these huge rolled up sails made out of sealskin leather, but they're in tatters, like centuries of mice have been nibbling away at them. Half the lines and the rigging are gone. There just isn't a hope in hell of making her sail-worthy.'

Mo tugged at Mark's arm. 'Lets go tuh-tuh-talk to thuh-the others.'

'If it'll make you happy. But I doubt it'll do any good.'

Half running to keep up with Mark's hurried strides, Mo had to dodge around the scurrying men with the brushwood. They found Alan still gazing up at the shaman on the quarterdeck, the old man's face pallid with concentration as he held himself erect before the rail. He was dressed in formal shaman regalia. On his brow he wore the skull of an eagle and over his shoulders a heavy necklace of whale's teeth. In his right hand he held the pointed horn of a narwhal and in his left he was cradling a bear's skull. His eyes were glazed, his attention focused inward, oblivious of worldly attentions. He intoned a prayer, deep and resonant.

As she heard a sudden loud crackling of burning brush and oil, Mo stood between Mark and Alan, and linked their arms. All three of them lifted their eyes above the shaman into the gathering thunderheads. Suddenly the longing returned, such a sense of despair it struck Mo like a physical blow.

Mark shouted above the growing wind, 'It's definitely coming from the ship.'

Alan shook his head, unable to explain it. He shouted to gain the shaman's attention again, 'Kemtuk!'

But the shaman didn't respond.

Mo had to raise her voice to be heard above the human commotion and the rising wind. 'Shuh-shuh-shuh-show him!' She touched Mark's hand.

Mark held open his left hand so Alan could see for himself.

Alan's eyes widened. 'I don't get it.'

'Neither do we,' Mark retorted. 'Maybe the crystal egg is doing something to me in the same way the ruby's changing you, only more slowly. It's interacting with me in some way.'

'Wow!'

'I wuh-wuh-wuh-woke up with an idea.' Mo concentrated

as hard as she could to try to control her stammer. 'Luh-luh-like . . .' She gave up and held her hand against her ear.

'What – something to do with a mobile?'

She nodded.

Mark shook his head. 'I think Mo is wondering if the crystals have taken on some kind of property from the mobiles.'

'Maybe you're right, Mo. I guess it would make some loopy kind of sense.'

Mark shrugged. 'But how do we check it?'

'What do you mean? Like some way of testing mind-to-mind?'

'Shouldn't be that difficult.'

Alan gestured so the three friends gathered together in a close huddle. 'Okay, let's see if we can call Kate. Just think it while you're clenching your fist around your egg. I'll do something similar through the crystal in my head. On my count to three. One, two, three!'

They stood together and waited. Within seconds they heard Kate's shriek and she came careering through the Olhyiu, with an excited look on her face.

'You got the message?'

'I heard you calling me.'

Alan, Mo and Mark laughed as one. Mark unclasped his fist to show Kate the flickering matrix in his palm. 'Open your hand and show us yours.'

Kate seemed unaware that her right hand was tight-clenched about her crystal. Now, exposing the palm, they all saw the same soft green matrix embedded in her flesh, speckled with motes of yellow and gold.

Mo gasped.

Alan explained, 'Mo's excited because we didn't actually call out your name. We called you through Mark's crystal and my ruby triangle.'

'Ah, go on!' She shook her head and laughed. 'For goodness sake – you people must think I'm an idiot!'

Alan hugged her. 'It's true, Kate.'

Kate looked at him questioningly, then stepped back, her hands clapped to her mouth and her eyes wide.

'Makes you wonder what else we can do.' Alan looked thoughtfully around at the milling people. 'I have an idea.' He picked one of the women who appeared to be scolding her children. She was shouting, distractedly, in Olhyiu. 'Mark, Kate – get a grip of your crystals. I want us to form a circle. You too, Mo – I want you to be our neutral observer here. Now, guys, let's all of us focus on that woman over there, listen to what she is shouting, and try to project ourselves through the crystals.'

The woman was married. They could tell this now because they knew married women among the Olhyiu displayed jewels on a chain around their necks, rather than rings on their fingers, and she was shouting from the deck of her boat to some children frolicking on the ice.

'Monkeys!' Mark and Kate exclaimed it together. The woman was calling her children monkeys.

'Yee-hah!' They all roared with triumph, clapping arms around each other's shoulders and jumping with glee on the trampled ice.

'Mo?' Alan was gazing down at her, a question in his eyes.

'I – I . . . I thuh-thuh-thuh-thought . . .' Mo stared from one to another of her friends, her lips trembling.

'You thought the experiment was a scam?'

Mo shook her head, far too excited to even try to explain through her stupid stammering lips what she wanted to tell them. She too had heard the word, 'monkeys'. How was that possible when she had no crystal? Even as she turned her head away from Alan, startled by the idea, a thunderclap erupted directly over their heads, causing all four friends to stare up into the sky.

Alan waited for the thunder to stop booming, so he could think more clearly. Something very strange, something as frightening as it was wonderful, was happening to him and his friends, and he couldn't even begin to understand it. Ordinarily he'd have asked the shaman for an explanation. But the shaman was preoccupied with spiritual forces, so that when Alan opened his mind to the shaman's words, he in his turn became the receptor for communications of meaning and vision somehow deeper than words. He knew that Kemtuk, in asking for his people to be freed from tyranny, was extolling the sacred visions that had been forbidden to him for all the long years his people had been held in captivity. Suddenly the hairs on Alan's neck stood up in awe.

He was gazing out on a vision of creation, at a time when there was but one existence, and his name was Akoli, the Creator.

'In that time,' the shaman spoke, 'he was in the form of the Great Spirit. In one day he created the world, lifting up the lofty peaks of the mountains and cloaking their shoulders with snow. Then he forced apart the mountains and into the deeps between he blew the moisture of his breath and created the oceans. Henceforth, these would become his spirit home.'

Alan saw the cataclysms as the mountains reared up out of the land. His body shook with the earthquake as their vastness was cleaved apart and, through the turbulent upheaval, a titanic gust of wind and rain surged and swelled through the birth of continents to become the storm-tossed oceans. Through the shaman's vision he tasted the bitter-damp mulch of the newborn world upon his tongue, he breathed the sulphurous first atmosphere, he stood on the brink of spuming calderas of gigantic volcanoes, and he watched the eruptions of boiling lava that would fashion and refashion the primal landscape in the dawn of time.

'Then the leviathan, Akoli, he that would henceforth be known as the Creator, took form in the eternal chaos of the deeps. From there he rose against the howling of beginnings, for then he came as the moon and as the fury of the storm. With wind and cloud he filled the skies and the world below, and then he wept so that the rain of his passion might make fertile the land and his joy would become the rainbow. Finally Akoli sang, and it was with the music that makes the tides rise and fall and the wind that rolls the clouds upon the air. He called together the mountains and the sky above, the stars and the planets that live within the sky, and he told the heavens: "Let there be night and day." He made the golden sun and bid it wander over the sky. He made the silver moon and had it swell as a woman with child each month. So sun and moon would rule the mysteries of creation as they made their journeys from the sea to the sky and back again.'

Alan focused on the figure of the shaman. A storm of energy was whirling about Kemtuk, flapping his ceremonial clothes and lifting his white hair in a startling nimbus. There was something profound beyond the words, something Alan desperately needed to understand.

Suddenly he moaned aloud, clenching his fists against his brow. The sudden swell of longing was so overwhelming, he fell to his knees. Kate helped him back up onto his feet. She was pointing – and Alan's eyes followed her finger, to the men with the brushwood.

'What's going on?' He had to shout to be heard.

'They're burning the Temple Ship.'

Alan whirled around, his eyes back on Kemtuk. He understood now. The shaman's homage was guilt, asking forgiveness for the great wrong the Olhyiu were about to commit.

Alan heard the closing words of the lament, 'At last Akoli, the leviathan, leaped over the oceans he had made with the flash of the rainbow. Then, tired from his labours, he pulled about him the blanket of the icy peaks, and closing his eyes, he rested there.' Kemtuk's silver eye had fallen onto the men, who waited for his word to fire the brushwood. But still the shaman hesitated, as if weighed down with the enormity of what he was about to command.

People were having difficulty keeping on their feet in the wind. Still they continued to lay the path of fire directly to the ship, piling the oil-soaked brushwood against the massive out-curved hull.

Mark shouted into Alan's ear, 'We all sense that it's wrong. But you're the only one who can stop it.'

But then what if he did? He'd be condemning them all to be killed by the Storm Wolves.

Alan thought back to the experience in the cave. To Granny Dew and her words. *'Duvaaaalll aaassskkksss – yeeesss! Duvaaaalll seeesss – nooo!'* What did he ask but not see? A meaning deeper than words? He shook his head, bewildered by riddles. He would have to trust his own feelings.

'Kemtuk – stop!' Alan shouted out his opposition through the triangle on his brow. 'Kemtuk, you must stop the burning!'

But Kemtuk was lost in his own grief, standing as stiff as a statue, his face like ravaged stone. His right hand fell, holding a thick bundle of oiled twigs.

Only now did Alan notice the standing crucible behind the old man, a small stone altar of whorled carvings, and an altar on which he had prepared the signal – the fall of the lighted firebrand onto the brushwood directly below the centre deck.

The thunderheads were erupting with lightning. Alan could smell ozone in the charged air. In a sudden violent swell of wind, all three of his friends were blown backwards, at first staggering, then completely losing their footing, crashing onto the ice. But the force of spiritual communication kept Alan erect. Whirling about himself on the trampled snow, he broke free of the communication with the shaman, and suddenly the maelstrom quietened. It was as if some other force, even greater than he or Kemtuk, had snuffed it out.

Alan was already pushing his way through the gathering throng to get to the gangway. Above him, Kemtuk had raised the blazing firebrand.

'Stop!'

Still the shaman was not listening. His mind was closed on the instrument of communication.

Running up the gangway, Alan stood, breathless, before Kemtuk. He grabbed the firebrand and snatched it away from the startled shaman's hand. Kemtuk's gaze turned gentle once more, and his hoary old head fell to face Alan.

'Tell me, Mage Lord, what I must do?'

'We have to save the ship!'

Kemtuk turned to look at the upturned faces of Olhyiu below the deck. The huge figure of Siam stood out among them. Kemtuk picked up the lance of the narwhal and raised it aloft. 'The Mage Lord commands that we cannot burn the Temple Ship. We must find another way.'

But, judging by the look of surprise on their faces, Alan's command was having very little effect. With a sudden roar from Siam, they began to apply their own firebrands to the brushwood. Then suddenly, in the centre of the turmoil, a running figure snatched the flaming bundle from Siam's own fist and hurled it away, across the ice. The huge Olhyiu reacted furiously. The figure turned its face up and Alan recognised Mark. A fight broke out, in which the Olhyiu easily overcame the youth. Mark was sent flying with a blow but he was immediately back on his feet, facing Siam's anger. Mo and Kate rushed to stand by him.

Kemtuk bent to whisper to Alan. On his face was a look of shame. 'Siam knows that in the night the traitor Kawkaw slipped his bonds, taking the lives of the two good men who guarded him. He has gone to forewarn the enemy. Though it grieves us, we must sacrifice the Temple Ship.'

Alan was shocked to hear of Kawkaw's escape. But this was not the time to dwell on it. 'No, Kemtuk. If we burn the ship, we're lost. I sense this.'

Kemtuk stared at Alan for a moment, as if in

contemplation, then he raised himself erect and brought back his arm, hurling the lance of the narwhal so it struck the ice directly in front of Siam. There it quivered, like an omen, before the huge man, causing him to raise his alarmed eyes once more to the shaman.

'Death at the hands of the Storm Wolves will be slow and unpleasant,' roared the chief. 'We have women and children. How, other than by the heat of the burning ship, do we break the grip of the ice?' Siam waited for counsel, and when none came from the shaman, he waved once more to the men with the firebrands.

Out there on the ice, Alan saw groups of Olhyiu arriving from a central brazier, carrying new firebrands.

'No!' Alan's voice roared out through the triangle. Even Siam stopped dead in his tracks. 'You know I carry the soul eye in my brow. And the soul eye tells me that you don't right a wrong with another wrong. You cannot burn the Temple Ship. With the help of the soul eye, we'll find another way. Meanwhile, Siam, please command the men to move the brushwood from around the ship and use it somewhere else. Add it to the piles they've already gathered over there!' Alan pointed to an area thirty or forty yards away, yet still close to the centre of the ice-trapped village.

Kemtuk shook his head. 'But it's futile anyway. Even if we preserve it, none can master the Temple Ship. Not even Siam, a seaman all his life. We dragged it here through ropes attached to the fishing fleet. We'll have to leave it behind, burnt or not, since it would only hinder us.'

Alan surprised himself with what he now said. 'I will be the master of the ship.'

'You – but you're merely a youth! One empowered, and perhaps more stubborn, than most – but a youth nevertheless.'

'You've got to trust me. I'll find a way.'

Alan left the shaman and went down onto the ice to put his hand on the powerful shoulder of the chief. 'I was foolish. I focused all of my attentions on your shaman, Kemtuk. I failed to realise the real leader of the Olhyiu. No one is braver or stronger than you, Siam.' He touched his brow. 'Here, I sense that you are a great leader. We should all put our trust in you.'

Although he looked like a man labouring under a dreadful burden, Siam accepted this challenge. He shouted to the people, who had crowded up close. 'You men – you cannot burn the ship. Burn elsewhere, wherever you deem it best to weaken the ice. And hurry! Meanwhile you women gather every family aboard the boats and use the harpoons to break open the ice.'

The First Power

The morning had turned to dusk under the towering thunderheads. On the central deck of the Temple Ship Alan's ears were full of the crackle of flames, his nostrils choked by the tarry smell of the burning brushwood. Already, the air was filled with the sounds of drumming. The womenfolk were following Siam's order, hammering the ice around their boats with long iron-tipped harpoons. Distant figures were also attacking the ice where it had been softened by the fire, using mallets to drive in staves of cedar to crack it open. But a glance confirmed what he already suspected: whatever their efforts, the thickness of the ice would prove too much. Even the burning of the great ship would ultimately be futile since it would take far too many hours to create enough heat to enable the flotilla to break through to the river. And with the escape and treachery of the renegade Kawkaw, there wasn't enough time for the villagers to make their escape.

Alan listened to the crackling of the melting ice, to the oaths and grunts of the men carried on the wind, to the steady hammering of the women. He gazed down at the frightened masses of elderly and children clambering on board their various boats. On their faces, he saw growing panic.

He hadn't noticed that Mo had come up beside him until she tugged at his arm to attract his attention. There was an intense look on her face.

'There's suh-suh-something huh-happening to me.'

'What is it, Mo?'

'Muh-muh-monkey!'

'Monkey?'

Mo gazed up at him, willing him to understand. 'I suh-suh-sensed it too.'

'What did you sense?'

Then his eyebrows lifted in astonishment at the realisation of what she was telling him.

Mo had heard the word 'monkey' on the lips of the Olhyiu woman.

Alan recalled that it had been Mo's song that had discovered Slievenamon, and that it had also evoked the symphony of the stones. It was another mystery. But it was no good trying to figure it now. 'I don't even pretend to know what's happening to us, Mo.'

She looked directly into his eyes a moment. 'I'm wuh-wuh-worried about whuh-whuh-what's happening to us!'

He reached out and held her shoulders, feeling how her

whole body trembled. 'We're all scared by what's happening, Mo.'

Even as he tried to reassure her, from nearby there was a crackling of fire. Siam had ignited the pyre not twenty yards away, at the centre of the ice. Alan could see the burly man, swaying slightly as if he were drunk, but showing the way to the others, applying a firebrand to a second place in the crackling pile of tinder. The chief tottered back as the flames sprang as high as the mastheads on the lesser boats.

'Time to call the others together, Mo. We need to gather here, on the Temple Ship.'

As if Mo's anxiety was contagious, Alan felt a constriction of alarm tighten about his chest. The Storm Wolves were nearing, close enough for him to sense the approaching minds and their vicious intentions. He shouted out to Siam over the heads of the crowd below, 'The enemy are almost here. Get your people to prepare the boats. Ask them to get ready to raise their sails to the wind. We, the huloima, will master the Temple Ship. But you've got to give us some experienced sailors to help man the sails.'

Siam lifted his face to growl up at him, 'Thirty of our best men would not suffice to man the sails, even if they were not already decayed. And once raised, the art of managing such a tangle of rigging – I doubt that all the men in this village could help you.'

'Well, let us have what help you can.' Alan turned to the silent but watchful shaman beside him. 'Will you stay on board to guide us? Have somebody else take care of your boat?'

Kemtuk inhaled deeply. 'I'll stay. But such actions will prove futile. Siam knows this, as I do. The ice has not melted.'

Alan turned back to gaze out over the rail and found the burly figure of Siam. In the chief's despairing mind he read the fear: *How can I make the people listen when we give them no reason for hope?*

'There is hope!' Alan shouted back at him.

'Where – where do I find it?'

'Look within yourself, Siam. To the spirit within you – to the courage and strength of the Olhyiu people.'

Siam waved him away, but nevertheless he began calling out to the men, gathering them about him, wiping his brow with his wide-brimmed hat before struggling to find the words to address them.

'I am not a clever man, and you all know that. But I love Kehloke and I love my son, Turkeya, and my daughter, Loloba.' He struck his chest, like a bass drum. 'It is true that I got drunk with those accursed abominations, the Storm Wolves, many times, when they came to our village. I would get drunk with them now if I thought that it would save us. So these are the words of a very stupid man. Maybe I am too stupid to lead the Tilikum Olhyiu.'

He crumpled his hat between his hands while a fresh squall of snow blustered about his bare head.

'But the youth above, whom the shaman calls Mage

Lord, has asked me to remember with pride when we, the Children of the Sea, were warriors. We didn't fear the deep. No more do we fear these abominations who would rob us of our pride. They underestimate us if they think we have forgotten the ways of battle. Perhaps it is time we blew alive the embers of our ancestors.'

Kemtuk drew back in shock and closed his eyes.

'What is it?' Alan asked him.

'Siam calls for the blood-rage.'

Alan shook his head, failing to understand. He watched as Siam walked out to where the brushwood was burning. He picked up some glowing embers in the cup of his hands. Ignoring the scorching of his flesh, he walked among his people, with his smoking offering held out before him.

'Blow on these embers. Punish with fire this oaf whose stupidity knows no bounds.'

When none would blow on the embers, Siam wiped the ash over his grizzled face. 'I am a stupid man who looks at death and still asks for a sign. But the gods have sent us a sign. Great Akoli! You have sent us this Mage Lord, Alan Duval, and three strangers. The shaman, Kemtuk Lapeep, tells us their lives are important. It seems that this Mage Lord, young as he is, is the one who will lead us. He will help us to escape to the sanctuary of Carfon by the Eastern Ocean.

'Now, go tell your women to prepare the sails. You men, join me in preparing for battle. If we die, let us die as warriors. I call upon the gods to grant me the blood-rage of legend.'

'Explain blood-rage to me, Kemtuk.'

Kemtuk shook his head. 'It is nothing more than a legend, grown foolish with time. A sacrilege even to invoke it.'

Alan thought back. He recalled Kemtuk closing his eye, the deep blue crystal gripped in the palm of his left hand, while his right hand . . . had changed. Five long bear-like claws had appeared from the tips of the fingers. Alan thought about that. He thought, perhaps, he understood why the shaman refused even to consider what blood-rage might mean.

There was a renewed outbreak of shouting, then the sight of old men and younger boys running here and there, taking over the fanning of the flames. All men of fighting age were now gathered in a circle about the chief. With a cry of determination a tall sleek figure broke through into the circle. Kehloke lifted her fist into the air. 'If fight we must, then let us women shed our blood together with our men!'

A cheer erupted from the people, and the drumming of ice harpoons against the ice became as loud as thunder.

Kemtuk dropped his head. His voice was a whisper. 'It is merely a dream, born of despair. It is worse than a dream, it is madness.'

But Siam stood large beside his wife, his two fists raised high into the air, his eyes wide and staring. His voice was a battle cry. 'All my life, and that of my father and many grandfathers before him, the Olhyiu have waited to find one who could master the Temple Ship. That too was thought to be legend. Yet the young Mage Lord tells us he will master it. If one legend be true, why not another! May we not invoke the blood-rage of legend?'

As another great cheer swept through the Olhyiu, the shaman took up a position at the head of the oak gangway, gazing not at Alan but outwards, to the periphery of the ice, his head tilted as if listening. Alan was startled to hear Mark's voice, his friend now on board, asking help to unfurl the leather sails of the three great masts. He turned to see Mark taking hold of the great wheel. Mark was doing his best to help. In moments, Kate and Mo were by his side. He reached out and put a protective arm about each of them, all three looking out over the ice and waiting.

'Kemtuk – where's the spear I brought with me?'

The shaman shook his head. 'I cannot tell you.'

'Surely Siam can trust me now?'

Kemtuk's eye fell from contact with Alan's.

Alan turned his face away from the shaman, his eyes falling on the frantic scene below.

The lake itself was a few hundred yards across within a clearing that extended for at least three miles to a scrabble of snow-covered pines. Soon Alan heard a sound in the far distance that caused the hairs to prickle on the back of his neck. It was a fearful sound, buried deep in the folk memory, even for somebody who had grown up in cities: the howling of wolves. His grip around the girls' shoulders tightened.

Kemtuk informed him, 'First they send their wolves to bite and maim. They will harry us until the war machines arrive.'

The Olhyiu started to chant in support of Siam, a deep-throated anthem of clan and blood, in time with the hammering of the harpoons against the echoing ice. Alan shook his head, 'Kemtuk! You've got to let me help them!'

Through the triangle Alan focused his attention on Siam, who was pacing among the great gathering of men and women.

In the turmoil of the chief's thoughts, Alan searched for something, anything – a feeling, a mood, some race memory the chief was looking for, a truth beyond words, yet a truth that Alan might understand. It was as if, within the very spirit of Siam, Alan found himself at the eye of an intensely personal storm. Somehow, in this strange landscape, he must find the ancestral inheritance. In an inner projection of all his outward senses – of vision, hearing, touch, smell and taste – Alan hunted for what he imagined must be a kind of soul spirit common to Siam's people.

At first he encountered nothing but confusion. Recalling the advice of Granny Dew, he did his best to abandon his logical self. The hunter that moved through the spiritual landscape of Siam shed all assumptions until it felt as if one shadowy being hunted another.

When he first sensed what he was looking for he barely recognised it. He had expected a force of power and violence, lost from memory but imprinted in some deeper, unfathomable trace of being. What he actually found was no more substantial than a wisp of longing, curled up on itself, an abandoned embryo of what once had been. Alan focused on that tiny essence, breathed passion into it, as if to give it life. But there was no response. No matter how hard he tried, it seemed inadequate.

He poured his own being into the attempt. His heartbeat rose to become a rolling drum in his ears and a black mist of unconsciousness threatened to blind both his external and internal vision. Still he persisted, willing life into the embryo of longing.

He reminded it of the feel of rain, the visions of clouds and sunsets, the smell of blood and soil, until the soul spirit appeared to blink alive and notice its own existence. He felt how it began to take a feeble strength from him. He encouraged it to do so, reminding it of the visions he had seen in the mind of the shaman, of how the leviathan, Akoli, the Creator, took form from chaos and rose against the howling of beginnings to become as the moon and as the fury of the storm. He felt the longing grow and expand, as, like a spiritual cannibal, the embryo devoured what it needed from his own soul spirit to become real flesh and blood, real sight and smell, at once snarling to break free.

Staggering against the supporting arms of Kate and Mo,

Alan opened his eyes and all three of them recoiled with shock.

In the centre of the Olhyiu, where Siam had stood with his fists uplifted, now stood an enormous grizzly bear. The bear, which looked as tall as a house, reared at full stretch on its hind legs. It wheeled about in fury. Alan glimpsed the fallen indigo hat and the shreds of clothing torn asunder by the metamorphosis of size and power. Suddenly the giant grizzly threw back its head and its jaws gaped wide on a steaming red maw, glistening with huge yellow fangs. It roared, a challenge so deep it appeared to reverberate from a chasm, shaking the ice and ships, echoing around the lake and causing a hysterical cheer to arise from every throat.

The approaching wolves slowed a moment as the roar was carried to them on the wind, then resumed their headlong rush towards the lake.

Alan closed his eyes once more and was one with Siam's soul spirit. He smelled the burning firebrands, a thousand times stronger now, but there was a more important smell – the hated smell of wolf. That hatred mushroomed until it had become a red mist of loathing. In moments, the great shape was bounding over the trodden ice, huge feet designed for snow, six-inch claws extended for battle. Alan shared the violent swell of Siam's emotions, the blue-white blur of snow passing below his racing form, the swell of massive muscles in a coordination of four instead of two feet, pounding and pressing the land until it seemed the very world was spinning beneath the flash of fur and claw. The focus was already clear ahead, fixed in the glare of those rage-filled eyes. Behind the great bear streamed the charge of Olhyiu, including Kehloke, with sharpened harpoons at the ready. There was no fear in their hearts any more.

Battle was engaged, sudden and fierce.

Slavering shapes leaped upon the great bear, snapping for its throat. There was no time for thought, only the automatic lunge of jaws, bared teeth, the lash of paws, talons outstretched. All senses dissolved in the mountainous impact of brute force against brute force, the lightning flash of combat, the violence of vision, the overwhelming smell and taste of blood . . .

Alan withdrew his senses from that terrible confrontation. Siam and the others were merely buying them time.

Kemtuk stood a few paces apart from them before the rail. He had taken a handful of pollen from a pouch before his heart and was sprinkling it on the wind so it would be carried to the boats of his people, blessing them as he did so. That completed, the old man stood gravely still, his tall frame silhouetted against the smoke and flames, watchful as the elderly among them, and the remaining Olhyiu women and older children, all raised their hammering to a new crescendo.

Alan glimpsed a new movement, a gathering flurry of snow between the trees in the distance, a few miles beyond the bloodied snow where the bodies of wolves were now rent and scattered. Suddenly a new deep-throated howling tore the air.

'Leloo!' muttered the shaman. 'Worse than wolves – they pull their sleds!'

Alan heard a tinkling sound, like distant sleigh bells. The Storm Wolves were arriving, with machines of war pulled by giant snow beasts. Here were battle-hardened troops armed with glittering weaponry. Now the howling of the Leloo carried for miles as the harnesses sent a twinkling glitter across the ice. They were moving much faster than he could have anticipated.

There was a final great roar from Siam, and the Olhyiu, several limping and bloodied, turned and ran back in the direction of the boats, where the gangways were lowered to welcome them back.

Mo's hand, clutching Alan's arm, was shaking with terror. The thunderheads above them spurted lightning.

There was a hammering of heavy feet on wood as the blood-covered bear bounded back up the gangway to the Temple Ship. Alan felt the impact as the giant grizzly leaped the final yards to the mid-deck, where it howled, as if impatient for the arrival of Kehloke. Within a few minutes she ran up the gangway to join her husband and lay down in the curl of his almighty embrace, panting heavily. Alan entered the bear's mind again and felt the ebbing of power from the shadow being. Siam was returning to his wife and his people.

The sleds of the enemy were easily visible now, no more than half a mile distant. Alan caught his first clear sight of the Storm Wolves themselves, powerful warriors with chainmail glittering under their surcoats of fur, with guns strapped across their backs and helmets of a matt-black metal. As they approached the edge of the ice, the air carried their curses and the cracks of their whips, the snarling Leloo driven to a frenzied galloping under the lashes of the drivers, with perhaps ten or so of the soldiers astride every sled. Close to, he confirmed that these beasts were not wolves. The Leloo were bigger and meaner. He glimpsed their bright yellow eyes, rippling shoulders and big splayed feet, fur-padded against the cold and through which curved talons scored the ice under its covering of snow.

While the main group slewed around to a halt and began to set up cannon positions at the edge of the ice, at least thirty sleds invaded the frozen lake. He heard the lick of metal on snow, even the laboured panting of the beasts that pulled them as they ate up the ground between them and the ice-locked boats.

Kemtuk took hold of Alan's left shoulder and shook it, to draw his attention. Alan felt the familiar shape and weight of the Spear of Lug pressed into his right hand.

'Forgive us, Mage Lord! Help us – help us now! Or all is lost before ever we begin our journey!'

He felt Mo's renewed trembling under his left hand. He said, quietly, to Kemtuk, 'Tell your people to raise their sails!'

'But the ice still holds.'

'Tell them to do it – now!'

Kemtuk's eyebrows lifted incredulously, but he picked up a great horn and blew it, hard and long into the wind. Over the little cluster of boats the waxed leathers climbed the masts. Alan heard the final blessing of the shaman, 'Grant us your protection in this peril, as you protected our fathers before us through many perils. Whether it leads to death or salvation, yet your will be done, O great Akoli.'

'Alan?'

He heard Kate's tremulous voice add to Mo's trembling fear.

'I know.'

He looked up into a sky that seemed to fill his mind with violent notions. The triangle in his brow was pulsing fast and powerfully with his heartbeat. Tentatively, relying on nothing more than instinct, he raised his right arm, the spear firmly grasped in his clenched fist. He felt the throbbing power of the Ogham invocation invade his fingers and thumb. Through the channel of the blade he directed the power of the ruby crystal into the fury of those whirling masses. Fashioning the command within his mind, he entered the wheeling thunderheads and opened his senses to the gathering storm.

The Storm Wolves were among them. He ignored the murderous hatred on their faces, the bloodlust in the slavering jaws of their beasts, the levelling of weapons on board the sleds. All his senses streamed upwards, on the flickering tongues of lightning that were tumbling from cloud to cloud. He heard the thunder of cannons. An explosion of green fire ravaged the sail and superstructure of one of the boats. He heard the screams of the injured on the deck, as they were consumed by the living furnace. Anger rose in him. Through the triangle on his brow, Alan became one with the immensity of the elements. He forced his being into that communication.

His eyes followed a single flickering river of lightning that played over the black underbelly of the tempest, and as his mind found the mark, one river of lightning joined another, until they coalesced to become a single great cataract of force, and the cataract itself began to twist and turn about the point of his focus.

A second boat erupted into foul green fire. Still the Olhyiu men and women maintained their furious hammering while the timbers of their boats cracked and splintered against the huge force of wind bending the sails against the rigid entrapment of the ice. Several Olhyiu gave up their hammering and hurled their harpoons at the encircling enemy.

Alan steadied his arm as the tempest raged over the frozen lake, and then, holding the eye of the storm above, he turned a new awareness onto the Temple Ship.

'Now!'

He gave the command with his lips drawn back over gritted teeth, his focus never faltering upon that centre of seething energy in the sky. His arm tensed and his fingers closed even tighter on the Spear of Lug, until it felt as if it were one with his white-knuckled fist. Abruptly, he brought the spear down and directed all of his will at the ship. The bolt of lightning struck the central mast with a brilliant explosion of light, which cascaded downwards, over decks and rigging, before finally erupting out over the lake. Where the army of sleds had been circling, a fountain of ice and water now erupted, a spuming mushroom of dissipating energy, flooding the landscape from the white-glowing superstructure of the great galleon. Alan stood rigidly still, his eyes blinded by the light, his hearing deafened by the thunder. From what appeared to be some distance away, he heard a great roar of triumph from the Olhyiu as the surface of the frozen lake shattered into myriad fragments, the boats tossing and bucking as they began to move under the wind. The tempest billowed sails as their ears were filled by the roars of beasts trapped in their harnesses and the shouts of drowning men against the gale.

In his clearing vision Alan beheld a new wonder. The Temple Ship was moving, heaving about in the fractured ice. His gaze snapped skywards to witness the rigging. The great sails were rising and unfurling, although no hands were pulling at any ropes. All the holes in the leather were self-healing before his bewildered eyes.

Beside him Siam also gazed aloft, his voice husky in an exhausted throat, his face bleeding from several deep lacerations, and with a fur cape wrapped around his naked body. He placed his heavy hand on Alan's shoulder, his eyes aglow with astonishment.

'Truly the Temple Ship has found its master!'

All around them, the small scattering of sailors were staring up open-mouthed. Mark spun the great wheel, laughing like a maniac at his new-found role, his legs parted wide for balance. He swung the enormous vessel about through an arc of one hundred and eighty degrees, its bow inclined at such an angle that the starboard deck was lapping with splintered shards of ice. Overhead the sails snapped at their summit, tensing sheets of leather as broad as a two-storey house, catching the full swell of the wind, and causing the superstructure to murmur and groan like an awakening titan. In moments, they overcame the inertia of the heavy galleon and the prow surged forward, cutting through the fissured ice that still stood between the fishing fleet and the central thaw in the nearby river.

As they neared the safety of the channel, Alan lowered the spear, which now felt too heavy to bear. He passed it back to Kemtuk, his eyes meeting the good eye of the shaman. There was relief in the old man's gaze, but more. Things to think about, things to question in the days that lay ahead. The main force of Storm Wolves had not been destroyed. They were already pulling back, redirecting their sleds around the shattered ice, in pursuit of the fleet. But for the moment that could be put to one side. There was room only for joy as the fleet, flagged by the majestic beauty of the Temple Ship, broached the central melt of the Snowmelt River and turned its prow southwards, following the stream.

The Song of the River

With the sails billowed by the following winds, they soon left the ice-bound lake behind them. The sky was still laden with storm clouds but the reflected snow illuminated the waves that spread from the prows of the fleet, with the Temple Ship cleaving the way. On every boat voices grew hoarse from cheering. Meanwhile, from the makeshift kitchen area in the stern of the Temple Ship, the smell of cooking filled the air, the grilled slabs of winter salmon reminding everyone that they had not eaten since yesterday. Mo left Mark at the wheel so she could gossip with Kate, who was helping Turkeya cook the food.

Kate said, 'Turkeya is amazing. Did you know he can recognise more than fifty different herbs? The trouble is he doesn't write anything down. He keeps it all in his head. But he's promised me that when we get the chance he'll teach me to recognise some of them – and what they're used for.'

Mo looked over to where Turkeya was pulling wry faces as he turned the chunks of fish over so they cooked in their own oil. She realised that the cooking must appear very strange to him.

Kate spoke softly, 'Mo, will you for goodness sake tell me the truth – do you have the slightest inkling of what happened back there?'

Mo could only shake her head.

Kate peered forward to where Alan's figure stood on the foredeck, his dark hair tossed by the wind. 'I'm not sure I know him any more.'

'Wuh-wuh-we're all chuh-changing.'

Frowning pensively, Kate accepted a bowl of steaming soup from Turkeya, while gazing about herself at the passing landscape of snow-covered forest. Mists coiled over the water so that it seemed that they were journeying into an enchanted world of cloud and light.

There was a perpetual cacophony of hissing and sighing from the river. By degrees the free channel widened so that by late afternoon of the first day the ice had receded to both banks. Still the mists swirled about them, solid enough to blur the passing landscape. At times snow fell so heavily they could see nothing at all of the way ahead, relying on the helmsmanship of Mark to keep the ship in the central stream. The nearby trees were grey shadows against the milky haze of light, with ice glittering in their beards of lichen and, seen in gaps in the mist, the giant conifers at the forest edge were so laden with snow they resembled a great cliff wall. On the first night of their journey the mists lifted and there was a cry of wonder from an old woman, who believed she saw the spirits of her ancestors observing their passage from among the trees. And peering through snow-grimed lashes into the shadows of dappled greys and silvers, Kate could imagine that the ghosts of her parents were there also, Daddy and Mammy, and her brother Billy.

Tears filled Kate's eyes as she thought about her family, and what had happened to them, tears of anger and resentment at what she herself had lost, at the fact she had been robbed of all she had ever wanted – just an ordinary life. Her heart brooded on the unfairness of it all as she gazed, hour after hour, at the wraiths of mist that peeped back at her from between the darkening trees.

The four friends gathered together about midday on the second day in the empty great chamber, sitting on a pallet of rushes spread out over the floor beneath the harpoon and surrounded by the murals of the Olhyiu history.

Kate couldn't hide her feelings. 'Have you boys gone altogether mad? Look at you. You're behaving as if this is some great adventure. It's bonkers. We could all have been killed back there!'

Alan's fingers brushed self-consciously against his brow. 'Okay – so what's been happening to us is crazy. But crazy or not, we're here. We've got to make the best of it.'

Kate refused to be placated. 'What if we never go home?'

Alan shrugged. 'Hey, don't think I wasn't scared too!'

'You boys are just enjoying yourselves. It's time the girls were allowed to speak. We, that is Mo and I, have something else we want to say.'

'Okay – let's hear it.'

Mo, through the impediment of her stammer, explained to Mark and Kate what she had already intimated to Alan, the fact that she could understand the Olhyiu without needing a crystal.

'So what does it mean?'

Kate held up her left hand so everyone could see the green matrix, flecked with gold, that had been impressed into her palm from her crystal. 'I don't have a clue what it means. All I can say is that I don't need to hold the crystal any more to understand the Olhyiu.'

Mark shook his head.

Mo stammered, 'I'll tuh-tuh-tell you what. Kuh-Kuh-Kate is telling you thuh-thuh-truth.'

Kate nodded. 'Mo and I, we've been talking things over. Granny Dew, whatever it was she did to us—'

'The bag lady?'

Kate slapped Mark on the shoulder, to shut him up. 'You realise that whatever Granny Dew put into the crystals – it's in *us* now.'

'There's another explanation,' muttered Mark. 'It's some kind of mass hallucination. We're all kidding ourselves.'

'Mark, we're not!' Kate exclaimed.

'You're the one who needs to get a grip on yourself.' Alan also allowed his impatience with Mark to show.

Kate reached out and tried to look at Mark's left hand, which still grasped his silver-speckled obsidian crystal. But with a look of disgust, he hurled the crystal against the opposite wall, where it shattered into glassy fragments. He stared at the fragments for a moment, as if shocked at his own action, then stormed out of the chamber, his steps clattering up the wooden stairs in the direction of the main deck.

Kate urged Mo to stay while she ran after Mark. She discovered him in the sleeping cabin he shared with Alan. He was squatting on a pallet of rushes, playing a blues number on his harmonica. Kate touched his shoulder. The muscles there were tensed, making her heart go out to him.

'What's up with you?'

'Go squeeze your zits!'

'I don't have any zits.' She sat cross-legged on the floor and began the beat with the flat of her hands on the bare wood planks.

He stopped playing the harmonica. He refused to look at her. 'He's not one for sharing, is he?'

'You have to stop resenting Alan.'

'Kate – oh, just get lost!'

'No, I want to talk to you about things – about what is happening to us.'

Mark muttered, 'It's taken you long enough to notice that this is a seriously weird place!'

'Perhaps it's not a lot weirder than where we came from?'

Mark thought about that. 'Okay, so you've done your good Samaritan stuff. Now get lost!' He turned the harmonica over in his hands.

Her voice softened. 'Your crystal's broken!'

'I don't care!'

'But you've still got its magic in you.'

Mark held out his palm and put it right in front of Kate's face. The patterning had gone from the palm of his hand.

Alan left the chamber feeling uneasy about Mark. He was joined by Mo in climbing the oak staircase, emerging onto a swaying deck that smelled of wood smoke. Snow drifted like the breath of winter over the riverbanks. For the moment, Mark appeared to have abandoned the wheel to Siam.

Kate appeared from the sleeping area and huddled with Mo, after which Mo went in search of Mark.

'I guess we've got problems?'

'I don't know what to think.' Kate told Alan the markings had gone from Mark's palm.

'What's eating that guy?'

'Don't tell me you're not frightened by what's happening. What you did, back there on the ice?'

'I don't rightly know how I feel. Heck, Kate – how could I possibly know what's going on!'

Kate shook her head. 'Where's the spear?'

'Kemtuk is looking after it.'

She sighed.

'I know it's unbelievable, what's happening.' He spoke softly into the cold air, without looking directly at her.

'I was hoping you might know some of the answers.'

Glancing astern, Alan saw that the following boats looked as insubstantial as shadows in the mist. He allowed his senses to wander, his ears lulled with the rush of water and his eyes filled with those haunting woods against the backdrop of the high snow-covered mountains.

'Honestly, I'm as baffled as you are.'

'You did it, Alan. You lifted the spear into the air and the lightning struck.'

'Yeah, I know!'

In all that had gone before, he had been a passive ingredient. But he had influenced the storm over the lake. He mulled that over without understanding it.

'It must have been something Granny Dew did to you. She made it possible. Do you remember what she did to you, what you felt?'

'I don't rightly know what she did to me, Kate. All I recall . . . I just felt something fantastic was happening to me. I guess like I was invaded by a sense of . . . of power.'

'It must have felt awesome!'

'Hey – scary, Kate.' He recalled those growling words, coming out of that strange being, the implication that he asked too many questions and failed to see what should be obvious. 'It feels as if I'm discovering some kind of instinct. Like I just sensed what to do back there. But don't ask me how such a thing is possible.'

Kate sighed again.

With his eyes narrowed against the biting wind, Alan watched the snowy banks give way to rock and shingle, moist with a scum of yellow-green algae. He murmured, 'And you, what did you feel back in the cave?'

'Nothing I could put into words any better than you can. Just as you say, it was more a sort of feeling. A sort of communication. It was like I remember when I was seven years old and had my first communion. I felt a kind of overwhelming sense of fulfilment. Like . . . like grace.'

Alan stared across at the passing landscape.

When Kate left him to go and talk to Mo, Alan searched out Kemtuk. He found the shaman on the foredeck with Siam, both men alert for every whim of the wind or weather. Already it seemed that they were fearful of an attack from either bank.

Alan asked Siam, 'Why not an attack by water?'

The Olhyiu chief shook his head. 'On the river we are the masters. The attack will come from land, and at a time that disadvantages us and favours their malengins. Not for nothing are they called Storm Wolves.'

'Tell me more about these Storm Wolves.'

'They are soldiers blood-sworn to the Tyrant of the Wastelands.'

'Who is this tyrant?'

'The enemy of all who live in this continent of Monisle. For years beyond count we fought against him, continent against continent, through an ocean of blood and destruction. But then, and the shaman here claims to understand what I do not, the High Architect of Ossierel, our spiritual capital, lost the will to fight on.'

'Ussha De Danaan did not lose the will to fight,' interrupted Kemtuk. 'She abandoned her own protection, though for reasons none have ever understood.'

Siam's eyes darkened with anger. 'Yet the shaman cannot deny that she allowed the Death Legion to massacre all on the island capital. And the consequence is our domination by these cruel forces. These are a hard and dangerous enemy, trained to live and fight in these wastelands.'

'The Storm Wolves are part of this Tyrant's army?'

'They are the most northerly of his army of occupation, which calls itself the Death Legion.'

While absorbing this, Alan noticed how Kemtuk's eyes were avoiding his. Was it possible that the shaman had grown frightened of him? Alan realised that the old man was not to be persuaded or hurried. He left the Olhyiu leaders to make his way to the stern rail, prepared to bide his time for a more suitable moment.

'My goodness! It's suh-suh-suh-so lovely. Huh-huh-haunting!'

Alan hadn't heard Mo approach. But now he smiled at her. 'You're right, Mo. It is haunting.'

Maybe she wanted to talk to him about Mark. He decided he would let her bring it up if it was what she wanted. For now he relaxed in her company as they stared out into the continuing thaw in the wilderness that was gliding by. Black tors still filled the gaps between the trees, shoulder pressed against shoulder, crushing the light from two thirds of the sky. Shags posed on the frosted crags of rock under the shadows of the banks and they disappeared, with barely a ripple, into the surface stream.

She said, 'There's fuh-food enough for the fuh-fuh-fish and the buh-birds buh-buh-buh . . .'

'But not for hungry people?'

Mo nodded.

Always on the threshold of starvation in the ice-bound lake, the Olhyiu were already low on food. Alan knew that there was plenty of food in the river and on the banks but to get hold of it they would have to stop. And to stop meant delays, and the ever-present risk of attack.

On the evening of the fourth day, after they had made a rapid passage with long hours of sailing, Siam felt that it was safe to draw up the keels against a bank of shingle. Hunters made preparations to enter the forest in search of meat. Some of the elders disembarked with the hunters to sit about fires on the snow-covered shore.

Alan joined the shaman's group around one of the campfires.

Inland the ash-white barks of birch trees faded into

shadows, while at the waterside, the bleached forms of the boats were glimmering with moonlight.

He shook his head at the leaf of tobacco, offered by one of the Olhyiu. But he welcomed a bowl of broth, warmed in the embers about the edge of the fire. Sipping it gratefully, with his shoulders hunched against the cold, he watched the shaman's wrinkled face, the glitter in the pupil of his right eye. The old man was deeply thoughtful, his pipe aglow. Alan had grown fond of Kemtuk, and he was reluctant to intrude on his reflections. Waiting until the shaman was filling a new pipe, he broached the curious nature of the Temple Ship.

'As you suggest, such a wonder was not constructed by the Olhyiu – nor by any craftsmen known to us. Its origins date from before the age of the wandering.'

'How far back is that?'

For a moment or two, Kemtuk drew on his pipe in a thinking silence against the glowing bowl of his pipe.

'Older than we might dream. In the earliest days, when the Tilikum Olhyiu were spread three thousand miles along the coast from Carfon in the south to this northern world of the Whitestar Mountains, the ship was ancient even then.' Kemtuk shrugged. 'Its makers are a mystery. But what is a world without mystery?'

Alan nodded, welcoming the approaching Kate to share his rug. She snuggled up to his warmth, shivering with cold. It was obvious that Kemtuk had nothing more to say, since his face had fallen into contemplation. Alan stroked Kate's face, then kissed the top of her head as she found a comfortable position against his neck. His eyes wandered about them, towards the red glow that played about the shining faces of the other elders. He pulled his cloak tighter about them both.

Mark felt too tense to fall asleep with the others, reflecting back on the stupid impulse that had resulted in him shattering his own crystal. In the moonlight he could see them – Alan, so proud of his ruby triangle, spending all that time earlier chatting to the shaman, and now falling asleep by the fire with Kate snuggling up against his shoulder. He had never seen Kate look as beautiful as she looked in this world. Her body was filling out, growing into the figure of a woman, and her auburn hair seemed to grow thicker and more luxurious day by day. And just looking at her now as she lay there, lovely and vulnerable in her sleep, with her fingers trailing around Alan's neck, he couldn't bear to see them so warm and cosy under their shared rug!

Still sleepless, an hour or two later, Mark slid out from under his own rug and walked softly away into the snow, stooping twice, first to lift a leaf-roll of tobacco from a sleeping elder's pouch, and then to pick up an ember from the fire. He felt so angry, and lonely, he could hardly bear it. Soon, he was hidden behind a coppice of birch saplings. He blew on the ember to heighten its glow before he made to light the leaf-roll with it.

'They are so lovely together, are they not?'

Mark spun around, looking for the source of the whisper, which had been softer than the breeze. 'Who's there?'

He caught a hint of movement, something diaphanous gliding closer behind some shrubbery. The ember fell from his hand, guttering in the snow.

With his heart pounding, he saw the shrubbery part and in a moment a young woman was standing there. She had picked up the ember and was blowing on it through pouted lips, now and then flicking her eyes in his direction. The ember grew to a tiny blaze and in the reflection of its glow he saw that she had platinum blonde hair brought forward over her shoulders, falling all the way down to her waist. Her eyes were a lustrous turquoise in a face like porcelain. She was too beautiful to be real, more perfect than any actress or pop star he had ever seen, more like a princess from a fairy tale.

His taut lips struggled to speak. 'Who . . .?'

'I can see,' she whispered, 'why you might envy him.' She glided up closer, so he could breathe in her fragrance. She glanced across to where, through the trees, his friends and the Olhyiu were sleeping around the fire. 'Yet she is but a child and I am a woman.'

His mind told his legs to run but his legs refused to obey. His muscles were frozen. 'You're not real . . . You can't be!'

'I am Siri.' She laughed, a bewitching sound, like the

tinkling of a musical box. 'Do you not have wood sprites in the world you come from?'

He tried to swallow, but his mouth was ash dry. 'You – you're a mirage – some kind of a trick of the light!'

'Touch me, then. See if I'm real.'

Mark tried to take a step backwards. But his legs wouldn't move.

She put the leaf-roll in her mouth and inhaled the smoke, then reached up to press her lips against his. She parted his lips and teeth with her tongue, breathing the honey-sweet smoke into his mouth and nostrils.

It's a dream. It isn't happening. Not wildly possible . . .

But it was happening. And it was the most enchanting dream he could ever have imagined.

In some distant corner of his mind, he heard the gravelly warning of Granny Dew in the cave: *Daaannngggerrr!*

But his heart didn't care. His heart was lost to the dream. His heart wished it would never stop when she kissed him softly. It faltered when he felt her scented breath move across his cheek and neck as her lips drew back.

Mark moaned. He felt dizzy. He had a throat full of smoke and he coughed and spluttered. But he couldn't move. The doll-like face studied him with her head aslant. He wanted to breathe her fragrance in, inhale her beauty so it filled his lungs, but he just stood there, his eyes staring at her, his mouth agape.

Her long-fingered hand reached up to cosset his cheek. Her touch was as delicate as the wings of a butterfly. 'Will you share a secret with me, my lovely, and tell me what the old crone said to you in the cave?'

Mark tried to think beyond the desire for her lips. His heart felt faint and his legs felt jittery. 'How . . . how did you know?'

She cradled his face with her hands, cupping the boyish smoothness of his cheeks, bringing his mouth to hers with a deeper kiss, moving upwards, with a feathery touch, to brush her lips over his momentarily closed eyes. Then she put her arms about his neck and she kissed him again, passionately and languorously. No girl had ever kissed Mark like that in his life. He could not turn from her kiss, his lips drinking in the padded softness of her mouth. Her delicate pink tongue pierced his lips again, moistened his own tongue with a caress that thrilled with pleasure. 'Oh, my lovely, I would dearly like to know what she said to you.'

In his spirit he groaned aloud while his mouth could not stop itself from intoning hoarsely, 'She said that one day I would find . . .' With all of his will, he forced it to stop, his heart pounding so hard in his chest he thought he was going to die.

'Yes! Yes, my darling, what would you find?' She pressed the wonderful curves of her body against his, thrilling him so he felt gooseflesh rise over his entire skin. Her lips brushed against his ear, her breath tingling in his very mind, a whisper of delight. 'Oooh, my lovely – you only have to let me help you make true your secret longing!'

Tears erupted into his eyes. 'I . . . I would find love.'

'Ah!'

As if waking from a dream, Mark found himself sitting beside her in the snow. How long they had spent together, he didn't know. He stood up, staggering with weakness in every muscle, attempted to turn away. She took his hand, which appeared to have a will of its own, helping her to her feet. There was no gooseflesh on her skin, no response to the cold at all. Her body was so lithe, it might have been weightless.

'I must go now, my beautiful boy.' She was already receding from him into the pitch-black shadows of the trees.

His voice quavered. 'No. Don't go.'

'I must.'

The anguish of her leaving, of losing her, crushed his heart.

'Will I never see you again?'

'If you wish, I might come to you in your sleep.'

A mixture of delight and dread caused a sweat to erupt over his brow and cheeks. 'Only in my sleep?'

'Oh, my dearest love!' She came forward and embraced him again, as if she couldn't bear to let him go, her hands stroking his hair, then falling to caress the skin on the back of his neck. 'Every night, if that would please you.'

He was trembling uncontrollably. 'Yes.'

'But beware. If those others knew! This boy they call

Mage Lord – the one you recognise to be your enemy – he would stop me coming to you. You must be discreet or he would part us forever.'

Mark was panting for breath, his heart breaking. Still his reedy voice proclaimed, 'Alan is not my enemy.'

'Oh, beloved, give me your word. Will you promise me, upon your heart and soul?'

'Yes.'

'I must hear it – you must speak the words.'

He sensed the spirit dying in him as his lips spoke the words, 'Upon my heart and soul, I give you my promise.'

'Go back now and tell them nothing. Go now. Hurry, before they notice your absence! And I will come to you every night, without fail.'

When the youth had gone, two figures with folded, membranous wings emerged from the deep shadows behind the woman. They were gigantically tall and skeletally thin, with bat-like heads that peered down at her from between the lower branches of the trees, and their grey-blue oily skins reflected the moonlight in iridescent gleams. They watched the retreat of the boy, following his stumbling progress until he had rejoined the primitives by their campfires.

The woman gloated, in a harsh purr, very different from the silken tones she had employed in addressing the youth, 'He is mine!'

This was observed with liquid hisses of pleasure, and a

chameleon-like darkening of the creatures' skins. A thumb extended from the first bend of a great wing and pointed directly into the woman's face. From the thumb, a single claw, as long as a dagger, emerged to exude venom only inches from her eyes. She averted her face, but it was more from the stink of the creature's secretion than from fear. When the bat creature spoke, it was through a series of clefts high up in its neck, somewhat like gills, so that its voice emerged as a warbling hiss.

'You have done well, succubus!'

Her lips drew back wide in triumph, and there was a flash of ivory, as four needle-point canines captured the white glitter of the moon.

'My mistress will be pleased.'

The Dragon's Teeth

On the second week they lost one of their company, the old woman who had seen her ancestors on the bank. Kemtuk told them that she had given up the will to live and so had slipped away during a hunting stop to die ashore. A party of men, led by Turkeya, followed her tracks for a few hundred yards among the rushes and sedges lining the bank until they found her body, frozen to the ground. They left her there, erecting a small mound of stones over her body to mark her grave.

The old woman's death startled the Olhyiu, and fearful eyes peered more anxiously at the snowbound forest as they moved out again into the increasingly turbulent river. The landscape was unchanging, that frighteningly stark contrast between the snowy ground and the shadowy indigo of the trees.

Kate did her best to keep track of the days.

Today was two weeks and six days since they had first

sailed out from their ice-bound captivity. She estimated they were travelling from twenty to fifty miles each day, depending on the difficulty they experienced with navigating the river. And those difficulties were mounting.

Later in the morning they came to a complete stop while the women passed out ropes to the men standing on the bank. They had to edge each boat past treacherous rapids, while all still on board pressed with poles from the decks. For the Temple Ship, progress became a major undertaking. The steam of their breaths bathed their heads like haloes, and on the banks thick reeds, coated with hoarfrost, crackled like gunshots under the feet of the men as they heaved and tugged on ropes attached to the prows. Hearts faltered when one of the fishing boats ran aground on a trap of breakers. With anxious eyes scanning the trees, this family home was finally saved by cantilevering it over the rocks using fulcrums hacked out of young tree trunks and lubricated by slippery inner bark.

But they had lost an entire day negotiating a few miles of water, and meanwhile the sense of menace increased as the food reserves dwindled. The meat caught by the hunters had long run out, and even their stores of fish and oil were almost spent. Kate's heart sank with the plaintive sound of children wailing from hunger. That night, sitting around another fire on the bank, with her sleepy head against Alan's shoulder, she heard a loud flapping in the air, a leathery sound, like great wings beating. Craning her eyes through the dark, she saw nothing more than shadows. But to her nostrils came a foul stench, left on the air in the wake of the wings. Shivering involuntarily, she peered into the forest, blue-black against the virgin white of the snow, as the sighing, lapping river carried them ever southwards through the alien landscape.

'Isn't it awful,' she murmured to Alan, 'that Mark and Mo only have bad memories of home?'

His sigh was a vibration deep in his chest.

Kate blinked away the moistness in her eyes. 'It's just that I don't want my memories to be just the bad things. I want to remember some of the good things. Like when Daddy would forget his work and play with us.' Kate recalled her father's face, his kindness not of touch or declared affection but of simply being with them, a shyness about the eyes which extended even to his only daughter. 'Mammy had a beautiful singing voice. She'd sing African songs from the Mission School. Have you ever heard the *Missa Lumba*?'

Alan squeezed her. 'No.'

'It's the mass, sung in an African language. It's haunting.'

With a small smile, Kate also recalled her grandad, Liam, who had introduced her to his love of plants, and she remembered the small comforts her kind but distracted uncle had been able to provide for her in the heartbreaking time after the death of her parents, and in the awkward years that followed. The fact that he had offered her his home instead of packing her off to boarding school, allowing her to live half-wild with Darkie and her dreams.

'I really miss my family – don't you?'

'I sure do.'

At dawn Alan didn't hear Turkeya come up beside him. The youth's voice cut like a knife through sleep, waking him. 'I worry about the journey ahead, Mage Lord.' Alan moaned with the stiffness in his back, sitting up on the bank next to the ash of last night's fire. He yawned and rubbed the sleep out of his eyes and then climbed to his feet. Kate was still sleeping and he didn't want to wake her so he kept his voice down until he and Turkeya had walked a short distance along the shore.

'Please call me Alan.'

Turkeya looked uncomfortable at the suggestion of such intimacy. A breeze ruffled the more youthful version of Siam's whiskers that thickened the fine fur at the sides of his face.

Alan looked at Turkeya. 'What's worrying you?'

The Olhyiu raised his right hand, in which a single claw sprang like a pointer aimed down the river. 'There are hazards close ahead. The water will boil over the rocks we know as the Dragon's Teeth.'

They walked on a short distance further while Alan thought about this, sharing the steam of his breath with the river mist. 'Tell me – are all the tribes like you, the Olhyiu?'

'Few live as we do. Once our people left the oceans to live in the cities, where we offered our labours for menial work or toiled on the land as farmers. But we could not settle there. We rediscovered our wild hearts.'

Alan hesitated, looking thoughtful. 'Is there no way around this obstacle ahead?'

'None other than we might fly.'

Hunger was so pressing that after only a few more miles Siam ordered the keels to be drawn up against a shingle shore. High cliffs reared on either side, making ambush difficult, while within the undergrowth of the narrow river valley were bushes laden with snow berries. As the women set out with their baskets, the children gathered on the decks and watched fretfully for their return. Soon happy cries sounded out as hungry stomachs were filled with the honey-sweet fruit. Alan watched as Turkeya led a party of several men into the forests by the water's edge, aware that the shaman was somewhere close to him. The old man smelled of tobacco even when his pipe was unlit.

Refreshing his face with a handful of snow, Alan spoke as he turned to face him. 'You're kind of watching me and all the while you're avoiding me, Kemtuk. There's no need for that. You and I should be friends.'

The old man was carrying the Spear of Lug. When he spoke it was with a voice husky with anxiety. 'If I am anxious, it is for other reasons. Take back your weapon, warded with magic – you may have need of it.'

'What's going on, Kemtuk?'

'I have felt hostile eyes upon us these last few days.'

Alan was shocked. How could Kemtuk stand there so calmly, knowing what he did? 'We've got to get the people back into the boats.'

'Do not distress yourself. Siam knows. That hunting party is also a scouting party.'

Alan's eyes darted about, worrying about Kate. How right she was when she complained of how dangerous this world really was. He sat down on a rocky projection and took a good look at their surroundings. The river was mere yards away, with coils of mist rising from its surface like phantoms. In full daylight the wilderness looked more desolate than ever. The vastness of the landscape dwarfed their presence. They seemed insignificant here, minuscule and vulnerable.

Lost in his brooding, Alan was hardly aware of Mark until his friend came up alongside him. He tried to be cheerful. 'Hi! How's it going?'

'I'm fine. Just bored.'

Alan was startled by the bitterness in Mark's voice. 'How's Mo?'

'She has a cold. Sneezing and blowing her nose like a bitch!'

Mark seemed different somehow. Alan tensed as Mark sat next to him on the rock and took the harmonica out of his pocket. Hunching forward, to rest his elbows on his knees, he played a few bluesy riffs. Then, abruptly he played

'Little Red Rooster', so brilliantly everybody just stopped what they were doing and stared.

Alan clapped. 'That was really something. You ever thought of forming a band at that boarding school?'

'Nobody at school was interested in blues – other than me.'

'You don't say!'

'I just said it.'

'Aw, c'mon, Mark – loosen up.'

Mark snorted, went through the pantomime of shaking out the joints of his arms and rolling around his shoulders, as if taking Alan literally.

They both laughed, if a little awkwardly.

'Ooh, lovely! Are you going to play us a dance tune!' The Clonmel accent caused them both to swivel around to see Kate join them, blowing steam through the tunnel of her red-raw hands.

Mark opened up with 'Cajun Girl'. A group of children came up close in the snow behind Mark and they started laughing and dancing to the music. Kate joined them, clapping her hands in time.

'Aren't they gorgeous!'

Alan grinned. The Olhyiu had such a natural feel for dancing he could have watched them all day, these little ones, with the tips of their noses and their lips blue-black and their bewhiskered faces cherry pink with underlying cold, their tufts of brown and silvery hair poking out from fur caps and bonnets. Steam rose from Mark's breath, shrouding his face even while he was playing. The tune complete, he rose to his feet, bowing ceremoniously to Kate before playing dodgem with the little ones, who chased after him, calling for him to play some more.

Kate took Mark's place, sitting next to Alan. A little girl – they called her Amoté – darted up behind her and ran her fingers through Kate's auburn curls before she ran away, shrieking. Everybody laughed, gazing after the little girl, who had bright red poppies painted over her cheeks. Then Alan joined Kate and Mark in a snow fight, with the Olhyiu children joining in. Afterwards, breathless and tousled, Mark smiled at Kate in a wistful way. He spoke softly, almost a whisper. 'I'd never do anything to hurt you – you know that?'

Kate flushed in embarrassment before turning away.

When Mark left them to play a little more with the children, Alan frowned at Kate. 'Something's eating him. I don't rightly know what.'

Kate agreed with him. 'He's never been happy since breaking his crystal.'

'Yeah. But whose fault was that?'

'Ah, sure, I know. But still, maybe I should go and talk to Mo and see if she knows what's going on.'

The tension only served to remind Alan of what the shaman had told him earlier – that danger still surrounded them. After Kate had left he picked up the spear and returned to Kemtuk, not caring that many of the elders were close and listening. He indicated the triangle in his brow. 'I need to understand this – what it is and how it works.'

There was a prickling silence, and then a murmuring of muted voices among the elders, who glanced from one to another under lowered brows. The shaman puffed at intervals on his pipe, so that Alan began to wonder if he would answer at all, until eventually he spoke.

'All can read the worry in your eyes. But I cannot help you.' The old man took his pipe from his mouth and tapped the bowl against a stone, while looking towards the nearby river. 'I would help if I could. But I do not have the knowledge. Only one mage in all the land has such knowledge, or so legend has it. He lives in Isscan, where we are headed. He is known as the Mage of Dreams.'

Later that same evening, sitting on his bunk by the porthole in the Temple Ship, Mark peered out at the campfires spread over the shore. Even his sister was resting in the warmth of one of them, deep in conversation with Kate. How he wished that he could join his friends. But Mark could no longer share his sleep with anyone. He couldn't possibly afford to let them see how, with the dark, things changed. How, at the very edges of sleep, things became distinctly weird – and more than a little scary.

Something in him really was changing, just as it was in all of the others. In spite of the fact he had smashed his crystal and there were no marks he could see in his hand, or anywhere else, he still understood the Olhyiu when they growled and grunted. And every night, whether truly in sleep or in some peculiar half-awake state, his wood sprite, Siri, came to visit him. She kissed and caressed him and made him hunger for more. Tonight he would beg her, as he begged her every night, to become real for him. He longed for a real girlfriend, somebody he could fool around with during the day, somebody he could really touch and hold, somebody he could talk to about his hopes and worries, like Alan talked to Kate.

When, later that same night, she came to him, he beat his fists against the hard oak of the porthole. 'It isn't fair. It isn't.' Tears rose in his eyes.

'Oh, Mark – my lovely, do not distress yourself. I am here for you. I shall always be here for you.'

'It's no good.' He buried his face in his hands. 'A dream is not enough. It's not! It just isn't.'

He felt her tapering fingers curl about his neck, like wisps of silk, gently stroking his skin. 'Does it not feel real when I am by your side?'

'But you're not really here. You're just a dream. You're tormenting me – worse than Grimstone!'

'Uncover your eyes and look at me. Here, remove your hands from your face and let me kiss your tears away.'

Her hands took hold of his and moved them down so they were encircling her waist. Through the veil of his tears he saw her incline her face to kiss his lips, then, with that sharply pointed pink tongue, she licked the tears from his cheeks and eyes.

'If . . . if only it was really happening, like that first night.'

'Perhaps there is a way we could be together.'

His heart leaped. 'How?'

'There is one who could make it possible. If you could persuade her that you truly deserve her favour.'

He snorted. 'What – some stupid goddess, like the Trídédana that old Padraig was going on about?'

'Such beings are hardly stupid. Truly one such goddess might make your dreams come true.' She kissed him again, lingeringly, and coiled his hair around her fingers, tugging him down to lie with her on his bunk.

'There are no goddesses.'

'Oh, but there is one powerful enough to make it happen.'

'Yeah? Like who?'

'My mistress has that power.'

Mark sighed. 'All right – so how do we persuade your mistress to make you real?'

'This you might achieve by demonstrating to her that you no longer love the auburn-haired girl.'

'But I don't.'

'I watched you today, when you made the children dance. You could not hide your longing for her.'

'But I wasn't trying to—'

'As ever, you allowed this mere girl to humiliate you. Oh, my lovely – all your friends saw the unrequited love in your eyes.'

'I don't love her. I love you.'

'Well then,' she nuzzled her lips over the naked skin of his neck before lifting her mouth to nibble his ear with the tantalising pin-pricks of her needle-sharp teeth, 'prove that you no longer harbour desire for the girl in the deepest reaches of your heart. Show my mistress how you spurn her.'

He sat up on the bunk, trapped in a twilight world of being half-asleep and half-awake, his hands gripping his head, trying to discover some level of understanding. The freezing air through the open porthole dusted his gooseflesh with ice-crystals as her turquoise eyes gazed longingly, cravingly, into his. 'If you would only make it so we could truly be together, you must push this girl away from your thoughts.'

'Push her from me?'

'You must do it soon. When the opportunity arises. I will come to you and whisper the moment in your ear.'

'But where – how?'

'On the deck of the ship, by the rail over the torrent – where and when hidden eyes can confirm your love for me.'

'Push Kate? You mean, just push her away from me?'

'Oh, my lovely, is it not such a small thing to ask for our love?'

Yes – yes, he thought, again and again, over the extending hours of darkness. He pondered and mulled it over, again and again, his thoughts confused, as his arms and legs jerked with the cold invading his muscles. He pondered it over and over, his hands rubbing at his face, making the frozen skin crackle, like leather encased in a morning's hoar frost. He would shake his head before nodding, or nod, then shake his head. *No – not actually* push *Kate!* But then, *Yes*, he thought. *Just one small push. It is such a simple thing.* It surely couldn't hurt Kate, other than in her feelings – Kate, who had never held back from hurting him from the day that they had first met.

At daybreak Alan heard the murmur of the rapids. An hour later the murmur had risen to a thundering. Siam roared instructions that had the Olhyiu running here and there, yet it seemed to Alan that the rigging was adjusting itself, the great sails furling in until only one tiny sail at the front, the spinnaker, billowed for the assistance of navigation. Mark's fair-haired figure clung to the wheel on the afterdeck as Siam continued to bellow orders to all the following boats that children should be stowed safely beneath the decks. Alan suggested to Kate and Mo that they should go below to their sleeping cabin but they took no notice. They went forward to the prow to watch what was happening up ahead.

The valley sides became jagged cliffs, like sinews of iron tethering the mountains about the swollen river. Between them the torrent was squeezed between a narrow pass, whipped into a frenzy by the speed of its passage. The current broke into heaving waves, seething where it struck the sharp edges of submerged boulders. The sails were all down but still the boats raced among the breakers, and pole-wielding men and women were hard-pressed to keep their keels clear of the rocks. Alan saw how the poles bent with the pressure. From time to time one splintered, the cracks inaudible against the background thunder.

Beside him, he heard Kemtuk groan aloud, 'These are not the normal rapids. A madness has invaded the pass!'

Jagged teeth of rock gnashed at the keels. Siam was hoarse from shouting to the sailors on board the Temple Ship, every hand pressing their long poles against the rocks. Just moments later the ship shuddered as it crashed against a reef. The decks shelved at a crazy angle, and an immense wave swept over them before the craft righted itself again. From the boat closest to them, a woman was flung, with a single heart-rending scream, into the maelstrom. Her husband fought to save his family but in moments all were lost, the boat disintegrating, as if caught in an explosion.

Kate and Mo hugged each other, their fingers white around the forward rail, fallen onto their knees to get as close as possible to the deck. Suddenly Mo clutched Kate's arm and stared back. Kate saw that Mark had appeared at the top of the staircase to the foredeck and was making his way towards them against the gale, his eyes blank in a face that was as white as moonlight. Mo was looking back at her brother, her head shaking from side to side, her voice stammering.

'Guh-guh-guh-go back!'

'Mark – stay where you are!' Kate shouted her agreement with Mo. 'You can't help us. We don't dare move.' She had to cling to the rail to avoid being thrown off her feet.

But Mark appeared to take no notice. He lurched away from the head of the stairs, clinging to rigging and bulkheads to try to keep to his feet. His lips were moving and he was shaking his head, as if arguing with the storm about him. With a massive lurch of the ship, he fell onto his side and skidded across the foredeck until he collided with the rail, about fifteen feet from where Kate hung on next to Mo. He struggled back to his feet, braced his legs wide, then began to inch his body in their direction.

Kate called out to him, 'What are you doing?'

Mark's eyes were bloodshot and staring.

'What's the matter with him?' she murmured into Mo's ear.

Mo stared at her approaching brother, her eyes wide with fright.

From just five feet away, Mark appeared to turn his face to the sky, and she could see his mouth opening as if he was shouting aloud. She caught snatches of words, but she couldn't make sense of them.

Then he lowered his gaze to Mo, his face distorted by the howling wind, his eyes tormented.

'Run!' he shouted.

Mo clutched at Kate's hand, hanging on to her friend

with a desperate grip. Kate whispered, 'What, for the love of God . . .?'

Mark lurched a foot nearer. Kate could see the tendons of his wrists standing out as his hands clutched the rail against another huge lurch of the ship. Suddenly he was within arm's reach. He reached out and tried to grab hold of Kate's arm. Instinctively, she jerked herself away.

'Mark – you're frightening me!'

Amidships, with the Spear of Lug stowed safely below deck and a pole clenched in his spray-soaked hands, Alan added his efforts to those of the Olhyiu to keep the ship off the rocks. A movement on the foredeck caught his eye. Two figures were struggling to keep themselves from being washed overboard. He could barely make them out in the spray-fogged air, but he could see that they were too small to be Olhyiu. They had to be Kate and Mo. They were holding onto each other with one arm, their other arms gripping the rail for dear life. He shouted encouragement, but his words were lost in the thunder of the water. Suddenly he glimpsed a third figure, pushing itself between the two girls. He glimpsed fair hair. It had to be Mark.

What on earth was Mark doing away from the wheel? Alan almost lost his own footing, he was so distracted by concern for them.

Mark looked like he was trying to put his arm around Kate, but she appeared to be resisting him. Suddenly Mark turned and Alan could make out his expression: he looked half-crazy, his eyes wide and staring.

Alan tried to run, but he lost his footing and crashed against the wooden staircase to the foredeck, his head barely level with the upper deck. In a lull, he could hear Mark's voice raised in an appeal, 'Run – Kate!'

How could she run?

Alan started crawling up the staircase on his hands and knees, clinging to the rail as he rose. What in God's name was Mo doing? She was trying to tear Mark's arm from around Kate's shoulders. Suddenly, with a bewildered shake of his head, Mark pushed Mo away from him, causing her to sprawl over the boards, sliding over the deck until she came to rest against the base of the forward mast. She pulled on some rigging to help her back to her feet. Alan inched out onto the forward deck. He crab-walked over slippery black boards. He tried to climb to his feet, but an almighty heave of the deck threw him sideways against the rail.

'Mo – go below!'

Alan heard Mark's shout to his sister.

But Mo took no notice. Her small figure was stumbling and sliding over the slippery boards, towards Kate and her brother. With horrified eyes, Alan watched as Mo clattered into them both, reaching out towards Kate, who still held onto the rail with one desperate arm. Spray drenched Mo's hair so it was flat with the oval of her head. Her eyes were protruding. Mark held out his hand to her but she refused his help, her feet slipping and sliding over the icy deck. Suddenly the prow caught on another reef. There was a great shudder as the stern jerked high out of the water and another foaming torrent rushed over the deck. Through the mist, Alan caught a glimpse of something monstrous, a creature larger than a man, with a long lizard-like tail and huge fangs bared in its bat-like mouth. Its leathery wings were battering through the storm-tossed air and its clawed feet were extended out towards the struggling three friends.

'No!' Mark cried, letting go of Kate and throwing his body forward, so he was sliding towards the staggering figure of his sister.

As he reached Mo, she evaded him again, her arm stretched out as if struggling to clutch Kate's outstretched hand. Against the roar of the surf Alan faintly heard both girls scream. The clawed foot of the monster caught Mo by her hair and she was raised aloft. Then, as she writhed and reeled in its grasp, the creature opened its claws and dropped her into the moiling water. Mark clutched the terrified figure of Kate in his arms, while his teeth clenched together in despair.

Terror! Alan's mind was suddenly flooded with the sensations in Mo's bewildered brain.

In that instant, he knew that Mo was drowning somewhere in the wake of the ship. He dived in and was swallowed by the tumult, crashing against ship and boulders, yet struggling to search with open eyes in the swirling currents beneath the surface. Shaking the confusion from his mind, he struck upward, his legs and arms flailing until his face broke the surface. But he could see nothing. Mo was nowhere near him.

'Mo!' he shouted, his voice torn from his lips and lost in the background thunder.

A moment later he was sucked back under.

Mo!

He expressed his call through the triangle in his brow. In answer there was the faintest whimper. If they were communicating it was through thought alone. Through Mo's open eyes he glimpsed the race of water, a whirling current around a huge black stone. She too was under the surface, still alive, but she would not survive long. He tried to shake off his fur-lined boots but they were too tightly laced. His surcoat, heavy with water, was dragging him under. But his fingers were too numbed to unfasten it. There was no time. Mo's terror was overwhelming him. Her mental screams had become an explosion in his brain. But where was she? She couldn't be far from him.

Think, Mo – think!

Panic lunged at him from her frightened mind. The terror was so great, no sensible message could possibly get through it.

Alan's body had been thrown close to one of the following boats and his flailing hand clutched a guardrail that ran just above the waterline. He hauled himself above the surface, held on, rising and falling with the heaving timber. His eyes scanned the river in front of him. He saw a great fang of rock that bisected the stream. It looked like the stone he had glimpsed in the terrified mind of his friend. Pushing hard with his feet against the hull, he swam away from the sanctuary of the boat and back into the raging water.

He forced all awareness from his mind, tethering everything to that flickering mote of life. *Mo!*, he called again, his eyes closed to focus through the triangle, searching desperately for the presence of Mo's mind with every ounce of strength.

Alan . . . Alan . . . *Alan!* In her mind, as in her singing, Mo did not stammer. She was answering at last, as if the oxygen deprivation of drowning had numbed her terror. Yet how powerful still was that communication from her will to live. It was as if he had searched for a distant star and encountered a nearby sun. His senses were overwhelmed by the immensity of her terror.

Then he saw the rock again. The fang-like shape of it flashed across his vision, as if through the open eyes of the half-conscious girl.

Diving under the surface currents, he saw her. Mo's body, bent and limp, was brought up against the submerged portion of rock, held against it by the force of the river. Thrusting out with his lungs bursting, he caught hold of her under her arms and he lunged to the surface.

He broke into air with his right arm wrapped under

her chest. His breath came in gasps. After a few seconds of rising panic, he drove away from the rock.

Thrashing out against the current, he glimpsed how the raging water lifted one of the stragglers among the boats clear out of the water, dripping spume and spray, then broke its back on a boulder. He heard the screams of the family on board, soon silenced as they too were dashed against the rock.

He held more tightly to Mo, forcing her unconscious face above the wave-lashed surface. He communicated to her, mind to mind, urgently: *Hold on!*

Even as he did so, an arc of livid green cut through the spray and another boat exploded into flame.

The Storm Wolves had timed their attack to perfection. There would be no counterattack with thunder and lightning here. He tried to recall his dad's life-saving lessons. Struggling to stay alive in the tumult, he brought Mo's back against his chest and, encircling her body under the armpits with his left arm, he turned on his side, manoeuvred his own position so her head was out of the water, then he kicked out with his feet, treading water.

Mo's eyes flickered open.

Swim!

A new voice entered his mind, alien and strange. The voice was a deep contralto, devoid of emotion.

Where to? He pressed his own mental voice back, like a gasp.

He was so drained that he could barely float, let alone

swim. The air was full of oaths and curses as more arcs of the sinister green cut through the storm-tossed air to find their targets. Alan had the impression of fierce conflict close to the bank – then an armoured figure plunged into the water not twenty feet away from him.

'Blasphemer's brat!' He heard the hate-filled growl. 'The Master would relish your impious heart.'

Alan searched for a small reserve of strength. Still clinging to Mo, he attempted to get her away from the bank into deeper water. But within moments a mailed fist gripped his hair. A brutal strength was plunging him back under the surface. Gasping to surface from under the water, Alan saw the soldier's other hand reach to his submerged waist and extract a dagger. Alan's head was dragged clear of the surface – he reeled from the blow of the dagger's pommel. But even as he struggled to fight unconsciousness, the soldier's own head parted company with his body and fell, trailing blood, spinning and dancing into the current before Alan's failing vision.

Struggling to find his legs, Alan's hand never relinquished his hold on Mo. Bloodied, exhausted, his head still reeling from the blow of the dagger's pommel, he lifted her face once more above the surface.

They were tumbling over a mill-race of smaller boulders, descending through the jarring impacts into a white-frothed basin. His body was numb. For a moment or two, he thought he was suffocating again, his face below the deluge. Then, suddenly, the storm was over. The water, beyond the cauldron of mist and spume, was fast-running, but there were no longer any rocks.

He felt the weight of his burden increase and realised that his feet were touching the bottom of the river. He willed his exhausted legs to stagger towards the bank, though his numbed feet could barely register the hard surface beneath him.

Shoving Mo out of the water onto a gravelly shelf by the river's edge, he was too weary to climb out himself. He remained submerged up to chest level, holding on to the shelf, which sloped gently up to the forest floor. His ears were filled by the sounds of continuing attack. His vision caught the flickering green light of the Storm Wolves' weaponry. In moments mailed arms grabbed hold of him and he was dragged out of the water and onto the sloping shingle. A sharp crack at the back of his head was followed by darkness.

Captured

When Alan recovered consciousness, Mo was gone. The Storm Wolves must have dragged her away. Breathless and bewildered, he was aware of hoarse shouts and curses from nearby.

Those guttural commands, accompanied by jabs of weapons and kicks, were coming from faces hidden behind fur-covered masks that made the Storm Wolves seem more animal than human. Their helmets were constructed of a metal alloy that resembled matte steel. Black bearskin surcoats covered their trunks and limbs over chainmail bodices of the same black alloy. Their black-booted feet were also fur-wrapped, and their hands were protected by leathery mittens that seemed extensions of the fur tunic, designed for combat in the extreme cold.

Rescuing Mo had exhausted him so he couldn't resist them as they dragged him up the bank of gravel. At the top, they beat him again until he was almost unconscious.

As he fell onto his hands and knees, he caught their derogatory reference to him, 'beardless cur'.

A single thought remained, and that was Mo. Where was she? Where had they taken her?

A group of Storm Wolves came running back out of the trees. They carried two sinewy poles, covered by bark. Ripping off his Olhyiu surcoat and boots, they made a cross by tying together the springy poles at their centres and bending each pole into a bow, then lashed his wrists and ankles to their extremities with leather thongs. The effect was to stretch all four of his limbs on a rack, the tension in the bowed poles tearing at every joint in his body. A gag of filthy leather was rammed between his teeth before they threw him, face upwards, onto the trampled snow and shingle.

A huge soldier – the legionary rank of a centurion entered Alan's mind – leaned over him to test his bonds. The fur-mittened hands also carried sharp metal spikes, sharpened to claws at the finger tips, so the probing left him scratched and bleeding. The pain in his joints was agonising. As minutes passed, the pain grew steadily worse. It made it almost impossible for Alan to think. Yet he had to try to think clearly. He had to focus his mind on the fact that some kind of battle was taking place nearby. Who was fighting the Storm Wolves? Had the Olhyiu stopped and come out onto the banks to fight? If they had, they would surely be beaten in hand-to-hand fighting with these professional killers. And what then would happen to Kate?

Alan couldn't bear to think of them harming Kate.

If he could just focus on that, on the sounds of battle; if he could sense through the triangle in his brow what was happening and where.

Fight against it! Use the pain!

He heard the calm contralto voice again in his head – surely some kind of communication, mind-to-mind. But who was attempting to communicate with him? Alan concentrated on his tormented joints, accepting the agony, bringing it into focus in his mind.

Then, through the curtain of his pain, came the memory of that soldier's head falling into the water. A sword had done that. But the Olhyiu had no swords. Who could it be that was wielding that sword? Whoever it was, he must be part of some bigger group of fighters, an army of a different kind, and that army was fighting the Storm Wolves in this battle that raged around him.

He heard the sounds of heavy feet approaching, then six or seven Storm Wolves burst out of the undergrowth to join the group holding him prisoner. One was carrying a body over one of his shoulders, and now he cast it down like a sack of firewood onto the trampled snow next to him. Alan struggled to see who his fellow prisoner might be, hoping it was Mo.

'Snakoil Kawkaw!' he hissed, inside his gag.

It was with difficulty that he recognised the Olhyiu traitor. Kawkaw's weasel-thin face was bloodied and swollen. His grey-furred neck was encircled by a leather thong, tethered to his shackled feet so it arched his body backwards. Alan assumed that Kawkaw's overlords had punished him for leading them into the trap on the ice-bound lake. Even now, the guard who had thrown Kawkaw onto the frozen ground gave his body a bone-crunching kick. Alan heard the slobbering sound that came from the traitor's split lips.

'Kawkaw!' he hissed again, trying to force some sort of communication through the triangle.

The shock of hearing his name caused the figure to stop moaning. He twisted his neck in Alan's direction, his eyes wildly staring.

'Huloima!' Even in his mind the evil man snarled. 'How is it I hear you in my mind? Are you a demon?'

Alan shook his head, and his eyes turned upwards, towards his brow, where the triangle must be visibly pulsating, judging from the throbbing he felt.

Kawkaw jerked his eyes to the triangle. A cough sounded deep in his throat, and his tongue forced a gobbet of blood from his lips. His senses, from what Alan could make of them through the triangle, were overwhelmed with fear – yet still he was full of the spite and cunning of old. As if fallen back upon the very dregs of his soul, hatred had become an inspiration for this depraved creature. And in the traitor's mind Alan confirmed the fate that lay in store for them both.

They were to be ritually sacrificed.

Torture and death was the way of life in the brutal existence of these legionaries. Cruelty was their pleasure, the reward they coveted for their work of oppression and killing.

The centurion had returned. Kawkaw knocked his foot against Alan to make him aware of something, though he couldn't read what it was on that face, contorted as it was with pain.

He spoke to Kawkaw through the triangle, 'What is it? What are you trying to say?'

'I am accursed,' he wheedled, 'a renegade from my own kind.'

'Through your own greed and betrayal!'

'So it may be. Yet I spit upon it!' That ravaged face twisted into a snarl again as he twisted around his constrained neck, so he was squinting at Alan from the corners of his eyes. 'Siam, the stupid! Who could make such a man leader in place of me? I had the guile of a true leader. As to that shambling hogsturd, Lapeep! What shaman would shackle the soul of his people into such servility and bondage? If I betrayed them, it was out of contempt because they had betrayed themselves. What was left for me but to gather the crumbs before even they were taken from them?'

One of the guards noticed the looks they were exchanging and he ran at Alan and kicked him viciously in the ribs. The pain, when he was forced to breathe, was agony. It was several minutes before he could focus his thoughts. He kept his head averted from Kawkaw as he attempted communication again.

'What are they waiting for?'

'The service of their god.' Kawkaw's lips parted in a broken cackle.

Alan glimpsed horrible scenes in the memories lodged in Kawkaw's mind. The traitor had seen the Storm Wolves at play.

'What god?'

'The slime of offal that is their leader.'

This made Alan forget his caution of just moments before. 'Help me, Kawkaw. Now you have a chance for redemption – atonement!'

Hatred contorted the face of the traitor, even the muscles of his neck. 'I shit on your atonement. Those miserable rabble who thought themselves my people! Ah but I relish their doom, as they forced my own upon me. Hah! These abominations of flesh-spoilers will exterminate them, just as they will see you and me off, and soon enough, this I promise you. But I don't give a damn that they will kill me. I have had enough of suffering. But you – if you can but live – might be the tool of my vengeance on these abominations.'

Alan wasn't so stupid he couldn't see the calculating intelligence in Kawkaw's mind. 'But how? When I'm as doomed as you are!'

'Hearken to the battle! Who do you think attacks these

excremental scum with such deadly earnest? Not those fish-gutters.'

Alan did his best to probe what Kawkaw was talking about. He had to force his mind to think against the agony in his limbs. 'Who, then?'

'Those self-abasing witches!'

Witches? In Kawkaw's mind the derogatory term was accompanied by a vision of fierce-looking women. But there was no time to question him about this because the centurion was back. He stamped down hard on the crossed poles, causing a new agony to rack Alan's spine. Then, abruptly, Alan found an unexpected respite. Kawkaw kicked out with all of the strength of both tethered feet at the crutch of their tormentor. In spite of the tightening this caused in the leather noose around his own throat, the Olhyiu was distracting attention from Alan to himself.

Kawkaw's diversion saved Alan further torment. But he had no time to feel gratitude. He needed that moment to return to his previous thought.

The fierce women that Kawkaw called witches – who were they? In Kawkaw's mind they clearly evoked fear. Could it have been one of their weapons that had decapitated the Storm Wolf while Alan was being forced under the icy water? The calm contralto voice that had made contact during his struggle in the river . . .

Swim!

That communication had been authoritative. Think, he urged himself through the distraction of his pain – *think!*

It had not been a voice. Or, rather, the authority who spoke it had known how to communicate mind-to-mind. Somebody who understood the triangle in his brow? Yet it had been a female voice, of that he was sure, a very deep and calm female voice, and definitely not the voice of Granny Dew. If this female warrior was still nearby, there was a chance he could communicate back with her. Alan didn't waste any more time. The call burst from his tormented mind, cutting through the surrounding shadows of forest.

In that same moment a scream from Kawkaw brought him back to the reality of his position.

With horror he watched the centurion tighten the noose about Kawkaw's throat as he writhed on the ground. The other legionaries gathered to enjoy the spectacle. Kawkaw's face went purple and his nose began to bleed, yet still his eyes stared with a savage intensity in Alan's direction, and his thoughts were still focused on him.

'Beware . . . Isscan.' His words came in gasps. 'If you but live . . . beware the treachery of the flesh-spoilers.'

A Storm Wolf grabbed hold of Alan's hair to lift his face and inspect the triangle. He read his mind: more curses, declaiming the sorcery of witches. Through a new storm of pain in his spine and limbs, Alan kept his concentration on what was happening to Kawkaw. Two soldiers had taken hold of the traitor's upper arms, while two more brought up a leash of the Leloo that pulled their sleds. Seen from close quarters, the beasts were even more dreadful than

Alan remembered, with jaws slavering at the prospect of blood. The centurion shoved Kawkaw's face into the snow to restore full consciousness. Urgently, Alan projected his thoughts, 'I will tell your people of your final courage, if I survive to meet them again!'

'Spare me . . . such sentimental slobbering!'

'Tell me – what have they done with the girl?'

For a long moment, as they forced the spitting and snarling man into a kneeling posture, there was no reply in Kawkaw's mind. But hatred so dominated the soul of the traitor that it revived in him the dregs of a final defiance. 'Nature's abominations . . . Ah, such pain!' Two of the legionaries had cut his bonds and were stretching out his arms to the right and left of him, forcing his head forward so it was no more than a foot above the frozen ground. The centurion braced his legs wide to steady himself as he wielded his sword.

Even then the traitor's eyes squirmed Alan's way, to snarl, 'The girl . . . They fear her . . . Dare not kill her . . . Sorceress!'

Those were Kawkaw's last conscious thoughts as the centurion brought the blade down, not upon his neck but upon his right arm, cleaving it midway between the elbow and the wrist. Arterial blood spurted out over the snow.

The legionaries threw back their heads and howled, in a ritual parody of the wolves their company was named after. Then the snarling beasts were unleashed, taking up the howling from their masters as they fought one another over the bloodied hand and lower arm.

Disgusted, Alan turned his attentions away and used what force was left in the triangle to probe the surrounding forest. Horrifying as the spectacle he had just witnessed appeared, his concern was not for the traitor, Kawkaw, but all the more for his friend Mo, who was also a prisoner of these same brutal soldiers. Along the river, northward, he picked up the cries and the fury of battle, but there was no impression of anybody responding to his earlier call for help. The respite was brief. Kawkaw's stump of arm was bound with a thong, presumably just to keep him alive for more torture. Now it appeared to be Alan's turn. The legionaries dragged him across the blood-spattered snow until he lay stretched out in the centre of the small clearing. One of them pulled his head back to expose his neck. The circle of helmeted heads gathered about him, eyes closed as they intoned some propitiation of their foul god and leader. The centurion lifted his sword, still scarlet with Kawkaw's blood.

But the strike was averted as a new figure materialised from the shadows close by Alan.

The newcomer lifted his hand to stay the centurion. Alan squinted up at a small man with a pock-marked face under a black cowl, a face so emaciated it resembled a skull, and from which two sunken eyes now examined him. Alan could smell rank breath as the man bent close enough to inspect the triangle. Curiosity, and even a little fear, contorted those emaciated features as from his side he slipped out a dagger with a matt-black blade. Alan sensed power emanating from the blade, which wasn't straight like a normal dagger but rather twisted into a spiral, like the coil of a serpent, to end in a needle-sharp tip.

A ritual weapon.

From the common minds of the Storm Wolves he also sensed a fearful respect for the emaciated man: they called him 'Preceptor'.

The Preceptor laid the dagger over the fingers of his outstretched hands, holding it out lovingly before him, then bringing it to his lips, so he could kiss its handle in prayer. Alan caught a glimpse of something silvery embossed into the handle. Then his heart faltered. It was a triple infinity. He recognised the sigil Mark had described on Grimstone's dagger, the same sigil he had seen for himself on the helm of Feimhin's sword entombed in Padraig's woods . . . the blade on which the insects had burned. And now, as the Preceptor gripped the handle in both his hands and turned its point so it was touching the triangle in Alan's brow, his heartbeat weakened to an irregular spidery pattering. It felt as if his life energy was leaking away from him through the triangle. The will of that cowled figure was so powerful that Alan felt closer to drowning in its darkness than he had felt in the turmoil of the river.

He had come to this world in anger. And now a final

spurt of that anger rose in him. It took a firm hold within his spirit. The force of it struck back from the triangle against the Preceptor's blade. The thin man was taken by surprise, thrown backwards onto the bloodied ground.

But the Preceptor was too powerful to be more than temporarily overcome by this small show of resistance.

With a hiss, he urged the encircling Storm Wolves closer. 'This one is dangerous. Kill him immediately. I want his head and the bauble on it!'

As if from a disembodied distance, Alan felt his head drawn back once more to expose his neck. The howling began again as the legionaries celebrated their lust for blood. In those same few moments, through the flaring triangle, Alan sensed other minds closing in on them from the surrounding trees. He sensed the feral instincts of born hunters, moving too stealthily and quickly for his confused mind to follow. Through the ruby on his brow he heard another mind communicate an order: *Blood-rage!*

Immensely powerful, the order radiated from that single focus, as, from the shadows, Alan sensed how the same mind was now focused on the centurion, with his sword arm rising. Through the triangle, Alan saw how, in the glare of the watching eyes, the figure of the centurion was haloed in blood-red.

As if sensing his own danger, the centurion whirled, his sword arm still rising. In that same instant Alan felt the blood-rage turn to fury. It was lightning quick – far quicker than he recalled of Siam. He sensed a huge body contract, as if timing the precise moment to spring, then the whip-like arc of that streamlined shape, the shriek of contact and the quick snap of fangs and rip of claws that ended combat so quickly the attacker was gone before the fountain of gore was spent. Even before the clawed feet had retouched the ground, the blood-rage had already focused on another red-haloed figure. Alan's head jerked back with fright at the terrifying nature of the combat and the grisly sound that had accompanied the snap of jaws.

Shackled by the crucifixion of his limbs, all he could do was swing his head from side to side in an attempt to see what was happening.

His breath caught in fits and starts as the deadly warfare ebbed and flowed around him, the blurs of movement that were all he could make out of the attack of . . . of what? Through the triangle, the sensations of hunting and attack were too strange and inchoate to remain focused on them for more than seconds. The guttural shouting of Storm Wolves was quickly submerged under a rising thunder of snarls and roars.

By degrees, Alan sensed how the attack on the Storm Wolves was precisely coordinated. A single focus of power controlled the attack, a single mind, yet a mind that seemed to be accompanied by a feral soul spirit guided by instinct, much as he had sensed with Siam at the ice-bound lake, but a mind and soul spirit far more intelligent and deadly than Siam's. From that focus, instructions swept over the battleground, fusing spirit with purpose, and translating to a deliberate and controlled fury and annihilation.

Then, abruptly, he had his first clear vision of that focus. His heartbeat quickened, in a moment rising into his throat.

A massive snow tigress emerged into the clearing. With a swirl of her head, two implacable blue eyes gazed at his bound and trapped figure, and blinked; then she was gone, returning to her command of a hunting party of great cats that pursued the Storm Wolves among the trees.

Shit, shit – sheeeeee-it!

Sweat drenched Alan's face. His breath caught in his throat. His limbs writhed in a useless effort to break his bonds and his skin contracted with fright as, in a continuing ballet of death, these furies took control of the clearing, panting steam through slavering jaws, great heads swivelling through wide arcs, dilated nostrils scenting the air.

With wild eyes, the Preceptor rose out of concealment and stabbed with his twisted blade at the eyes of the leading tigress, but she evaded the weapon with a toss of a great head with a crystal embedded in its brow. A flash of power from the crystal threw the Preceptor high into the air, his snarling figure smashed back into the undergrowth.

Within minutes the battle was over. Slender dark-skinned women were appearing out of the trees, organising the aftermath with urgent whispers. They carried clothing and armour to clothe the gigantic figures who were manifesting, like liberated souls, among the shadows of the trees. Alan clenched his eyes shut with shock. The great cats were the soul spirits of . . . of some kind of warrior women.

He shouted with pain as he was lifted from the ground, his limbs cut free, then assisted in standing by the attendant women. He found himself in a circle of dead legionaries and Leloo, their carcasses still oozing blood into the snow. Kawkaw was the only other survivor within the clearing, although he appeared to be unconscious. Alan ignored him, grinding his teeth at the agony of release in his joints and ligaments. He felt shattered, mentally and physically, and the sense of intense cold was returning to his skin. But he had no inclination to feel sorry for himself.

Mo was still missing.

With an effort of will, he lifted his head to confront the gaze of a statuesque, bronze-skinned woman who was studying him with luminous eyes the speckled brown of tortoiseshell. He had no idea who she was, or what army she represented. But he was in no doubt as to what was needed, and needed urgently. He spoke with a voice croaky with exhaustion and pain:

'I need your help to find my friend!'

The Shee

'Save your strength!' The woman waved to one of her companions, who took a fur-lined greatcoat from one of the dead Storm Wolves and wrapped it around Alan's shoulders. Then, with the help of one of the others, she offered him a turquoise flask containing a honey-coloured elixir.

'This is healwell, from the Guhttan Mountains, the homeland of the Shee.'

'The Shee?'

'Those who saved you.'

For a moment his eyes darted about the clearing, contemplating the slaughter, the tall female warriors now encircled by ministering smaller women.

'Drink!' she urged him. 'Take no more than a sip. It will help you to recover your strength.'

He coughed, wincing with pain where the legionary had kicked his ribs. He murmured, 'Oh, man!'

Then he took a sip from the flask. The elixir was as thick as syrup and it burnt his mouth, like his grandfather's poteen. But it worked. It dimmed his pain so quickly it must have entered his blood through the lining of his mouth and throat. His strength improved and the pain lessened in his limbs. He felt a little better able to think about what he had just witnessed.

A rhythmic chanting began in the distance, somewhere behind the line of trees. It sounded like a much larger force of Storm Wolves, raising the hackles on his neck. Glancing past the woman, he eyed her astonishing companions. None other than this woman had spoken a word to him.

'Who are you?' He turned back to address the bronze-skinned woman, his voice still weak but now with much less pain.

'Forgive me. I am failing in my duties as diplomat.' She allowed him a second sip of the honey-coloured elixir before taking it back and passing it to one of the assistants. Then, after closely inspecting the triangle in his brow, she bowed deeply before him.

'You are the Mage Lord, Alan Duval?'

Alan stared at her in confusion.

The woman's words implied a familiarity with his name that he didn't understand. The tall figures standing in the background were now clothed with long capes that appeared to offer them some camouflage. Through the triangle he sensed a vision that still shocked him. Unlike

Siam, where the bear soul spirit had been embryonic, the great cat soul spirit crouched immediately beneath the surface of these tall female warriors. It was an integral part of them, as if the two beings existed as one in the same person. He saw swords now being fitted to their belts by the smaller ministering women.

Great cats turning into women, armed with swords!

He realised that the spokeswoman was studying him closely. Her voice had become urgent, impatient.

'We have come in haste to meet you. Permit me to introduce myself and my company.' She stood self-consciously erect. 'My name is Milish Essyne Xhosa. My matrilineage is that of a Princess of Laàsa. I was until recently a stateswoman of the Council-in-Exile. But need demands honesty between us. No council edict has sanctioned our coming here. Yet still you might regard me as an ambassador for my world.'

Alan sighed. 'Hey, look!' He still winced with pain from the bruised ribs. 'I don't understand a word of what you're saying to me.'

Desperate as he was to rescue Mo, he realised that a few minutes of composure would be more likely to help her than going out on a reckless hunt on his own. Somehow he had to enlist the help of these powerful women and, to do that, he needed to understand them. He inspected Milish, who, even without her headdress, must have been six feet tall. Her face was haughty, perfectly proportioned even to the deep shadows below the high cheekbones. His eyes darted past her once again, drawn with open incredulity to the armed women watching him from the background.

'My companions are bred for war since ancient times. The others are their helpers, known as Aides.' She bowed in the direction of her taller companion. 'Ainé bears the Oraculum of Bree upon her brow. It is the mark of Kyra – the hereditary leadership among the Shee.'

Alan studied the ferocious-looking woman called Ainé. Her hair extended, in luxuriant tufts of sideburns the colour of ivory, down the sides of her down-covered face to the angles of her jaws, and there were symmetrical markings, like large brown freckles, over her brow. There was a scar, like a sword cut, running from her left brow down onto her cheek. Her eyes were the same eyes he had seen in the snow tigress – huge and a glacial blue. There was a rippling strength in her broad arms and shoulders. Her facial markings resembled Maori war-tattoos, but the thick brown marbling that followed the centre of her brow in two widening tracks, with stripes like broad ribs moving out to either side and dappling down over her cheeks to fuse with the luxuriant sideburns, was as natural as the decorations on the wings of a butterfly. He saw a puckering of scar tissue in the centre of her forehead, broken veins about a flat oval of glistening crystal that was embedded there, like his own ruby triangle – what the stateswoman, Milish, had called 'the Oraculum of Bree'.

There could be no doubting that this giantess, Ainé,

had been the fulcrum of command during the battle action, and that her soul spirit had been the snow tigress that had thrown off the Preceptor. Inspecting the crystal in her brow more closely, it looked as if a wafer of jade, perhaps an inch long by two-thirds of an inch across, had been welded to her skull. Its surface was as smooth as a pearl's, yet deep within its surface he saw a constantly changing patterning that pulsated and changed, like silk held at a constantly varying angle to the light.

'The Kyra's companions are Muîrne, the teacher, and, by her side the warrior-in-noviciate, Valéra. If you cheat death on the road that lies before you, this will be your debt to them.'

Although there were other Shee present, Milish did not trouble herself to name them. Alan turned from Milish to speak urgently to the Kyra, Ainé. 'There was a girl with me. Her name is Maureen – Mo. The Storm Wolves have taken her. We have to save her.'

The Kyra met his gaze. She was astonishingly tall, at least seven feet, with thick fair hair coiled into a braid and fastened over her left shoulder with a plain silver pin. But there was nothing romantic about her: she looked more like a bloodied survivor from countless battles. 'Why risk many lives to save one girl?'

He recognised that deep, authoritative voice. It was the same voice that had called out to him in the river.

She took a step closer, grasping the hilt of the sword that dangled from her belt. 'A cloud of blood hangs over the province of Ulisswe. Word has spread of the arrival of the Mage Lord Alan Duval, the Redeemer of the Olhyiu, bearing the Oraculum of the First Power of the Holy Trídédana on his brow. And now we see that the rumour is true. The hearts and souls of the oppressed have been set aflame. Already new rumours are spreading of the destruction of a platoon of Storm Wolves in the icy north. Such hopes have been stirred even more by the flight of the Temple Ship, its new master heading south to confront the Council-in-Exile at Carfon.'

Redeemer of the Olhyiu! The Oraculum of the First Power of the Holy Trídédana . . . Alan's hand reached, instinctively, to the ruby triangle embedded in his brow.

Was that what the old woman had really done to him – embedded an oraculum of power in his head? And how had word spread about him – or for that matter the killing of the Storm Wolves around the lake? He shook his head, desperate for explanations, yet aware that it just wasn't the right time.

'We have to save my friend.'

'Tell me why we should save one girl when the armies of the Death Legion have taken to war. They are fanning out over all the occupied lands. Rebellion is in the air. Many villages and towns are in open insurrection. It was this rumour of the Mage Lord that led us to you. It is also the reason why so few of the Storm Wolves could be diverted to this ambush. The Shee are moving eastward from the Guhttan Mountains in such numbers as have not been seen since the fall of Ossierel, though they are too distant yet to assist us.'

'Mo isn't Olhyiu. Four of us were brought here from another world. If I'm important, then so is she.'

The Kyra reared back in astonishment and Milish joined her in confronting Alan. But he had no time to waste in argument. 'There's a thin man among the Storm Wolves, armed with a twist-bladed dagger. They call him Preceptor. If we find him, maybe we'll find Mo.'

Milish whirled to gaze eye-to-eye with the Kyra. No words were exchanged between them but Alan glimpsed a more intense flickering in the patterns of the Kyra's oraculum. Then, in a blur of camouflaged movement, the Kyra was gone. Milish also melted away, as if under a cloak of invisibility, into the surrounding forest. Meanwhile the remaining Shee formed a guard around him. They included the novice, Valéra, who had amber eyes and golden blonde hair fastened with a silver pin, and Muîrne, the smallest and sleekest of them, who had creamy white hair that contrasted with eyes as grey as granite. Like Ainé, Valéra conveyed the soul spirit and strength of a tigress, while in Muîrne Alan sensed a soul spirit more akin to the speed and cunning of a snow leopard.

Under Valéra's direction, the Shee led him through the trees. Their movements were lithely graceful for such large and weapon-encumbered women. Under their camouflage cloaks, which fell almost to the ground, they wore loose-fitting trousers of olive green cotton, tied at mid-calf over the cross-lacing of leggings, and above boots made from the same material as the cloaks. Their downy arms were tattooed with fantastic imagery of animals.

In the gaps between the foliage, Alan saw that it was late in the day, with no more than a couple of hours of daylight left.

They emerged onto a sandy beach upriver of where Alan had been dragged ashore, and here he saw several long canoes that had been beached in a hurry. These, he assumed, were the vessels that had carried the Shee into the battle zone. They were powerful craft, adzed from whole trunks of cedar, their prows uplifted six feet out of the water, and Y-shaped in their end sections. Sleek in design, they contained packs that Alan guessed must belong to the assistants they called Aides, but the lead canoe also contained a trunk of polished ebony, inlaid with silver, which looked so ornate it had to belong to Milish.

Alan could find no trace of the Olhyiu boats, including the Temple Ship. He hoped that the bulk of them had escaped from the trap – and Kate too. He didn't want to have to worry about Kate as well as Mo.

Above the sand, a series of tracks led away into the forest. The Shee led him among the trees, away from the river and in a new direction, until they arrived at a clearing that looked as if it had served the main body of Storm Wolves as an encampment. Here, what appeared to be several dozen Shee, led by Ainé, had spread out to encircle a force of about sixty Storm Wolves, who had assumed a close-knit circular battle formation.

Milish appeared by his side, her voice sounding weary. 'These will prove difficult to defeat. They are the Chosen, from the fighting arenas of Ghork Mega.'

Peering about the clearing, Alan could see no sign of Mo. Then a new chanting began. It was the Shee who were chanting now, a deep-throated battle-hymn, then, suddenly, as if goaded into fighting, the ranks of Storm Wolves appeared to dissolve, the legionaries already among the encircling Shee in a fury of hand-to-hand combat.

Alan had never seen hand-to-hand fighting move with such speed. It seemed that the Shee could fight ferociously in human or animal form. He saw the flashing green of their sword blades, eerily luminescent. But the battle was far from one-sided. Ainé's reluctance to divert her forces for one missing girl now made sense, for these Storm Wolves fought back with a maniacal passion, glad, it seemed, of this opportunity of killing Shee. Alan saw several Shee stagger and fall, the movement of the legionaries' blades so deadly it happened in a blur. Suddenly, with the same lightning change as had begun the fighting, the surviving legionaries fell back into their common defensive formation and the Shee closed ranks to complete the encirclement.

Alan studied the shields of the Storm Wolves. They were long and rectangular, decorated with the same symbol he had seen on the handle of the Preceptor's dagger, a triple-looped infinity. He also noticed that the shields were curved in their transverse section, so they slotted together along their long sides to form an interlocking wall. Others carried their shields aloft, creating a defensive dome. Even from this distance, he sensed the same darkness that had recently enveloped him. The Preceptor had to be among them.

'Ask the Shee if they have seen anything of a girl, Milish.'

Word came back that several Shee had glimpsed a small bound captive among the legionaries, but that the head was covered in a sack. 'It's got to be Mo,' he muttered, with a surge of hope. 'That has to be the reason they are being so defensive. And the Preceptor is there. I can sense his presence.'

The soldiers were performing another coordinated battle strategy, with a harsh, guttural chanting.

A filthy looking smoke curled from the fissures between the shields and then coalesced over them, to envelop the shield-wall, as if welding them together in a power-charged unity. The calculation involved in this strange warfare, the rhythms and formalities of it, appeared important. The Shee were passing items from one woman to another. Alan glimpsed a jade-green glow, like the colour of Ainé's oraculum. It looked as if they were charging the points of arrows and the blades of swords, using crystals that were carried by each of the women. For several minutes nothing happened other than a repeat of the ritualistic chanting. Yet the Shee were tensing as if with a tangible expectancy. Then sporadic fire, with long plumes of white smoke, broke out of the shell of shields, and with the erratic volley the Shee became a blur of movement, dodging the smoking trails.

The smoking missiles streaked through the air, trailing a putrescent green glow. Alan remembered the green fire during the attack at the frozen lake and more recently in the attack on the river. There was that same stink coming from the burning missiles, a vile sulphurous smell.

With a groan, one of the Shee was hit. In a final act of defiance, she hurled her sword into the glistening force of the shield wall, but it fell where it struck, incapable of penetration. Alan saw that there was something crawling over the sword. It appeared to be a living growth of some sort, a glistening contagion that proliferated as it spread, as if attempting to devour the metal it came into contact with. Even the fallen giantess was being consumed by the same living poison of the legionaries' weapon. It invaded every organ and tissue with horrible speed and malignancy. Within minutes, he saw that the charnel-green was glowing inside the dead warrior's eyes.

'What's happening, Milish? Why will nothing get through their shields?'

'Such is the power of their malengin.'

A malengin? Studying the shield wall he noticed its resemblance to a glassy prism, in the way it reflected light in a rainbow sheen.

'Quickly, Milish – explain this malengin.'

'The Tyrant uses the enslaved people of the Daemos to plunder the Wastelands and thus find the malignancy that exists in the dark side of nature. The Preceptor among them has the power to project it thus.'

Even as he was considering her words, a glowing fragment hissed between him and Milish, setting fire to the tree behind them and showering them with malodorous smoke. It forced them back, coughing, their eyes watering. 'If this continues, Milish, the Shee will be defeated.'

'If they die, they will die with honour.'

Wheeling around, he addressed Ainé directly. 'If I can breach the malengin, can you attack through the breach while still keeping the girl alive?' In moments, he found himself explaining his idea under the questioning gazes of both Ainé and Milish.

Alan knelt down by the smouldering remains of the dead Shee while Milish and Ainé stood back, repulsed by the sight and charnel stench of the brightly glowing corruption that still devoured her flesh.

He shook his head. 'What I'm thinking is that, even if we don't understand their weapon, maybe we can turn it against them.'

'How?'

Alan climbed back onto his feet, his eyes meeting those of the Kyra. 'Can you find me a javelin – one with a good strong point?'

He was handed the javelin within moments and he spent a little while examining the tip. The head was made of no substance he was familiar with. It didn't look like iron, or copper, or bronze. It might have been some kind of amalgam of a metal and crystal – he really had no idea. He closed his eyes, focusing on the point through the oraculum.

He felt his imagination expand, sensing an additional ingredient, a spiritual force within the point. He assumed that this was the force linked to the jade-green glow he had seen passing between the Shee earlier, a force that must have been put there by the Kyra. He didn't need to remind himself of the urging of Granny Dew: not to question, but to see what needed to be done. He recalled the feeling he had had in the presence of the Preceptor, that had also felt like some kind of spiritual force, if one of a dark malignancy. What it all meant, he had no idea. Alan had begun to sweat with worry, and his voice was husky, knowing the risk of what he was proposing.

'I'm going to see if I can help you to penetrate the wall of force around their shields.'

In the dirt, he drew a dome, representing the shield wall. 'Here,' he declared, jabbing his finger at the apex, 'is its strongest point. But if I'm right, it could also be its greatest weakness. It's a bit like a keystone in an arch.'

Under the horrified eyes of Milish and Ainé, he twisted the tip of the javelin in the putrefying flesh of the dead Shee. Probing it again through the vision of the oraculum, he sensed a darker spiritual force that now inhabited the head of the lance. Then he focused his mind onto the tip of the lance head, moving slowly backwards along the two backwardly separating cutting edges, infusing into it every ounce of power he possessed.

But how could he be sure it wouldn't harm Mo? He had to pretend to be more confident than he really was. He turned to Ainé. 'Can you throw it so it strikes at the dead centre of the dome? Then have your Shee ready for an immediate attack.'

A few minutes later, he watched as Ainé bent her gigantic frame, then cast the javelin. He heard the faint screeching sound as it arced through the air, striking the centre of the dome of shields. He saw it explode on impact. A stellate web of brighter green spread over the shield wall. Then the Storm Wolves began to howl. The force of the impact disrupted the shield wall and penetrated further, to the arms steadying it from within. The dome burst asunder and the legionaries pitched and tumbled, in torment and panic, over a ground that was already proliferating with that slimy green poison.

Alan hadn't anticipated the violence of what he had conjured up. The Storm Wolves were throwing aside their own weapons, which had been invaded by the vile green poison. If Mo was in the centre of the battle group, she was in grave danger.

The attacking Shee darted skilfully among them, dispatching the enemy with a pitiless efficiency while searching for the captive child before the green contagion could spread to infect everybody. But all the while, the web of green was still spreading over the ground, subtly metamorphosing about its edges, as if the deadly force of the malengin was actively combining with the power Alan had infused into it. He picked his own careful way through the confusion of bodies. He saw many dead but he found no sign of the Preceptor or of Mo. The Shee were already leaving the battle zone in pursuit of the escaping soldiers, probing the encircling forest.

Milish helped Alan to continue his search, with fresh snow matting in individual large flakes in her hair.

'Over here!' It was Ainé's voice from some distance away, and Alan hurried towards her.

The Preceptor was still alive.

Without Ainé's cry, Alan's nostrils might have led him to him. The deathly luminescence leached into his skeletal features, causing him to shrink back for support against the bole of a great tree. Hate contorted his face as he clutched a small, bound figure, whose naked legs protruded from a filthy sack.

Desperately, Alan probed the bound figure, attempting to make contact mind-to-mind to reassure himself it really was Mo. But the mind inside the hood was as cloaked as the body. Meanwhile, the Preceptor's other hand pressed the black-bladed dagger against his victim's neck. A mist of green vapour exuded from his stinking flesh, and the foul glow was in his eyes. Dark blood trickled between his gritted teeth, dribbling down onto his captive's head as he clutched the bundle even more savagely against his chest. All the while those hate-filled eyes stared deeply into Alan's own, as if daring him to come and rescue her. The Preceptor's voice was rasping, his throat already partly consumed by the spreading plague.

'Witches obsequium! Chance has favoured you today but it will not long save you. Stand back! The merest prick of my blade and the insect-spawn dies in torment.'

Alan spoke grimly, urgently. 'Let her go and we'll end your suffering.'

The thin man cackled again. 'Decide then which death is dearer to you? Is it to be this brat's, or would you exchange your life for it?'

'No, Mage Lord!' Ainé laid a restraining hand on his arm. 'Beware the scheming nature of this creature. Though weakened, he retains malice beyond your comprehension.'

Alan wasn't sure what to do. He couldn't expose Mo to danger. But no more did he expect that the Preceptor would hold back until he died from his wounds, even though the spreading malignancy burned more fiercely by the moment in his tormented flesh. If only he could delay the dagger for seconds longer . . . 'How do I know you'll release the girl if I volunteer to take her place?'

'I have no concern to reassure you!' He paused, as if to savour the mere contemplation of it. 'I am the instrument of my master's will. For such an honour, I would sacrifice an infinite number of brats such as this.'

Alan used the triangle to probe the Preceptor's state of mind. Here he discovered no resemblance to the human envy and malice of Kawkaw. This was a mind perverted to darkness. And the brooding malevolence was not entirely spent. It attacked him back, still strong enough mind-to-mind to gain a fleeting hold over his will. Alan's limbs were stiffening again in that creeping paralysis. He knew that the dagger was extending towards his own throat. Waves of shock reeled through his mind. But even as the dagger lunged forward, he registered a furious movement at his side.

Faster it seemed than thought itself, he felt his body being pushed aside, and in that twinkling of time his mind was released.

'No!' Alan's shout was a second too late.

In that distracted moment, the Preceptor, with blade extended, was pulled violently backwards, his body rising up off the ground, pressed tight against the tree. Still the knuckles enclosing the black-bladed dagger were white with tension. The cackling voice still hissed with loathing.

'Infidel!'

Powerful arms encircled the Preceptor from behind. It was the golden-haired noviciate, Valéra, her arms long enough to encircle the entire bole of the tree and crush the throat of the Preceptor against the wood.

Alan had already grabbed Mo from the Preceptor's arm, pulling her back towards him, tearing at the sack that covered her head. But when he ripped it off he found it wasn't Mo at all. It wasn't even a girl, but some other sacrificial innocent, an Olhyiu boy, perhaps one of those who had been lost overboard in the rapids, and who now sagged, barely conscious, in Alan's arms.

Ainé had to stop him rushing at the creature. He could only watch with fury as a final sneer came over the marbled decay in the Preceptor's face, the eyes aglow with the green death, the poisoned blood dribbling between his bared teeth.

'Valéra!'

Protecting Alan had distracted the Kyra's attention, but now a cry rang from her lips. It was too late. Even as Valéra crushed the Preceptor's throat, the dagger was thrust backwards, burying its sinuous blade to the hilt in the young Shee's abdomen.

Mo's Secret

At times her mind wandered so that Mo could almost convince herself that it was just a nightmare, but then a sudden cramping pain in her feet wrenched her back to the terrifying reality of darkness and fear.

I'm buried alive in a pit in the ground.

She had screamed out Alan's name, again and again, searching for the communication mind-to-mind of the triangle in his brow, but he hadn't answered.

Alan was not going to come and rescue her.

The realisation that he would not be coming provoked such a giddy wave of panic she had to cast her mind wide again, to call out, hoping he would hear her and come for her. But there was no sign that he heard her, no answer except the pounding of her heartbeat. It must be night above the ground but she couldn't really tell because down here it was pitch dark all the time. The last thing she remembered was the thin man's face leering cruelly down at her from the small opening above her head before the soldiers had dragged a slab of stone over the pit, followed by noises that told her they were covering the stone with debris and snow, hiding her away so that nobody in the world would ever find her.

It made her remember the many times Grimstone had locked her in the dark cellar at home.

The first time she had been only three years old, and she had searched for a box to stand on so she could look for the light in the low ceiling. The bulb socket had been empty and her finger had gone up into it, throwing her through the air with an electric shock. At the memory, gooseflesh erupted over her skin. And such a wave of terror came over her that she closed her eyes tightly and dared not open them after that. This time it wasn't just a night in the cellar.

Why is this happening? What have I done to deserve it?

Mo recalled what had happened on the deck of the ship. How Mark had frightened her and Kate during the storm on the river. From the first moment of seeing him come out of the door, with his white face and tormented eyes, she had felt such an ominous feeling. In the past, when Grimstone had made her afraid, she had found strength inside her. Now she recalled what Alan had done to Siam at the ice-bound lake. He had awakened the soul spirit of the grizzly bear in Siam. She wondered if the part of her she had sometimes sensed, like a source of strength inside her, was her own soul spirit. Right there, on the lurching and heaving deck, she had sensed the wrongness of what was about to happen in that part of her – she had sensed it so strongly, so awesomely, that it was very hard to imagine that the dark would ever go away, as it always had in the past . . . that things would ever be all right again.

Make me strong! she begged the soul spirit inside her. *Tell me what to do!*

But even her soul spirit had no answer to her terror. No help came. There was only silence.

It felt like ages since the soldiers had put her down here in the pit, and all that time she had been unable to move. Her hands were tied behind her back with leather strips which dug painfully into her skin, and her ankles were tied together in much the same way. But most terrifying of all was the leather noose the thin man had pulled tight around her neck and attached to an iron ring above her head. That was the cruellest trick the thin man could imagine. He had forced her to balance on a narrow pole that crossed the pit below her feet, so that if she slipped off the pole the noose would choke her. Even when she was down in the pit Mo had heard his rasping murmur up above her, as he was praying to his Master – a horrible kind of prayer – just to make doubly sure that nobody in the world would ever know she was trapped down here. Only then had the soldiers put the stone on top so she was left balancing on the pole in utter darkness.

Her feet were already so swollen and sore that they

could hardly bear her weight, and her muscles were jerking and shivering in the effort to balance on the pole. And now her feet were cramping and hurting and her muscles were tired from having to stand all the time. And yet, if she slipped an inch . . .

'Oh Muh-Muh-Muh – *Mark!*'

Tears came to her eyes as she called out to her brother. She had seen how lost and frightened he had looked on the deck and, in spite of her terror, she wanted to reassure him that, whatever happened, she would die still loving him. But Mark couldn't hear her any more than Alan could. Nobody could hear her. Mark had changed since they had come into this strange and frightening world. Why had Mark changed like that? Why had he frightened her and Kate? Why, when she went to help Kate, had he pushed her away?

In her mind, she screamed all over again with fright when she remembered that bat creature, that wasn't really a bat but a . . . a kind of demon with wings, that had swooped out of the storm and caught her by the hair.

Alan – why can't you hear me?

She projected her thoughts in another wild, desperate search for the triangle in his brow, repeating his name over and over for what seemed a very long time, weeping his name with her imploring mind.

The cramping pain in her feet was becoming unbearable, and dizziness was filling her head in debilitating waves. Her legs began to judder and shake.

Soon, she knew, she would lose her balance. In final desperation she thought of the only person in this terrifying world who had ever seemed to care about her. She thought of Granny Dew. She called out her name inside her mind. In her soul spirit she wept and implored it, even as a new wave of dizziness invaded her head. Terror overcame her efforts at self-control, and she suddenly felt herself toppling. Then, just as everything seemed hopeless, she heard a growl, from way back, from so very far away, and she hoped it wasn't just the wishful thinking of her panicking mind.

Mo spoke, 'Is thuh-thuh-thuh-that you, Guh-Guh-Granny Duh-Duh . . . ?'

I am here, Little One.

From so far away, but coming closer – she found the will to hold on for just a few moments longer.

'Is it ruh-ruh-ruh-really yuh-yuh-you? I'm fuh-fuh-fuh-frightened it muh-muh-muh-might buh-be my i-muh-magination.'

Granny Dew knows where you are, precious one. Hold on, just a little longer.

'I duh-duh-duh-don't know if I cuh-cuh-can hold on. I'm nuh-nuh-nuh-not buh-brave enough.'

The bravest always doubt themselves.

Mo clenched her teeth. She clenched shut her eyes. She clenched tight every muscle in her neck, her back, her legs, but still she couldn't stop the wobbling of her whole body from her head to her feet. She knew she was about to fall off the pole. She was about to slip, and the noose would choke her.

'I cuh-cuh-cuh-cuh-can't . . .'

The wobbling became a shaking and jerking in her thighs. She couldn't stop it.

Hold on, little one!

Her legs no longer belonged to her. Her knees were giving way.

'Cuh-cuh-cuh-cuh . . .'

A moment longer . . .

She felt a movement through her hair, as if cobwebby fingers were stroking her brow. Then, suddenly, there was a scratching in the wall of the pit, close to her face, and she smelled as much as heard something small and furtive come out of the dirt – something, she imagined, that must look very much like a rat or a mole. She no longer felt alone.

'Whu-whu-whu-what . . .?'

A small mind that will gladly do my bidding. But first we must take care of your dizziness. Your breathing is poor and that's what is making you dizzy. There now – take a deep breath.

Mo took several deep breaths, one after another. Tears were pouring through her clenched eyelids and over her cheeks. She felt the little creature lick at her tears. Then it began to nibble and tear at the leather that bound her wrists. It seemed to take several fraught minutes before her hands broke free.

'Thuh-thuh-thuh-thank you!' She coughed to clear the tears that had run down her nose and into her mouth.

'Oh, thuh-thuh-thank you so muh-muh-muh-much!' She blinked her wet eyes open, but the darkness was still complete. 'I cuh-cuh-cuh-can't fuh-fuh-feel my feet.'

Patience, child.

Mo felt the little creature pulling at the thongs around her ankles, but the focus on her ankles made her wobble horribly and she nearly slipped. And the thong around her neck was too tight for her shaking hands to free.

Hah! We must think again. The Preceptor is wily – the nature of what confronts us is tricky indeed. Fate, it would appear, has set us a riddle.

'A ruh-ruh-ruh-ruh – ruh-riddle?'

What else? The Preceptor sensed that he dare not kill you directly. So he set you a trap in which a mistake on your part would result in your death. But he has warded the trap with danger. We must discover a subtle solution. Yet not too subtle for you, I imagine?

'Whuh-whuh-whuh – whuh-what sort of ruh-ruh-ruh-riddle?'

Perhaps we should make a game of it? Do you like to play games?

'Yuh–yuh-yuh-yes. I duh-do!'

Well now. Riddle-me-ree! But what is the answer, hmm?

> *In my case three into one will go*
> *But have a care if you test me so*
> *Need not greed should come to mind*
> *Or fate might choose to be unkind*

A cackle in the voice of Granny Dew: *What am I, child?*

Mo so loved riddles and had often played with them in her daydreams. She knew the answer straight away. 'Thuh-thuh-thuh . . . thuh-three wuh-wuh-wuh-wishes.'

Three wishes it is. But think carefully now! First wish?

Mo felt so pleased with herself that she nearly lost her balance again and she had to stop everything, even her thoughts, just to breathe in and out very slowly and regain her composure. She closed her eyes again, to concentrate with all of her might.

'I wuh-wuh-wuh-wish to get out of this puh-puh-puh . . . puh-puh-pit.'

This, sadly, I cannot grant. It is the nature of the ward the thin man has set for you. You must choose another.

Mo's heart, which had so rapidly risen, fell back into despair.

Think, child – as I know you capable!

'I wuh-wuh-wuh-wuh-wish to wuh-wuh-weigh . . . to wuh-weigh no muh-muh-muh-more than . . . than muh-muh-muh-my eyebrows.'

Then as eyebrows you are!

Mo felt herself float up off the pole so she was dangling from the noose around the neck, floating up and down, like a yo-yo. She felt so light that her feet no longer hurt at all and the tight noose became looser so she floated just an inch or two above the pole. With her freed hands, she loosened the noose and, after a struggle lasting a minute or so, slipped it off her neck. Immediately, she felt for the bog-oak talisman and breathed a sigh of relief to find it still dangling around her neck. She clutched it, fiercely, instinctively.

'Oh, thuh-thuh-thuh-thank you – a muh-muh-muh . . . a muh-million times, Guh-Guh-Granny Dew. Yuh-yuh-yuh . . . you're my fuh-fuh . . .'

Fairy godmother, I am not. A creature of the earth am I, and the earth of me.

'Thuh-thuh-thuh-then you ruh-ruh-ruh . . . ruh-ruh-really are the Earth Muh-Muh-Muh . . .?'

Not questions – only wishes. Two more wishes you are granted. But you must discover wisdom beyond your years. Dannngggerrrr beckons!

'I've stuh-stuh-stuh-stammered all muh-muh-my life. I duh-duh-don't want to stuh-stuh-stuh-stammer any muh-more.'

So, let it be!

Mo's heart leaped in her chest. Her mouth was so dry she had to moisten her lips with her tongue to speak. 'Whuh-whuh-when?'

When you discover your true name!

'Buh-buh-buh-buh-buh . . .'

Precious to you is the name your birth mother gave you, on a silver chain around your neck when you were abandoned.

'Muh-muh-muh-my real muh-muh-muh . . .?'

They hid your true name from you.

Outrage flared in Mo's mind. She forgot her desperate situation, so powerful was her need to know more about her real Australian mother. Was she dead? Did she really hate her baby daughter so much that she gave her to Grimstone and Bethal without a backwards glance?

'Whuh-whuh-whuh . . . whuh-why?'

Little one, there are reasons for secrets. Your real name has searched for you, and now it has found you. Mira is the name your real mother gave you. In her eyes your name ever brought a smile.

In spite of the terror that surrounded her, Mo smiled too, and it seemed that in that same moment the shy, stammering Mo was gone. Her fingers rose and touched her lips.

'Mira? My name is Mira?' Mo's heart leaped in her chest as she realised that she really had lost her stammer. 'I want to know so much. I want to know about my mother – and my father too. I want to know about my real parents.'

No questions for now! Such answers will find you in time. The truth, for the present, is dangerous.

'Oh, please?'

Your mother was herself a lost and bewildered soul. She died of sorrow when you were not yet one year old.

Mo's head dropped. 'My mother died?'

Yet still she loved you. You sensed it, child, even as you lay curled within her, how you were the fulcrum of her world – as one day, if fate is just, you will become the fulcrum of another.

'I don't understand you, Granny Dew. Only that you say that my mother is dead. Oh – I didn't want to hear that.'

Truth is pain.

'I knew she loved me. I always knew.'

Hush now. And remember this. Mira must not speak of this, not to a soul. A time will come when it is right to tell, and Mira will know it when that time comes. But not until the time is right can you speak your name. You will promise Granny Dew?

'Oh! Must I?'

The whisper became a guttural roar: *Dannngggerrr – child!*

Mo's head fell. 'Then, yes, I promise.'

All depends on your keeping that secret. Yet there is one more wish, and you must think very hard and make it the cleverest wish of all.

Above the pit Mo heard a scuffling noise. Somebody – or something – was scratching and scraping over the slab of stone.

'My third wish is that you care for me – that you never leave me. So I shall never be alone again.'

So be it!

Immediately, there was a rush of cold air and Mo looked up at the towering figure that was faintly outlined against the moonlight. Her heart faltered as she recognised that cunning and vicious face.

'Trust the guile of old Snakoil Kawkaw to know the tricks of those back-stabbing Storm Wolves! Eh! What say you, brat?'

The Sister Child

A fire of brushwood flickered by the head of the dying Valéra, as Ainé and Muîrne sat cross-legged on either side of their wounded companion, under a rough bower of pine branches. The remaining Shee had withdrawn to the forest, leaving these two to tend her through the night. The only concession to the presence of Milish was the acceptance of healwell from her hands, yet even this Muîrne insisted on administering herself in the privacy of the bower.

It had been snowing gently all night, and dawn of the following day broke with a leaden sky, heavy with foreboding.

During the intervals when Muîrne left the sickbed to fetch more brushwood, Alan caught glimpses of Ainé, her cloak covering her sagging shoulders, her great frame rocking slowly with the litany of her night-long lament.

His Olhyiu surcoat and fur-lined boots had been

recovered from the main encampment of the Storm Wolves and the Aides, which, as Alan had discovered, was pronounced Ay-des, and was the same term for one or many. He had dried these over a fire and resealed the leather with a rubbing of tallow and a thin, pine-scented oil, ready for wear. He was glad to have them back, since the cold, even several hours after dawn, was still extreme. The boy they had rescued slept more soundly than any of them, thanks to herbs administered by Milish, who came to join Alan by the fireside for a breakfast of bread and salted meat. She asked about his aching joints but, given Valéra's condition, he was in no mood to grumble about his own aches and pains. Then Milish made a signal, to hush any further discussion, before leading him away from the scene of tragedy.

'I still don't understand.' Alan shook his head at her as they were walking into the pine woods. 'Other Shee have died and there was less grieving over them. And Valéra's condition, surely you could do more to help her? You've got herbs, and I guess you also have knowledge too that might help her.'

'There is a deeper injury to Valéra than a mortal wound, even from the blade of a Preceptor.' The eyes of the Ambassador caught Alan's and he glimpsed there some special grief he didn't understand.

Alan couldn't help thinking about Mo, and the fact that they had been unable to find her. He couldn't bear to think of what those sadistic soldiers might have done to her. For all he knew, she might be dead by now. Milish had to shake his shoulder, to bring him back to full attention. They walked over the snow-dappled forest floor for another thirty yards or so, a time in which Alan studied Milish more closely.

Her hair was a lustrous blue-black, the long straight strands parted centrally over her forehead, swept down in careful arcs over her temples, with folds that hid the upper third of her big-lobed, fleshy ears, then swept back to be brought together and lifted above her head in a plume of silver filigree at least nine inches high. The plume was kept in place by a heavy clasp of that same antique silver. It was a beautiful creation, encircled at the base by bottle-green and copper-blue enamelwork of intertwined foliage and blossoms that extended halfway up the plume.

He spoke softly, reflectively. 'I can't see how you knew my name. You talked as if you were expecting me.'

'Mage Lord – all of Monisle has been expecting you and your companions for a generation.'

'Then maybe you can tell me why we're here. Why us? How come my friends and I were brought here?'

'Is it possible that you know nothing of the sacred honour that was entrusted to you? Are you not the chosen ones of the last High Architect of Ossierel, Ussha De Danaan – falsely scorned as the Great Blasphemer?'

Alan sighed with irritation. All he ever seemed to get in answer to his questions was more riddles. 'I don't understand anything of what you're telling me.'

Then, suddenly, Milish was embracing his head with passion. Her eyes roamed his features in what appeared to be wonderment.

'Oh, believe it, Alan Duval! There can be no mistaking the Oraculum of the First Power of the Holy Trídédana! The force of the land – of the very elements! It is true! You bear it on your brow. You, and the companions you speak of, are the hope of an entire world!'

He just shook his head in disbelief. There were so many questions he would have liked to ask Milish. But she escorted him onward, leading them further away from the scene of lamentation to emerge from the trees into the smaller battle arena, where the bodies of seven or eight Storm Wolves still lay in the scatter of their deaths, their spilled blood frozen to the snowy ground.

Only now did Alan remember to look for Kawkaw. He scanned the ground for his body but there was no sign of it. He did find the leather thongs that had bound the traitor but they were neatly cut, manoeuvred against the edge of one of many fallen swords. How likely was it that the hateful man, exhausted and maimed, would have survived the night in this bitter landscape?

Alan shook his head without knowing the answer. In the drama of Valéra's nightlong suffering he hadn't given a thought to Kawkaw, or to the Storm Wolves. But now he gazed at the horror of so much death. Some of their insignia, on epaulettes and over the right breast of the matt-black chest armour of the centurion, must signify military rank. On every helmet, hammered out of that same metal, he found the malevolent symbol of the triple infinity.

'What does this symbol mean, Milish?'

'It is the mark of the Tyrant. Every division of his army of occupation – aptly named the Death Legion – wears this accursed sign.'

Alan recalled how Kawkaw had talked about the Master, who appeared to be a god to the Storm Wolves.

'Look at them! Even in death they look fierce,' Milish spoke in wonder. 'The Tyrant does not permit children to be reared as any normal child might be, in a family or a village. The soldiers are culled as children from the Daemos.'

He asked, 'The Daemos?'

'The barbarous peoples who populate the Wastelands across the Eastern Ocean. Some say it wasn't always like this: that the Wastelands were once fertile and well governed. But the Tyrant spoiled that. Now his overlords harvest people as a breeder might select dogs – or wolves.'

'That's vile!'

Alan gazed over the carnage in silence. What kind of world was this? A world, it seemed, in which magic was accepted as normal and where forces, spiritual forces, whether for good or evil, openly played a part in people's lives. It had begun to snow again, in hard, dry flakes, as large as petals. There was a chill in the air that made him shiver.

'Why does the Tyrant do these monstrous things?'

'I lack the wisdom of a High Architect.' Milish's eyes returned his gaze. 'Yet it seems to me that in the wonder of existence there is dark and there is light. The impulse that attracts one spirit towards the light might lead another to a darker, more desperate path.' She hesitated, shook her head. 'Some say the Tyrant came from another world, as you do. If so, he has escaped the bonds of natural control. Has he not lived for several thousand years, and perhaps a great deal longer? Speak to Ainé if you wish to learn more of it. But choose your moment carefully, for the Kyra does not care to be reminded of her trials as a child in the great arena of Ghork Mega.'

'It's incredible.'

'Yet it is true that every advance in truth and understanding on Monisle has been opposed in war and despoliation by the Tyrant and his malice. Where the Council at Ossierel valued and treasured life, the Tyrant was ever bent on pillage and destruction. Soon every river in his land was polluted, and with that the very oceans they flowed into. Mountains of spoil grew where his slaves were made to tear elements from the earth. Not a forest was left standing, but the wood was hacked and burnt, always to fuel even more destruction until all that was left was a wasteland that covered an entire continent. Thus war between our peoples became inevitable. Mine is a world that, for all the history we know, has never known peace.'

Alan caught an inflection in her voice, a hint of an unasked question in her eyes, but it wasn't the right time to probe this. They had already begun to walk back to the fires when a young Aides came running.

'Come quickly – the Kyra is calling for you.'

They hurried back to the clearing, where Ainé stood outside the bower, her downcast face evidence enough of Valéra's condition.

'My sister-in-arms is dying,' she stated bluntly. Then, lifting her eyes to look directly into Alan's, she added tersely, 'I have tormented myself through wondering why you, a mere youth, should be granted the First Power of the holy Trídédana. Why so? Unless through a grace that I am not given to understand . . .' She checked herself, inhaled deeply. 'Yet in asking assistance of you, what I ask I dread, for it is anathema to my race.'

Then, her eyes sweeping across to the snow-encrusted bower, she continued, 'I know that it is beyond hope to save Valéra, but if only there were some power that might yet grant her peace by saving the immortality of her lineage!'

Alan turned in puzzlement to Milish, whose eyes opened wide in a deeply anxious and troubled face. He felt out of his depth. But still he murmured simply, 'Valéra took the wound that was intended for me.'

Ainé led him into the bower, where the overnight fire still burned. There was a strong smell of healwell and applied liniments. Valéra tossed in a stupor on her bed of rushes. Her golden blonde hair had been freed in a sweat-soaked halo about her face, and the amber eyes that had once smiled at him were now restless in their sunken orbits. A lean, wizened woman with leathery brown skin and white hair wiped sweat from the warrior-in-noviciate's face. Muîrne stood in the background, as if awaiting his arrival.

It was Muîrne rather than Ainé who now addressed him in a whisper. 'We saw how you destroyed the shield dome, turning their green malice back against the Storm Wolves. Here we face a malice even more vicious. The poison of a Preceptor's blade runs deep within her. If you cannot help us, the daughter-sister will be lost.'

Alan shook his head, looking at the Shee teacher. 'This crystal in my head – this oraculum, whatever power it is supposed to give me – I don't know if it has any kind of healing property.'

The Kyra shifted restlessly on her feet behind him. 'Rather than anticipate failure, will you use the oraculum to probe her wound? Then you will understand the nature of our despair.'

'Maybe Muîrne could help explain things to me so I get a better idea what you really want of me.'

The teacher instructed Alan to copy her in washing his hands in a bowl of herb-scented water. Then, gently, she lifted aside the packing cloths to show him Valéra's wound. It was to the right of her abdomen, low down, barely above the pubic bone. It was almost a foot long, ragged and livid about its edges. He had seen the black and twisted blade plunge to its hilt so he knew it had to be deep. Now the reek of gangrenous flesh made him gag.

'Feel it!'

'Aw, gee!' He gagged again. As soon as his fingers touched her skin, Valéra stiffened and moaned.

Alan spun aside, and could not stop himself retching. 'I . . . I don't know if I can go any further.'

Behind him the Kyra grew angry with him. 'Did you not admit mere moments ago that Valéra accepted the blade intended for you?'

The Aides woman stepped forward and put her hand on his arm. 'I am Layheas, skilled in herb lore and battle wounds. If the young Mage Lord will permit me, I will help him.'

Alan nodded his gratitude, breathing slowly and deeply through his open mouth.

He gazed down once again on that terrible wound, then, as gently as he could, he prised apart the edges, eliciting another tormented moan. He spoke to Layheas, whose eyes willed him on. 'I can't see into the wound. It's too narrow and dark. Do you want me to see what I can feel?'

Layheas nodded.

With his left hand Alan probed the flesh deep within the wound. The muscles, membranes, organs – everything within reach of the twisted blade had been ripped open. He had to pause so he could overcome a new wave of nausea.

Layheas nodded again, encouraging him.

'I'm going to feel a bit deeper.' Swallowing hard, he inserted his hand as far as the wrist. Suddenly he encountered the shock of the venom that had been implanted there. An intense pain froze his fingers. It gnawed deep into his bones. The shock made him stagger back, and shove his hand instinctively into the bowl of hot water. When he lifted it out again, his fingers had turned a livid purple.

'What the heck . . . ?'

Layheas grasped his hand with surprising strength and stopped the trembling so she could inspect the fingers. 'The blade of a Preceptor carries more than just a physical poison. It is infused with the malice of its Master. The Preceptor discharged the evil of his life force through that debased weapon before he died.'

Alan clenched his teeth against the agony that was already ascending into his wrist from the poisoned fingers. He tottered back against the bower wall, feeling the structure sway. With a heightened alertness, he heard a shuffling patter of snow falling from its disturbed branches. He saw the anguish on the faces of Muîrne and Ainé. Only Layheas had remained absolutely calm. 'The Mage Lord must use the oraculum.'

The Aides woman was right. But how could he relax his mind when his fingers were in such torment? *Don't think about your own pain*, he urged himself. *Think of Valéra – how she has suffered all through the night!* Forcing his fingers back into the wound, he pushed them deeper than before, as deep as they would go. Then a new shock of realisation entered his unprepared mind. He jerked his arm, blood-stained to halfway up the forearm, out of the wound.

'She's . . . she's pregnant!'

'Yes,' Ainé responded tersely. 'The warrior-in-noviciate carries her own sister-child.'

'I don't understand what's going on here.'

Muîrne's stone-grey eyes confronted his own. 'Is it not obvious? Surely it is the point of everything. Such is the focus of Valéra's torment and the grief that consumes us.'

Alan fell onto his knees and retched. Now he understood that the Preceptor's dagger-thrust had not been random.

Layheas took hold of his shoulder, a look of pleading in her eyes.

But he just couldn't take any more of this. Tearing himself free from the Aides' hand, he blundered out of the bower, running blindly into the snow. The bitter wind excoriated his skin, like a swarm of stinging wasps. Hunching forward against the elements, he called out, with great urgency, 'Granny Dew!'

The cry was ripped from his lips by the spite of the wind.

Never in his life had he felt so useless. He fell onto his knees, his head bowed, his arms adrift by his side, his fists clenched.

He was so exhausted with his own fever, and the cold was so bitter, that within moments he felt exhaustion fall

over him like a heavy blanket. He poured his anguish into
the oraculum. It evoked an unreal, disorientating feeling,
one similar to that he had experienced when he had seen
those visions in the mind of the shaman on the icy lake.
It seemed as if he had abandoned the snowy landscape to
find himself standing in a flat wilderness that stretched
to the horizon in every direction. A presence hovered before
him. Though the presence assumed a human form, it
remained as insubstantial as moonlight reflecting off the
surface of a dancing ocean, glimmering and metamorphosing from moment to moment.

'Are you Granny Dew?'

*I am not the one you call, yet I might have the answers you
seek.*

The voice was calm, little more than a whisper, but he
heard it with the utmost clarity. He hesitated, peering
into the region where eyes might be. 'I've had it with
mysteries. I need more explanation than anybody appears
willing or able to give me.'

Ask then what you will.

'Where is this place?'

*It is all places and all times and therefore nowhere and timeless.
To some it does not exist while to others it is the only reason for
existing. But take care – for those of good heart are not the only
True Believers.*

In exasperation he called out, 'What the hell is that
supposed to mean? What is a True Believer?'

One who enters here.

'Why won't you give me clear answers to my questions? I need to understand where this journey is leading me. I need to understand – *why the hell me?*'

You ask too much in this place and this time. Such understanding is surely the object of your journey.

'What's the goddamned use!'

But no anger on his part seemed capable of fracturing the calm of that answering voice.

Be patient in your search for answers. There is great danger even in a single word, for the understanding you seek is power unlimited. In Carfon is one of the three portals that lead to the very gates of eternity.

He shook his head again in bewilderment. 'What does that mean – a power unlimited?'

I must caution you again. Do not question such things in this unguarded moment. It is enough that it holds all truths, including the truth of Dromenon.

'Dromenon?'

Here you stand on its exalted plain. You are not entirely unfamiliar with it, for it was through Dromenon that you entered Tír from Earth.

'Tír?'

The ancient name for this world.

He clutched at a single important possibility. 'What are you really implying? Are you saying that we can return to Earth? My friends and I, we can use this – this Dromenon – to go back to our world?'

Your will is your blade, though you must discover through trial how best to wield it.

Alan hesitated, considering this. When he spoke again, he did so thoughtfully. 'What is the importance of Dromenon to the Shee, Valéra?'

She knows it as the Harbour of Souls.

'Does that mean that Valéra must die? That nothing can save her?'

Silence only in answer.

Then it seemed that something in his own grief triggered the metamorphosis: the being became brilliantly incandescent so that it flooded his senses with wonder.

'Is my friend, Mo, dead?'

The one you call Mo is not dead.

What did that mean? *The one he called Mo?* 'Then where is she? Is she a prisoner of the Storm Wolves?'

She is a prisoner, though not of the Storm Wolves.

'For goodness sake, tell me where to find her.'

There is another whose endurance will be rewarded. It is already preordained that your paths will cross.

He shook his head with bewilderment. 'What does that mean? Why can't you speak plainly?'

I will give you a guide to what you seek. All wisdom is contained within the Fáil. Yet such wisdom is perilous beyond your understanding. You must approach your purpose elliptically, not directly.

While Alan struggled to understand this communication, the being returned to human form, though the voice now sounded like a chorus of many speaking urgently within his mind. *The future is shrouded in uncertainty. The seed of chaos, long dormant, is coming into flower.*

'Gee – don't confuse me with any more mysteries. If you want to help me, show me how I can save Valéra's baby.'

In a moment the spirit of the golden-haired Shee stood before him. She appeared on the white plain, her form a shimmering transparency, barely visible in the light of the glowing luminosity of the first presence. Then, Alan noticed that what he was seeing was not a single figure but two. Before the towering shape of the Shee warrior-in-noviciate was a much smaller body, so slender and delicate as to be almost invisible, yet also standing perfectly still, no higher than mid-calf. The two shapes seemed almost to mingle as if identical in spirit, as if Valéra's spirit cradled that of her unborn child.

Alan's voice was taut with emotion. 'Valéra's daughter is born from her alone? There is no father, only Valéra as mother?'

She is the sister-child of Valéra's lineage. Thus do you witness the mystery of her immortality.

The full realisation of Valéra's pregnancy was clear now to Alan – and it was astonishing. A Shee was born from the cloning of her mother's egg. Every sister-mother was replaced by her identical sister-daughter. It *was* a form of immortality. If Valéra's sister-daughter could be saved, Valéra would live again. But if her sister-daughter died, Valéra's lineage was lost forever.

Shocked by this knowledge, Alan found himself back within the snowy landscape. The storm had heightened, as if the dark forces had strengthened against him. He just had to feel it, to make his way to the solution, through instinct.

Your will is your blade.

He clenched his fists, frustrated still by this vagueness. Then he realised that there was no longer any pain in his fingers. He tried to look at his left hand but he was so blinded by the snow he found it difficult to see his hand before his eyes. But he could feel that it was healed. *My will!* He thought about that. He recalled the way the poison had so quickly invaded his fingers, how, within what appeared to be moments, it had run up his wrist and into his arm. That had to mean some kind of bloodstream spread. Yet now the poison had completely cleared. There was only one explanation he could think of. The First Power had saved him. It had made him immune to the poison.

He stood once more in front of the bower, pausing only long enough to gather his courage before returning to the side of Valéra.

'I need a sharp, clean blade.'

The Aides passed him a bone-handled knife.

Under the watchful eyes of Layheas and the two Shee, he exposed his left arm, then cut across a vein in the crook of his elbow. He squeezed his upper arm until the blood began to flow from it, then held his arm out horizontally over Valéra's abdomen so that his blood could pour down into the poisoned wound.

Valéra's need was great, and Alan gave generously of his blood. His heart pumped the precious gift of immunity into her, so that, minute by minute, he weakened and her tissues strengthened. He couldn't expect to cure her. Valéra's condition was too far advanced for any false hope. But he was determined to do all in his power to save her sister-child. By degrees, through the progressive loss of his blood, Alan drifted into a physical stupor before Layheas removed his arm from over the wound and stopped the bleeding.

Alan would have only a vague awareness of events as they unfolded, although his memory would retain the cry of a newborn baby, more lusty and powerful than any he had heard before. He dozed off and on, lulled by the night-long litany of lamentation that accompanied the birth within that bower, buffeted and tossed by the wind and snow.

Shikarr's Hunger

In the moonlight Snakoil Kawkaw was forced to rest in the shadow of an old lightning-struck oak whose maimed form dangled precariously out over the shallows by the bank of the great river. He was peering up at the night sky, as if bemoaning the fact that, although the snow had lightened, the wind still sighed through the forests and the ground snow whirled and eddied in their faces.

Mo sighed, 'I can't go on.'

He yanked hard on the thong that tethered him to her hands, causing her to totter and fall. She could tell from his face that it was all he could do to resist the temptation of kicking her. It wasn't kindness on his part that stopped him but his own exhaustion from the bleeding stump of his arm. Leaning over her, he cursed her softly. 'Any more whining from you and I'll throw you into the river.'

Mo trembled, climbing back onto her feet.

'What in a rat's pelt are you?' He peered down at her

now, where she sat hunched up on the riverbank. 'When I kick you, I encounter no weight, nothing solid.' He shook the dizziness out of his head in an attempt to figure her out. 'Stop that – do you think I can't see that your mouth is jabbering. Who in a witch's teat are you talking to? What tricks are you up to?'

'I'm thinking of riddles.'

'Pah! Get going!' He yanked her back to her feet by her hair, then shoved her ahead of him with his foot. 'Save those pitiful eyes for looking for a boat. There must be a raft or a canoe hereabouts. Fish gutters work these waters. Sooner or later my luck will turn.'

He forced the pace for several more miles before the weariness of blood loss made him stop again. Using a dagger he had stolen from the Storm Wolves, he cut off several long strips from her sealskin coat, tying them into a longer thong and shackling her ankles with it. It was a clumsy business, using just one hand and his teeth, and it took him a long time to satisfy himself that she was secure, after which he slumped down on the bank and stared at her, as if trying to figure out what to do with her.

'How tempting,' he whispered in her ear, 'merely to plunge my knife into your soft young belly! Make life a lot easier for old Snakoil Kawkaw. I could start again somewhere far from here.'

'But then,' Mo countered, 'you wouldn't be able to sell me in Isscan.'

'Don't tempt me, brat. Here I must rest – get some sleep. If you so much as fart out of turn, I will dangle your head down into the water. You think the pit was bad, but there are hungry mouths aplenty in this river.'

In her mind, as she called for her, Mo heard the comforting voice of Granny Dew.

Hush, now! I am here.

'He terrifies me. He's just like the thin man. He wants to kill me. I can sense it in him.'

No, little one. This man is bad, but not like the other. The other was evil for evil's sake, but this one is driven by his own selfish reasons. You are only valuable to him while whole and healthy. He will not harm you unless he becomes angry or mindlessly desperate.

Before falling asleep Kawkaw had added a new thong and tethered her shackled ankles to him, binding her so close that there was no possibility for Mo of sleeping in comfort, even if the cold would allow it. Her clothes were still soaked from her immersion in the river; she shivered and her teeth chattered with the cold. When she moved even a fraction, the thong pulled on his hand, around which he had looped it three or four times. If she even tried to move he would surely waken. So the best she could hope for was to doze, half-awake.

'I can't bear it. He will sleep again for a few hours and then we'll have to walk again, all through the night.'

Then do something to prevent it.

'What can I do? The leather is twisted around his hand. He will wake immediately if I try to escape. He'll do what he said. He'll dangle me over the river for . . . for horrible things to come and eat me.'

He preys on your mind, child. He's a cunning one, and experienced in the ways of tormenting. Yet still there is a wish granted that might enable you to help yourself.

Cautiously Mo sat up. It had stopped snowing and the bright ball of the moon peered between blankets of cloud like a lamp through net curtains. A bank of mist rose from the river, heavy and still. Trembling with fear, she inched her body around so she was kneeling on the cold damp earth within a few yards of the riverbank. She peered at Kawkaw under the moonlight. He looked sick as well as wounded, with a filthy rag wrapped around the stump of his right arm. A thick sealskin cape was pulled tightly around him, and his hair was standing up in wild tufts, so he looked half-bear, half-man. Mo wept while she thought again about Granny Dew's advice. *Do something to prevent it . . .* What could she do? Why couldn't she just ask Granny Dew to untie her and let her escape?

She stared at the loops, where they curled in and out of his paw-like fist, as if wishing them to unravel. But, of course, they didn't.

Still there is a wish granted . . .

But what – what could she do? Then into her mind came an idea. She still weighed no more than her eyebrows. Perhaps she could use her weightlessness to help her uncurl the leather thong from around that hand without the sleeping Kawkaw noticing?

Little by little she brought her face to within inches of his hand. She took hold of the thong, very close to his hand, and began untwisting the first loop as carefully as if she were brushing a baby's face in sleep. The first loop undone, she rested a moment to allow her heartbeat to slow down. Maybe just one more loop and it would become easier. But fear made her hand jerk and pull on the thong. His eyes sprang open. He was instantly wide awake.

'Scheming vermin! You think you can better old Snakoil Kawkaw? Well I warned you what I would do to you if you tried to escape. And now at least I'll have my sport even if I miss the ransom you would fetch in Isscan.'

With his fist pulling her this way and that, he found the dagger and waved it in front of her eyes. She could smell his foul breath as he snarled in her face. Then, with a twirl, the blade was under her chin and pressed against her neck as he forced her over to the water's edge. Here, struggling one-handedly, he kicked her down onto the sloping bank, and then, bathed in sweat from his exertions, he used his feet to shove her further, until he could dangle her, head down, over the shallows.

'No – please!'

Ignoring her squirming, he shoved her far enough out so that her head entered the freezing water, and then toyed with her, lifting her in and out, so she was coughing and choking for breath.

'Come gather round, hungry mouths. Come nibble this titbit!'

Suddenly there was a loud hissing sound from nearby. With a twist of her neck, Mo managed to raise her head clear of the water. She saw Kawkaw's narrow face above her, squinting out into the river. She heard him curse with fright. Twisting back to look at the river, she saw something monstrous rising out of the swirling mist – a serpent so huge its gaping jaws could have swallowed her whole. Its glowing eyes, faceted like a fly's, were focused on Mo, where she dangled upside down between bank and water. Its forked tongue, blue as slate, probed the air as the great head descended to inspect her plight.

Kawkaw had fallen onto his back with terror. Now he struggled to free his hand from the thong tethering him to Mo, biting at it with his teeth while using his heels in the snow to make a slithering retreat. Mo felt the tether snap. She slithered further down the bank until she was half-immersed in the shallow water.

'My offering,' he wheedled. 'It is yours. I – I make it freely in your honour, Great One.'

'Offering accepted, mmmm! Though so little flesh we perceive on these bonesss.'

With a shriek, Kawkaw attempted to flee. Mo, with her feet now freed, scrambled to climb back up the bank. She found herself ignored as a huge coil struck out of the river, cutting off Kawkaw's escape amid a deluge of water that almost dragged Mo back into the river. The coil closed around him, as high in its diameter as his shoulders were off the ground, and it began to drag him closer to the lip of the bank, so he too could be inspected.

Kawkaw shrieked, 'What demon from the shades are you?'

'No demon are we. Has the memory of the fish robbers become so poor that you have forgotten the true name of this river? Fair Shikarr are we, queen of the river that once bore our name. A hundred years have we slumbered only to find ourselves aroused by you. Now awake, we find ourselves hungry to excess.'

'River serpents feed on fish!'

'Fish flesh is tasssty, but cold. Man flesh isss warm, and a nice warm meal isss the delicacy we covet.'

Mo shook her fist at the great head above her. 'You cannot eat us.'

'We cannot?' The head swung, the terrible eyes coming to focus again on the girl.

'Granny Dew won't let you.'

The head rose high into the air then descended with lightning speed, hesitating only when the great fangs, longer than scimitars, gaped around Mo. The huge, forked tongue gathered her scent only inches from her face.

'Well now – what have we here? Though terror of Shikarr we read in its eyes, yet such obstinacy do we read in its spirit. Few would dare to challenge Shikarr in our hunger. Many indeed have died merely at the sight of us. Perhaps, little one, we should do you the honour of becoming the first bite of my meal – a tasssty morsel before the main feast?'

'I'm not worth the trouble of eating, your highness,' Mo said firmly. 'I will show you if you put out your tongue and lift me to the bank.'

'Oh – it sports with usss!'

Mo's voice chattered with fear but still she played the game with the serpent. 'But first only weigh me before you think of tasting me.'

The blue-black forked tongue, its individual forks as thick as Mo's thighs, flicked delicately down through the water and they lifted her clear, until her whole shivering figure stood dripping within the great coil on the bank.

'Why, you weigh no more than a fish scale.'

'I am not worth a bite.'

'Oh my – this game becomesss interesssting!'

The serpent's head swept from side to side, as if suddenly wary. Her eyes, like glowing braziers, searched the surrounding shadows before returning to focus on Mo. 'You like to play gamesss?'

'I love to play riddles.'

The serpent's voice dropped to a sigh. 'What sorcery isss this? Could it be the reason Shikarr was woken from our century-long slumber? If so, Shikarr must surely share in the mystery. But, wait – patience is called for! Could it be that the bait isss a trap?'

'I'm not a trap.'

'Hmmmm?' The hissing voice had become so loud it blew like a wind through the surrounding foliage. The head yawned close again, falling back ready to swoop. The great eyes closed, as if savouring the moment. 'Oh, deliciousss morsel, we are willing to take the risssk!'

Mo's hand closed on the bog-oak figurine still laced around her neck.

Abruptly, from the shadows behind her, a staff struck the earth and a thunderous shockwave rolled out under her feet, sending eddies out into the deep waters of the river. The serpent whirled, her eyes searching the shadows where a small triangular figure stood, as if in protection, behind the girl. The small size of the figure belied a will as adamantine as the mountains. A new voice, carried on all senses, erupted into all consciousness.

'Shikkkaaarrr the perfidious!'

The serpent reared back, her eyes glaring, the blue-black tongue probing the air about the triangular shadow.

'Isss not perfidy the fate you bequeathed to serpents such as we? We are woken from our slumbers, and sacrifice is offered, be it no more than the miserable flesh of a bear-man – and an insolent urchin!'

The triangular figure lifted its staff and made a gesture, like a summons, to the cold night air. In less than a moment, a lightning bolt struck the river only yards from the serpent, singeing its flesh and choking its nostrils with the stink of ozone.

'Isss the urchin too much to ask for? Oh, let us settle

for the bear-thing then. T'isss a poor joint of meat, sickly and incomplete – though warm and tasssty.'

The triangle increased in density until it became the absence of light. An earthquake trembled through rock and water.

The serpent shrieked. But still her monstrous jaws slavered above the man and the girl. 'Shikarr wantsss! Shikarr mussst feed!'

The triangle expanded until it became a great pyramid high above the ground and, like the forward-leaning shadow of a mountain at sunset, it encompassed Mo, the serpent and the quivering Snakoil Kawkaw.

'Eons have you ruled, Shikarr, Queen of the River, but immortality is not your true legacy. Even you cannot escape death, if it should be decided that your time has come.'

In the water surrounding the serpent a seething life gathered, composed of many hungry mouths and flashing teeth. In moments the water, from bank to bank, seethed, and the gnawing and snipping of teeth and claws were louder than the wind. The serpent squealed.

'Enough! *Enough!* Oh, Mother of All – you can be ssso cruel. Shikarr will not harm the urchin child. But leave usss a small mouthful. Give us the bear-man.'

The pyramidal shadow diminished in size. Its voice fell to a whisper on the wind, but it was a more threatening whisper than the thunder and lightning. 'Shikarr will feed on neither child nor man. Instead your purpose is to ferry them, safe from danger, to the city of stone.'

'But—'

'Hssst! I will brook neither confrontation nor delay!'

The fury of snapping jaws increased. The serpent shrieked and, suddenly, Mo and the bewildered Snakoil Kawkaw found themselves enclosed within the enormous coils, lifted high from bank to river, and from there borne swiftly into the centre stream. A stinking cloud of serpent breath hid their presence there, as with immense undulations of her great body, Shikarr bore her unwanted burden downstream.

A Baited Trap

Alan lay back against the keel of the canoe in a distracted mood. He could smell the river, a very different aroma from the Suir back in friendly Clonmel: this smelled stranger, more bitter, the quintessence of dark magic in an alien and frightening world. Snow gusted around him in the darkness. He was still dosed with healwell to treat his damaged joints, and his weakness through blood loss was being gradually restored with strange-smelling potions administered by the Aides woman, Layheas.

Nobody spoke a word.

He thought about Mo, the fact that she was still missing, and he thought about Kate. He missed his friends. He had to pray that they were safe, that soon they would all be together again, as he listened to the soft and steady rhythm of the rag-quieted oars wielded by Ainé and her companions, their canoe the lead of many carrying the fighting band of Shee southwards towards Isscan through the inky-black current.

During those long hours of silence, Alan also thought about the young Shee who had died to save him. He saw again the great funeral pyre, with its orange flame, as it had engulfed Valéra and her dead companions, their heads positioned so that they faced northwest, across the great landmass of continental Monisle towards their ancestral home in the Guhttan mountains. In this same canoe, Muîrne cradled the sleeping crescent of Valéra's sister-child, so startlingly reminiscent of her mother, with the first wispy tresses of golden-blonde hair and the first twinkling of babyish curiosity in the same lambent amber eyes.

So hope had been born out of despair.

At daybreak, once they had pulled in the canoes and rested, he had a little more time for a whispered conversation with Milish. He learnt that only noviciates among the Shee carried their daughters in the womb. The mature warriors had long ago given birth. Their daughter-sisters were safe from their enemies, back in the heavily defended mountains of their homeland, where they were in turn schooled in their warrior history and trained in arms. All the other Shee who had died in the recent battle had been full warriors, so that, in a sense, they had not died at all. It was a thought Alan would need time to get used to, even as he listened to Milish's explanations.

He presumed that Ainé also had a daughter-sister, though in the Kyra's brooding silence he also sensed a tragic family secret, one he knew better than to enquire into. In his heart he felt a growing apprehension about his role in this world as, with his new companions, he lay down to get some sleep in the daylight hours. Even his dreams were pervaded by foreboding so that he woke frequently, afraid of shadows.

Then on the third night of travel, the southern sky became increasingly aglow – the reflection of the night lamps of Isscan.

A few hours before dawn, as they pulled the canoes under the canopies of some riverside trees, Milish told him the history of the city states of Monisle, and that of Isscan in particular, this great inland port and market centre from the days when it was a proud regional capital renowned for its trading wealth and ancient traditions. But a shake of her head and the lowering of her eyes suggested that things had changed since the coming of the Death Legion. As they whispered together, Ainé and Muîrne were rigging a cover of pine branches over an already shadowed hollow, so that they could sleep a few hours before entering the city.

Alan felt guilty about the fact that he was concealing from Milish the real focus of his thoughts and hopes. He never mentioned the fireside chat with Kemtuk, or the shaman's belief that a great mage lived here in Isscan: a mage more ancient than any other and whose art could probe the labyrinths of the mind. The shaman had called him the Mage of Dreams.

When, a few hours later, Milish, Alan and Layheas emerged from their hiding place disguised as a merchant woman with her two servants, the Ambassador led them towards the city with a jaunty step. Alan did his best to look the part with a worn and tattered seal cape, lagging tiredly in the wake of his mistress. For many a mile they walked through farm lanes surrounded by winter pasture. They encountered few people at this early hour, and those they saw ignored them, little interested in strangers. But one farmer, a bald-headed man with a pale, round face, leaned on a field wall and watched them pass, his expression surly and suspicious.

Milish wished him good morning in a guttural language new to Alan, without even a momentary pause in her step. Once past the man, however, she fell back abreast of Alan to murmur, 'A farmer with the face of a townsman – if I am not mistaken, we have encountered the first spy of the Death Legion.'

During their rest by the riverside, Milish had explained a little more about the occupying army, and why they had not plundered and destroyed Isscan as they had so many other towns and cities. Having witnessed the brutality of the Storm Wolves, Alan guessed that it could only mean that the city was useful to them. Now he understood that the Storm Wolves were only a minority of the main army of Death Legion, a force of occupation that, in Milish's reckoning, numbered millions. An army that size must need its belly fed. And Isscan, as the great trading centre and confluence of river, forest and farms, provided an important source of grain, fuel and fish.

The ramshackle outer city gathered itself about them, the dispersed farmsteads condensing into villages – viper pits of gossip, as Milish took care to warn him – then dirt-lined streets, their meanderings too higgledy-piggledy to owe anything to any architect's pen.

Alan disliked these slum-warrens, devoid of clean water or sanitation, where desperation bred greed, cruelty, and disease.

There was no longer any possibility of being ignored. Sharp eyes in unwashed faces watched their every step. More intrusive still were the outstretched hands of beggars, the sight of deliberately blinded and maimed children. Here he saw a mixture of peoples, much as you might see in a shanty-town around some developing city back on Earth. But a great many of these people looked distinctly feral, with downy or frankly hairy faces, a medley of furry skins, claw-like hands and scaly bare feet.

They had to pass a gauntlet of offerings: unwholesome sweetmeats and alcoholic drinks, as well as trinkets, often gaudy and increasingly vulgar. In one section, where the proliferating shanties hung back in the shadow of the massive city walls, the offerings were a good deal darker. Here, in the frames of rickety doorways, the most perverse of fantasies were openly advertised. Sadistic deviations of pain and pleasure were paraded before their averted eyes.

'Stop and indulge your wildest dreams!' a man with

black stumps of teeth wheeled, running among and about them. 'What could be more tasty than these fruits of the secret passions?'

'None, I grant you.' Milish concocted a smile. 'And perhaps we shall have time to dally after our business is done.'

Alan struck out at the clawing hands, or the beckoning fingers, but Milish, with a squeeze of his arm, maintained her calm. 'Keep your distaste to yourself. There is much at stake. Remember your friend, Mo, and endure it.'

For what seemed the hundredth time, Mo explored what appeared to be a corridor of ivory-smooth stone. She stopped and looked up high in the wall to one of the tiny circular openings that was the source of daylight. The light diffused rather than fell into the featureless space. There was no clear angle where the floor met the walls or where the walls met the vaulted ceiling, high above. Everything seemed to melt into a blur of whiteness. When she held up her hands to examine the effects of the light falling on them, her flesh looked too bland to be real, as if her presence had no more substance than a ghost. Even her dress – what should be a lovely dress, from her throat to her ankles, made of what appeared to be gossamer-white silk – couldn't possibly be real. And when she tried to remember where she was, how she had come to be here, her memory too was blank, as if her very personality had been stolen from her.

She cried her thoughts aloud, into the white-glowing air. 'I'm not some doll, or puppet in . . . in somebody else's imagination!'

The worst thing, the very worst thing of all, was the fact that she could not sleep. Oh, she felt so tired, so needful of lying down and abandoning her aching limbs to rest! But there was no bed, no rug on the floor, not even a simple chair to sit on. She inhabited a world of utter blandness, no more than an endless circular corridor made out of faintly glowing smooth white stone.

Nothing appeared to make sense – unless, of course, it made an altogether too perfect sense.

'There should be windows!' she cried.

Abruptly, as if she had willed it into being, a tall narrow window, like an arrow-slit in a castle, appeared in the outer wall. When she ran over and looked out through the slit, she saw a sunlit garden, a garden which, the more she looked into it, was broodingly still, with a mirror-like pond in its centre. On one side of the pond was a rounded grey stone on which a large white bird was perched. The bird was as big as a grey stork, with long spindly legs and a bright yellow beak. It was perfectly motionless. Its head was averted so the face was in profile and it was peering fixedly back at her with one huge yellow eye.

Mo's hand reached up to her throat. Her fingers searched for something that should be there, but whatever they searched for was missing.

Mo panicked. She began to run down the circular

corridor, stopping to peer out of one window slit after another. In every window she saw that identical view, the garden with the large white bird. She retracted her gaze, sensing the awful malice that looked back at her in that single great eye.

'There should be a bed, or a rug, or a chair – and food!'

But no bed, rug or chair – or food – appeared.

She flopped down listlessly on the featureless white floor, sitting upright, with her legs crossed. Her hands brushed her face, touched the skin of her arms, and felt nothing substantial. Nothing was real. A frantic restlessness invaded her, causing her arms and legs to jump and her mind to wander, as if her very thoughts as well as her memories were trapped in the white labyrinth.

She took a deep breath. With a trembling voice, she tried to calm her fears by speaking aloud a new riddle:

'What is eternal
Yet everywhere dies?
Its skirt of many colours
Bewitches the eyes.
Its home is the earth,
Yet its birth is the skies.'

Into her mind crept a voice, like a whispered secret at the very edge of consciousness, 'The answer, pretty one, is the rain!'

Mo gasped, whirling from one side to another, to try

to find the source of the whisper but there was nobody near her. The voice appeared to have washed into her consciousness through the very glow in the air.

'Who are you?'

The reply came again, like a breath in her mind:

> 'For some they are barriers,
> Like the encircling moat.
> For others they are comforting,
> Like a familiar old coat.
> In its pockets two trumpets
> That play not a note.'

Mo easily solved the riddle. The barriers and old coat were walls that keep some out while keeping others safe within. And the trumpets were ears.

The riddle was a warning: *These walls have ears!*

She climbed to her feet, dashed to the nearest slit window and stared out again: that same bird was watching her with its huge yellow eye. She thought that the walls had eyes as well as ears!

She returned to sitting down in the corridor and she murmured, 'So I must be careful what I say.'

'Very careful indeed!'

She hesitated, attempting to think this through. 'Since I can't see you, how can we be talking to each other?'

'In a world of magic, everything is possible.'

Her heart leaped. Was this truly a world of magic? 'Where is this place?'

'You are the prisoner of one who calls itself the Mage of Dreams.'

Her heart lurched. She had to swallow a moment and her head dropped. 'You said "itself", not "himself" or "herself".'

'It is not human, though it takes human form when the need arises.'

'But why – why should this Mage of Dreams want me?'

'You are the honey in its trap.'

'What does that mean?'

'Can you not imagine for yourself?'

'I have lost my memories. I know little more than that my name is Mo. That and the fact that this – this Mage of Dreams – will not let me sleep.'

'Ah, now, there is the puzzle.'

'But surely my dreams could not threaten one who calls itself the Mage of Dreams?'

'How clever you truly are, pretty one. And no wonder the Mage fears something about you!'

She paused again, her mind as bewildered as ever. 'But you never told me your name. Who are you?'

'I'm afraid that I'm not yet ready to tell you that. Though you may freely set eyes on me.'

Into her imagination came an image of a squat but very heavily set little man with shoulder-length hair the red of copper and eyes as green as emeralds.

'Are you a . . . a dwarf?'

'Indeed I am, from the distinguished warrior race of the Fir Bolg.'

Even in her tired mind, his words evoked a memory. Mo blinked, trying to recall . . . There was something familiar about that name, the 'Fir Bolg' . . . Why couldn't she remember what it was? Now Mo studied the face still hovering in her imagination. It was a strange face, heavy and brooding, with bronze-coloured skin and a broad flat nose, and lips as proud and wide as an African's, yet now fiercely sad. It was a face in which she sensed great strength of character as well as pride and determination.

'Are you breaking some rule in talking to me like this?'

'At the risk of my life.'

'Oh!' She sat back with another jolt of fright.

'But who cares for risk when a companion is so pretty, and so resourceful, as you!'

'You must be very brave.'

'No braver than you, little one! You see, in your mind I have discovered a little of your journey and purpose here.'

'My name is Maureen Grimstone, although everyone calls me Mo. And I don't understand what you're saying. Can you tell me what I'm doing here?'

'Mo it is then. And I should explain that you have been imprisoned for a single purpose – to lure another to the Mage's chamber.'

'I – I still don't understand. Who am I supposed to lure?'

'You know who – but you try not to think of it.'

'I try not to think of it?'

'It is your own mind rather than the will of the Mage of Dreams that has suppressed what might be unpleasant, even dangerous, from your memories.'

'My mind would never suppress my memories, no matter how unpleasant or dangerous they were. If you can help me, please help me now. I can't bear another moment like this.'

'If you so wish, pretty one – Mo!'

Suddenly memories flooded her mind. Terrible memories. The dwarf was right, and it might have been better to have remained forgetful. She now recalled everything about coming to this world. The cave with Granny Dew, the desperate series of journeys through the snow, the Snowmelt River, the attack at the rapids where she had been picked up by some terrifying bat-creature and cast down into the violent rush of water . . .

Alan!

She almost called his name out loud, but only stopped her tongue with a major effort of will. She remembered the pit and the horrible thin man – and Snakoil Kawkaw, who, of all people, rescued her but only so that he could sell her like a slave girl in the marketplace of Isscan. She remembered Shikarr . . .

Terror almost made Mo faint as she recalled the journey within the coils of the great serpent, during which Shikarr questioned her relentlessly about who she was and where she had come from, and about her three companions, especially the one who carried the ruby triangle in his brow.

When Mo had refused to answer her questions, the serpent tried many tricks and strategies, from mockery to hypnotic mind-power, in which she allowed Mo to peer into her many senses, including the second sight that allowed her to see the warm heart of every living creature within devouring range, or at least the warm-blooded ones, and the sense of smell that could paint a picture every bit as detailed as Mo's own vision and which came not from her nostrils but from the blue-black forked tongue. There was a deep, wild wonder in feeling as well as seeing new colours, even tasting colours and the shapes of things, and sharing a great proud memory of ancient triumphs and humiliations. But here too, in every sigh and brush of contact with the great serpent, Mo had sensed an abiding hatred of all warm creatures, and of humankind especially, that was as deep and raw as blood.

Infuriated by her resistance, Shikarr had finally shrieked, 'Do not think to escape me, child. Wherever you go, I shall follow. For in your wake isss great opportunity. Blood, flesh and bone will be my reward – in certainty and plentiful. For an innocence such asss yours leads inevitably to battle and ssslaughter.'

Mo had understood nothing of this.

When, in the first light of dawn, the serpent had eventually pulled in close to the bank and deposited Mo and Snakoil Kawkaw a few miles from Isscan, a small rowing boat had come up and beached itself next to them. Kawkaw just lay on the bank in an exhausted sleep. Two desperate-looking men had jumped out and encircled Mo, one with an oar upraised as a club and the other with a sharp-bladed knife, both their faces leering. They had their backs to the river and didn't see the great shape that suddenly lunged out of it. Mo had screamed in terror and squeezed her eyes tightly shut . . .

There had been barely time for two screams of terror, causing birds to clatter out of the trees. When Mo opened her eyes again, the great serpent was gone, and so too were the men. And the boat, now empty, offered itself to Kawkaw, who had been roused by the screams. 'Get in there, and be quick about it. For there's one in this marketplace that will pay me a pocketful of gold for a witch's brat such as you.'

With her memories restored, Mo readily understood her role as the honey pot. The trap was intended for Alan. And that thought frightened and oppressed her, so that she whispered fearfully through her mind: 'Are you still there?'

'I am.'

'I remember now – I remember where I heard about the Fir Bolg. Padraig talked about you. When we were in the barrow grave.' Mo recalled the feeling of dread, as the four friends stood before the mortal remains of the terrible warrior prince. She remembered the Ogham inscriptions cut into the walls, which were a ward against great evil from the distant past. The inscriptions told the story of a warrior tribe who were not native to Ireland, a tribe of little people, yet the fiercest warriors. Padraig had called them Fir Bolg.

'Please – oh, please, Fir Bolg, or whatever your name really is – can't you just help me to go to sleep?'

'My name is Qwenqwo Cuatzel.'

'Qwenqwo Cuatzel – that's a very strange name.'

'No stranger than Maureen Grimstone sounds to my ears!'

'Will you help me?'

'This I cannot do.'

'Oh, Qwenqwo Cuatzel, if that is really your name, I'm so exhausted and frightened. And . . .' She stopped herself suddenly, aware that she had nearly exposed her secret. She had nearly blurted out to this supposed new friend and helper the secret she had sworn to keep with Granny Dew. And now that she thought of it, she understood at last why it was that she was not permitted to sleep. Qwenqwo was right: it was her own instinct that was preventing her from falling asleep. In sleep, the big yellow eye would see all, and the Mage of Dreams would know her secret – her real name.

'I'm so weary, and you've already been so kind to me. Surely, if I can't be allowed to sleep, is there not something you could do, at least to help me rest?'

'I could tell you a story.'

'What kind of story?'

'A dreamtime rather than a bedtime story.'

'Would you – please?'

'Do you have a request?'

She remembered Padraig's stories about a magical place known as the Wildwoods. 'Do you know any stories about the Wildwoods?' she asked, rubbing at her eyes.

'A tale of the Wildwoods it is.'

'A long story, long enough to help me pass the hours?'

'Your wish is granted. But on one condition. Will you sing a little song for me as I tell it? Your song will distract the Mage while it entertains me.'

'What song shall I sing for you?'

'A song that comes from the purest of hearts. A song of innocence, such as the thrush or the blackbird sings to greet the sun in the morning.'

'I'm really tired, but I'll do my best,' she yawned, blinking slowly.

'And as you sing, I will tell you the tale of an epic battle of wits between the last little wren and Gorra, the earwig.'

Mo sensed the song growing in her heart, like a tiny harp tuning its chords, and then suddenly the first notes were born from her lips, as if from the magic of her true inner being, and its magic echoed in rills and rivulets through the never-ending corridor, with its fusion of light and air and stone. Qwenqwo's voice also tuned itself to the same wonder of need, so his words bathed her spirit like a calming potion.

'Of course the Wildwoods, as we both know, were the home of a great king of magic, known to all the fairy creatures as Ree Nashee. And today they are filled with the most beautiful blossom of flower and shrub, and the air trills with the lovely sweet songs of the birds. But it wasn't always the case. For the new king was conceited and gullible, unlike his famed and less arrogant father. He would admire his reflection in mirrors they made for him out of sand-polished quartz. And do you know what it was about himself he was most proud of?'

'No – do tell me.'

'His ears.'

'His ears?'

'His ears, indeed! You see, the king had ears so tall they reached quite to the top of his head, and they were wonderfully pointy.'

'He had pointy ears?'

'Indeed they drew out to tips as fine as the finest pine needles, and were capped with little tufts of golden hair that he would wax and twirl, like others wax moustaches, until they curled high above his head, like the feelers of a butterfly.'

'Oh, you've drawn such a lovely picture that I can see him – he is here quite clearly in my mind!'

'Sing then, Mo Grimstone. Sing your song of innocence while I continue my story . . . For now I must inform you that the conceited king, Ree Nashee, was married to the most beautiful wood sprite, Nimue Guinevere, who wove dresses from daisies and the summery blue of the brightest flag irises, and she pranced through the Wildwoods on Dovera, her gold-maned unicorn.'

'A gold-maned unicorn?' Mo questioned, then continued to sing.

'So sparkling that it captured the light of the morning and haloed the great horn of ivory and outshone the reins and saddle, though they glittered with elvish diamonds and jewels. But to return to the king, it was this pride in his ears that gave Balor his chance to take control of the Wildwoods.'

'Who was this Balor?'

'Why Balor, of course, was a titan of the sort you would call a Cyclops, with a single eye in the centre of his brow. He had long been jealous of the kings of the Wildwoods. And now he cast the wickedest of all his spells. But Ree Nashee was also powerful in magic, and that spell was only capable of making the king go to sleep. But it wasn't an ordinary sleep. It was the kind of sleep that lasted for ever. And the way he conceived it was deviously brilliant. You see, Balor spat into the palm of his hand and turned his spittle into an earwig called Gorra, into which Balor infused all of his malice. Then he instructed the earwig to climb into the left ear of the king while he was sleeping, and once hidden within the king's ear, Gorra was to whisper the most powerful enchantment direct to his mind.'

Mo's eyelids drooped. 'I like this story.'

'So it was that Gorra the earwig began plotting and planning. He climbed into the left ear of Ree Nashee and there he whispered every despicable thing it was possible to conceive. He proved to be as wicked as Balor himself, and twice as cunning. Soon he was plotting how he would end the enchantment of the Wildwoods with his mischief. Above all, earwigs have a dislike of birds. So he saw to it through stealing the magic of the sleeping king that there wasn't a single bird left singing in the Wildwoods – that is, except for one that Gorra was not sharp-eyed enough to see. And do you know why he could not see her?'

'Why?'

'Why, because it was none other than Aieve, the mother wren, and the smallest bird of all. Nimue Guinevere, seeing what had happened to her husband, the king, had conceived of a plan of her own and had managed to hide Aieve under the sleeping king's hat. Aieve flew out of that hat, landing on the left shoulder of the sleeping king, where she peered deep into that great pointy ear and saw where the earwig was hiding. Suddenly she sang out in a piping shriek of a voice, because you could hardly expect a wren to sing deep like a bull, and the words of her challenge will never be forgotten.'

'What did she sing?'

'She sang, "Since everybody knows that earwigs are the stupidest of all creatures, and since everybody also knows that riddling is the wisest and wittiest of occupations, then, to prove that I am right and you are wrong, I challenge you to a duel of riddles.'''

'A duel of riddles?'

'The fiercest of duels there ever was.'

'How fierce?'

'A duel without quarter – riddler takes all!'

'The riddling of all riddles?'

'So it was! Now I wager you might know a riddle or two for such an occasion?'

Mo's eyelids half opened, and she nodded.

'Then,' the coppery-haired dwarf laughed loudly, 'shall we say that I will play the part of Gorra and you the part of Aieve?'

Mo clapped her hands and began:

'I dance without legs round a song without rhyme;
My sigh is the sky and my dress the springtime.'

'You are surely the wind in the tree tops!' The dwarf answered Mo's riddle before returning to the earwig's story: 'So the riddling continued, hour after hour, and day after day, from the eyes of the peacock to the song of the lyre bird, through the birth of muses, to carpets woven from snow-white angels' feathers, until at last, Gorra sang aloud his final challenge:

'I, for one, in glass am set
And I, for two, am found in jet

For three I'm seen to hide in tin,
For four I'm found a box within,
But if determined you pursue
For five I can't escape from you.

'Aieve cried out in frustration, for Gorra had her stumped. She racked and racked her little wren brains, but she could find no answer to Gorra's riddle. And then Gorra, so overcome with his own vanity and pride, called on all his relatives to join him for the feast of wren flesh. And soon the Wildwoods were filled with the squeaking and rustling of every earwig who heard the invitation, Gorra's brothers and sisters and uncles and aunts and his cousins three hundred times removed, until the whole forest floor appeared to be on the move. Gorra called out to them to hurry, poking his head out of Ree Nashee's left ear, wearing such a look of triumph on his earwiggy face, and gazing out at Aieve's plump little body with a slavering, rat-a-tat gnashing of his side-to-side jaws.

'But now, if you like, you might help Aieve solve the riddle?'

Mo chuckled:

'What jewels every word adorning,
Like the memory of joy in flower and morning,
Are the vowels sounds a, e, i, o, u
And the rhythm and rhyme of my answer true.'

It was the dwarf's turn to chuckle with delight. 'Alas, like every good tale, it must come to an end.'

Mo grinned. 'And I think I know how Gorra's story ends.'

'Oh, you do – do you?'

Mo closed her eyes and laid down her head, if not to sleep, at least to the contentment of daydreams. And in her daydream she chuckled:

'If the conclusion to this duel you seek,
Look no more to a riddle but the snap of a beak.'

'Aha!' laughed Qwenqwo. 'Who is spinning this yarn – you or me?'

The trembling ceased in Mo's body, though not even a great story of the Wildwoods could entirely ease her sense of dread. For, like Balor, a sorcerer had baited his trap. The Mage of Dreams would draw Alan into that trap. He would send some kind of a message – an enchantment. And instead of an earwig hidden in the king's ear, she, Maureen Grimstone, was the bait set to capture Alan, and her friends.

Isscan

For Alan, the teeming slums outside the city had become so unsettling he found distraction in a memory when, as the canoe was being hidden, he had noticed a curious action on the part of Ainé, the merest touch of her hand on the brow of Valéra's baby. During that fleeting caress the oraculum in Ainé's forehead had pulsed, a single intense throb from deep within the matrix.

He sensed that it had been important. But what had it meant?

His ruminations were interrupted by Milish, who whispered last-minute advice as they neared the gates. 'Be wary at all times. Isscan holds many perils. The Death Legion have already erected one of their accursed arenas within the city walls. We have no desire to become the entertainment.'

Before setting out, Milish had encouraged Alan to wear a broad-brimmed yokel's hat, which Layheas had woven

out of reeds. 'Even if your face isn't known, the oraculum
is a beacon. You must keep your brow well shaded.'

No amount of disguise would conceal the stature of the
Shee so it had been decided that they could not accompany
them into the city. The Kyra was unhappy about this, and
furious debate had taken place during the hours of
darkness until they had arrived at an uncomfortable
compromise. Layheas had a means of calling for help, if
help was needed. Now, walking in the shadow of the walls,
Alan was astonished by their grandeur. Masoned from huge
blocks of granite, they towered a hundred feet high on
their aprons, and another twenty feet where hexagonal
towers buttressed their angles. The ramparts sloped in
from their base to about two-thirds of their ascent, after
which the summits sloped out again, in a gigantic collar
that would make attack by scaling virtually impossible.
Isscan appeared to be so large and sprawling, it would
have required a vast army to defend, or encircle, it. It made
no sense that he saw no evidence of soldiers. But he took
Milish's caution to heart and kept his guard.

In the distance, unapproachable by road from this
northern direction, he glimpsed the forest of masts and
cranes that marked the docks. If the need proved desperate,
this was where they had agreed to meet: the old harbour
under the city walls. The Temple Ship had to be somewhere
within that forest. And that meant Kate was nearby.

Kate! Even to think about Kate – the thought of holding
her in his arms again – was so exciting he could hardly

bear to wait another moment. He found himself rubbing at his brow, as if to force his thoughts to concentrate on the reality of the moment, and the dangers that surrounded their every step.

The North Gate had been removed from its great iron hinges allowing a ramshackle collection of stalls and booths to curl through the massive portal, with its sculpted coat of arms and leafy decoration. Alan made out two sheaves of corn crossed and a fish leaping over the balances that once symbolised its free-trading status. Again, it appeared that no guards or sentinels controlled this northern entrance.

Once inside, the lanes were carpeted by a thick settling of dung, wetted to a foul sticky mud by snow. The poor trod barefoot in this filth, which was churned to spray by the traffic of carts pulled by short, stout ponies, their passage spattering the legs of the people about them. Other riders, on grander horses, wore greatcoats of velvet, embroidered with stitching of gold and silver in clever geometrical patterns. The farmers had their horses and flat-bottomed carts, loaded with provisions to sell in the markets. Here at least it was a bustle he felt more comfortable with.

Barefoot children went running by and shrieking. More wealthy townsfolk, men and women, jostled with one another, warmly wrapped in long coats, or dresses, that fell down to their laced leather boots. In some of the side alleys the houses overhung the pavements, like Tudor shambles. Between the alleyways he saw dicing houses and what his mother would have called 'houses of ill-repute'. At every corner he found a multitude of beggars, their hair whitened by snow and their dishevelled clothes caked in the foul-smelling muck.

In Isscan, as Milish now informed him, every day was a market day, so that in spite of the snow and the cold there was a bustle of activity, with music, entertainers, hawkers, and peddlers. Open stalls were selling vegetables, a variety of fish and bloody joints of meat. In one cobbled area, where heat blasted their eyes from an open hearth, an entire hog carcass was being turned on a spit. Throughout the teeming market, the scent of burning wood mingled with the smell of the roast meat, with glowing braziers reflected in the red cheeks of the men and women who tended them. Some of the braziers had griddles over them, where they cooked flat pancakes of corn. Others served soup in chunky bowls, so hot they had to be held in straw mats. Alan was hungry, and the savoury smells made his mouth water.

His hunger must have shown because a boy with a running nose ran beside him, pestering him to buy the carcasses of small birds, roasted on sticks. In response to Milish's gesture of refusal, he cursed them, screeching obscenities in their wake. Alan was glad to escape the congested streets of the marketplace to trudge at last along cobbled inner-city streets, over walkways lined with timeworn paving stones.

Begrimed buildings of two, three and even four storeys hung over them, masoned in grey-blue granite, some built around stout oak frames. The mason's love of ornament appeared on jambs and lintels, reminding him of the intricate wood carving on the Temple Ship. Then, as they emerged from the side streets in the heart of the city, he was awestruck.

Confronting them was a great boulevard with a tree-flanked highway enclosing a central island of magnificent architecture. The boulevard had been densely planted with decorative trees, now irregularly hacked down to fuel fires in the shanties. Riverward, two great battlemented horns embraced the plaza, which was completed by a three-sided buttress on the harbour walls. Great bronze cannons extended out over the masts of the ships. From this elevated platform, high above the moored ships and gantries, the eye was drawn to the confluence of the two rivers below, which dictated the shape of the plaza, and from which the city had derived its strategic importance.

Isscan, as Milish explained, was the province's largest inland fishing port, being situated at the meeting of the two great rivers, the Ezel, or East River, and the Snowmelt, or Tshis-Cole, as it was known locally. From here, the confluent Snowmelt River continued southwards to enter the mountainous pass of Kloshe Lamah. 'There it meanders,' she whispered, as if she were in fear of being overheard, 'through the Forest of the Undying in the Vale of Tazan, dividing around the holy isle of Ossierel, to meet again in a new majesty, running southeast until it meets the Eastern Ocean at Carfon, the last sanctuary of freedom among the great cities of Monisle, and where we are bound.'

Alan considered what she had whispered, confused by notions of undying forests and a holy isle, as he gazed for a moment around the plaza, with its stepped platform, where a multitude gathered about its steps. 'My God!'

From a distance of fifty or sixty yards, he recognised the obscene carnival of a public execution. And not of a single prisoner, but of a series of a dozen or more men and women, their hands manacled behind their backs and their ankles shackled and linked from one person to the next by a long black chain. Some of them looked hardly older than children.

'Mask your aversion,' hissed Milish. 'Yet witness how grief follows in the wake of the Death Legion, as flies follow the reek of corruption.'

With nausea rising from the pit of his stomach, Alan made out the distant figure of a tall, white-robed man, who appeared to be presiding over the executions. He looked like some venerable priest, with flowing white hair and beard. Lofting a glittering chalice before the exultant mob, he brought the chalice to his lips and drank its contents. The mob cheered. Alan had an awful presentiment of what filled the chalice.

Milish led them away from the grand boulevard, though her gait was stiffer than before. 'Damn the Tyrant!' she muttered. 'Damn him and his minions to the pits of hell!'

Quickening their steps, they entered a street that was more functional, paved with granite, cobbled for commercial traffic and lined with three-storey buildings of unadorned stone. Midway along this street she stopped by an entrance with windows guarded by spiked embrasures and its door head decorated with hieroglyphs. It appeared to house some of the civic offices. The gap-toothed man who answered Milish's knock eyed them with suspicion, but Milish was persuasive enough to get them over the threshold. The doorkeeper told them to wait in a corridor. He brought his mistress, a squat civil servant, who eyed them with a contemptuous stare.

She led them to a wide and high-ceilinged chamber where other men and women, busy at desks or tables, did not trouble even to glance in their direction. Strangers were not welcomed by these townspeople. Nevertheless business was business, and now Alan witnessed how business was done.

The woman took a seat in a padded mahogany chair, leaning her fleshy arms on a desk of similar wood while listening to Milish's prevarications.

There had been a flood caused by an untimely spring, as Milish explained, disguising her voice under a more earthy accent. This had forced a village of fisher people to abandon their winter quarters to seek sanctuary in Isscan. Among these simple people was her brother by marriage. She begged this good lady, busy as she was with her public duty, to assist them. Was not Isscan's reputation for shelter famous throughout Monisle! Perhaps this council woman might have heard word of some new arrivals that fitted Milish's description?

The woman yawned, making it clear that she had no interest in homeless rabble.

Milish produced a purse that jingled with coins, which she now tipped onto the desk. The coinage was gold, of different sizes and geometric patterns, some triangular, square, or hexagonal, each denomination decorated with a symbol from nature: corn, flowers, animals, birds and insects.

Alan watched the official closely to see if she showed any signs of undue curiosity. But he saw nothing other than ill-concealed greed in her eyes. 'A village of fisher people, you say?'

'They would have registered their boats with the harbourmaster – and very recently.' Milish scooped the coins back into her purse and held it firmly to her breast. 'The waterfront is such a warren, they could be anywhere. We are wearied in our search for them. We have no place for the night but would be pleased to share what simple refuge they might have found.'

The barter lasted several more minutes, during which the official tested Milish, making sure that there was no more gold to be extracted. Only then, taking the purse and having asked several of her clerks to check their records for the fisher people's arrival, did she dismiss them with a peremptory nod, barking to the doorkeeper, who was instructed to lead them to an address. Once back in the streets the gap-toothed lackey took Milish's last triangular gold coin before he would lead them more than a block from his mistress's offices.

They soon abandoned the grander streets to enter a maze of shambling alleys lined by taverns. In the yards of some of the larger taverns were sunken arenas that looked like fighting pits. From time to time, Alan caught the furtive swivel of Gaptooth's eyes, as though he were attempting to probe Alan's face under the low brim of his hat. Unlike the official, Gaptooth appeared decidedly curious about the strangers. Meanwhile the smell on the air told them that their guide was leading them back to the waterfront.

The end of their mission was a wooden building on the wharf-side, sunken at one corner into the foul-smelling mud, where the piles that sustained it had rotted away. Its weatherboarding was splintered and peeling, and many of the deformed planks had sprung their nails at the corners. Here, Gaptooth bowed before them with a mocking flourish before kicking ajar one half of the rickety gate.

The stench of fish assaulted their nostrils as they stepped inside the barn-like building.

Amid the shouts of surprise and welcome, Alan was almost bowled over by the tearful Kate. He lifted her off her feet, twirling her round in a circle and hugging her so hard she could hardly breathe.

She kissed him fiercely, then murmured into his ear, 'Ah, and sure I could kill you! I've been bawling my eyes out, thinking you were dead.'

They hugged again, until they simply had to let go to breathe.

'Where's Mark?'

'Here – somewhere.'

'I want a few words with him.'

'Go easy on him, Alan.'

'Go easy?'

There was no time to discuss it further. Now it was Siam's turn to lift Alan off the floor in a bear hug, then curl a burly arm around his shoulders and drag him away to greet Kehloke, Turkeya and Loloba, Turkeya's sister, who were just three among the hundreds of astonished faces that peered at him from the shadows. Alan introduced Milish and Layheas to everybody, then let them all chatter among themselves while he found Kate again. But they were given precious little chance to be alone. Kemtuk limped over the irregular floor to come and clasp his hands, with evident relief.

'My friend!' the shaman exclaimed. Then he leaned over and whispered in Alan's ear, 'We are in great danger. Isscan has proved to be a trap.'

'I saw enough already to have figured that.'

The lack of guards at the gates, the absence of soldiers

on the walls and throughout the streets when an occupied city the size of Isscan should be teeming with them, all made sense only when you realised that it had to be a deliberate strategy. And Gaptooth knew who he was, Alan was certain of it. He put his hand on the shaman's shoulder, escorting him over to Milish, who was being questioned, in urgent whispers, by Siam.

'But tell me quietly,' Alan spoke quietly in Kemtuk's ear while they waited, 'how many were lost?'

'Sixteen. Three whole families. The others from different families. We had assumed we had lost you too.'

'I wouldn't be here, Kemtuk, if Milish and the Shee hadn't arrived to save me.'

'You speak of Shee?'

'They're waiting just outside the town. They know we've got to get away from here.'

The shaman nodded, then took a step back to examine Alan in amazement. 'You appear to have matured years in mere days.'

Alan's gaze turned to Mark, who had just appeared from the shadows to one side, his head bowed. Kate, who was standing next to him, put her arm around his shoulders and looked at Alan, a warning expression in her eyes.

Alan and Mark embraced each other, though there was none of the passion he had felt with the others. Mark looked tired. His red-rimmed eyes lifted to look directly into Alan's. 'Where's Mo?'

'Hey – I'm really sorry! She was taken by the Storm Wolves. We did our best to find her.'

'Are you telling me that Mo's gone?' Tear's glistened in Mark's eyes, which shied away from contact with Alan.

Alan recalled the words of the figure of light in the forest. 'I don't know – but I think, maybe, she's still alive. If so she has to be here, in Isscan. Where else can they have taken her other than here?'

Mark shook his head, unable to believe him, then dashed away. Alan felt like chasing after him, but Kate held him back. Nevertheless, there were urgent questions he needed to ask Mark, and no matter how much he chose to avoid him, Alan was determined to get answers to those questions.

Siam found him again, accompanied by Kemtuk and Milish. He spoke in that same urgent undertone: 'Though you have just arrived, and doubtless are tired and in need of rest, nevertheless we need to make plans to flee.'

The shaman nodded his head. 'I have been pressing Siam to make plans for immediate departure.'

Milish also nodded in complete agreement.

'Not without first trying to find Mo,' Alan insisted. 'Make all the plans you have to, but I have plans of my own.'

Siam grasped Alan's shoulders, gazing at him eye-to-eye. 'We have no time.'

'I'm not going to abandon her.'

'In war, sacrifices must be made!'

'Plan we must, with the council woman, Milish,'

interrupted Kehloke, taking hold of her husband's arm. 'In the meantime, we shall leave the Mage Lord to the welcoming arms of Kate. Surely we must show our guests a little of the traditional Olhyiu courtesies. Food and shelter we do possess, though the quality of both is meagre.'

Kate took the hint to drag Alan away, taking him on a tour of the warehouse, meanwhile holding tight to his arm the whole time, as if still only half believing that he was back with her.

The Olhyiu occupied three communal rooms, with pallets made up from grimy old sacks distributed about the floor. Most of the ground level was a single huge chamber, its ceiling supported by beams fashioned from whole trunks of trees, many still retaining the bark. The reek of fish came from two long tables set aside for fish-gutting and packing, work that the Olhyiu – men, women and children – had taken on in return for food and shelter. The whole chamber was thick with dust, old packing cases and piles of the moth-eaten sacks. At least the plentiful supply of packing cases fuelled a grate in a great brick fireplace. Here, in the shadows, they found a few moments of privacy to really talk.

'Don't you miss your uncle, and Bridey – the Doctor's House?'

Her eyes moistened. 'I never stop thinking about them – and Darkie.'

'Me too! I can't help thinking about things. Grandad!' He brought her close to him and kissed each of her tear-filled eyes.

She kissed him back, long and passionate. 'I'm never going to let you out of my sight again, Alan Duval!'

'I don't ever want to let you out of my arms.'

Their giddy heads were only brought back to reality by the clanging of two great copper pans being beaten together.

'Everybody – let me have all of your attention!'

It was Kehloke, standing on the top of a table, and swirling from one side to the other with a spin of her elegant body and a wave of her pan-wielding arms. She called for a celebration.

'The Mage Lord has returned from what we all assumed to be a watery grave to give us new purpose! Put aside your fears for one evening and gather more timber to feed the fire. Let our guests warm their weary bones. And then we shall feast as best we can in these limited circumstances.'

While Kehloke oversaw the preparations for the meal, Alan, Milish, Kemtuk, Siam and Kate sat around one of the fish-gutting tables and shared information. Siam described how they had been forced to pawn any precious objects they still had to buy vegetables and corn from the market, always with the certainty they were being cheated. 'Every little coin or trinket is gone. They have even robbed us of the wedding amulets from husbands to their wives on the first night of their marriage.'

Alan remembered the tiny jewels that had once decorated the married women's throats. Clearly for Siam this had been the greatest act of betrayal by these corrupted city people. Yet in return for accommodation and shelter, the fisher people had taken on the lowly task of fish-gutting and packing for the fleets of others, working all the waking hours in this rat-infested ruin. They were allowed enough fish to guarantee their supper, which tonight would accompany a soup of vegetables in which to soften their corn bread.

Alan was puzzled by what Siam had said about gutting and packing for others. Surely the Olhyiu had the use of their boats?

A scowl contorted Siam's face. 'All confiscated, from the moment of our arrival in the harbour!'

'Confiscated?' Milish questioned sharply, glancing with alarm at Alan. 'For what transgression?'

'None! We are compelled to join the legions of beggars.' It was Kemtuk who replied on behalf of the furious Siam. 'They call us primitives to our faces. We, the Olhyiu! All our boats lie chained and guarded, even the Temple Ship itself, pending the decision of the High Preband.'

Alan turned to Milish, whose anxious face reflected his own. 'How can you flee,' she asked, 'without boats?'

'It is still worse, I fear,' Kemtuk spoke up. 'Even if we could somehow free our boats, the Death Legion has placed a boom, a great spiked chain, across the river. No vessel can leave the port without the boom being lowered.'

Silence fell over the gathered company.

Milish nodded, her worst fears now confirmed. 'The

Mage Lord's arrival was surely anticipated. It was foolish to imagine otherwise. I am now convinced that there are forces of Death Legion massing within the city.'

Kemtuk confirmed her fears. 'Aye! The town and the surrounding district has more legionaries than a rotting tree has termites. Some, if our sources are confirmed, have already moved on southwards in large numbers by land and river.'

'What can it mean?'

Kemtuk shook his grizzled head. 'It can only mean that they intend to breach the power that guards the ancient Vale of Tazan, with its forbidden forests.'

Milish clutched at Alan's arm. 'Ainé must be made aware of this. If they succeed, Carfon will be vulnerable to attack.'

Alan said, 'Tell me more about Carfon. What about this council – the Council-in-Exile, as you called it?'

'There will be time enough to introduce you to the politics of Carfon if we succeed in passing through the Vale of Tazan ourselves,' she murmured. 'Suffice it to say that our mission to save you was an act of rebellion, contravening the orders of the Council-in-Exile.'

A common foreboding weighed on every heart as they settled down for the frugal meal around the bare wood tables that stank of fish. The Olhyiu ate the meal raw and spicy but they made provision for those who preferred their fish cooked. Alan deliberately took a seat next to Mark. He kept his voice to an urgent whisper.

'What happened back there on the ship?'

'What do you mean?'

'I saw you struggling with Kate. You pushed Mo.'

Mark's face went beetroot. 'I wasn't struggling with Kate. I was trying to save her. I – I sensed she was in danger. I was trying to persuade Kate and Mo to get below deck.'

Alan gazed at Mark, eye-to-eye. Was Mark telling him the truth? Why did he feel that Mark was keeping something important from him? He shook his head, not satisfied with Mark's explanation. He would talk to Kate about it. But for the moment, with all that was threatening, his main concern was Mo.

The Mage of Dreams

With nightfall, as a cold wind rattled the clinkered walls of the warehouse, scraping the wood with a bitter mix of sleet and snow, the company was entertained by a dance of three young men in the centre of the floor. Turkeya organised the music, which sounded a little like pan pipes but was played on a mixture of pipes made out of the bones of animals and pots that resembled ocarina, but longer and more carrot-shaped. Alan's eyes darted about the large room, searching for Mark, who wouldn't normally be left out when it came to music, but Mark had made no effort to join in.

He returned his attentions to the festivities, noticing three young women who stood back, shy in their demeanour, yet with eyes excited by the dancing of the youths. Milish, who had come to sit beside him, accepted a cup of corn liquor from a proffered hand, passed it to Alan as soon as the tray moved on and explained the significance of the dance. Three families had perished and three couples were being bonded. Alan smiled across to Kehloke, who returned his smile. While they had young men to dance and young brides to respond, death would have no hegemony over the Olhyiu people.

The bonding ended with the young men carrying away their brides and it was followed by merriment and more dance music. Kate dragged Alan onto to the dance floor.

'I'm not sure I'm capable, thanks to the attentions of the Storm Wolves.'

'I think we should at least pretend to join in,' she whispered in his ear.

In fact he needed no persuasion to take Kate into his arms.

Siam also joined his people on the floor, dancing with Kehloke, who swirled through the couples with all the grace of the swan in her name. The couple split up, as did others, exchanging dance partners. Alan glimpsed Siam's daughter, Loloba, taking to the floor with a young Olhyiu in tow. Siam was the natural ringmaster, as with jokes and suggestive movements of his hands and body he circulated among his people, a jar in his hand to fill up their cups. And frequently, when their eyes met, the chief would hold the jar aloft, with liquor trickling from his laughing cheeks, before downing some more of the contents, then belching loudly.

Siam's brown eye winked at him, and his head nodded to one side. Alan's gaze drifted in that direction, registering the fact that Kemtuk was signalling him to join him.

Something important was happening. When he manoeuvred Kate up next to the shaman, he explained, 'Turkeya has led a party of men outside – looking for spies.'

Alan gave up any pretence at continuing to dance, considering what this might mean. In a moment, Milish was by his side, her left arm thrown around Kate's shoulders. With her right she pressed a cup into Alan's hands. 'Drink – and let any watching eyes observe your slurring speech and drunken limbs.'

He brought the cup to his lips, noticing it was nothing more than water. He made a play of taking a hearty swig. 'Watching eyes?' he enquired.

Milish transferred her arm from Kate to Alan, as if to merrily entice him back onto the dance floor. 'The walls are full of holes, easy to peer into. None,' she whispered, 'are as drunk as they appear.'

Not needing to feign exhaustion, Alan sat down on a sack by the fireside, where through the plank floor he could hear rats squeaking and scurrying about the half-sunken wharf below. Minutes later he heard a scuffling outside the entrance and several men rushed in, led by Turkeya, who was holding a knife against the throat of a stranger. 'Caught this one peering through the cracks in the wall.'

The stranger was on his knees in the dirt, his hands outstretched, his voice beseeching mercy. Siam took him by the scruff of the neck and exposed his features to the light of a firebrand. Alan recognised the cringing face. 'This is Gaptooth, the servant who led us here.'

'Save me, Mage Lord!' the man whined, his forehead dashed against Alan's feet. 'I do not come to spy, but to serve you. I bear a message from one who would offer you counsel.'

'What treachery is this?' Siam demanded. 'How do you know to call our friend Mage Lord?'

'No treachery, I swear upon my honour.'

'You have no honour.' Siam took the hunting knife from Turkeya and pressed its point up against the spy's scrawny throat.

In one of their captive's pockets they discovered a dagger. But they found no money, not even the small gold coin he had haggled from them earlier. His beery breath suggested how that had been spent. However, they did discover a flattened oval of jade as big as a fist, which was inscribed on both surfaces with intricate carving. Kemtuk took the jade from the searcher's hands and marvelled at the art of it.

'This is strange indeed. It is ancient – I wonder just how ancient and what power might have made it. What remarkable skill guided the hand that inscribed such runes on an unyielding surface!'

The shaman passed the runestone to Alan, who weighed it in his hands, his eyes unable to read its message.

'What does this tell you, Kemtuk?'

The old man hesitated, as if his instincts were torn by contradictions. 'Certainly it doesn't belong to this dolt.'

Gaptooth whined, 'It is as I have tried to explain – an invitation, from one who calls himself the Mage of Dreams.'

The man screamed as Siam's knife blade drew a bead of blood from the cords of his throat. 'The choice of emissary is evidence enough of treachery,' growled Siam. 'I say kill the spy and make haste to the harbour.'

'Master, I beg you! I would not wish upon you the fate that beckons if you tried to cut free your boats.'

Alan said, 'Siam – hold on a moment. Let him explain.'

'A thousand thanks, Mage Lord. I beg you and your companions to consider. I speak the truth. The Mage of Dreams is greatly venerated in this city. But his location is difficult since, with the perils of these dark times, his chamber must be hidden from the merely curious. I have been bidden to take you to him.'

'Why would the Mage of Dreams want to meet me?'

'Read the message in full, Mage Lord. Its truth is sealed within the runestone.'

Alan returned the runestone to Kemtuk, who crossed to the fireside, where he spent many minutes running his fingers over its surfaces, even sniffing at it – exploring it through every sense before he returned.

'There can be no doubting that this is indeed a stone of power. It is very ancient, with markings unlike any I have ever seen. If I am not mistaken, it is powerful – the property of a great and powerful Mage. There may well be a message concealed within it, though what message, I cannot tell.'

Kemtuk returned the runestone to Alan, who moved across to kneel in the firelight, where he could illuminate the jade in the cradle of his hands. Then, closing his eyes, he probed it with the oraculum.

'Oh my God! Kate – take a look!'

'What is it?' Kate hurried over to join him in front of the fire.

Alan held out the runestone so she could gaze into its crystal depths. Kate's expression changed to astonishment as she saw, imprisoned there, the ghostly spectre of Mo's face peering back at her.

'But . . . but what on earth does it mean?'

'Mo's lips are moving. It's as if she's trying to tell us something!'

'To warn you, perhaps?' Kemtuk spoke.

Alan could hear the murmur of excited and cautionary voices around him, although they seemed to come from a thousand miles away. He exhaled slowly, before climbing back onto his feet.

'All I need to know is that Mo's alive! And she's here, somewhere in Isscan!' He clenched the runestone so tightly his fingers crackled.

Kate hugged him. Mark's worn face appeared out of the shadows to join them, his wide-staring eyes focused on the runestone.

'You believe what you see in that thing?'

'What do you think, Kemtuk?'

'There is much here that confuses and alarms me. Our enemies know where we are. They allowed us entry on the open river. The gates and walls are such as to put up a false impression of being unguarded. Once here, the authorities block our escape. They spy on all that we do. Yet still they withhold their attack. The logical inference is that they fear you, Mage Lord. Indeed I would wager that their overlords sit in counsel even now, considering a way in which they might destroy your power before they are ready to attack.'

'The shaman's words express the thought I have dreaded every hour since entering this fallen citadel,' Milish agreed.

Alan nodded. 'Thanks, all of you, for your concern. But I'll have to take whatever risk is necessary to meet this Mage of Dreams. I can't ignore the fact that Mo's life is in danger.'

'I'll come with you,' blurted Mark.

'No! It must be you alone, Mage Lord,' insisted Gaptooth, his eyes squinting with a sudden cunning. Even as he winced as Siam jabbed the blade harder against his throat, he insisted. 'Entry to the Mage's chamber is forbidden except to those he has invited.'

Kemtuk took Alan's arm to draw him out of earshot.

'Let me offer my protection. For the lore of such a mage will be powerful indeed. And his presence here, in a city that has fallen to the Tyrant, might imply a malicious allegiance. I will follow your path tonight and will be nearby if danger threatens.'

A bitter wind scoured the streets, blowing sleet as cutting as ice against Alan's face as Gaptooth took him on a winding route, no doubt deliberately clouding any sense he might have of their direction. They passed the night's drunks, lurching between hostelries in the meaner streets, with wooden houses almost meeting as they fell towards one another in their upper storeys across the refuse-soiled passages. On and on they wove, through a degenerate labyrinth that seemed to extend for miles, arriving at a district of tall and rickety buildings closely gathered about walkways of iced-over cobbles. Here, they entered a poorly illuminated inner maze, ascending and descending staircases of age-worn stone, moving through hunched arches and uneven avenues.

At last his guide peered back into the darkness, listening hard to make sure that they had not been followed before opening a latch-gate concealed in a soot-begrimed wall of irregular and deeply shadowed boulders. They were close enough to the waterfront for Alan's ears to pick up the creaking of rigging and for his nose to pick up the smell of polluted brine. The Mage's chamber was a few hundred yards further on in the twist and turn in what increasingly felt like a three-dimensional maze in solid stone. It was Alan's impression that they had entered the fabric of the ancient city walls. He was unaware of having entered a building, so confusing was the approach through tunnels and portals, yet immediately he felt the triangle in his brow pulse with a sense of numinous power as they arrived at an antechamber with a narrow window, looking down eighty feet onto the masts of ships. There was no time for him to see if the triple mast of the Temple Ship was among them.

A figure was waiting by a window, his white-cowled face in shadow. Alan spotted Gaptooth's furtive hand return the runestone to its master.

With his guide melting away through the closing doorway, Alan saw the cowl drawn back on a face harrowed with age and bent forward over a frame as spare and fragile as a heron's. The Mage of Dreams was a good half foot taller than Alan, even though he was bent over the staff he held in his right hand. He seemed old beyond the threshold where one bothers to count the decades. His locks of hair, thinning over the front and crown of his head, fell down over his neck and shoulders in a cataract of white, as fine as silk threads. As Alan's hand was clasped in the Mage's withered fingers, a dwarf with coppery red hair appeared from a gothic doorway, swaying in hesitation like a drunken man. The dwarf made a guttural sound, as if he had lost his tongue, and then, with a clumsy bow, led them down a sloping passage with damp-stained walls, into a close-walled chamber where a fire crackled and roared in a corbelled fireplace.

As he turned to leave them, the dwarf appeared to totter against the wall of the entrance passage, causing a flicker of amusement to cross the eyes of the Mage. 'Forgive my servant his unfortunate habit. I retain him out of loyalty after many years of service.' The Mage's face wrinkled to a wry smile. 'Would you indulge an old man in his amusement? In this poor dungeon, I nourish such simple creatures for the joy of their beauty.'

With a gentle clap of the Mage's hands, clouds of brilliant colour filled the air between them, dazzling and shimmering. They spiralled and fluttered until they filled the chamber, like the fall of blossom in a breeze. Alan was astonished to discover that they were butterflies, of a diaphanous sapphire blue. Several alighted about the Mage's eyes to create the illusion of a carnival mask around the clouded irises of venerable age. Alan couldn't help sensing great power behind the gentleness. From the fire a fragrant incense cloaked a reek that Alan assumed must be rising out of the harbour.

For a moment, in the poor light of a chandelier and the flames of the fire, the Mage made a point of putting aside his staff to stand erect before Alan and, intertwining the fingers of his hands, as if in a refinement of passion, gazed even more deeply into Alan's eyes. 'These are troubled times. Yet such determination and courage do I read in your character!'

Those gentle eyes had curious pinpoints of gold invading the blue, like myriad fairy lights in a constant motion of weaving and whorling. For a moment Alan felt a dizziness pass over him but, with a pulse of his brow, it quickly cleared. The Mage stepped back a pace, as if in surprise, before his voice returned with a new tenor of respect underlying the prodigious intelligence and learning.

'Indeed, young sir!' Those skeletal hands, dappled with liver spots, waved him to a comfortable leather armchair by the fireside, while the Mage took his seat in an identical one opposite, with a low round table in between. 'A gentleman is a gentleman in all worlds – and it is such a rare pleasure to meet one these days. And the bearer of such a portal of power – known to the ignorant as the Oraculum of the Three Witches. You grace a lonely scholar with your visit. Alas, I am compelled to endure these reduced circumstances. But still I am able to offer some refreshment.'

The Mage's blue eyes twinkled with merriment as he picked up a tiny silver hand bell and tinkled it above his head. Only four of his teeth still survived, all canines, which gave his smile the look of an old cat yawning. His nostrils, as if suffused with the emotion of their meeting, had begun to run with mucus, and the tip of his nose had turned a bright scarlet. With the forgetfulness of an old man, he wiped his running nose on a pendulous sleeve as silkily white as his hair and interwoven with cabbalistic symbols in gold and silver threads. Then, with a flourish of his hand, he beckoned entry to the dwarf, who stood cautiously in the inner door. Alan inspected the small yet heavily shouldered servant, whose features were different from those of any dwarf he had ever seen before. His skin was reddish bronze, his face square and heavy, his nose broad and flattened and his lips thick and wide. There was a sense of unbreakable pride in his emerald-green eyes that belied the status of a servant.

'Ah!' the Mage cried. 'A noggin, my dear Zoda. A refreshing sup of our special reserve that will aid our guest to unburden himself of his apprehensions.' Then, as the servant hesitated, those aged eyes fell upon Alan and the thick brows arched in a moment's benign contemplation.

'Forgive my boldness, yet I already know the reason you have come. I have been expecting you.'

'How do you know about me?'

'My goodness! He is the direct one, is he not, Zoda?'

Inclining his head, the rheumy eyes widened with a mischievous amusement. 'Of course we adept have long awaited your arrival. You, my dear young man, are the incarnation of prophecy. But enough of this! Zoda! Have I not called for refreshment?'

Alan felt increasingly uncomfortable with the obsequious tone of the Mage. He nodded his appreciation while his voice remained firm. 'I don't have the time to chat. My friend, Mo, is missing. You sent me your runestone with Mo's face in it. Can't you just tell me where to find her?'

A more knowing smile crinkled the corners of the Mage's withered mouth. 'The young gentleman is in a great hurry. Ah, but surely we can help him, can we not, Zoda, on the condition that each of us is prepared to share a secret or two with the other?'

Alan sighed. 'I don't have any secrets.'

'No secrets! Hark at the gentleman!'

'I just don't have time to be fooling around. All I want is your help in finding my friend.'

The Mage of Dreams nodded his wise old head. 'It is true – I did send you her image. And I assure you that I will do all within my power to help you. But first I must have a little information in return. I am curious to know more about your companions. A she-cat of the Western Mountains, a Kyra who bears an oraculum of power upon her brow, and a rebel princess from the Council-in-Exile. Tell me more of these. Why have they accompanied you to Isscan? What business have they in coming here?'

Alan tried to conceal his surprise. How could the Mage of Dreams know about Ainé and Milish? He had no awareness of his mind being probed.

He wondered if he dared to use the triangle to probe the mind that lay behind the rheumy blue eyes. Even as he considered this the dwarf re-entered the chamber and handed Alan a goblet of heavy silver, chased with glittering symbols over its bowl. The dwarf filled the goblet almost to the brim with a clear, thick liqueur, poured from a decanter of turquoise crystal. Alan took a sip to find that it tasted sweet and strong. His senses reeled from an immediate intoxication.

'Where's my friend?'

The Mage of Dreams accepted a similar goblet and he took a delicate sip from its contents before replying. 'We should not hurry this conversation. First, a toast! To the pleasure of your visit, my dear young sir!'

Though he was increasingly irritated by this time-wasting nonsense, Alan went through the motions of taking another sip. The Mage of Dreams also took a second, noisier, swig. 'But to business! I can tell you that your friend has indeed been brought to Isscan. By a one-armed bear-man, one of the ferals.'

Alan sat back, startled. 'Snakoil Kawkaw?' Somehow the traitor had not only escaped but must have known where Mo was and taken her with him.

'Is she okay?'

The Mage of Dreams shrank back, as if shocked. 'Such concern! You really do care deeply about this young friend. To my knowledge, she is unhurt.'

'Why won't you just tell me where she is?'

'Patience – *patience*! I must know more before I can help you. To answer your needs, I would know of your secret. What is the source of your power? Who bequeathed you, so obviously ignorant in such matters, such an oraculum of destiny?'

'I've had enough of your questions.'

'Had enough of my questions? Such discourtesy is

disappointing. I merely enquire as to its source. Ah – hmm! I have in mind a perfidious being, enamoured of spiders, worms and slime! But one who is yet careful to conceal her machinations. Have you by chance encountered such a being?'

'I don't give a damn about this.' Alan attempted to stand up again, but immediately fell back in his chair, his senses reeling.

The Mage's eyes glittered, then widened. 'Ah – forgive my rambling! Replenish the goblets, Zoda. And you, my friend, drink up! It will relax your mind and help me to help you in your need. Yes, that's it – that's the way!' Suddenly Alan felt an overwhelming compulsion to take another drink of the clear liqueur. The Mage nodded, watching him lift the heavy silver goblet to his lips. He waited until Alan had taken a much deeper draught, then smiled a great wide yawn, with those four pointed teeth bared. 'Yes . . . um! But can it be true that you know nothing at all about the source of your power?'

Alan's mouth began to speak, as if against his will. 'I . . . I might have seen somebody like you describe . . .'

'How fascinating! And did she give you a purpose – one that has led you here to my door in search of your poor friend, who, alas, is lost and calling out your name?' He clapped his hands and the sad-looking dwarf reappeared.

'More refreshment, clumsy oaf!' The Mage struck the dwarf a sharp blow across his face, causing him to totter back, striking the wall with a wince of pain. 'Get to it!'

The Mage dismissed the servant to take a rasping slurp at his goblet, draining its contents, before returning to Alan. 'How should I put it, my fine young sir? Perhaps you have spent too much time in the company of witches.'

Alan was startled at the grimace of loathing that accompanied the Mage's derogatory reference to women.

'Ummm – I wonder if these witches have been telling you lies? Oh, you will think me overly suspicious no doubt, but experience has made me wonder if all women are not born with lying tongues. Is it not conceivable that at the very least you have been misled by them – these witches who pretend to be your friends and yet have broken the edicts of their own High Council-in-Exile?'

The Mage's tone had taken on a growling quality, and his brow had fissured into a spider's web of wrinkles. 'My good young man, you must ask yourself that simple question, as indeed have I. Have you been beguiled? Yes, beguiled I say!' The yawning smile appeared no longer to be a smile at all, but a triumphant baring of teeth. 'Consider all that has befallen you since you first arrived in this blighted land.'

Alan felt the compulsion to reply, to tell all, to agree with the preposterous insinuations the Mage was making as, meanwhile, the Mage waited, with ill-concealed impatience, for the frightened dwarf to refill both goblets, all the while studying Alan with intense speculation. A covetous look flickered across a face that now seemed more scaly than lined. His lips drew back thin and wide, to drain in a single swallow the contents of the goblet. His shoulders seemed to fill out and hunch massively about his neck. Suddenly Alan sensed a violent invasion of his mind.

A deeper growl replaced the old Mage's quaver. 'Do not have the insolence to resist me!' The changing figure stretched enormously long arms, as if to reach out to claw at Alan's oraculum. Alan found a deep reserve of self-preservation that pulsed momentarily in the triangle, causing those long arms to retract. The Mage's face contracted, revealing a huge, alien, contortion, which he covered with a hand, as if to suppress a yawn, after which he widened his eyes and shook his weary head. 'The first power you appear to have discovered – if poorly. You derive a modest strength from it. But still you have much to learn.' A hateful glee transfigured the Mage's restored face. The inner beast was so close to the surface that his expression seemed to vary from moment to moment. 'My, my . . . So much that puzzled me is now revealed. The witches' plans – I see them now. Confound them and their execrable trinity!'

Alan was sweating freely from his struggle to block the mental probing. He found his voice, though it caught in his throat. 'I – I don't understand anything you're saying.'

With what appeared an immense struggle, tranquillity again cloaked the Mage's features, though his eyes still stared suspiciously into Alan's own. 'Such a power, as you, young sir, have now discovered, may be a trial as much as a blessing. For nobody could carry this accursed mark without knowing the secrets of their plans. Secrets you will volunteer to me. Ah, confound the witches!'

Alan forced his will into the oraculum again, to discover some last well of strength to oppose the Mage. 'You look sick, old man . . . confused?'

'Do not play games with me, foolish manling! Oh, devour the witches! Lick their blood!' Those bony fingers scratched at the ancient brow, the overly long nails in what were increasingly metamorphosing from aged hands to claws, gouged the skin to either side of his wrinkled face. 'How deviously they have plotted against the Master! Well, their plans are now undone.'

Alan had noticed how, with every slurp of his drink, the scarlet of the old man's nose was spreading further to become a butterfly mask of thick red scales that was spreading over his cheeks. 'Pain cleanses. Pain,' the monstrous face now seethed, 'is the delight that lies at the core of debased womankind. Does she not cry out in the ecstasy of it as she presents her very offspring from her foul cloaca?' Two large animal eyes now peered out of their enfolding wrinkles with the hard black glitter of polished jet.

'Where the hell is my friend Mo?'

The metamorphosing thing opposite growled, the words barely distinguishable. 'Drink, manling! Zoda, you scabrous excrement! Fill the goblets – to the brim!'

Alan had no intention of drinking what the Mage was

forcing on him. He tried to create a barrier within his mind. But he was unable to resist picking up the glittering silver goblet, unable to resist drinking again, though his senses swooned almost until he was unconscious. And the Mage, with lip-smacking relish, drained his own in another noisy slurp.

'Soon you will stock my larder, you and all your brattish friends.' The Mage's hands had tightened about the bony swelling that formed the head of his staff, fingers arched about it like claws over a skull. 'You will forget all about the answers you seek when I introduce you to the delights of torment. In such circumstances your cries for mercy will become a music of their very own!'

With growing horror, Alan realised that he was losing control of his will. 'You'll never win!'

'Thus would you repartee with me?'

The increasingly beast-like face, with elongating snout, reached across the table to snap its teeth in Alan's face. 'Hark at the fool! What a poor rival you have proved, in truth.'

Through his increasingly clouded senses, Alan remembered the white-robed figure lifting the chalice to his lips before the exultant crowd in the plaza. He had been too distant to see that figure's face. But now he knew who that figure must have been. He used the oraculum to enter the mind behind the curtain of those alien eyes. And in so doing, he confronted an alien intelligence, dreadful and ominous. A dew of sweat oozed out of his brow and plastered his hair to his head. There was nothing at all that he could do to prevent the talon that reached out to his brow, that touched with a contemptuous ivory point the recoiling matrix of the oraculum.

'Ah,' growled the voice, now crackling with glee, 'you so desperately wish to find your friend? Perhaps the information you seek is in the possession of my Master. Surely then it is my Master you would like to meet!'

Saving Mo

A black vapour materialised over the table that stood between them. It solidified as a perfect pentagon. Though it seemed smoother than still water, no reflection showed upon its surface. In its depths Alan perceived an expanding matrix of awesome power. With that twinkling smile returned to his malleable features, the Mage had taken a blood-red prism, shaped like a multifaceted inverted cone, from a pocket in his capacious robe and caused it to rise into the air, suspended, it seemed, without any visible attachment over the centre of the pentagon.

Suddenly the bloodstone began spinning rapidly about its vertical axis, and the Mage's growl became distant and hypnotic.

'In search of enlightenment you came to me. Well, now, enlightenment has found you. For this key will open the door to the most secret and hallowed of labyrinths, my foolish young friend.'

The withered Mage was eclipsed by a third presence, a more formidable figure by far, its features shadowed like coals within a blood-red flame. Even to look at this presence pained Alan's eyes. But he could not avert his gaze any more than he was able to blink. Slowly the cowled head lifted, and he saw there a being of utter darkness. The figure willed him closer, and his limbs ached to comply with that instruction, though he fought back with all of his might.

'No withholding. All resistance must be abandoned.' The voice of the Mage of Dreams echoed within his skull.

Then, abruptly, his mind was penetrated as sharply as if a blade had entered it, and Alan was gazing down upon himself and his three friends. Though he knew the scene, Alan felt a strange, cold detachment. They were gathered about the tumulus of stone on the summit of Slievenamon, under a dreadful sky that wheeled about them. He saw the expression on every face, including his own . . . the look of horror as the guardian of the gate attacked them.

'A pernicious little cabal!' exclaimed the Mage. 'But now you will disown them. You will spurn them and kneel in homage of my Master!'

Alan resisted that command. Yet the compulsion to obey it overwhelmed his mind. 'Surely my young friend has not imbibed enough. Another drink, scabrous Zoda – let our young friend show the Master a token of his veneration!'

Though he did not know the nature of the Mage's poison, Alan's mind reeled with its intoxication already. Fighting back with every fibre of his resistance, he used the oraculum to scour his blood for evidence of the chemical nature of the poison, so he could fight it. But still he found nothing. A thought struck him with the suddenness of revelation: he remembered the spiritual essence that had charged the weaponry of the Kyra in the riverside battle. He felt certain that the Mage had infused some similar potion into the drinks, a potion that had no effect on the Mage but which was undermining his own spirit. Sweat poured from Alan's brow as, physically weakened by the poison, he resisted the force of compulsion that rose again within him. As the dwarf brought the glittering goblet to his lips, an icy darkness enclosed him, as if to physically devour him.

A glimpse alone and Alan almost died from the horror of it: a vision as through the pupil of a monstrous eye that enclosed an entire universe of darkness. And the deep and dreadful voice that addressed him as a whisper in his mind was no longer that of the Mage, but his Master.

So we meet! And you, in your ignorance, imagine yourself my adversary?

'Who . . . who are you?'

Why, I go by many names. To those, such as my servant who has so readily trapped you in his lair, I am the cusp of reason and veneration. To the Shee-witch who ruled Ossierel until her final abject surrender to my conquest, I was the other side of grace, the left hand of darkness. Like her, you will discover, in opposing me, that my power, like my will, is infinite.

Alan shrank back into his chair by the fire, its flames now cold as tombstones, his limbs withering with an increasing paralysis, aware only of his hands writhing uselessly over one another, until the knuckles crackled.

That figure was gesticulating with a single ebony talon, its cowled head so close it could have stretched out and touched him.

There is an answer I would have of you before I leave you to the Mage's passions. There is one among you who bears a secret name – Mira. I must know which of you it is.

He saw, as if through a pitiless eye, the four friends again. His gaze could not blink over the vision in which terror was frozen on all of their faces. A gigantic shadow was bisecting the sky. In his eyes the orange of flames, in his ears the howl of battle. The howling condensed, in a moment, to become a bell that was pealing, distant in his mind.

Very well, if you will not speak, I will enter your mind!

The figure extended an arm of darkness out of the cavern of its sleeve. The claw on the end of a stygian finger was reaching towards his brow . . .

'No!' Though his heartbeat faltered, like the irregular pealing of his own doom, he found the inner strength to resist it for one final moment.

In that same moment, a clatter startled him from his entrancement. The dwarf, who had refilled their goblets, stumbled as he left the chamber through the door that now seemed more the portal to a shadowed crypt. The clatter was the turquoise decanter shattering against the floor, releasing elemental forces to flash and explode about the chamber.

The Mage's howl of wrath filled Alan's ears as the dwarf bowed repeatedly in a profuse apology, while collecting the fragments in his hands.

The black pentagon melted away.

The voice of the Mage was a snarl, issuing in slurring cadences through grotesquely elongating lips. 'Clumsy fool – I shall take pleasure in the multiplication of your pain!'

Alan was still shaken with horror by the memory of that figure of darkness, yet he knew he had to deflect the Mage's wrath from the dwarf. He intoned not through speech alone but subtly, through the oraculum, fawning over the beast's head that now capped the figure of the Mage, a reptilian mask of black glistening eyes and slavering jaws from which protruded four venomous fangs.

'Anger does not become such . . . such a sublime mind.' He racked his brain to find the right flowery words to fit the archaic language of the Mage. 'I have never encountered a mind as powerful as yours before. Not even, I daresay, the mind of the Tyrant himself!'

'A mind as powerful, you say?' the Mage growled. 'None – not even the Great One – not even the Master?'

Alan saw in that moment how the dwarf was signalling

to him. He made a drinking motion, then shook his head. With his face looking ominous, the dwarf pointed to his own wide-staring eyes before he scuttled away, with head bowed, through the door.

A conflict of rage and self-preening fought within the grotesquely metamorphosing figure opposite Alan. For a moment, the kindly old man dominated. 'But you flatter me, surely?'

Alan tried to continue his deception while struggling to interpret the dwarf's signals. 'I think you'd see through flattery in an instant, an intellect that's so superior . . . well, I guess, in all that is ignoble?'

'Ah – indeed I would!' The Mage's head became that of a bird, a tall bird, like a great heron, of snowy plumage with eyes of a sulphurous yellow, fissured with red. In a moment, the eyes switched back to the black of the reptile, lusting for blood. Only now did Alan understand what the dwarf had been trying to communicate. The power of the Mage – the entrancement – was not solely located in the drink. The greater danger lay in the eyes. He recalled how the enchantment had begun with the very first trick – the sapphire mask of the butterflies that had drawn his attention to the Mage's eyes.

Alan broke eye contact, pretending to examine his silver goblet, as if in admiration.

'Yes!' The snout hissed, its mucousy breath right up against his ear. 'We must partake of the civilities. Yeeesss!' A contemptuous gloating sounded at the back of a lengthening throat, edged by fangs. The eyes careened through hypnotic blue within their mask of butterflies, yet all the while coldly observant, basking in the anticipation of devouring him.

'I can see,' gurgled the Mage, 'how you might adore the likes of me. Savour, while you can, your eclipse by no small captain of darkness.' A muscular tongue, glistening blue-black and forked at its tip, darted from between the fangs in the gaping maw as it licked its stretched lips before swigging its drink in a single gulp. Alan watched with horror the changes that continued to invade the Mage's body. He was rising out of his chair, a darkling shape that had abandoned any pretence to being human, elongating at one end into a tail and at the other into a gaping snout. From its paws sprang three claws as it reached out towards Alan's brow.

The dwarf was back in the chamber. His face was contorted as if in an agony of effort. He was holding something in his outstretched hand – the runestone of polished jade. By some sleight of hand – or will, perhaps – during the confusion of the dropped ewer, he had stolen the runestone from the Mage. Now he was pressing it forward with an extended arm, fighting every inch against a resisting force that caused the veins on his temples to bulge and knot, and reaching towards Alan's brow.

Still the distance that separated them, though mere inches, was too much for him.

The dwarf's face was grotesque with effort. A flare of scarlet ignited his features. But he was losing his struggle.

Alan turned his head, willing his paralysed limbs to move. The claws, like pincers, had caught hold of his hair. They twisted and turned, attempting to bring his face closer to the slavering maw. He tried to tear himself loose. He focused his desperation through his mind, searching for the weakened power of the oraculum. Suddenly there was a thunderclap and a flash of lightning, causing the beast to stagger off balance. But its strength was enormous. The outstretched paw slackened momentarily, but did not release him. Instead, the claws tore deeper, twisting wildly, as powerfully as a hawser shackling his head.

Bringing himself an inch closer to the runestone, Alan felt blood start to trickle under his hair. He forced his head to move further towards the jade, his scalp stretching through the hurricane of pain.

The beast roared, re-tightening its grip. Its head was lolling from side to side with the force of its struggle to pull him towards it. The jaws were gaping, the tongue flicking about violently, through and around the slavering fangs. The agony mounted until Alan could no longer see the dwarf, could hear nothing but the roaring of the beast's fury, its ravening lust almost touching his face. Then, abruptly, he felt the oraculum make contact with the jade, and a force, like a breaking dam, flowed from him and into the runestone. The chamber exploded into a fury of thunder and lightning.

He found himself on hands and knees on the flagstones, in front of the extinguished fire. The storm raged about him, hurling the table and chairs against the walls and ceiling. The dwarf had been thrown down on the floor beside him, yet still he managed to hold the runestone aloft, its matrix exploding a hurricane of power against the cowering beast.

Alan struggled to think. Somehow his oraculum had awoken great power in the runestone and the dwarf had known how to use it. But there was no time to dwell on this. Suddenly the jade was extinguished, pressed into some inner pocket of the small man's tattered clothes, and he was helping Alan to his feet, taking hold of his face between his hands, rubbing Alan's cold, perspiring skin, slapping him on either cheek to hasten his recovery.

Opposite them the Mage flickered uncertainly between metamorphoses, yet a single eye, alternately blue and dreadful yellow, still watched Alan as the tongue lolled over the fangs.

'Go! Run for your life!' the dwarf shouted. 'The force of the runestone will not hold it for long.'

'Did you see?' Alan's voice was croaky, forced from a throat still husky with horror.

'Yes, I saw. His fear of you must be great for the Tyrant to challenge you in person. But quickly now – we must escape this prison while there is time.'

'I came here to find my friend. But now I've failed.' Shaking his head in despair, Alan was still only gathering his own senses as the dwarf threw open the side door leading into a pitch-dark chamber. He disappeared into the gloom, then returned with his arm around the shoulders of a small and trembling figure. She rushed into Alan's arms.

'Mo!'

'Alan! Oh, you're hurt! You're bleeding.'

'Never mind me. How are you?'

Tears rushed into Mo's eyes and she hugged him tighter. 'I knew you'd come. I knew you'd find me.'

Suddenly Alan held her back from him so he could look at her in amazement. 'Mo – you didn't stammer.'

'No. I didn't. Alan, there's so much to tell you. I don't know how I could even start to explain.'

But the dwarf interrupted them, grabbing each of them by the arm and hurrying them out of the Mage's chamber.

'Thank you, whoever you are. I owe you my life!' Alan gasped his gratitude, as they arrived at the gate in the wall of boulders. It was still night, although the first promise of dawn was in the sky.

All of a sudden, the dwarf stamped his foot and, seizing both of Alan's wrists in a fierce clasp, his face scowled and their eyes met. 'Don't you realise who I am?' In the half light of daybreak, Alan was confronted by those emerald-green eyes, which were blazing with pride. The dwarf struck his chest with a gnarly fist and stretched to his full height, his rage making him seem a foot taller than his diminutive stature. He raised the runestone out of a pocket. 'My property – and so, with your help, I have reclaimed it. I am Qwenqwo Cuatzel, the true Mage of Dreams.'

Mo laughed with delight. 'I knew it! I knew you were special when you risked your life to comfort me in that terrible place!' She threw her arms around the dwarf's thick neck and hugged him with all of her might.

'And I, in my turn, owe my liberation to you both. You are remarkable young people. It is my honour to consider you my friends.'

For a moment longer, all three held one another. But then Qwenqwo Cuatzel shook himself free, shaking his head. 'Later! There will be a time for talking around a campfire. Now there is a need for haste.'

Alan nodded. 'Just tell me who – or what he is?'

'A warlock from the realms of chaos. Do you imagine that he alone would have had power enough to usurp me? None other than the Tyrant himself could have cast me down! I was forced to be the amanuensis and slave to that hypocrite and liar, while his shadow grew and spread. But enough of explanations! Hurry now! With every moment, the danger increases.'

He led Alan and Mo through the labyrinth of shadows, to where Kemtuk appeared out of the shade of a doorway, his face racked with contrition.

'Mage Lord, I followed through the most difficult of tracks to this point, when an ague came over my mind. I awoke only minutes ago, convinced that we had lost you.'

Alan grabbed the shaman's hand and squeezed it. 'No time for apologies! We've rescued Mo. All thanks to the real Mage of Dreams.'

The dwarf mage waved them away. 'You have sprung the warlock's trap. But still another trap ensnares you.'

'The Death Legion!'

Qwenqwo took a renewed grip on Alan's arm. His breath was hot on Alan's face. 'You people are its target. Save yourselves! There is nothing left for me here. I shall join you in escape.'

'But we have vulnerable people to protect.'

'Then take them with you. Any who are left will be hunted down.'

Alan turned to Kemtuk. 'Can you find your way back to the warehouse?'

'Yes.'

'We must call Ainé. Get help.'

Qwenqwo squeezed Alan's arm even tighter. 'There is no more time for talk.'

Kemtuk still shook his head. 'But how can we possibly escape? The boats of the Olhyiu are confiscated and guarded.'

The dwarf mage twisted his neck a moment, as if he had heard a distant growl on the night air, his twisted back hunched and gnarled as an old tree root.

Kemtuk decided. 'The Temple Ship is our only hope. All other boats will have to be sacrificed. We must flee downriver to the Vale of Tazan. The Legion will follow but we may yet elude them. I know that for all their boasting, they have not yet defeated the ancient power that still inhabits the Forest of the Undying. If only we can pass through that haunted valley, sanctuary awaits us in Carfon.'

From his pocket Qwenqwo picked out the runestone and fondled its engraved surface a moment before pressing it into Alan's hands. 'Keep it safe – for I must return to the chamber for some unfinished business.'

Alan's eyes met those of the dwarf mage. 'Be careful!'

'You also – hurry now! May the Powers grant you wings!'

The Flight from Isscan

There was barely time for the people gathered in the rickety warehouse to welcome Mo back – this strange new Mo, who had lost her stammer – before the whole company made ready to flee. It seemed an impossible task to move an entire village of men, women and children out of a town in the first light of morning and not attract attention. But these were people skilled in the art of moving silently. And fear gave urgency to their feet. Now, with their bundles of possessions carried on their heads or strapped to their backs, the Olhyiu followed the meaner streets, cutting through the yards of closed and derelict buildings where locked gates were no barrier for desperate people. The sun had half crested the horizon, its rapidly growing light obscured by the haze of smoke from wood-burning fires in a city of open hearths. Then, on the upper wharf-side, and no more than half a mile from their destination, a company of black-armoured soldiers sprang from the shadows to confront them.

The platoon of Death Legion, though more than matched in numbers by the fisher people, was made up of lightly armoured soldiers, each of them better trained and much better armed than the Olhyiu. The officer-at-arms struck a woman in the face with his mailed fist, causing her to drop the infant she was clutching to her breast. Her husband pressed himself in front of his dazed wife, his only weapon a wooden staff. A heavy-set man with the face of a bully, the officer pretended to quake with fear, his arm trembling as he pulled his black-bladed sword from its scabbard. Several soldiers laughed in anticipation of the coming sport.

'What have we here – a dawn plague of rats?'

With a play of bravado he whirled the blade in a feint and parry before pressing its tip against the throat of the husband.

'Squeak now, vermin! But what is that you say? I can't hear you!'

Alan tugged Kate back so she was hidden behind him, then brandished the Spear of Lug, getting ready to throw it. But before he could carry out his intention a gleaming blade flashed through the air and parted the officer's head from his shoulders. The dwarf mage, Qwenqwo Cuatzel, barely recognisable under a heavy helmet of embossed bronze, clinking shoulder plates and chainmail to his mid-calves, caught the returning blade and stepped

out to confront the platoon of soldiers. His green eyes
blazed as he twirled a double-headed bronze battle-axe
above his head in one gnarled hand. Runes identical to
those on the blade that Padraig had shown them – the
Fir Bolg battle-axe that had killed the warrior prince,
Feimhin – glittered over the cutting edges.

'Which ten of you cowards will desist from tormenting
women and engage in battle a single Fir Bolg warrior!'

None of the soldiers moved to attack him but no more
did they pull back. And additional heavily armed soldiers
were arriving by the second, blocking all progress down
into the harbour.

Alan closed his eyes and focused his exhausted senses
into the oraculum. He called out Ainé's name. But Siam's
hand on his shoulder pulled him back to reality. 'The
helper, Layheas, has already summoned the Shee.
Meanwhile, we must look to ourselves!'

The Olhyiu chief was already organising a simple
defensive circle around the vulnerable. Fish-gutting knives
and staves were all that armed the Olhyiu, but they
intended to fight for their lives. The soldiers closed around
them, their armour rattling as they took up positions to
attack.

'Mage Lord, give me the blood-rage,' Siam demanded of
Alan.

Alan probed the chief's spirit, found the embryonic form
there, a lot stronger and more ready to emerge than before.
He poured energy into it, saw the change complete in

mere moments. The grizzly bear rushed forward and battered through the near ranks of soldiers before retreating to guard the knot of his people. Its battle roar echoed far and wide through the streets and walls of Isscan.

Although eyes widened among the soldiers, they still held their ground. A new officer-at-arms appeared among them. His sword arm rose, preparing for the attack. Suddenly a new chanting could be heard on the air. Such a strange medley of voices and throats that the hackles rose on Alan's skin. He remembered it from the skirmish by the river. It was the battle hymn of the Shee. The outer circle of Death Legion spun round to face attack from this new quarter while the inner circle continued to surround the Olhyiu. The officer, with his sword still aloft, rallied his men. 'Is the Death Legion to be routed by women, a midget and a bear?'

The soldiers laughed and cheered.

But even as the officer's sword arm fell, an explosion of white fire closed about his throat, and the head of a tigress tore itself free from his falling body, its eyes red pits and its body an incandescent furnace of lightning and flame.

Ainé!

It was the Kyra, but in a form Alan had never witnessed before. It was as if she had turned the force of her oraculum inwards, melding its terrible power with her flesh and blood.

The dwarf mage shook Alan's shoulder. 'Make ready to run!'

The soldiers were falling back, step by step, fear etched into their faces. And through the oraculum, Alan detected the looming approach of fighting Shee, a terrifying vision of snarling jaws and extending talons. Suddenly the tigress lifted her huge head and bared her maw. Rivulets of lightning flickered over the ground and a crackling white fire flared outwards through the air, reflecting by a wall of approaching Shee blades. With this, a coordinated attack descended on the soldiers and the noise of battle echoed far and wide through the streets and boulevards.

'To the harbour!' shouted Alan.

The Olhyiu hurried onward, with the giant bear tearing a way through the panicked soldiers, and soon there was the renewed pattering of many feet into the awakening morning.

At the harbour, Alan and Kate found themselves wreathed in a heavy mist that was rising out of the confluence of the two rivers. They heard their names spoken in an urgent whisper. They might have walked by a high white wall, faintly luminescent in the pearly light, had they not heard the urgent summons.

'Alan . . . Kate!'

Glancing upwards, they saw Mo's face peering down at them over a white wall that must be the hull of the Temple Ship.

Through gaps in the mist they glimpsed a towering superstructure, aglow with a strange lambency, dressed in a wraithlike maze of rope ladders and rigging that ascended into the murky air. The Temple Ship appeared ghostly, as if illuminated by a diffuse, pale light that flickered and danced in the timbers and rigging. What had happened to the black oak, fissured and worn with time and weather? A new metamorphosis was changing the superstructure, extending and swelling into this spectral monolith. It was as if the ship was responding to their needs.

Tall shapes were materialising out of the harbour mists. Alan and Kate glimpsed the flash of warded green blades.

Kate clutched at his arm.

'It's okay – they're Shee!' He hugged her to him with his free left arm. 'They wear camouflage cloaks. It makes it difficult to see them clearly.'

Many more Shee were arriving. Alan assumed that Muîrne would no longer be with them. He knew that the plan had been that she escort Valéra's baby back to the safety of their homeland in the Guhttan Mountains. Now the swirling camouflage of the warriors' capes made it difficult for him to count the numbers of arriving Shee, though there were a lot more of them than he had left at the edge of the trees, perhaps as many as a hundred. He caught a glimpse of Milish, followed by two Aides carrying her ornate trunk.

'No time to wonder!' Qwenqwo hissed at both their elbows. 'We must flee while the mist still cloaks our passage!'

As they scrambled up the gangway, the ship appeared

to judder and move. Alan and Kate headed aft, where they found Mo waiting for them with Mark at the great wheel, his feet widely planted on the aft deck.

Mo tugged at Alan's arm. 'His eyes!' she whispered.

Alan and Kate peered into the face of their friend, whose eyes appeared to be glazed, as if registering nothing of the hustle and bustle on the deck around him.

But then Kate took up Mo's alarm. 'Oh, Alan – look more closely!'

When Alan did so he saw that the whites and irises of Mark's eyes had disappeared, replaced by darkness, black as obsidian, in which motes of a silvery light flickered and changed.

In a tremulous voice, Mo pressed him, 'What's happening to him?'

'I don't know, but the pattern is the same as his crystal.'

'But he broke the crystal!'

Alan shrugged. 'I'm not sure what it means, Mo.'

Mo said, 'I think it's something to do with his closeness to the ship.'

Kate turned to look at Mo, her eyes wide as if still only coming to terms with a great many different surprises. 'What do you mean?'

'Do you remember how we all felt that terrible sadness when the Olhyiu were going to burn the ship, back at the frozen lake? Mark was just standing there on his own. He sensed it before anyone else. He knew the feeling was coming from the ship. Then he just took the wheel as if

. . . as if the ship had summoned him. And look at him now. He has that same look on his face.'

Alan studied Mark again. He hardly seemed to register any of their presences. It was if he and the ship were in some intense, intimate communication.

Suddenly the matrix in Mark's eyes began to pulsate rhythmically and powerfully, as if with his heartbeat. Everybody jumped with fright as a crackling force shook the massive timbers. All three of them spun around, marvelling at the changes that continued to pervade the creaking and groaning superstructure. Moment by moment the ship glowed brighter, a light that seemed hardly to reflect the dawn but to exude from every surface and line of the vessel, as if the ship itself had become the cradle of light. Ainé, restored to human form, had come on board without Alan noticing, and now she stared about her with an expression of wary incredulity. She reached out to touch a glowing rail and withdrew her hand sharply, as if it had given her an electric shock.

Siam, also restored, stood and stared, his eyes wide with astonishment, interrupted in the order to raise the gangway. Regaining his senses, he shouted orders to his sailors. But without their help the great sails were already rising. Ainé called out to the Shee, ordering them to take up defensive positions on the port side, where they faced the battlemented walls. Alan, now probing with his oraculum, sensed the immense and mysterious charge of energy that surrounded them.

'The chains!' Siam roared, his alarm too urgent for whispers.

Running sternwards in Ainé's wake, Alan found the Kyra with legs astride a massive anchor chain. Each individual link was a foot in diameter and cast of the same matt-black metal as the armour of the Storm Wolves. The chains manacled the ship to the huge iron capstans of the dock. With jaws clenched in warlike incantation, Ainé raised her sword to its extremity and crashed its glittering blade against a single link, causing an explosion of brilliant sparks but barely making a dent on its surface. Milish placed a cautionary hand on the upper arm of the Shee. The Kyra's blade was not indestructible, and they might have need of it in days to come.

With an oath, Ainé sheathed her sword and glared with rage at this shackling of their escape.

Alan was equally appalled by the massive girth of the chains. Powerful and strange as the Temple Ship had become, there would be no escape without first breaking through these bonds.

A shout from above caused the Olhyiu to crouch down on the deck, already rolling and shuddering as the power of the unfurled sails battered against the obstruction. The Death Legion was proliferating on the walls above the dockside. They had the advantage of the harbour side of the great plaza, which brought them high above the level of the groaning deck. Others among them were swinging cannons into position so they could direct them at the

Temple Ship. Alan shouted at Kate and Mo to go below. It was pointless risking their lives here on deck when they were unarmed and couldn't contribute to the fighting.

'We're here to tend the wounded!' Kate insisted.

'That will keep for when the fighting is over.'

He saw them reluctantly head for the stairs. He glanced over at Mark, who appeared to have become one with the wheel. He heard the first thunder of cannon fire, followed by flame and smoke. The discharge struck the super-structure about the mainmast, and a conflagration of sparks exploded in the rigging. He recoiled, gagging, from the foul green fire, noticing how an answering counter-force rose out of the deck, smothering the flames, causing them to splutter and die.

The Shee were hurling javelins with deadly accuracy at the Death Legion on the harbour walls. Bodies were tumbling down onto the quayside. But there was no shortage of reinforcements.

Confronting the chains, Alan focused on them through the power of the oraculum. The red glow from his brow caused the people to shrink away from him. From above, two more cannons were being pulled into position, their muzzles trained directly onto the crowded decks. Ainé's voice of command sounded out like a clarion call, exhorting the Shee to greater battle. A fierce flare from Alan's oraculum caught a single link in the chain, and within moments it glowed red. Sparks of hot metal began to crackle from its incandescent surface. But its massive strength resisted the force of his attack. Several more detonations of green fire descended on them from above; the burning conflagration and foul stench of one struck no more than yards from Alan.

Suddenly Qwenqwo was by his side. A glare of determination contorted his features as he lifted his arms into the air, as if invoking the assistance of the elements. Alan felt a gale of wind rise about him and catch in the heaving rigging.

A roar of triumph came from above as a gigantic cannon was dragged into place. The legionaries rammed the huge barrel through the fabric of the masonry, toppling a shower of stones into the water, meanwhile enabling them to direct it downward. And now they were wheeling it back again to load it, before training it onto the central mast of the ship.

Alan stood still, his legs parted on either side of the chain, his brow cast down, furrowed with the intensity of his concentration. Desperation consumed him. There was an almighty flare from his brow and the link blazed white-hot. A cataract of sparks erupted into the air from the blazing link.

The passionate voice of Ainé was ringing out, concentrating a deadly fire onto those commanding the great cannon. Qwenqwo was howling at the wind. Suddenly there was a cry from Mark at the wheel.

'C'mon, old girl! Time to show us what you're made of!'

Alan whirled to look at his friend, who was embracing

the wheel with his entire body. Was it Alan's imagination that from his friend's outstretched body, flickering lines of force connected him to the decks, the masts, the rigging, as if the matrix within him was one with the ship?

With all of his remaining strength Alan focused even more desperately on the link that tethered them to this deadly harbour. There was a massive lurch, as if the ship itself was coming to his assistance. A great new force of energy pressed against the restraining chain as the sails cracked taut in the gathering wind. There was a shuddering jerk that almost threw Alan down onto the deck as the ship surged against its restraints, and then, with an almighty crack, the weakened chain sundered. Alan watched, blinking furiously, as the splintered edges tore apart, streaming sparks. He watched them still as the fractured links slipped out from between his stiffened legs, tumbling over the decks, hissing deep into the storm-whipped water. From above, and rapidly receding, rage-filled faces howled as they watched the great ship pull away from its moorings with sails billowing on its towering masts, the tallest complete with a crow's nest in which Turkeya was shouting his triumph.

In a blinding conflagration of force and light the Temple Ship forced its passage through the hindering maze of other vessels in the harbour, battering a path through into clear water, and throwing up a mountainous wave of spray across its bow as it approached the pincers of the harbour mouth.

'Danger! Up ahead!' screamed Turkeya from high above. His hand was pointing to the river.

Peering out over the prow, Alan saw massive iron teeth looming out of the depths, about fifty yards downstream. A trap for the unwary, the boom spanned the entire harbour mouth.

Alan ran to the stern rail, the oraculum bursting into a brilliant red flare even before he got there. He leaned forward against the broad rail, his fists raised, his eyes glazed. He heard the screams and shouts from all around him as they approached to within twenty-five yards of the trap. Then he brought his fists down, invoking all of his power, directing the First Power deep into the turbulent water. In moments a great sea-spout whirled into the sky, raising an enormous wave that lifted the great ship high on its crest, carrying it, bucking and heaving, over the danger.

Once clear, the ship drummed in its depths and sang in its rigging, so that Kate and Mo, and every man, woman and child that had been cowering below decks, came up into the salt-drenched air to join them, sharing in their hearts the pure, sweet joy of the freed leviathan as it struck a majestic course southwards, towards the Forest of the Undying in the haunted Vale of Tazan.

PART III

Ossierel

Mysteries and Silences

The thrust of wind in the sails was so perfectly balanced with the direction and purpose of the ship that the waters appeared to surge by with scarcely any resistance, so that, although the thunder of cannons still cracked and boomed behind them, they were soon out of range of the batteries on the walls. Mark still took the helm, but his posture was more relaxed now. His eyes had cleared and the lines of force had slowly melted away from his body. Alan and the other two friends had watched it happen. None of them knew if Mark simply did not remember what had happened or if he just didn't want to talk about it, so maybe he was genuinely unaware of the changes that had taken place in him. Either that or he was deliberately avoiding having to discuss it, even with Mo. The truth, as they acknowledged discreetly to each other, was that there appeared to be two different Marks at war with each other within the same body, and the upshot was that their friend was growing increasingly distant from them.

Within an hour or so of sailing, the mist had blown away, and no boats had been speedy enough to give chase from the harbour. No more could they see signs of organised pursuit on either bank.

But Alan was not so naïve as to imagine that they had won. He couldn't help but recall the horror of what he had witnessed in the false Mage's chamber. The memory so shocked and bewildered him that even now, aboard the escaping ship, a lingering fear lurked below the surface, so that he wondered how anyone, let alone himself and his friends, could possibly challenge that terrible malice. And so it was that, as all around him the happiness of liberation thrilled and excited the people crowding the deck, the lingering awareness of unseen menace still oppressed Alan from all sides as they sailed in full majesty through a hinterland of devastated nature.

Kemtuk arrived to stand by him, as if sensing his mood. 'When an Olhyiu fells a cedar to construct his boat, he keeps vigil for a night and a day to ask forgiveness of the spirit of the forest. Yet here you see no evidence of respect, let alone repentance, only a greed that might cause an entire forest to fall. The hearts of the people of Isscan have become as stone under the brutal overlordship of the Tyrant.'

Alan could see that the shaman spoke the truth. Although they must have travelled thirty miles or more since Isscan, not a single stand of trees had survived the destruction. In places the rape of nature had been so recent that smoke still rose from the smouldering ruins of charcoal and ash. He steeled himself for another hour or so, until the first green forests appeared, before he persuaded Mark to leave the wheel, leaving Siam to keep a steady course. The two friends collected the girls together so that Alan could take them through the decks, congested with Shee, Aides and Olhyiu, affording him the opportunity of introducing them, in a more organised way, to their new friends and fellow travellers.

He began with Qwenqwo Cuatzel, whom they found on the forward angle of the prow, his battle-axe, with its curved bronze heads, suspended from a leather harness across his back, and his enraptured face lifted up into the misty sky to inhale the fresh air of freedom. Qwenqwo insisted on embracing each of the four in turn, including the somewhat reluctant Mark. 'Any friend of the oraculum-bearer is a friend of mine!'

'Oraculum-bearer?' several voices whispered among themselves.

'You must tell me about yourselves.'

So the Mage of Dreams learnt each of their names.

'Do you know what it all means – or why we in particular were chosen?' Kate was a little cautious in befriending the dwarf mage, yet eager to know more of what role she had to play.

'Might I examine your crystal?'

She hesitated a moment before passing it to him.

Qwenqwo folded his gnarled hands around the egg-shaped stone, with its green matrix speckled with metamorphosing arabesques of gold. He closed his eyes, deep in thought for many seconds. Then he passed it back to her with a wide-eyed glance.

'What did you see in it?'

'A force powerful indeed, yet close to nature. Perhaps, if I judge true, yours will be the gift of healing.'

Kate liked the idea of a gift of healing, but she wasn't altogether convinced by the vagueness of his reply. 'You're not just being nice to me?'

Qwenqwo inclined his head, but his eyes sparkled at her through his bushy red eyebrows. 'In your crystal, as in your heart, I truly sense great mystery and even greater latency of purpose.'

'Mystery?' Mo piped up.

'Why certainly, Mo! What else?' Then, with a sly grin, Qwenqwo reached into his pocket, withdrew Mo's bog-oak talisman and handed it to her. 'I found it hidden in the false mage's chamber.'

'Oh, brilliant! I thought it was gone forever.'

Qwenqwo turned as if to leave them. But Mo put her hand on his arm. 'What about my brother, Mark? His crystal was broken.'

Qwenqwo nodded gravely. 'That was indeed unfortunate. But you must understand that runestones are merely conduits to evoke the power vested in individual spirits.'

'Then it really is true. Each of us really does have a special role to play?'

'I do not doubt it.'

'And Mark hasn't lost his special role?'

Qwenqwo looked at Mark, observing how he was shaking his head, as if disbelievingly, at all this.

Kate interrupted the awkward silence to thump Alan on the shoulder. 'I don't know about you omadawns, but I have a whole sackful of questions that need answering. And I'm going to start with you, Alan Duval – Mage Lord, my eye! Like, what really happened to Mo? And would you kindly explain what really went on back there in the harbour?'

Alan laughed. 'Hey, Kate – what do you think? You think I don't have a whole bunch of questions too?'

She punched his shoulder again. But he just lifted her up off the deck with a big hug. He refused to take his arms from around her waist.

'Later – okay! We'll have a long talk about everything.'

'You promise?'

'I promise! But right now, I have some more introducing to do.'

He took his friends in search of Milish and Ainé, explaining along the way what little he really knew about the Shee.

Mark appeared to have recovered a little of his sarcastic humour. 'Aw, gee,' he muttered, 'so now we can add pussy cats to teddy bears!'

Only twenty feet away, through a throng of Shee and Aides, Alan caught sight of Ainé's gigantic battle-scarred form. She whirled around, as if sensing their approach. Alan dropped his voice to whisper into Mark's ear. 'If I were you, I wouldn't let the Kyra hear you talk about pussy cats.'

Later, Alan spoke to Milish on the foredeck, her eyes watchful over the elements and river currents. 'You still anticipate danger?'

'We can take no comfort from the fact that the Death Legion is not visibly in our wake.'

'But why do you look south rather than north?'

Milish said nothing, gazing straight ahead to where far-distant mountains were faintly outlined, copper-tipped in the morning sun, above the horizon of a smoky-blue mantle of forests. Row after row of scarps and jagged peaks arose in an overlapping sequence, like the waves of a limitless ocean, as he gazed further southwards into the blue-hazed distance.

'To my people,' she confided, 'these are the foothills of the Blue Mountains. But to the Kyra they are the Mountains of Mourning. Great passions and tragedy have ravaged this land in times all too recent as well as in the distant past.' Milish turned and Alan saw tears moisten the elegant woman's eyes. 'Ossierel approaches, with all of its terrible memories. It was, until recently, not just the spiritual capital of all of Monisle, and the seat of the governing council, but also a haven of beauty and tranquillity. It grieves me beyond words to witness it as it is now reduced to ruin. For proud Ossierel was also the scene of the martyrdom of the last High Architect, Ussha De Danaan.'

'I've heard Kemtuk mention her, Milish. But nobody has explained what really happened.'

'The De Danaan was herself an oraculum-bearer, gifted with immense knowledge and the power of prophecy. For these gifts she is all the more condemned throughout Monisle since few can forgive her disastrous final decision, made even while Ossierel was being overrun by a great army of the Death Legion. She dismissed the Shee, whose sworn duty it was to defend the capital. Ainé's sister-mother was the Kyra then – and that surrender cost her her life. Perhaps now you grasp something of the anger that still rages in the Kyra herself. No explanation was given as to why the High Architect abandoned her main defence. The survivors of her council – the Council-in-Exile – have denigrated her as a traitor. Yet, though I cannot explain her decision, no more can I bring myself to see her as a traitor.'

'Aye,' interrupted a loud and angry voice, 'but what the council woman does not explain is an even more profound and terrible mystery.' Alan spun round to find the dwarf mage standing close by, his feet splayed wide and an indignant rage contorting his face. 'Ossierel,' he countered, 'stands on the great island of the same name in the legendary Vale of Tazan. On that island long ago, in the time of the Dark Queen, Nantosueta, warring armies faced the same enemy as we do today, and it was the queen herself who called for assistance from all of the warrior people of Monisle. Thus twice have the armies of this continent fought the forces of darkness there.'

Milish stood erect in silence, staring into the distance, as if reluctant to discuss such sensitive matters.

'Aye,' Qwenqwo continued, 'and it is also rumoured, though the council woman would no more inform you of this, that the Shee were a different race in those times: women such as any others, who knew men. But they allied themselves with the Dark Queen and it was she who changed them.'

Milish snorted. 'Now you speak nonsense.'

The dwarf mage shook his head, and a terrible sadness transfixed his features, as if the council woman's comment had silenced him entirely.

But Alan wasn't satisfied. He turned to Qwenqwo, his curiosity piqued. 'Who was this queen you mentioned – Nantosueta?'

Qwenqwo blinked for several moments and swallowed, as if struggling even to speak because of some inner grief. 'Some call her the girl-queen. For a girl she was, of no more than fifteen years during that ancient and disastrous war. Rumour has it that she aligned herself with a force of darkness that still reigns over her haunted valley. Indeed it is Nantosueta who, from her ancient tower above the island fortress, still casts her dark shadow over the valley through which we must pass. There the great river narrows as it cleaves the mountains, a slow and twisting course called in the language of my people "Kiwa Hahn", which means "the crooked throat".'

Kemtuk and Siam had also come to join what now appeared to be a conference, and wishing – or so it appeared in Kemtuk's case – to contribute some wisdom.

'The dwarf mage is right. Many and strange are the tales that warn against entering the Vale of Tazan. After the guardians of the pass are behind us, and within the long and winding valley, the river passes through a blighted land in which an ancient and forbidden forest has long endured. The trees of this forest are strange, such as are not seen anywhere else in our world. You might laugh at such foolishness. But I have met battle-worn men who told tales as we sat around the campfires of winter – tales that speak of ghosts of human origin, warriors who were sacrificed for the vanity of eternity. Other legends claim that they are not ghosts of warriors but the first people, the human animals created by the Earth Mother to please Akoli after his great slumber. Fearful for their survival at the hands of their children's children, who threatened them with fire, they took the long and wearying journey to that valley, to preserve the old ways.'

'Who knows,' interrupted Milish, as if to divert conversation from realms that were disturbing to her, 'where truth lies in the Vale of Tazan? But great are the powers of that forest. And if I dread to speak of it, it is because death itself is said to have protected the sanctuary with accursed powers. None dare profane the Rath that stands atop the pinnacle, not even the Death Legion. Such was once the protection of Ossierel, and even today it remains the last outer defence of Carfon from the degradation we have witnessed in Isscan.'

Siam frowned, as if coming to terms with the clash of passions aroused by mysteries recent and ancient, and his fretful gaze flickered about him and over the altered timbers, with their pearly glow. 'Believe me,' he growled, 'when I say that even we, the Olhyiu people – who are the most experienced mariners in all of the land – must pass through this accursed vale, we dare not delay in those strange shadows or gaze long at the ruins that straddle the slopes but keep our prows steady in the centre stream.'

Then the chief's eyes darted aloft to where the soaring wings of an eagle appeared to be following the course of the ship. Alan stared at the eagle with a prickling sense of disquiet before he deliberately brought them back to practicalities. 'Siam, how far are we from this pass?'

'A hundred leagues, or thereabouts.'

Alan did the calculation in his mind. A league was three miles – roughly three hundred miles! They would reach it, travelling at their present speed, the day after tomorrow.

He thought about the Mage of Dreams, realising how little he really knew about him. With a sudden realisation, he reached into his pocket and withdrew the runestone given to him when the dwarf mage had feared his own death and the capture of the runestone by the enemy. Holding it up against the pearly sky, Alan saw deeper than the etchings over the polished surface the symbol of an emerald eye. Even as he held the stone to the light, the image of the eye fell onto the deck at his feet, as if projected through a prism. Kemtuk cursed and backed away.

In a blur of movement, Ainé appeared from the congested deck. With her face averted from the green eye, she seized the runestone and hurled it far out over the water.

Qwenqwo's roar of outrage exploded high into the air in the wake of the runestone. Yet another figure moved faster still, a cruciate shape of gold and grey, mantled with white, swooping in a lightning-fast arc from sky to water, the speed of movement faster than Alan's eyes could follow, though he caught a glimpse of the ferocious raptor's beak and talons. He barely had time to recognise the eagle that had been monitoring their passage before, in a swoop, it had snatched the runestone as it struck the surface of the water, perhaps a hundred yards distant from the ship, and, with a piercing shriek, beat its ascent back into the air, swivelling around to swoop low over the Temple Ship and drop the precious cargo into the dwarf's outstretched hands.

Ainé did not so much as blink as the outraged Qwenqwo Cuatzel confronted her on the foredeck, his eyes ablaze. The runestone was aloft in his left hand. In a moment, Ainé had drawn her sword. The blade was glittering a fearsome green, and the Oraculum of the Kyra was pulsating powerfully. 'It would appear that poison still arrives in small bottles!'

'Perhaps,' hissed the dwarf, his right hand drawing his battle-axe, and stretching to his full height, at which he barely reached the Kyra's chest, 'this is a witch warrior who would prove less arrogant if her legs were reduced to the level of her knees.'

Alan reached out and took the stone from Qwenqwo's hand, wrapping both his own hands about it. Closing his eyes he held it in the focus of his oraculum. Though his spirit became invaded by a sense of anger and loss, he could detect no evil. Opening his eyes and gazing deeply into the dwarf's, no more did he witness any trace of treachery there. If anything the shadow that hung behind the eyes shared a common loss with the runestone.

Alan returned the runestone to its master, then turned to question Ainé. 'Why did you throw it away?'

Ainé refused to reply, staring over all their heads towards the distant pass in the Blue Mountains.

The dwarf's face flushed redder than his hair. 'Ask the witch warrior to talk of mendacity and slaughter – ask her of treachery in the Undying Forest!'

'Ainé!' Alan spoke urgently to the silent Kyra, whose sword was only now returned to its scabbard. 'What has happened in the past to cause you and Qwenqwo to distrust one another?'

Neither dwarf mage nor Shee seemed prepared to enlighten him but continued to stand apart in an irreconcilable posture and gaze.

'Qwenqwo – what's going on?'

The dwarf mage bristled for several more moments, then muttered, 'Oracula are not confined to the almighty Trídédana any more than they are to be found solely upon the brow. My runestone, like the crystals of our young friends, is also a portal of power. Though it was no threat to you, Mage Lord, the Kyra, with her suspicious nature, misunderstood its purpose. To some it might appear to threaten, as a doubter might question loyalty.'

'I don't understand.'

'I was deceived, as you know, by a force of darkness more powerful and malevolent than any warlock. Yet ever, throughout my captivity, I vowed that, once free and the runestone returned to me, I would place there an eye such as you saw – not for malice but as a ward that looks into the heart of any who holds it, searching there for good or evil.'

'And did my heart pass its test?' Alan asked, with the hint of a smile.

'Your heart would pass all tests. You saw for yourself how the eye glowed. If it had discovered evil in you, it would have closed, thus becoming a consumer of the light for the one who attempted to use the stone.'

'Yet,' Kate pressed him, 'the false mage put Mo's face into it! That was how he drew Alan into his trap.'

'So it might appear – but is it not possible that one other than the false Mage was calling Alan?'

'You?'

'Not I!' Qwenqwo inhaled and his eyebrows drew close together. 'But one whose need was far greater than my own!'

Alan looked at Mo, who had so mysteriously lost her stammer. There was more in Qwenqwo's eyes than he was saying, and Alan wondered if he should press him more for answers. But suddenly there was a delighted cry further back along the deck. Alan's gaze turned to a small cluster of women gathered about the stern who were urging their men to cast their nets into the water. Everybody hurried to join them, where a shoal of silvery salmon leaped and flashed in the ship's white wake. The fish followed them like a living cloud, glittering and sparkling, intent, it seemed, on offering themselves.

Alan couldn't help glancing at Mo, who was standing quietly to one side, a look of entrancement about her features as her gaze met that of the Mage of Dreams. For the moment Kemtuk hammered with his staff on the deck to attract everybody's attention.

'Providence has offered to feed us. We should put aside our differences and spend an hour filling up the hold.'

Many hours later, and with every belly satisfied with the feast of fresh fish, Qwenqwo was persuaded to tell them a story that might throw light on the history of the Temple Ship.

The Ark of the Arinn

Sharing a pipe of tobacco with Kemtuk Lapeep, the Mage of Dreams joined the shaman in sitting cross-legged on the deck, joined in their inner circle by the four friends, Milish and the tribal elders. Ainé refused to join the circle but stood apart, while making no secret of the fact that she was listening intently.

It had been Mo's question that had prompted Qwenqwo to tell them more about the Temple Ship. 'Can you solve a mystery for me? When Mark went funny back there and the crystal patterns appeared in his eyes, he talked to the ship as if he were talking to a real person.'

Qwenqwo shifted his bottom to get himself comfortable, then smiled at Mo, his eyes appearing to glow an even brighter green. 'Sailors are apt to talk to ships. But even so, it reminds me of a story – and you, Mo, more than any among your company knows how loath I am to tell stories!'

Mo's peal of laughter drew everybody's attention to her blushing face. But already more people were gathering around Qwenqwo, drawing up a second circle, and there was a sharing of anticipation as the dwarf mage puffed on his pipe. 'But now I see that there are too many curious faces to be disappointed. So I will share a little of what I know. For I am acquainted with a legend that tells of a very ancient people, of what the Olhyiu might call First Man and First Woman. Now, if you believe the legends, this man was known as Ará and the first woman as Quorinn and these people were henceforth known as the Ará-Quorinn – so that in the telling from one fireside to another they became known simply as the Arinn.

'Whatever the truth of such legends, all people who now live in Monisle know them in some shape or form, whether by different names or in their stories of beginnings, for these were the first people to gather the fruits of land and shore. Some stories suggest they came here from another world in a great ship, which was known as the Ark of the Arinn. For, if the legends are to be believed, their vessel had powers bequeathed to it by the Changers themselves.'

'The Changers?' asked Mo.

'Another name for the Arinn, my friend. You see, the Ark responded, sense for sense, with the Changers' wishes and desires. As you might imagine, such a wonder was beyond the comprehension of ordinary senses, for it was one thing and all things to those who travelled within it. Some believed it retained the capacity to fly through the air, with great wings beating, like the black-headed swan. Others that it could transform its substance, according to the instruction of its masters, even as the creatures, whether of myth or fact I cannot pretend to tell, known as changelings.'

Qwenqwo's eyes caught Mo's fleetingly, and their sparkle of delight reminded her of their mind-games in the false Mage's chamber.

'Stranger still are the stories of the Arinn themselves. For it appears that above all they venerated knowledge. If the oldest legends are true, so arrogant did they become that they challenged the very immortality of the gods. Such arrogance became their downfall.'

Of the many faces enraptured by the storytelling, none was more intrigued than Mark, though he made sure to conceal his interest from his friends, waiting behind until the stories were over and everybody but he had withdrawn to other tasks and interests, so that he could be alone with the dwarf mage.

'I've heard stories,' he spoke with a show of scepticism, 'of women, with faces like dolls, who visit men in their dreams. In your tales around campfires, have you ever come across any mention of these?'

'Possibly I have, and possibly I have not.'

'You're not really answering my question.'

'If I am reticent it is because I wonder why a young man like you would be interested in succubi?'

'Succubi?'

'Supposedly, in all manners and appearances they are deceivers and seducers, whose purpose is to ensnare the souls of men.'

'Supposedly? Does that mean you don't believe in them? You're just talking about legends?'

'Oh, I suspect they are real enough. Though, thank the Powers, I have never set eyes on such.'

'I don't understand. I mean, how is it possible for these – these succubi – to control the men they prey on?'

'If legend is to be believed, they do so not merely through the seduction of the eyes but even more so through a hidden scent.'

'A scent?' Mark shook his head disbelievingly.

'A scent, in its capacity for seduction, can be a thousand times more powerful than sight or hearing. Surely it cannot be sight or sound that attracts the moth to its mate, across miles of forest, against the wildest storm and in the dark of night.'

Mark pretended to laugh. 'Oh, come on – it's just myths and fairy tales!'

The dwarf mage shrugged his shoulders. 'Perhaps it is a myth, also, that they serve a mistress mighty and foul, a mistress so wicked I would not wish to describe her lest I burden you with nightmares.'

'What mistress?'

'One who stands second in the powers of evil in this world, eclipsed only by the Tyrant himself. I speak of the Great Witch, known as Olc, whose domain is far from here, in the southernmost region of the Wastelands, and whose purpose it is to harvest the souls of men.'

Mark could not hide the pallor that invaded his face. He fell back onto his haunches, blinking rapidly, while the dwarf mage inclined his head and studied the youth through the arched red hairs of his eyebrows. 'Will you not speak to me, young Mark, openly and honestly?'

'Please, Qwenqwo – don't tell the others.'

'It is foolish to conceal the truth from them.'

'Please. You have to promise me.'

'Very well! I give you my word.' The dwarf mage inspected the bowl of his pipe, which contained nothing but ash. He tapped the ash away against the rail of the ship, his face still deeply thoughtful. 'You do have a friend, of a curious kind – as I have increasingly witnessed.'

'What friend?'

'Your friend is the ship – or am I altogether mistaken?'

'I . . . I don't know what you mean.'

'Perhaps you do not sense it as I do. Yet it is true. You care deeply for her – as no doubt she cares for you.'

Mark placed his left hand on the bare oak of the deck and brushed the wood, an unconscious movement, as if stroking it. 'Ships can't hurt you. Not like . . .'

'Not like people – is that what you mean?'

'Oh, God – is there no hope? I mean, what would I have to do . . .?'

The dwarf mage saw how Mark's throat tightened. He saw how sweat glistened over his face. Qwenqwo's voice fell to a kindly whisper. 'When, my friend, did the succubus seduce you?'

Mark began to tremble. He could not answer.

'Let me guess. It was before the capture of your sister?'

He nodded.

'During the river journey, then?'

He dropped his head.

'She made promises. You gave yourself to her?'

He nodded again.

'And in return? She made demands of you?'

He shook his head. He would die before he answered.

'Her price was your betrayal of your friends?'

'No – *no*! I'd . . . I would never . . . !'

'If I am to help you, Mark, you must tell me everything.'

'I . . . I just can't talk about it.'

Qwenqwo put his hand on Mark's shoulder. 'Your sister talked to me a great deal while we were prisoners of the warlock. I know some of what happened. I would like to hear your explanation.'

'I . . . I was asked just to push her.'

'To push Mo on the deck of the ship at the Dragon's Teeth?'

He shook his head. 'Not Mo.'

Qwenqwo fell silent a moment, deep in thought. 'Yet

there were but two others with you: Mo and Kate.' He frowned, then his eyes widened. 'It was Kate?'

Mark nodded. 'But honestly, I fought her will – the succubus. I fought and fought. I tried to warn Kate. Oh – if only Mo hadn't been there. All I did . . . I put my arm around her. I tried to save Kate. I never pushed her.'

'You pushed Mo instead?'

'Not instead . . . by accident. I just pushed her out of the way. She was trying to get between us, between Kate and me. I sensed that Kate was in terrible danger. I wanted to protect her. I didn't think . . .'

'You never realised that when the Garg saw you push Mo, it assumed the girl you pushed was the target of the succubus?'

'The Garg?'

'The bat creature that carried Mo overboard.'

'That's the horrible memory that keeps going through my mind. That creature carrying off Mo. It's been haunting my nightmares, over and over.'

Qwenqwo fell deeply in thought. 'So it was Kate the succubus was really after?'

'It isn't over, Qwenqwo. I can't sleep. I daren't. I know she'll come again. I keep thinking maybe I should throw myself overboard.'

'Such thinking ill becomes you.'

'What else can I do? Tell me what to do.'

'You spurned the power offered to you by one who might have protected you.'

'I didn't mean to smash the crystal . . . Oh, God – what a mess I've made of everything! Qwenqwo – what can I do?'

'Perhaps there is a way. Perhaps there is only one way – through asking for forgiveness.'

'Forgiveness?'

'The Powers, believe me, have long recognised the folly of human passions. Yet true contrition would count for much if it came from the heart – in the circumstances it surely must be from your heart alone, in honest and open repentance.'

On the second day after leaving Isscan, the wind blew from the north, and its chilly breath whipped about the decks and rigging. Winter howled about Mark's ears as he walked the decks, and men and women passed by in his vision as dark silhouettes, bent into their fur capes against the cold. The night landscape was once again showered with snow, and the bitter squalls cleared all but the essential mariners from the deck. Yet Mark felt safer here in these harsh circumstances, when the ship's timbers were folded around him.

Qwenqwo was right, he did love the ship. He loved her in a strange, altogether secret way – maybe like he loved music. A ship, like music, rewarded your love with what it had to give in return. Neither was capable of hurting you.

Mark's eyes watered with the cold as he peered out

through a porthole in the cabin he shared with Alan, currently busy on deck.

The succubus had not yet reappeared. The ship, somehow, had something to do with that. The ship was protecting him. Mark sensed this although he didn't know how. He just felt it. But he knew it was only a question of time. Her first attempt had failed. He had not pushed Kate overboard, as she had asked him to, and so, here, in this terrible valley, she would try again. He knew it, sensed it deep within him, and the dread of it made sleep impossible. In the lonely hours of darkness, prowling the decks and avoiding the company of the Shee or the Olhyiu sailors, he had overheard snatches of their conversations about Alan.

'Is the Mage Lord a demon?'

He had recognised the voice of Topgal, Siam's brother-in-law. Topgal never seemed to speak without bitterness. It seemed that the Olhyiu alternated in thinking Alan might be a demon or a god, but never just a youth, as he was.

With morning, the land to either side of them seemed to rise in scarps, capped by plateaus, hills and valleys, gripped in the white thrall of winter. He gazed out at the passing copses of evergreens, often in clefts of hills or rills. Great trees overhung the water, and sparks of light glittered in the green-black depths of their shadows. A deep and brooding menace was gathering in those black rocks, as if the angry landscape was showing through its sparse cover of mist and snow. The sky was massing with clouds, their edges shrouding the caps of the mountains so that they became a single dome with the shoulders of rock and the coiling mists rising from the river. Everybody saw that they were drawing closer to the jaws of the pass, through which they would enter a valley where new dangers awaited them.

Mark had never felt so frightened and alone as he felt right now. He welcomed the piercing barbs of snow that whipped his face in the bitter wind, ignoring the pain as his lips cracked and his ears became numbed. He avoided his friends, even his sister, Mo – especially Mo after his confession to Qwenqwo.

The dwarf mage knew the truth. Would he keep his word? Who would he tell about it? Who had he told already?

Back in his cabin, the grief of his betrayal tormented him like an iron fist closing around his heart. And now, with another night drawing in, he peered morosely through the porthole at the wraiths of mist that ran among the great trees like hunting wolves, his growing alienation making him consider all over again whether they might all be better off without him.

Such thinking ill becomes you . . .

Inside his mind, his own voice berated him, 'What . . . what can I do? *What can I do?*'

The dwarf had talked about forgiveness. Forgiveness from whom? Granny Dew, the bag lady he had ridiculed, the one into whose black eyes and wrinkled face he had shone his mobile screen light?

Mark sneaked out to stand disconsolately before the stern rail, hearing the sigh of the water under the flanks of the great ship, watching the ripples spread out towards the wide-spaced banks, reflecting the moonlight. He took a deep breath and imagined what it would feel like, falling into the darkness, the cold . . . An end to this torment. He recalled Granny Dew's very words:

When the darkness is worst, child, then will you find love.

He licked his lips, bowed his head. 'Granny Dew! It was a really stupid thing I did with the crystal you gave me. I know I've gone too far for forgiveness, but please help me at least to pay back my friends.'

No voice answered his call. Instead, he felt an intense pain flare in his left shoulder. The pain was so agonising, he ripped off his shirt and rubbed at the skin. There was no point calling again for help. It was useless. She had abandoned him, like everybody had always abandoned him. A new stab of pain brought him to his knees on the hard oak deck. It was so agonising his whole body began to tremble. He couldn't help the rush of tears that came into his eyes. When he touched the skin over his shoulder, it burned.

He staggered back to the tiny cabin, sat on his bunk, hugging his shoulder. Sweat ran in rivulets over his face and dripped off his chin. He staggered over to the basin of water, examining his reflection in the pallid lamplight.

His face was haggard and drawn, with blue crescents under his eyes. He went to dip his hands into the icy-cold water, thinking that he could splash it onto his burning skin. In doing so, he saw in his own reflection what was happening to him. A dark oval, like scorched flesh, covered his left shoulder. With a cry of anguish, he twisted his upper body one way and then another, to examine it closer. Within the black oval, whorls and arabesques of silver were pulsating with his heartbeat. That same heartbeat quickened to a sickening acceleration. It pounded in his head and throat. He fell back onto the bunk and just lay there in a daze.

Mark spoke not a word to Alan when, exhausted by some duties on deck, he arrived back in the sleeping quarters an hour or so later, threw off his clothes and fell into his bunk. He no longer cared that he couldn't sleep. He spent the night thinking about what had happened.

What did it really mean? Was he forgiven? Was the mark on his shoulder the hope he had begged for?

He was still lying there, sleepless, as the first pale rays of dawn peered in through the porthole. Moments later, he heard the shout – it was the deep throaty voice of Qwenqwo from high in the crow's nest. The words appeared to expand, like the light, as they entered the chamber, and they invaded his half-dazed mind. Mark ignored his sleeping friend and walked out onto the deck even as the dwarf mage shouted again, his cry flowing like a liquid, half proclamation and half warning, over the decks of awakening figures, and through every crack and crevice that led into the coursing labyrinth that was the ship.

'Behold the Pass of Kloshe Lamah! Behold the face of Magcyn, keeper of the accursed Vale of Tazan and last king of the Fir Bolg, whose spirit in truth still guards it!'

The Vale of Tazan

Alan woke to excited voices shouting and calling. He dressed hurriedly and joined the multitude gathering over the decks. His searching gaze found Mark, who had taken up the helm in the stern. Then he headed forward, taking the steps to the foredeck two at a time to get to the prow, where Kemtuk Lapeep stood like a sentinel, peering through the dawn mists at the extraordinary vision that confronted them. Here the river had become deep and fast-moving, its great waters compressed to no more than a hundred yards wide. Siam and the Olhyiu lined the rails, peering up into the ragged crags and escarpments that reared to dizzy heights on either side of them. Towering above them – it seemed impossible, for the scale appeared beyond any human undertaking – was a great figure of stone rising out of the bedrock and soaring to several hundred feet above the river.

People were shouting aloud the name of the figure

carved out of the mountain – Magcyn, last king of the Fir Bolg – and indeed you could not mistake the figure as anything other than a great and formidable king. He was seated on the shelf of rocky outcrop on the port side, as if on a throne, with his legs crossed at the ankles and his arms folded about the unmistakable double-bladed battle-axe.

Alan stared up at the massive sculpture, feeling so awed by its scale and power he had to hold onto the rail for support.

More than any other aspect, it was the head, a tumulus of granite as big as a two-storey house, that cast a brooding warning over their forward passage. The face was square, the nose broad, with prominent nostrils flattened across the bridge, and the eye-sockets were caves of shadow. The likeness to Qwenqwo was unmistakable.

Alan's attention wheeled to the portal on the starboard side, but there, though equally massive as the figure on the left, the shape that remained was only vaguely human. Some calamity more destructive than wind or rain had ruined the image – and recently, too. The upper portion was shattered into a profusion of jagged ledges and scattered fragments. Boulders of detached rock had tumbled down over the shoulders and torso, masking the presence that had once reigned opposite the figure of the king.

'The profaned image was that of the youthful queen, Nantosueta!' Alan heard Milish's shocked whisper from his side as the council woman came to join him. And now, as they dropped sail to slow their passage, Alan did sense a bedraggled femininity in the desecrated right portal.

'What does it mean?'

'A malignancy has preceded us. As to what terrible malignancy would dare to profane the guardian – surely we journey into a vortex of danger!'

With a grim set to his jaws Mark piloted the ship deeper, passing through Lamah's pass and into the blue-black shadows of the crooked throat, or Kiwa Hahn. Towering cliffs overhung their passage, as if they were gigantic beasts that had slunk down to the water's edge to drink. Even the Shee who stood guard on the deck looked apprehensive. The air became still and humid, and it seemed that the beating of their hearts echoed back at them from the massive keeps to either side for the hour or more that Mark picked his course, twisting and turning between these dreadful cliffs. And judging from Siam's expression as he paced the decks, at every moment he expected those jaws to close about them and end it all in a splintering of oak and bone. All the while, the eagle followed their course, soaring high overhead, as if wherever the dwarf mage journeyed, his guardian would follow.

But then abruptly, as if entering a new dawn out of the darkest night, they were through the pass and a secret world opened before them.

The sails were once more hoisted to catch the moisture-laden winds that drenched the decks with a blustering rain. Lichens, thick and furry, carpeted every rocky outcrop. A tributary rushed to join the river in a white-water furnace over timeworn rocks, its spray sending up clouds of water droplets in which a series of rainbows shimmered. Kate joined Alan and Milish in the prow to watch a pair of dippers, their grey-brown plumage dusted with a chalky blue, diving and bobbing in the gossamer curtain.

'Oh, Alan – it's gorgeous!' Kate exclaimed.

After the barren cold of their approach to the pass, it was a wonderland. And its wonder extended for mile after mile.

The weather would change without warning. One minute a clear rain washed the view to a sparkling clarity. The next minute a wetting fog would close about them, plunging the day into twilight. Everywhere life proliferated, wild and strange. They might have been entering the primeval forest at the beginnings of time.

She felt the muscles in Alan's arm tighten and wondered why. Her first glimpse of the trees was of great boughs, festooned with living curtains over green-carpeted banks. Every branch and twig was so bearded with moss and lichens it was difficult to make out their forms. In places the secondary growths were so dense as to become hanging gardens in the canopies. The giant green fingers of ferns proliferated in the sunlit openings.

In a hushed voice Milish spoke of a forest of giants. Meanwhile Alan, beside Kate, nodded, awestruck.

But still Kate sensed these trees meant something even more special to Alan. They had seen massive trees in the forests north of Isscan, but they had been no more than saplings in comparison. Great boles of trunks soared into the distant sky, their upper reaches lost in the fusion of mist and canopy. Kate struggled to identify even a few of the species – Douglas fir perhaps, and Sitka spruce and cedar – only to be forced to withdraw her gaze from leaf shapes that were completely unknown, or colours so bright they dazzled her eyes like spears of sunlight. Back in Clonmel, many of these plants would have been listed as rare, or more likely unknown.

Over the splintered caps of the encircling mountains to the northeast, smoke and fumes fed the discoloured clouds. She saw now that many of the peaks were volcanic cones, and she heard the cracks and rumbles of their restless violence, even at this great distance. Part way up the slope, heated air rose from vents in the rocks, billowing steam that fell down into the forests and ran like a tidal race between the trees.

Hour after hour they watched in amazement as the great ship sailed deeper into the pass, past streams yellow with sulphur from the discharges in the distant peaks. Here and there age had thinned out the woodland, where bedraggled survivors of some natural calamity lay scattered about open spaces, supporting an explosion of parasitic mantles, each its own intimate garden of delight.

Then, as they rounded a bend into a sunlit valley, Kate's

breath faltered and her heartbeat rose into her throat.

Rising, as if through an immense struggle from the arid rock of the waterside, was an extraordinary tree. Its roots were a gnarled battle of intertwining shapes, as ancient as the stones, and from that complex skein of roots, the trunk and branches were grotesquely twisted, their ends broken and repaired through the storms of thousands of bitter winters, until the golden heartwood was exposed, whorled and twisted like the eddies of whirlpools.

Although she knew it only from pictures, she recognised the tree. She whispered to Milish, 'What do you call these trees?'

'Ah – these are the Oleone. They are revered as the most ancient of living spirits in all of Tír, the elders of the Forbidden Forest.'

Kate put her hand on Alan's shoulder.

He reached up and cradled her hand. 'Yeah – I know!'

They both recognised the species from their own world, where it was also revered for its great longevity, known to live for six thousand years. Though gnarled and contorted almost beyond recognition, they were looking at a bristle-cone pine – it looked like the oldest bristle-cone pine that had ever lived. Its significance overwhelmed Kate, even as she heard Alan sigh with grief.

'What is it, Mage Lord?' Milish spoke softly.

'These are the trees of my native land, Milish.'

'What land is this, that it should arouse such passions?'

'America.'

'A-me-ri-ka!' The council woman tested the syllables, a look of astonishment on her bronzed face.

'Seeing them so unexpectedly – they reminded me of my loss, my parents . . .' Alan couldn't speak any more of it.

Kate hugged his arm, recognising other familiar trees among these leviathans. The rust-coloured tannin of their barks was unmistakable. These had to be giant redwoods, sequoia. The river hinterland was dense with them, tall and upstanding amid the Douglas firs and spruce.

For the first time Alan also realised what should long have been obvious – that there must be a link, a sister-like relationship, between Earth and this very different world. That thought stirred him at a level he could not altogether logically understand.

After another day-and-a-half's journey, the river expanded until it became a mile or more in width. Ahead of them its stream divided around a pinnacle of rock. Sailing closer, they saw that it was the northernmost prow of an island about which the river split into two unequal branches.

The main branch flowed right, while a lesser stream flowed left through a shadowed inlet.

On Siam's direction, Mark began to pull hard on the wheel to direct the prow into the broader tributary when a dreadful foreboding seized Alan.

'Hold it! Don't head that way!'

Siam turned round to confront Alan. 'We cannot take the leftward channel. That way leads to forbidden places.'

Through the pulsating oraculum, Alan sensed an even greater danger waiting for them on the broader tributary. That danger was so overwhelming he took a firm hold of the chief's shoulder.

'We have no choice. I'm sorry – but we have to turn aside! We're in great danger.'

A chorus of voices erupted into the air about them as the Olhyiu clustered around their chief.

'The Mage Lord is right.' It was the clear strong voice of Ainé that cut through the rising panic. Alan saw that the Kyra's oraculum was also pulsating strongly. 'I too sense the trap that awaits us upon the greater channel of the river.'

With a groan of disbelief and a continuing shaking of his head, Siam nodded to Mark, who brought the helm around so the ship was heading into the left channel. The chief glanced at Kemtuk, whose face was haggard with worry.

Alan and Kate were also joined in the prow by Mo, all watching intently as the island flowed steadily by them for mile after mile. 'Ossierel was the name of both the capital and the island itself, from ancient times,' said Milish. 'Such was it called in the tongue of those who first settled the valley.'

They saw that the island was densely forested over its

lower reaches, and rising in a series of scarps to a broad plateau on which they glimpsed walls and buildings of ruined stone – the fallen citadel. Blue in the distance, and capping the plateau, more scarps buttressed a tor that soared almost vertically upward, so steep and high its peak was lost in the mists of what was now afternoon.

'There is a tower, at present obscured by the mists, on that soaring pinnacle.' Milish's finger led their gazes far inland.

Then Siam's voice sounded from behind them. 'We sailors know it better as the Rath of the Dark Queen.'

'The Rath of Nantosueta!' echoed Qwenqwo Cuatzel, who had only just descended from his watch in the crow's nest to join their gathering on the prow. 'It is all that remains of the temples of her dark arts, elevated above forest and river, from where long ago her witches' coven could cast their spells over forest, mountain and river, and over the kingdoms of men.'

An hour and a half after entering the narrow channel Alan could see a small alluvial plain that broke out of the dense forest of the island's lower slopes, and now, as they approached it, he could make out the faint outline of a track winding up through the forest that cloaked the slopes over the river. It had to lead to the plateau, and ruins, high above. It looked like a difficult place to get to. Now, peering aloft through gaps in the mist, he was awed by the vast ascent that took his gaze to the level of the plateau, and beyond it, to the level of the clouds.

Suddenly Mo startled them all. She was standing stiffly before them, her face racked with alarm. In a piping voice she warned them, 'We must stop here – it's where we've been drawn to.'

Alan wheeled round to face her. He took her shoulders in his hands and gazed down into her startled eyes. 'What is it, Mo?'

'Don't you feel it too?'

Even as he began to shake his head, he felt it rise in him, so overwhelming with its closeness that he was almost thrown backwards. The ecstasy of contact came in a single great wave, causing gooseflesh to erupt over his skin. He heard the sighs of his friends and knew all of their mouths had fallen open.

The calling!

All four friends, even Mark, further back on the aft deck, looked upwards, towards the high plain on the mysterious island. The calling had come from here.

A chill of presentiment swept through Alan as he waited for the wave to ebb, then looked at Mo and Kate, then across to Mark, whose arms had fallen from the great wheel. He asked them, 'Are we all agreed?'

The two girls nodded but Mark was silent.

'Mark?' He had to call out across the intervening decks.

Mark shrugged, as if to say, 'What choice do I have?'

Alan realised that Mark, more than anyone, would naturally be reluctant to leave the ship. He turned to Ainé and Siam, his face pale. 'I'm sorry, but we have no choice but to leave the ship and answer this calling.'

'Abandon the Temple Ship?'

Alan heard the incredulous growl of Siam even as he felt his oraculum begin to pulsate so strongly his entire brow seemed to throb with it. The chief was insistent. 'You cannot ask this of my people. Not here!' His fearful gaze lifted up to look at the distant ruins that towered over them.

'Siam – I know you don't want to leave the safety of the ship. My friends and I have no choice, but you do. You don't have to come with us. We'll make our way up to the plateau on our own.'

Kemtuk's hand reached for Siam's shoulder, as if supporting him in his fears for the people now gathering about them in consternation.

'The Mage Lord asks that we abandon the ship,' Siam groaned to the sea of anxious faces. 'Here, in the very shadow of the Dark Queen's Rath!'

Ainé stood erect with a silent Qwenqwo Cuatzel, watching.

'Never has danger so threatened us in this journey as it does now.' The Kyra's deep voice rose above the clamour of debate. 'Can you not sense eyes upon our every movement?'

Topgal roared, 'Aye – and there is even greater danger in the forest and above these slopes. We are safer leaving this place. We shall pole our way back up these quieter waters and find the greater tributary.'

'Where you will discover a much greater peril!' Ainé raised her voice to a roar. 'Do you not yet understand the nature of what faces us? A Legun has surely passed through the pass of Kloshe Lamah. What other force could sunder the image of the queen, where she has guarded the gates for two thousand years? That Legun has cast a deathmaw over the wider course of the river. That is the peril that the Mage Lord sensed ahead. None would survive, for there would be no escape, trapped within the confines of the ship.'

A groan of fright went through those who heard her.

'What is a Legun – or a deathmaw?' Alan asked Ainé.

'A Legun is one of the seven orders of malice that forms the Tyrant's inner circle. It draws power directly from its master. The deathmaw is its malengin – a force invisible until you come up against it. Then it is deadly.'

'We are already doomed!' muttered Siam.

Ainé said firmly, 'We are not doomed. But we invite doom if our courage now fails us. The Mage Lord and his companions have heard their calling. Above us, in the ruins of Ossierel, he and his three friends will come face to face with their destiny. Is this not the purpose of his journey? Do not waste time on argument. Take heed instead of the gravity of our position. Dark forces close upon us from all sides. But on the plateau of Ossierel we can put up a better defence.' Ainé lifted an arm to calm their terrified babbling. 'We must enter these forests without delay – or abandon all hope of redemption for our peoples.'

Topgal's voice was raised among the Olhyiu. 'These are fine words. But we have children and elderly to care for. Darkness falls – it can be no more than a few hours at most. I say return to the main stream and sail on. Take our chances in spite of these faint-hearts with their womanish forebodings.'

'No!' Siam stood full-square against his brother-in-law. 'Not one among you dreads these accursed forests any more than I do, yet I trust the Mage Lord more than I fear death. How can you even consider denying his counsel?'

Ainé took her sword out of its scabbard and lifted it high above the fearful company. The blade glowed with the pulse of her slow steady heartbeat, like a beacon of resolution against the shadows of approaching evening. 'If you attempt to sail on, darkness will bring the attack you fear. The Legun will cast a new deathmaw further along this very channel. We Shee leave immediately, in protection of the Mage Lord and his companions. If you will take my counsel and accompany us, we will find concealment in the forest this night. That will give us respite to continue the climb with rested limbs tomorrow.'

'So be it!' Siam spoke quietly, without the heart to roar.

As they cast anchor against the shingle beach and made ready to unload supplies of weapons and food, Alan turned to examine the island, his face lifting to the temple plateau. He had a lot of sympathy with the Olhyiu's fears. The ruins of Ossierel, if ever they got to them, might prove to be another trap.

Brooding Heads

In the crepuscular shadows of the forest's edge the Shee spread themselves out, with Ainé leading and the others distributing themselves to guard the long column of Olhyiu. Mark stopped for a moment and looked back at the abandoned ship a final time with tears in his eyes. Within minutes, they were within the gloom of the canopy.

They made their way up the winding slopes, hacking through the undergrowth and climbing – ever climbing. Just as darkness fell they found their progress blocked by a wall of Cyclopean stones. In the twilight Alan saw how each stone was an individually shaped boulder of granite, so skilfully sculpted that the convexity of one stone exactly met the concavity of its neighbour. It was a fortification built to withstand a siege, and it stretched into the distance to either side of them.

Ainé explained, 'We have reached the first of three

defensive fosses, intended to delay any attackers and give time for the inner defences to organise.'

'Yet,' Qwenqwo countered, 'in spite of such defensive calculation, Ossierel was defeated?'

The Kyra glared down at the little man. 'Here,' she growled, 'the people can rest for the night. Warn them there can be no fires. In the meantime we must search along the wall to either side until we find a gate.'

'More likely a breach!' Qwenqwo muttered softly.

In the gloom, Kate was shivering from a mixture of cold and trepidation. Keeping close to Alan, she whispered, 'The Shee can see in the dark. But how can we help them search without some form of light, and that would only give our positions away?'

The dwarf mage came to their rescue. From one of his pockets he brought out a cluster of tiny stones, lumpy like knuckles, which, when he touched them against his runestone, glowed in the dark. He handed one each to Alan, Kate and Mark – Mark, who had not spoken a word since they left the ship.

'Hold the glowstones in your fists and let the light appear only through the gaps in your fingers. Thus to our enemies will it resemble the fire insects that abound in these forests.'

The Olhyiu put down their bundles and set about making a temporary camp, sharing out their rations and huddling together under their rugs. The Shee melted into the shadows, concealed under their camouflage capes. Meanwhile, Alan and Kate were forced to split up into two groups. Kate, visibly unhappy that she had been separated from Alan, headed left, led by Ainé, and Alan headed right, accompanied by Qwenqwo and Kemtuk. They used their machetes to clear a path through the undergrowth.

After Alan's group had covered a few hundred yards they came to a hexagonal buttress that marked an ancient guard tower. Through brief flashes of their glowstones they made out gargoyles on the tower wall, jutting monstrously over the surrounding forest.

Qwenqwo murmured softly, 'Though the Kyra did not mention it, this fortification was guarded by Fir Bolg warriors long ago.'

'How do you know?'

'Because of this!' The dwarf mage hacked aside some scrub immediately downslope of the wall tower until, in the glow of the pebbles, they peered at a monument of rounded stone, overgrown with creepers and ferns. Between them they cleared away more of the scrub to discover a giant head carved in granite which, though tilted askew and a quarter buried, still rose a good nine feet above the forest floor. The face had the same broad flat nose and wide-lipped features as Qwenqwo. While Alan was still staring up in amazement, a hand suddenly took hold of his shoulder, causing his heart to miss a beat.

A Shee voice whispered, 'We must go back. The Kyra has found a way.'

Qwenqwo, with a thoughtful expression, asked Alan to leave him behind. 'You should return to the camp while I spend a little time in this sacred place.'

Back in the dark and fireless camp, they satisfied their growing hunger with dried berries and salted fish. Alan asked Kemtuk if he knew the explanation of the stone head in front of the wall tower.

Kemtuk sucked on an unlit pipe, talking reflectively. 'I wonder about the masons who shaped these walls and towers. Here and there, in the marks I found on the stones, I recognised an ancient calendar – a year divided into the eighteen months of the moon cycles and the sacred nature of the five days.'

'Are you suggesting it wasn't just guarded but also built by Qwenqwo's people – the Fir Bolg?'

The shaman nodded. 'Legends do tell of a fierce warrior race of that name, stories of fearless valour from the days before even the Olhyiu were known in this land. And warriors such as these will have had engineers skilled at defending sieges. It may indeed be that the dwarf mage is a descendant of those who constructed these walls.'

The friends huddled together for warmth but none of them slept soundly in the oppressive darkness. Alan woke to the whispering of Mark and Mo, who appeared to be sleepless. He could make out nothing of their words, and could see only the vaguest shapes of their hunched-up figures in the dark.

'What is it with you guys?'

It was Mo who whispered a reply, 'Mark is pining for the ship.'

*

At the first pale glow of dawn, Alan threw off the rugs and made his way along the track they had cut in the night so he could take a better look at the giant head. The sculpture was even more impressive in the misty daylight, the face impassive yet charged with power. There was no doubt about it – the resemblance to the dwarf mage was unmistakable, even to the implacable stare he had seen in Qwenqwo's own eyes when he was angry.

A flicker in the oraculum warned him of another presence, and he said softly, without turning, 'I know you're still around, Qwenqwo. Have you spent the whole night here?'

The dwarf mage stepped out of the shadows. He spoke reverentially in the presence of the head. 'Yes. It comforted me. Mage Lord – what service can I offer you? You only need to ask and it is yours.'

'One thing you could do for me is to call me Alan.'

'Such honour I will reserve to times when it would appear appropriate.'

Alan sighed, then stared up at the impressive stone face. 'I sense, as you do, that we're surrounded by danger.' He hesitated, then looked Qwenqwo directly in the eyes. 'But if you really meant what you said, there is something you could do for me. I'd appreciate honest answers to some questions.'

Those green eyes gazed back at him with equal frankness. 'Your people – the Fir Bolg. Tell me about them.'

'They were the bravest and noblest of warriors.'

'But they died – I'm sorry, Qwenqwo, but even you have to admit that that was a long time ago.' He dropped his head, searching for the right words. He spoke softly, searchingly. 'I guess maybe I'm not putting this very well. The truth is it hardly makes any sense. But nevertheless I need to understand. What I'm asking is, do you still have some connection with these ancient guardians?'

A fierce pride glowed in Qwenqwo's eyes and he put his hand on the uppermost head of his battle-axe where it protruded above his left shoulder. 'I am the last of the Fir Bolg.'

Alan's pulse quickened. It had been a strange reply on Qwenqwo's part and he needed a moment to consider its implications. 'And your runestone – that has something to do with all this?'

The dwarf mage stood erect without a trace of tiredness, though his night must have been devoid of sleep. 'The runestone I inherited from my father, who was the lore-master to Magcyn. Most particularly did my father show me, and not through words alone, how the worth of a man is measured not by his stature but by the courage and integrity of his spirit.'

Alan started, 'I was recalling how you explained earlier how your runestone once held a much greater power.'

'You recall true.'

'How did it lose its force?'

'What does a mortal man know of such things as the plotting and scheming of immortals long ago?'

'Immortals?'

'Aye. It would be prudent for me to hold my tongue. Yet through such terrible loss, I retained the lore that was lodged within my mind and the result of my training. Yet the runestone – thus emasculated – promised more than could ever be fulfilled. Then you shocked me to my very soul when you appeared in the chamber of the impostor bearing the Oraculum of the First Power on your brow. Of course I had heard of such a thing, but only in legend. And I confess that the hope it kindled in my heart was so powerful that therein was born my selfish motive. I dared to pray that even the mere proximity of such power might reawaken the runestone to its former calling. But even then – and this I swear – if you had it in your gift to resurrect its power in full, I would have pledged that power to your service, as now, even in its weakened state, I pledge it.'

'I know you would.' He hesitated. 'What about the eagle – it is still there, in the sky above us?'

'Yes.'

'It's somehow linked to you?'

'The eagle and runestone are one in spirit – in a way it would be difficult for someone who is not a Fir Bolg to understand.'

Alan nodded. 'I can sympathise even if I don't understand. I need your friendship, Qwenqwo. Let's work together from now on. Maybe we could start by looking more closely at this stone head.'

Together they inspected the face, with its large protruding eyes, its flattened nose and wide, full lips – an almost African face under the heavy-domed helmet that capped the brow. The brow was buttressed by a thick broad strap. Although Qwenqwo wasn't wearing it right now, Alan recalled a similar strap of heavy bronze girdling Qwenqwo's helmet during the fight at the waterfront in Isscan. In the uncertain light, he saw a circular pit in the centre of the brow-strap. Qwenqwo's helmet had had some kind of crystal embedded in exactly the same place on the brow. 'I think this might have contained some kind of crystal.'

'So?'

'If so, it puzzles me,' Alan spoke softly. 'What possible purpose could it play in battle?'

After a thoughtful hesitation, Qwenqwo spoke. 'Perhaps you should look upon it through the lens of your own experiences. Is there not a common source of all power, as you have already discovered?'

Alan was taken aback by these words. 'Now you're talking about something I just don't get at all. We're called to this world by a power we've never identified or understood. We're led to the gateway on Slievenamon. From there we arrive on Tír close to a stone circle that in turn leads us to Granny Dew. She gives me this.' He indicated the triangle in his brow. 'She gives two of my friends egg-shaped crystals. The Olhyiu, with the Temple Ship, are nearby.' Alan sighed. 'Do you follow my reasoning?'

'You question fate?'

'There's been one coincidence after another. It just couldn't be accidental.'

'In the play of great powers, nothing is ever entirely accidental. Yet you might look upon fate as a marriage of soil and seed.'

'I still don't get it.'

'You are the seed as fate is the soil. The seed is not chosen by accident, any more than the soil responds by accident.'

'Heck! Just who does the choosing?'

Qwenqwo placed a finger to his lips.

Alan sighed before returning his gaze to the brooding head – a Fir Bolg head, with the Mage Lord of the Fir Bolg now standing next to him, and its spiritual emblem, if that was how he should think of the eagle – in the sky above them. 'Qwenqwo – what is it about the tower of the queen that has kept the Death Legion from passing through to Carfon?'

'You should not ask me this. It is not safe to talk of it.'

'That's a risk I have to take. Many lives may depend on it.'

'The Fir Bolg harboured great knowledge of war. Knowledge and power enough to challenge Nantosueta's own accursed Rath.' Qwenqwo's voice was urgent now. 'Yet it was she who triumphed.'

'What are you saying? It is she – the Dark Queen – whose power still preserves and protects the valley? It's Nantosueta the Death Legion fears?'

'If the rumours are to be believed.'

Alan hesitated. 'It just doesn't make any sense. The way I figure it, there has to be something else. There is something else, isn't there – something a good deal more terrifying about the Vale of Tazan?'

'Hush! I beg you. There are powers so dangerous it is dangerous to speak of them.'

Alan scanned the forest with the oraculum. 'I sense it as you do, Qwenqwo,' he murmured softly. 'There is something else here, a great power buried in the very earth and rocks.'

Back at the camp Alan found Siam berating Kate, who had returned from a dawn foray, her arms full of roots and herbs. Turkeya was missing. Earlier he had left the camp with Kate but had stayed in the forest when Kate had returned. Alan struggled to focus on the squabble, his mind still reeling from the conversation with Qwenqwo. 'Kate, it's understandable that Siam is angry. We can't sit around and wait for Turkeya to come back.'

'Well, I'm not just going to sit around and do nothing while you play at Conan the Barbarian. I'm interested in herbs, and Turkeya has been teaching me things.'

'Hey – I'm not saying— Oh, forget what I said. But we're just about ready to leave.'

'Besides, you don't need to wait for Turkeya. He knows how to track us down when he has what he's looking for.'

'Which is what?'

'He's spying on the enemy.'

'Kate, that's crazy!'

'Nobody's better than Turkeya at tracking and spying. He's determined to be our eyes and ears.'

Siam threw his hat on the ground and stamped on it. 'That stupid boy! I despair of the mischief he will think of next.'

Alan shook his head at Siam. 'Maybe Kate is right. We shouldn't underestimate Turkeya. He's already given you cause to be proud of him.'

But the chief merely picked up his hat and stormed away, lashing out at imaginary stupidities.

All around Alan people were settling down for a hasty breakfast of what little could be spared from the dwindling food resources before they tied up their bundles for the long day's march. Through breaks in the canopy those same dark clouds that had crept over the dawn horizon were now thickening, as if a storm of rain threatened. Alan was so lost in his thoughts he failed to notice Mo until she tugged at his sleeve. She led him a couple of hundred yards into the forest, where she pointed out the Kyra, her feet widely straddled on a buttress of rock that protruded from the slope. Ainé held herself erect, as if standing to attention, then suddenly her position altered and she moved through ninety degrees and took up a similar position.

Mo spoke in a whisper. 'She's calling for help, isn't she?'

Alan shook his head. 'Gee – I guess she must be.'

Suddenly his oraculum began to pulse strongly. Instinctively, he searched for the cause . . . and sensed something the Kyra must have sensed already. There was another presence – a malignant force nearby. As if detecting his probing, it turned its awareness from the Kyra towards him.

Then he heard the sound of screaming. Mo clutched his hand as they started running back to the camp.

Under Attack

The Olhyiu camp was in uproar, and Alan saw the cause of their alarm down in the river, where a pillar of crackling green fire was rising high into the sky. A dense mushroom of smoke billowed out of the flames, gusting and spiralling over the surrounding slopes, carrying an acrid odour on the wind, that same rank smell he remembered from the ambush north of Isscan.

'No!'

He heard Mark's cry even as his own heart fell. The fire and smoke were rising from the Temple Ship.

Siam was attempting to restore order. Milish reached out to hug the tearful Mo. Ainé had also returned, and she spoke decisively. 'We must leave this place immediately. We are too few to resist any coordinated attack and this position offers no protection.' She made no mention of her signalling for help. Alan assumed that she wanted to avoid increasing the panic that was already overwhelming the frightened people.

But the shock of the attack on the Temple Ship had resurrected all of the Olhyiu's fears. A frail old man spoke, his voice trembling with conviction. 'This forest strikes a chill in my heart. I will not take another step into this graveyard of history.' The old man turned his wrinkled neck about, eliciting the support of others, all equally fearful.

Siam took command of the situation, striding among the crowds of murmuring and gesticulating Olhyiu. 'Old Canim here fantasises in his dotage.'

'So you say,' someone else spoke up, 'but the hairs on our necks speak louder than words.'

Siam strode among them, knocking heads with his hat. 'Don't allow yourself to be panicked. The Olhyiu have prevailed in worse adversity than this. Go pick up your bundles or we leave you behind. And leave you we will, just like my witless son, who is still out there on some fool's errand.'

So it was, with the Temple Ship ablaze in the river below and with Turkeya still missing, the long column set off for the breach in the outer fosse. Mo appeared to huddle up close to Mark as, once more, they made their way through the trees, where sparks of wintry sunlight pierced the canopy, mottling green needles or a half-seen edge of granite, while flitting shadows hovered about their path or seemed to watch them from only a few yards away in the stillness. Soon they came upon another of the giant heads, half buried under a rotten tree that was festooned with brilliant yellow crescents of fungi.

Alan shivered, his eyes glancing skywards, where the eagle hovered, little more than a speck, high above them. Despite the chill, the effort of climbing brought out a sweat that trickled down over his back, where it felt like spiders' legs crawling down his spine.

During a subsequent halt about mid-morning, he watched one of the Aides pull down a creeper, hack it through with a knife and drink the juice that pattered from its cut surface. One family and then another copied the Aides in slaking their thirst. Ainé came to stand beside him in the gloom, her oraculum pulsating. 'You feel it as I do. We are not alone here. Something other than the Death Legion stalks us here.' As his eyes fell, Alan saw a third giant head, no more than yards from where he had halted. Brooding in the shadows, with those dark pits of eyes, it appeared to observe him as closely as he studied it. This one still retained a crystal insert in the brow strap.

'Here! Will somebody give me a hand to get a closer look?'

Siam threw his stout legs apart and signalled with his hand. 'Climb on my shoulders.'

Alan did so cautiously, bringing his face up to the level of the eyes. The steam of his breath bathed the stone as he reached up to touch the crystal in its brow. Its surface was hard, like polished glass, yet, as far as he could make out in the murky light, a dull, semi-opaque green.

'Jade, I think!'

They forced several more hours' march before pausing again at noon. Alan didn't need to search for long before he found another of the heads. He called out for Milish to come and give her opinion.

'Take a good look. See if you agree with me!'

Milish studied the head thoughtfully for several moments. 'I see what you mean – the face is different from the previous ones.'

'Right! Every face is different.'

He figured that the heads were spaced at regular intervals, and very close intervals at that, considering the ease with which they were coming across them. There must be a vast number of stone heads forming some kind of a grid through the forest.

After a brief rest, they struggled on to make the most of the afternoon daylight, the weak having to be supported or carried.

Resting again hours later, with his tired back against the bole of a tree, Alan noticed that the Shee were increasingly restless, searching and peering into the formless shadows.

After a wearying climb lasting several more hours, they arrived at another wall of massive stones, which proved to be the second fosse of the island's defences. Darkness had fallen as, through a gate with inwardly sloping stone jambs, they entered a cluster of buildings ravaged by time and lichened with age. One of these was clearly a temple, its walls sculpted with scenes of what appeared to be warriors fighting monsters.

It was enough to provoke renewed exclamations of fear among the Olhyiu. No one would shelter inside the walls.

Siam, with a worried glance about him, took Alan aside. 'It's even worse than before. There's a malevolence here that withers the spirit. Surely this place is one with those heads. Who among us does not feel their brooding evil, stalking us at every step we make? Mage Lord, I beg you – there can be no stopping here. We are but a day from sanctuary. Exhausted as we are, we must march through the night.'

Kemtuk cautioned against any night march, insisting that there were too many exhausted among them. But the chief was adamant. And Ainé did not disagree with him.

Struggling with fatigue and dread they pressed on deeper into the night, even as the slope became steeper and more difficult, so that at times they were sliding backwards down banks of mud coated in a slimy mulch of leaves and bracken. Alan found himself relying on the Spear of Lug, leaning heavily on its shaft for purchase. Yet even on these difficult inclines, mired in tangled roots, they still came across more stone heads. The Aides now took the lead, feeding back ropes to help the exhausted Olhyiu climb through rock-strewn slurry and thorny scrub.

The small wiry women appeared to be tireless as well as excellent climbers. So dark were their surroundings and so treacherous this terrain that the Olhyiu were obliged to forgo the meagre light of the glowstones and accept the risk of firebrands, even though it would inevitably give away their position. After three or four hours of halting progress they heard a distant thunder in the air. With every step the thundering became louder until they emerged into the open from a screen of giant ferns to be confronted by an astonishing spectacle.

The noise came from a cataract spilling over the table of rock at the top of the slope. Catching the pallid light of a scudding moon, it dissolved in a curtain of mist and spray that cascaded like rain through the moonlight and shadows over the cliff face. The thunder arose from the impact of the main waterfall against the rocky floor, where it threw up a freezing mist. A deluge of streams and rivulets ran downslope, fast flowing and bitterly cold. While the Shee and the stronger men among the Olhyiu might risk the crossing, for the majority it presented an impassable barrier.

Dismayed, they gathered on the wet rocks, buffeted by the wind and icy spray, the women and elderly sitting on their bundles, some quietly weeping or cuddling the fretful children.

Approaching the waterfall, Alan's hair was immediately soaked, his clothes moulded to the outline of his flesh. Ainé stood beside him in a watchful silence, her sword unsheathed. He felt a dreadful premonition that caused him to look around them into the encroaching night.

'Mage Lord,' the Kyra warned him, 'your brow is aflame.'

'I sense danger!'

'Do not speak of it aloud!' Ainé's eyes glanced over at the frightened women and children.

He lowered his voice to a whisper. 'This creature that terrifies you – this Legun! Tell me what you know about it.'

'The Tyrant has an inner circle, the Septemvile, each a reflection of a different facet of his malevolence.' Her fingers brushed the scarred left side of her face with a grim reflection. 'The one who did this to me is his captain. Its name is pride and its mask is death. Had it wished other than to torment me, my death would have followed that of my sister-mother in the arena of Ghork Mega.'

'Is this what I am sensing? Are we going to be attacked by a Legun?'

'Yes.'

His fist squeezed the shaft of his spear so tightly it hurt. 'Well – so what can we expect?'

'When a Legun attacks, it may do so in spirit as a bane of darkness – or it may attack as its incarnate self.' Her voice was lowered, so nobody other than Alan could hear her. 'In the spirit we may fight it. But if it attacks in the flesh no mortal force will prevail against it.'

'What are you saying? You're telling me that this thing, this Legun, is what – immortal?'

'So we believe.'

Alan's hand rubbed distractedly at his brow. His mouth felt as dry as a desert in this landscape of freezing waterfalls and streams. 'Oh, man! Jeez!'

Forcing himself to hide what he was feeling, Alan crossed to where Kate was helping Kemtuk distribute herbs among the Olhyiu, who were huddled in exhausted and demoralised groups. A few women, under the direction of Kehloke, were gathering brushwood. Ainé's voice cut through this activity as a commanding bark: she forbade it, though they were as fearful of the dark as they were of an attack.

Alan froze. The sense of menace was suddenly overwhelming.

Suddenly there was a woman's high-pitched scream, followed by a heart-stopping silence. Alan could feel a steady drip of sweat fall from his chin onto his chest. He made sure Kate was protected by Shee before heading off in the direction of the scream. His nostrils detected a heavy smell which his instincts told him was blood.

Somewhere nearby, a trembling voice called out, 'Great Akoli save us!'

An entire family had been slaughtered. As he neared he was sickened by the foulness in the air. He gagged on the excremental stench. He glimpsed terror-stricken faces, he heard the patter of running footsteps, the sobbing cries of terrified children. Several were ignoring Ainé's warning and lighting bundles of twigs to ward away the darkness.

One had already thrown burning tinder into the undergrowth, causing more smoke than fire. In the confusion, Alan tripped over a smooth, firm weight. He realised it must be a body. It was too dark to see but he felt the flesh still warm and slippery with blood. He moved his hands about, encountering a heavy leg, the exposed knee above a skin-tight boot.

A Shee – dead.

Inching forward, he peered into the shadows and smoking brush. He made out another body, then another. As he touched one of them, there was a shudder of life, as if the injured person was fighting him, cursing and aiming blows at his head.

'Easy – easy!' he whispered.

'Hah, my friend!' sounded the answering whisper. 'It is I, Qwenqwo Cuatzel! My arm is broken – but fortunately not the arm that wields my axe. You should not linger here. Danger is about me – I pray it does not find you.'

'Lie still. I'll come back for you.'

'Do not tarry over me. It takes more than a demon to make an end of the Fir Bolg!' In the sudden flare of light from the brushfire, Alan was heartened by the fierce courage of the dwarf, his eyes blazing.

But even as he left Qwenqwo where he lay, there was a grotesque tearing, as of a rib cage being ripped apart, and it was accompanied by an anguished moaning from nearby in the tall rushes. Alan forced aside some giant reeds to find the old man, Canim. He lay bleeding and broken in the reeking undergrowth. The moaning stopped as Alan arrived by his side. Alan's nostrils recoiled from that stink again and his stomach heaved. The stench was getting stronger. He was breathless with apprehension.

Duvaaalll!

He heard his name, a guttural whisper from the surrounding darkness. A rash of gooseflesh erupted over his skin.

Outside the clump of rushes, the night air seemed to whirl and glisten like an agitated vapour. Anticipation made the muscles in his legs tense, and rivulets of sweat ran from his brow, over the folds of his face, stinging the angles of his eyes. He could actually taste blood in the air.

A presence loomed between the bulk of two trees. He saw how it flickered as if willing itself into existence through the resisting dimensions of space and time. A livid vapour began to coil and then expand towards him, licking at the air, following his scent like a snake's tongue.

In the past, rage had activated the oraculum. But now, in spite of his rising anger, he felt only a weak throbbing from his brow. There was barely power enough to illuminate the shadows that deepened about him. Coming closer, only a little more substantial than the mist that wreathed the low ground, was a pale phosphorescence. It condensed to something resembling a wraithlike face a long distance above the ground. With the touch of the light from the oraculum, it retracted in hesitation, as if repulsed by it. And then, abruptly, with what sounded like a roar in his mind, it had gone. The effect was so rapid, its disappearance so complete, he might have imagined it.

For a minute Alan held his ground, staring into the grey darkness, gritting his teeth. Then he shouted for the Kyra. 'Ainé! Over here!'

There was shouting now in the background and the sound of running footsteps. Then a firebrand flared next to him. Ainé was examining him, from his face to his feet. 'Trídédana be praised – can it be that you are without a single wound?'

'It was here. Then it disappeared.'

The Kyra lifted the flame to peer into the shadows. With a shudder, she recoiled from the stench. 'Never has it been known for a Legun to withdraw from its murderous purpose. It is not over.'

Alan explained what he had seen. 'It spoke my name.' He shook his head, uncomprehendingly. 'I tried to use the oraculum. I tried to probe it, but only managed a feeble attempt.'

Wrinkling her brow, Ainé gazed about her at the impenetrable shadows. 'There are forces at work in these forests more mysterious than even the legends have foretold.' She took firm hold of Alan's arm. 'Where is the dwarf mage?'

'His left arm was broken during the attack.'

Her oraculum pulsed rapidly – some words of command, ordering the survivors of the Shee to regroup and maintain their guard. Then she asked Alan to lead her to Qwenqwo. But before he could do so, she murmured, as much to herself as to Alan, 'A Legun never attacks randomly. There is always a pattern. First it baits a deathmaw – but over the river some miles southward and not within the forest. It destroys the Temple Ship. Only then does it cast its spirit in search of us. Meanwhile its attack was directed not at you, its obvious rival in power, but at the Mage of Dreams.'

'What does it mean?'

'Who can say? Yet I wonder if this diminutive mage's understanding runs deeper than he tells.'

'I'll find Qwenqwo, Ainé. You have important tasks to organise. We've got to get away from here.'

Nodding, she declared, 'We have more than a dozen dead with no time for ceremony. All we can do is to cover them in haste with rocks. We must press on to the fortress, for it was constructed with defence in mind.' Pressing the blazing torch into Alan's hand, Ainé was away, issuing orders.

Alan ran to where he had left the dwarf mage. 'Qwenqwo – where the hell are you?' He turned in a circle, searching for him in the dark of the trees.

There was no immediate answer. Only the silence and the dark.

Alan wandered the gloom, peering into shadows. He almost fell again over the body of the dead Shee. Now, inspecting the gruesome remains with the torch, he saw the unfortunate woman had been bitten in two. Shivering with dread, he held out the brand against the encircling darkness, calling more loudly, 'Qwenqwo! If you're alive, answer me.'

'Can't a man take a quiet drink without the hounds baying?'

Alan heard the grumble from no more than yards away and saw that it came from a cavity in the tangled roots of a tree. Then, as if in a blink, Qwenqwo clambered out of it, a flask uplifted against his lips. 'Had the monster come back, broken arm or no, I would have left my mark upon its ugly neck.' Qwenqwo chuckled, while his eyes protruded with excitement. 'If a neck it truly possessed!'

'You're drunk!'

'As well a man might be who discovers he owes his life to the witch-warrior lying yonder.' He waved the bottle in the direction of the dead Shee, and hiccupped.

Alan helped Qwenqwo to his feet, calling out for the Aides to come and splint the broken bone.

A Lament for the Fir Bolg

As one by one the Shee prepared for further combat by going on one knee before Ainé and handing over their swords for recharging through contact with her oraculum, the four friends formed a ring about a single great fire, where they were joined by a dozen or so of the apprehensive Olhyiu elders, including Kemtuk, Siam and Topgal. The dwarf mage also joined them, as did the attentive Milish.

In the flickering light of the flames, Alan addressed them. 'The Kyra is certain that the Legun will return.' He paused to allow the horror of that realisation to sink in. 'Its target last time seems to have been the Mage of Dreams. And maybe that tells us something – a clue that might help us fight it. Does anybody have any thoughts or ideas they'd like to share?'

Kemtuk said thoughtfully, 'It seems to me that it was testing us, perhaps assessing our strengths and weaknesses?'

Alan nodded. 'The Kyra is determined that we press on.'

'The Kyra is right.' Kemtuk glanced towards Siam, who clearly had his reservations. 'We are already two thousand feet above the river. We must be very close to the plateau and the third wall of defence of Ossierel. Certainly we must hurry to complete that final march. However, I believe the heads may give us direction. If I gauge correctly, each faces directly outward on a line from the heart of Ossierel . . .'

'So if we stand exactly in the opposite direction from a head, we face directly towards that heart?'

Kemtuk nodded.

Siam said, 'Further progress will be hard. We have children and wounded to carry. The Kyra will grant us a two-hour rest – no more. The strong among us will have to bear the children and the wounded. We will crawl if necessary the final league until we reach the sanctuary.'

'Spoken like a true Olhyiu!' shouted Qwenqwo Cuatzel, his face breaking into a crooked grin, taking a sip from his flask before passing it to Siam.

'Perhaps,' spoke Kemtuk, with a sidelong glance at Alan, 'the Mage of Dreams might offer enlightenment to this company in the dark hours before we head into yet more peril?'

Alan took the hint from Kemtuk. He looked from the shaman to Qwenqwo, observing a glint in the dwarf mage's eyes.

'Truly,' Qwenqwo declared, filling his pipe with one

hand, 'the shaman is the wisest of men, for he recognises the importance of the history we confront on this island. It is a story both great and terrible, yet perhaps one that has been overdue in the telling. I will therefore explain a little of past events that might give you heart in this time of peril.'

A reflective silence prevailed over the company while the dwarf mage lit his pipe. Then, his voice a little more sobered, he began his story.

'These stone men – these brooding idols, as some have mistaken them – are all that mark the mortal remains of the bravest warriors ever to take up arms in a righteous cause. It is true that you see their likeness in my face, for they were my people, the Fir Bolg. And now, in this meeting of like minds around the campfire, I will share with you a sacred knowledge I have shared with none for two thousand years.

'Here, in this enchanted forest, you have sensed the hand of fate from a time so long ago that all but I have forgotten it. I carry the burden of that history. For I am the sole repository of the purpose that brought my people, an army of fifty thousand warriors, here into this accursed forest, where it was their destiny never to return home.'

'What dreadful power could condemn so great an army?' demanded Siam, who was staring at Qwenqwo, his eyes wide.

'What power, you ask?' Qwenqwo took the pipe from his lips to spit into the fire. 'You will see that I have more reason to hate the Dark Queen than you. There is much that I could tell, if I had as many years as we have minutes, of the ways in which a heartless woman, though young as Alan here and beautiful beyond men's dreams, plotted the destruction of a warrior nation! Ah, my friends . . .' He paused, his face wreathed with sorrow. 'Yet such is the peril we face that I see with new eyes the purpose of that wrathful queen.' The dwarf mage smoked his pipe, as if to give him a moment or two to indulge his grief, before continuing.

'At that time, when the army of the Fir Bolg came here, marching for months from a land far to the south, the Queen of the Valley – Nantosueta, she called herself – bade us welcome, for her realm was threatened. Even in those distant times the forces of darkness had long been stirring in the Wastelands across the Eastern Ocean. And had it not been for the courage of the Fir Bolg, that darkness would have been victorious long ago.

'But even after great slaughter of the forces of the enemy and terrible losses too among our own, our leaders knew that we were not fighting powers merely of flesh and blood. Indeed you saw such monsters carved on the walls below.'

'Leguns?' Milish whispered.

'Leguns indeed. And with them came a hatred of life that would have laid waste even these ancient forests. Some say the queen herself perished in the final battle, and that it is her spirit that has reigned ever more from the Rath that stands upon the fastness of rock that bisects the great river.

'I don't know all, for I was but a youth at that time, and it may be in consequence that my memory is prejudiced. Yet I know that it was Magcyn's command that our warriors were given the choice, each man and woman for himself or herself, whether to make a final stand against the forces of evil or return home to the peace of hearth and family. The Arch Mage of the Fir Bolg then cast the runes that foretold that the evil could not be crushed by mortal courage. Only then was Nantosueta's final recourse made plain. From her vaunted pinnacle she laid the hand of death over the entire valley. So she commanded, and so she watches over it still, making certain that all, who should have been allowed to choose their own fate, were compelled instead to remain in death, their souls enslaved to her terrible purpose.'

The dwarf mage wept openly, waving away the flask of healwell offered by Milish, for no healing balm could assuage the sorrow that had long brooded in his heart.

'Through such treachery,' he continued, 'was a warrior race condemned not merely unto death but for eternity. And now you know the true and terrible meaning of the heads. For the Dark Queen in her wrath invoked Mórígán, the raven of death, to accept the sacrifice so that such fealty would endure. Thus was the darkest enchantment cast – an enchantment that emasculated the runestone of the Arch Mage, guaranteeing the enslavement of my people – with every grave marked by the head of its warrior, drawn of his individual living features.'

Qwenqwo wept for a short time, so that those who sat on either side of him placed their arms about his shoulders and held him steady. Then, once recovered, in a voice of outrage, he continued:

'At the throat of the pass Nantosueta, in her arrogance, moulded the very mountains to the figures of herself and Magcyn, the last king of the Fir Bolg. As such they would forever guard the entrance to her valley like some benighted king and queen.'

The dwarf mage drew a great sigh and knocked out the ashes of his pipe on the makeshift hearth. 'My father was none other than the Arch Mage, Urox Zel. After him do I bear the name Cuatzel, for I am the son and heir of Zel. The Mage of Dreams I became in time, for my race was gone and with it my birthright. Thus now, as you see me, with my heart and spirit broken, did I accept this burden and bear it alone for two thousand years.

'So, I now answer you, Mage Lord, Alan Duval – I answer your question as to how the runestone of the Fir Bolg lost its power. And in telling my story I weep no more. For I thank the brave Olhyiu, and you, my friends, who have allowed me to unburden my grief at last. I ask only this of you, that when I fall my grave should be added to theirs, and so the sacrifice will be made complete.'

There was a hushed silence that lasted several minutes, for not a man or a woman among their circle was other than stirred to a new courage by the story of the sacrifice of an entire nation.

Alan put his arm around the gnarled shoulders of the dwarf. 'Thanks, Qwenqwo. I don't know what to say after hearing your story. Is there anything we can do for you?'

The dwarf mage lifted his head and, with tears in his eyes, he looked directly at Mo. 'There is one of you I came to know and love in our shared imprisonment. If there is a lament to be sung, she is surely the singer, for her voice is such as to charm a heart of stone. I would beg of my friend, Mo, to do me the honour of that song.'

All three friends looked at Mo, who had been silent throughout the entire gathering. Mo gazed across into the distressed face of Qwenqwo and smiled. 'Oh, Qwenqwo, of course I'll sing you a song – a sad song that came into my mind when the ship was burning. I'll sing it for you, and I'll think also of my brother, Mark, who has been mourning the ship as you have been mourning your people.'

Mo was helped to her feet by Mark, who put his arm around her shoulders to support her as her sweet voice sounded again in an alien world, singing her lament for the blood sacrifice of the Fir Bolg. And meanwhile the forest seemed to fall into a hush, and as though in a bog of darkness, the glimmering reflections of fifty thousand stars flickered into life and then faintly glowed for the duration of her song before darkness claimed them again.

All too soon, at Siam's command, the Olhyiu climbed wearily to their feet. The chief stood erect at the heart of them, his face ablaze with passion. 'Now we know at what price security was purchased in days beyond memory. It is time we showed our friends the answering courage of the Olhyiu people.' Though Siam did not speak of it, Alan knew he was thinking of Turkeya. Siam lifted his right fist and clenched it against the dark. 'We know that danger lurks in every shadow on the journey that lies ahead of us. Yet let us forget our wounds and let every man, woman and child march in pride with the memory of how precious is this liberty that we have come so far to win.'

So with their dependants and wounded on their backs, they forced their tired limbs into a renewed climb through roots and thorns. A wave of Shee melted into the trees to become the outer ring of defence. Alan climbed in company with Kate and Qwenqwo. Progress was laboured. The children did not understand what was happening, and in their exhaustion they cried out repeatedly to their struggling parents.

Waiting for the last of the stragglers to clear the top of the slope, the party paused only to account for all before driving on again.

They gasped for breath at every stride, shaking with weariness. But as they arrived at first one proud head and then another, they took direction and were encouraged where earlier they had been frightened. Increasingly, it was Alan now who forced the pace, his fingernails clawing at the slope, his feet kicking into the mud when he found himself sliding back down embankments. The dark was oppressive. Still an iron will in Alan's heart pushed him on. He needed no reminding of why he had come here. He remembered Mom and Dad and what had happened to them. He was going to find the guy, or guys, who had murdered them. And when he did find them . . .

That was what drove him on. Drawing on his need for vengeance, he ignored the moans of pain and frustration, the gasping breaths that rose from hanging jaws to form clouds in the torchlight.

On and on they persevered, each pace a further achievement through a gloom so oppressive they might have been threading their way through the depths of a cave. Torches were lit to illuminate their way between twisted trunks that seemed more like the merging of stalagmites and stalactites, so ancient they had fused into dense pillars that supported the roof of foliage.

At last, with dawn's first glimmerings invading the sky, and when few seemed able to take another step, they reached a third fosse, its footings cut into the very bedrock, and its lichen-encrusted boulders rising sheer to a battlemented summit fifty feet above their heads. With eyes hollowed with weariness, Alan lifted his gaze to the summit and beyond, where even higher than the inner fosse he could make out the ruined walls and towers of a great city. They had reached Ossierel.

Ramming the butt of the Spear of Lug into the ground,

he probed the city with his oraculum. There was no doubt about it: he knew, absolutely and overwhelmingly, that the calling had come from here. A sudden wave of anger rose in him. He felt it close dangerously around the oraculum. But then Kate was beside him, grasping his arm, calming him.

'Look into the sky!'

When he looked overhead, the sky had filled with thunderheads, and lightning crackled between them.

'It's you – it was you, back there, at the ice-bound lake!'

'I— I don't understand.'

'Oh, Alan, it's your oraculum. Be careful: you don't understand how powerful you've become.'

He shook his head, shut his eyes tightly. 'It's here – the calling came from this place.'

She kissed the back of his hand. 'Yes. I feel it too.'

He hugged her to him. 'Oh, Kate, I don't know who the hell has called us here, or why, but maybe – just maybe in this crazy world – we might find out what really happened to our parents!'

Ossierel

Straggling in a long, disordered column through a ruined arch in the inner fosse, the company climbed a steep ramp onto cobbled streets. Everywhere their eyes fell on delicate masonry, a tracery of ornate carving and shapes designed to rest the senses and delight the eye. Mullioned windows of stone gazed out even from the humblest building. No street or alley ran on straight lines, but followed curves and spirals to beguile the senses, as if love of nature had married the art of the mason with ornamental trees, now dead or overgrown, decorating every street. On and on, their tired gazes took in the beauty that had been Ossierel, its meandering streams and sculpted bridges, its fountains. There was a poet's eye in the curve and flow of form, the joy of permanent springtime in the weave of nature and architecture, the music of running water, cascades and fountains, the soul of a great spiritual capital framed on every twist and turn by the staggering views over the forests and blue distances of the Vale of Tazan.

Even in its ruined state it was breathtaking.

The Shee called a halt while they probed for any signs of an ambush in the dark caverns between broken walls. But they found none, only desolation. Street by street, and ruin by ruin, they searched for safety and shelter until, roughly central within the city, they entered a plaza in front of a building large enough and sufficiently preserved to accommodate the injured. Alan was amazed by the deep-carved entrance, flanked by the inwardly sloping jambs and surmounted by a great triangular lintel. Inside, the great chamber was so generous it must have been some kind of meeting place. Outside the entrance, to the west and east, paved roads led to walled gardens and courtyards.

The Shee wasted no time, making a careful inspection of the damaged defences. Alan left them mapping out the breaches; meanwhile he needed to assess the situation with the Olhyiu. Siam joined him, leaving Kehloke to organise the nursing of the exhausted and injured now scattered about the great hall.

'You have succeeded, Mage Lord, where none believed it possible.' Siam's voice was a ragged whisper. As he walked now by Alan's side, it was with the stagger of a man making the best of exhausted muscles and blistered feet. They halted next to one of the small fires that had been lit within the chamber. Alan nodded in sympathy with the chief, whose dark eyes reflected the orange glow of the fire. His own voice was little above a whisper. 'Siam, I know how many of your people have died.'

'I fear more will follow.'

The Kyra, arriving to discuss the situation with Siam, interrupted their conversation. 'The Death Legion will not attack today. Unlike the Legun, they are ordinary flesh and blood. They will have to endure the same journey through dense forest to get here, hauling malengins of war. Yet we should be wary of smaller groups – sporadic attack designed to harry our positions while testing our resolve and strength of numbers.'

Siam grunted, his calloused fingers twisting the crumpled hat he had preserved through attack and adversity. 'Rest we need first and foremost. Then if die we must, let us die bravely in the dignity of these hallowed ruins.'

Alan clapped his hand on the chief's tensed shoulder before he allowed Ainé to lead him away to speak with him in private. The Kyra had shown little emotion before, but now, looking up into her eyes, he couldn't mistake the gleam of desperation he saw there.

She spoke bluntly. 'Even a day's rest will not refresh these exhausted limbs and demoralised spirits. And there is little food left.'

'I know.' Alan's eyes swept over the huddled masses of frightened and demoralised people. 'I need to talk to Milish.'

They found the Ambassador, her hair awry, kneeling before a wounded mother. Milish's sleeves were rolled up, and her hands and forearms were stained with blood. Alan could see that the wounded Olhyiu was on the point of death. Her husband must have carried her all the way up the mountain.

'We have run out of healwell,' Milish whispered.

They drew the Ambassador away from the scene of anguish. Walking out into the plaza, where the fitter of the Olhyiu were settling, they watched the tired hands spreading their impoverished bundles about the fires. Others among the exhausted had fallen into stupors, with ice crystals condensing on their cooling flesh. How many, Alan wondered, would wake up again? Even as he gazed down on them, there was an explosion in the forest. He followed the sound to the pillar of fire, closer to the river, perhaps three or four miles downslope.

Ainé spoke softly. 'The Legun taunts us by destroying stone heads.'

Milish tugged at Alan's arm, drawing him to one side so she could confront him eye-to-eye, as if weighing what he must be thinking. 'Do not despair. Consider what has been achieved.'

'I'm not sure it counts for much.' He sighed. 'We are facing attack – and we're never going to be ready for it.'

A squall of wind rattled the needles of some nearby trees. 'I think the time has come for you and me to be a little more open with each other.' He hesitated before continuing. 'I've talked to Qwenqwo. I know about the Fáil, Milish – the fact that it is believed to hold all the answers.'

'You must stop such discussion!' Fear caused Milish's pupils to grow, as if devouring her speckled brown irises.

'I can't stop asking these questions. I need to know. And you've got to be honest with me.'

Milish was swaying on her feet with exhaustion. Alan reached out and supported her before she fainted. Yet still she shook her head at him, her exhausted eyes firmly shut.

'Why won't you answer my questions?'

'I cannot. There are dangers more perilous even than Leguns.'

Abruptly there was another explosion; another head destroyed.

Alan stared sightlessly into the distance. Then, suddenly, from the nearby forest came the clash of battle. It had to involve the Shee guarding the perimeter. He hurried back to join those sheltering in the great hall. Siam was alarmed by what was happening close to the sanctuary. 'Arouse yourselves, warriors of the Tilikum Olhyiu!' Siam did his best to sound confident, but he was unable to hide the hoarseness in his voice as he staggered among his people, attempting to inspire them to a final effort. 'Let a proud people make a valiant stand!'

Alan hefted the Spear of Lug. From outside, on the plaza, he heard Ainé's shout of command. The Kyra too was injecting her determined leadership into what could only be a hopeless battle. And then, plaintively, he heard the brave chant of the Shee. But the chanting of so few voices was drowned by the explosion of legionary weaponry.

Maybe the main army of Death Legion was still struggling with the ascent of the steep slopes, but a considerable advance guard must have arrived at the fosse. The sky nearby grew gangrenous with the flickering green fire. Alan's ears pricked in the direction of the nearby conflict. Surely it wouldn't take long for the small guard of Shee to be overwhelmed. Then he heard the Shee battle hymn begin again, louder, more powerfully – so powerfully . . . Siam tore past him, his blistered feet forgotten, running out into the plaza. Alan blinked repeatedly. No – it was mere wishful thinking that had entered his mind! All the same, through the weariness in his limbs he ran after Siam.

'By the Powers! Mage Lord – see who comes!' It was Siam's voice, laughing like a crazy man, throwing his hat into the air.

Alan saw the gangling figure of Turkeya making his way through the tide of human bodies on the plaza. Suddenly, Turkeya was running towards his father. Siam's hair was standing up wildly on his head, and his side-whiskers stood erect like outstretched bird's wings as father and son embraced.

And then the glinting of silver on the cape brooches was the first Alan saw of the new arrivals. An army of

Shee flowed into the plaza in a chanting wave. They expanded out to fill the space, eyes darting about warily as if searching for evidence of a trap. Their battle song overwhelmed that of Ainé and the small gathering of her companions. From the weary Olhyiu a great cheer broke the air, as bruised arms thrust their weapons aloft.

A wizened newcomer – she could have been Layheas's twin – pressed a flask of healwell into Alan's hand as he gazed about himself in amazement. He felt diminished by the stature of so many gigantic women. There appeared to be as many as two hundred of them already within the square, their great capes twisting and turning: an army of new faces, many bruised and bloodied from conflict, with different colours of braided hair, different armour and uniforms, and everywhere the flash of weaponry at the ready.

Alan found himself facing a remarkable woman whose skin was as magnificently black and fine-haired as that of a jaguar. Though she moved with the same stealth and grace as the other Shee, she was not quite as tall and she looked older. Her long hair, braided over her left shoulder, was threaded with white.

'I am Bétaald,' she said, in a clear, deep alto. 'And you are Duval! The Mage Lord who bears the Oraculum of the First Power of the most holy and sacred Trídédana. I am honoured to meet you!'

Between Bétaald and Ainé he sensed a wordless communication.

Bétaald bowed. 'It is the very air of legend I breathe.'

Alan could only gaze into her eyes, the orange yellow of sunflowers, with astonishment. More and more Shee were arriving by the moment. Already they greatly outnumbered the Olhyiu.

Milish rescued him from his confusion, arriving at his side to take his arm. As he struggled to comprehend all that was happening, Bétaald held a hand to the air as if to demand quiet, and Alan realised that the sounds of battle had ceased. An ominous silence pervaded the encircling forest.

'Fortunately we encountered only a scouting party of Death Legion. But they bore new weaponry, which may carry their foul discharge over greater distances – and Gargs in such numbers as have not been seen outside of the Wastelands. I fear that there is a great force of them at large in the forest – tens of thousands – and still more legionaries are arriving from Isscan by the river.'

Alan's heart sank with this news even as he took a welcome sip of the healwell. His gaze returned to Bétaald, noticing that Ainé treated the dark-skinned newcomer with respect. Bétaald herself carried no weaponry. He assumed that she was their spiritual leader.

Her return of his gaze was frankly assessing. 'We must conclude that this is the spearhead of the invasion we have long anticipated, a first step in their strategy to take Carfon.'

'Then,' declared an exhausted Olhyiu elder, 'all is surely lost!'

'Not so!' growled the voice of Qwenqwo Cuatzel, who had appeared from the hall, with Kate and the others in tow. "Not while the Vale of Tazan still holds them back. You might ask yourself why they move with such patience, destroying heads with the energy they might otherwise devote to city walls.'

Bétaald lifted her eyelids at the intrusion of the Mage of Dreams. She gazed at Qwenqwo with interest. 'Perhaps you are right, Fir Bolg – it may be that in such a vortex of ancient forces their malengins do not function well.'

Alan joined Kate, Mo and Mark in heading back to the circles of fires, where supplies of food and drink, and much-needed flasks of healwell, were being distributed among the Olhyiu. While Siam needed no more than the safe return of Turkeya to bolster his spirit, Aides were busy treating the wounded. Like Layheas, these were a curious-looking people, wiry and tough in build, with a dry, almost leathery skin. The newly arriving Aides had come decorated for war with broad lines of ochre, red and blue painted on their cheeks. Alan knew from conversations with Milish during the journey that they included metal-smiths, weapon makers and architects among them. In fact, the more he saw of them, the more he understood how essential they were as partners to the Shee.

Kate grabbed his arm and led him away from the bustle of the plaza to stare at the silhouette of the eagle, observing it in the process of alighting on the formidable crag that reared up through the morning mists to the north, dominating the ancient city.

'Do you see the staircase?'

Alan's gaze picked out the winding steps hacked out of the stone that led to the summit, where, soaring above the wheeling clouds, he saw the black fist of a pentagonal tower with its ancient roof remarkably intact. From one high corner protruded a single stellate window. The window appeared to be glazed, judging from its twinkling reflection of the mid-morning sunlight.

Beside him Kate shivered. A prickle of fear also invaded Alan as his gaze lifted beyond the lofty tower to the very pinnacle of the crag, immediately above it, where he now realised that Qwenqwo's eagle had alighted – atop the very statue of the Dark Queen, Nantosueta.

'Such omens does it conjure up within one's mind!'

Alan and Kate turned to welcome Qwenqwo, who joined them in staring up at the statue on the pinnacle.

For Alan it felt as if many pieces of the mysterious jigsaw were coming together here, in this ancient capital, where the High Architect, Ussha De Danaan, had met her death, and where two thousand years earlier Nantosueta had plotted and warred. In answer to the look in Kate's eyes, Alan squeezed her hand. He spoke quietly. 'Qwenqwo, I know how crazy this might sound. But this place, with all of its terrible history, has put an idea into my head. Is it possible that Ossierel holds memories – memories that could be recovered, like . . . well, like dreams?'

A frown invaded Qwenqwo's features, still staring skywards.

But Alan persisted, 'I think you know what I want you to do for me. I want you, the true Mage of Dreams, to see if you can recover those memories.'

The dwarf mage flinched, his right hand rubbing at his broken arm through the sling.

'I wouldn't ask it of you if I could see any alternative.'

The dwarf mage looked directly into Alan's eyes, making no attempt to hide his disquiet. 'I have anticipated such a request. Yet so fearful am I of its implications, I beg you to reconsider.'

Alan felt Kate's hand tighten on his.

A Heart of Iron

'It's a lot bigger than I thought – it'll be even harder to defend,' Mark remarked to Kate and Mo as they gazed out from the vantage of a roof terrace over the ruins that extended over several acres of the plateau. They were leaning over a corner that came close to the third fosse and from here they could enjoy a panoramic view of the river as it meandered through the valley. How glorious – and deceptively peaceful – it looked!

Alan was busy in the plaza with a war council of Shee and Olhyiu. Meanwhile Kate and Mo were preparing in their own intuitive ways. The girls had painted the Aides' lines of ochre, blue and black across their cheeks, with ribbons of the same colour knotted in their hair, which had deteriorated to wiry bushes of fiery red and mahogany in the absence of shampoo and hair-straighteners. 'The way I see it,' Kate had explained to Mark, determinedly, 'Alan isn't the only one who came here for a purpose.'

He could only admire their spirits. They knew, as he did, that even with the thousand or so of Shee that had arrived, they were still grossly outnumbered. The Legun had herded them into a killing zone.

'Ah! There you are!' All three wheeled round to hear the dwarf mage's voice coming from the spiral staircase that opened out onto the roof level. Qwenqwo emerged onto the windy terrace and strode towards them.

'Why,' he guffawed, in his boisterous way, 'I would be making no more than an inspired guess, but I see now that you girls have joined the Aides?'

The very presence of Qwenqwo lifted both the girls' spirits.

'However, it is young Mark here that I have most specifically come to address! I think that our young friend will understand.'

Mark looked up warily at the dwarf mage, who could hardly miss how bloodshot and puffy his eyes were from lack of sleep.

'My young friend – all I ask is that you remove your coat and shirt.'

Mark stared at Qwenqwo. 'Why – what are you up to?'

'On my honour, no harm will befall you.'

Mark sighed. His hands trembled as he removed his fur-lined coat and then his leather jacket and shirt. Kate and Mo gasped to see the black oval that covered his left shoulder.

'Oh, Mark!' Mo brought her hand to her mouth, seeing the flickering silver matrix within the oval.

'Are you satisfied now?' Mark dropped his head in shame.

'I would prefer to demonstrate rather than explain.' Qwenqwo produced his runestone and passed it to the tormented youth. 'Gaze into it and tell me what you see.'

Mark shook his head. 'Don't do this to me! Please, Qwenqwo – you know I can't do it.'

'Before doubt overwhelms you – observe!' Qwenqwo gazed up into the sky to where, a mere speck in the distance, the eagle once again hovered. He lifted Mark's hand so the plane of the runestone was perpendicular to that flight and an arm's breadth above a flagstone in the centre of their small circle, where it would be illuminated by sunlight. There on the flagstone all four of them could see the emerald eye projected onto the stone.

'The eye of truth!' Kate exclaimed.

'Indeed, the eye of truth – and you recall what the soul eye tests?'

'The heart of the holder!'

'So now you know – the heart of your friend is true. As well I anticipated, for I have been observing Mark's struggle with the dark force that sought to take his soul. Your friend has a heart of iron.'

Mark shuddered as Kate and Mo hugged him.

Qwenqwo accepted the runestone back from Mark. 'Now tell them what happened on the Temple Ship during the attack of the Storm Wolves.'

Red with embarrassment, Mark told them his story: how he had been seduced by the doll-faced woman, how his lips had been sealed by her wile and treachery. He explained how she had instructed him to push Kate. And how, rather than threaten her, he had tried to protect her in the confusion of the Dragon's Teeth pass.

The two girls stared at Mark in a shocked silence. Kate, blinking in bewilderment, turned to Qwenqwo. 'But what in heaven's name is a succubus – and why me?'

'One thing at a time!' The dwarf mage nodded. 'From Mark's tale we learn several things. We discover that you, Kate, are important to our enemies – so important that the succubus went to considerable lengths to have you destroyed. We also need to consider that the succubus does not act for herself. She has a mistress, a very terrible one, half in league with and half in violent jealousy of the Tyrant – a great witch, known as Olc, who inhabits the Wastelands beyond the Eastern Ocean.'

'Oh, Lord – I don't know what to believe!'

'There's much I don't yet understand myself,' continued Qwenqwo. 'But we know enough to conjecture. The succubus has not completed the will of her mistress. She will try again. And this time Mark must be ready for her. We must ensure that rather than becoming the puppet of her scheming he will become the instrument of her undoing.'

Mark's eyes narrowed. 'Just tell me how.'

The dwarf mage shouted a single word, 'Aides!'

They waited as lighter footsteps ascended the stairs and an old but sprightly figure emerged from the shadows of the stairwell holding a glittering weapon in a leather harness. They recognised the Aides, Layheas, who had been introduced to them by Alan. Layheas went down onto one knee and slid the weapon out into the sunlight, revealing a bronze twin-bladed battle-axe. It was smaller and lighter than Qwenqwo's weapon, but it was unmistakably a Fir Bolg battle-axe.

She laid the blade across her open palms.

Qwenqwo nodded to Mark. 'Take your blade. It is cast of bronze from the mines of the Geltigi Mountains, made rune-worthy with crystals of jet and cobalt. It was forged by weapons masters as skilled as any known to the Fir Bolg.'

Mark accepted the weapon with a clumsy bow to the Aides. He stared at the battle-axe in his hands, closely, disbelievingly.

'And now, if you will pass it to me. There is a gift in my power that even Layheas cannot provide.' Qwenqwo accepted the axe from Mark and sat down against the low wall, laying it across his knees and running the runestone along the cutting edges of the blades. His eyes were closed and his face turned skywards as he intoned a mantra. A patterning of runes appeared over the cutting edges, glittering in the sunlight as Qwenqwo returned the weapon to Mark.

'For a warrior his weapon must also be his friend. Perhaps its new master would test it for balance?'

Mark climbed to his feet and, ignoring the fact that his upper body was exposed to the bitter wind, he felt the battle-axe vibrating faintly in his left hand. He swung it through repeated figures of eight, as he had seen Qwenqwo exercise prior to combat. The matrix in his left shoulder pulsated. He could feel the pulsation over and above the vibration from the axe itself – and from the expressions on the girls' faces, they could see that something was happening too. He gazed down and saw for himself the flickering arabesques of silver that ran down his arm from the pulsating black oval on his left shoulder. He lifted the battle-axe high over his head, feeling his soul spirit become one with its being.

Qwenqwo pressed the runestone against Mark's left shoulder. 'Let warrior and weapon be united in life as in death!'

Too amazed to speak, Mark stared up at the bronze battle-axe, feeling its runes and arabesques pulsating with his heartbeat.

Layheas spoke. 'Every weapon calls for its name when newly presented to its warrior – but this is a deeply personal thing, something the warrior alone must share with it.'

Mark thought without hesitation: *I name you Vengeance!*

Qwenqwo laid down the runestone and clapped his hand on Mark's right shoulder. 'Now you must test the union of warrior and blade. Cast your weapon, as if at a distant enemy!'

'I'm not sure what you mean.'

The dwarf stood next to Mark, who was several inches taller than him, though Qwenqwo was as broad and gnarled as a truncated tree. 'Now cast it as far and high as you can into the air. As it reaches the point where you imagine it has struck your enemy, call it by its secret name – in the intimacy of your own heart and mind.'

Mark grasped the central hilt and twirled the battle-axe a few times to get a sense of balance. Then, bringing it back over his left shoulder, he spun his wrist at the same time as he hurled it with all of his might. Tempted to close his eyes from sheer panic, he waited, with his left hand stiffly extended. The axe emitted a high keening note as it flashed, spinning into the distance . . . But then he saw its whirling form returning, completing a broad arc, before smacking into his hand again, his fingers and thumb closing about it in an instinctive clasp.

Qwenqwo held the runestone against Mark's heart, and intoned, 'Swear in all that is good and just that you will fulfil the role I now entrust to you. I now charge you with the duty of Kate's protector. You will become not only her shadow but also her shield, if necessary to the death. Do you swear it?'

Mark looked for a moment into Kate's eyes. With tears dimming his own eyes, he nodded.

'You must say it in words – and mean it.'

'I will protect Kate to the death. I swear it.' Then, allowing the battle-axe to fall to his side, he turned to Qwenqwo and met his eyes. 'Thank you!'

The dwarf mage returned his gaze unflinchingly. 'You will best thank me by discovering your affinity with the weapon, and its affinity with you.'

Mark nodded, but he saw something else in the eyes of the dwarf mage, a barely concealed pain. 'What's really going on, Qwenqwo? There's something else – something you want me to do?'

Qwenqwo lowered his head and softened his voice, so that he spoke slowly, in a bitter whisper. 'Not you alone – both of you, Mark and Kate – your destinies must now be revealed to you. Though it pains me deeply to instruct you so, I speak of the Rath of the Dark Queen.'

Kate looked from Mark to Qwenqwo. 'Are you asking us – telling us – we're to climb up there . . . to the tower?'

There was no mistaking the look of anguish that invaded the dwarf mage's face as he instructed them with a sigh, 'Look for the shade of one whose fate it is to linger there. Long ago she faced a situation as grim as that which we face today. Discover what lesson, if any, is to be learnt from it.'

The Dark Queen

Kate turned back to look questioningly at Qwenqwo, his arm around Mo's shoulders, as, accompanied by Mark, she made her way in an awkward silence towards the great stairway, ascending to the Rath high above them.

Mark asked her, 'Are you all right, Kate?'

'I'm far from all right.' She paused to look at him, with his battle-axe strapped to his back within the leather harness. 'What in heaven's name was that all about?'

'I'm no wiser than you are.'

'Oh, come on, Mark. Our destinies – those were the words Qwenqwo used. What are we to make of that?'

'I know one thing. Qwenqwo is right – the succubus will come back.'

'And you're what – my protector? Even if it kills you? My God – do you have any idea how bonkers that sounds?'

'Hey – you're looking at Mark the Barbarian!'

The ghost of a smile dimpled Kate's cheeks as they

emerged from the paved streets at the very northern edge of the city, arriving at a point where any defensive wall would have been superfluous. Below them the mountainside fell sheer for several thousand feet. Kate exclaimed, 'You know what I think? This is the mountain we dreamed about, back home!'

'You're probably right.'

For a few moments they stood and gazed up at the stone staircase that led to the Rath, hacked out of the living stone of the crag and winding up hundreds of feet. The passage was so ancient that the treads had been worn down to saddle-shaped depressions. There were no handrails in spite of the precipices to either side. Awed into silence, they started to climb. The staircase twisted and turned, at this lower level delving under the canopies of evergreens or bridging over swiftly running streams. At one turn they passed under a gossamer fall of water, perhaps a hundred feet high, that fanned their sweating faces with a refreshing mist of rain. To look down was to invite a swooning dizziness.

Soon they were above all vegetation, so high their gazes soared over the entire Vale of Tazan, including the river that encircled the island and the forested slopes beyond the tributaries to either side.

'I'm sorry, Kate. Well, you know—'

'Oh, Mark!' She knew what he meant. But what did it matter any more? She just squeezed his arm for a moment.

'Still friends?'

'We never stopped being friends.' Kate blinked with embarrassment, looking past Mark and up to the tower that was surprisingly intact despite the fact it had been abandoned so long ago. Judging from the dense proliferation of lichens, it had remained uninhabited ever since. She said, wonderingly, 'That stuff – about fate – our destinies – you know Qwenqwo really has me in a panic, wondering what we're going to find.'

She stared up at the tower, with its single glazed window, and further above it at the statue of the queen, Nantosueta, now looming much larger than she would have imagined from below. 'Doesn't it strike you as odd that the Tyrant's armies – the Leguns – didn't trash all this?'

Mark blew out through pouched cheeks and did a cartoon voice, 'Thuffering thuffocats! Another mythery!'

Kate laughed, a jittery union of spirits.

'I think we're expected to explore the tower.'

There was a doorway up ahead under a triangular arch of stones. Some of the stones of the walls had tumbled out onto the approach. They skirted the rubble to enter an atrium, where a spiral of marble steps led higher. Here the sense of foreboding became so oppressive that Mark reached up and touched his battle-axe. With a rising nervousness, they continued to climb.

Step by step, they ascended the first storey to emerge into an elevated cloister. Mark warned Kate back from where broken pediments hovered over an abyss. Peering about herself carefully, she could see that a section of outer wall had collapsed, exposing the cloister to the howling wind. Mark helped her inch past the danger, passing through into a pentagonal loggia. This was lined by colonnaded arches, each double pillar of shining marble coral red and surmounted with carved reliefs. This inner architecture lacked the exquisite sophistication of Ossierel. It looked much older, more primitive. They padded, single file, along a narrow cloister, past openings leading to individual cells. Each cell was illuminated by a single unglazed window. Kate had the impression of some kind of a convent community, like the nuns back home.

Entering one of the cells, her instincts picked up an aura of violence. Though there were no bones – time would have withered bones to dust – the floors were littered with green-encrusted bronzes, scattered and broken, too precious to have been willingly abandoned. It confirmed what Qwenqwo had told them of the history. There had been a violent invasion of Nantosueta's religious order in this secret valley with its brooding forests. It had ended badly. Kate couldn't help but shiver, calling out for Mark to hold on for her.

They arrived at another entrance, cut deep into the wall at the end of the cloister. It was sealed by a bronze door, thickly encrusted with green verdigris. The door was battered and torn from its hinges, presumably a result of that same violence long ago.

'You want to call a halt here?'

'I . . . I don't know.' Kate was feeling increasingly scared.

'You don't have to go on. Just say the word and we'll head back down.'

Kate shook her head. 'You heard what Qwenqwo told us to do. He thought it was important. I think we've no choice but to carry on.'

Mark squeezed through the broken door and ascended a spiral staircase of marble. It was pretty obvious now where this was leading. He was inside the corner tower, with its flashing window, like an eye watching out over the valley. After a further climb of perhaps thirty steps he came to another bronze door, its hinges fractured like the last, and leading into the summit chamber. Dust as white as a swan's breast carpeted the floor.

The dust was inches deep, so undisturbed through time it looked like virgin snow. The dust was much thicker than Mark had seen in the ruins of Ossierel. It suggested that nobody had come here for centuries. His initial impression was of an empty room, at least thirty feet in diameter, his gaze lifting to the star-shaped window on one corner, glazed with stained glass. Though only a poor light penetrated the dusty panes, a profusion of colours flowed into the chamber, projecting shapes and hues onto the walls and floor like a slightly out of focus phantasmagoria of a coral lagoon.

Kate appeared in the doorway behind him.

He shook his head. 'There's nothing here – it's empty!'

'Let me have a look.'

She came into the chamber with a noiseless blur of footsteps, leaving impressions as clear as his own in the virgin dust. He watched her turn through a full circle at the centre of the chamber, as if examining the strange patterns of light and colour over the walls and ceiling, before blinking several times and then standing utterly still, her eyes falling shut. Mark had the impression that it was Kate, rather than the room, who was the focus of the light show coming in through the stellate window. Mark jumped when Kate reopened her eyes and he saw that they had been invaded by a brilliant matrix of green, in which motes of gold pulsed and flickered into life.

'Kate! What's happening to you?'

'I . . . I don't know.'

'Bloody hell!'

Mark tried to swallow but his mouth was too dry. Staring at Kate's familiar oval face framed by her auburn hair, he hardly recognised her any more, not this new Kate with the crystal matrix in her eyes. He murmured, 'What you said about the chamber – what did you mean, exactly, when you said it wasn't empty?'

Kate walked stiffly across the floor, as if moving in a dream, and confronted the stellate window. Then, hauling herself up onto the broad stone sill, she wiped the dust from the central portion of the stained glass. She held her crystal against it, so the incoming light passed through it. Mark's eye caught a sparkle of movement in the air, a rainbow diffraction of colours, before a series of what he initially took to be holograms took shape in the beam of light. But the images were too vivid for holograms. They seemed to be infused with life. With a gasp of surprise, he joined her at the window, wiping clear a greater portion.

He had mistaken the panes for stained glass. Now he saw that they were crystals of many different shapes and colours.

'What did you do, just then?'

'I . . . I don't know.'

The sun was still above the horizon, and its bright glow pervaded the chamber. Mark sat in a bewildered panic next to Kate on the window sill and looked at the fantastic play of light and shadow that now filled the chamber. The patterns were increasing in complexity and wonder, thrilling his senses with a flickering motion of reds and indigos, leaf-greens and gold– as if threatening to become alive. He stiffened, his heart beating violently, as suddenly there was a more powerful burst of illumination – as if the sun out there in the Valley of Tazan had come out from behind a cloud.

He turned to Kate and whispered, 'How can this be happening?'

Kate didn't reply.

Turning to the chamber, Mark found himself looking into a summery glade. Young saplings hung over a dappled stream. He could have reached out and touched the bluebells and forget-me-nots that grew on the banks. He could hear the burbling of the water, the faint sigh of the breeze through the leaves and the trembling lances of reeds. Then, no matter how impossible it ought to be, he heard birdsong. He saw a dark-haired girl laughing as she pirouetted among the slender trunks, as abandoned as the breeze, now dancing forward to take his hand and lead him down to the stream.

An exquisite thrill ran through his fingers at the touch of her hand. He looked at her face, saw that it really was human – the face of a real girl and not a doll, like the succubus. She was beautiful – *lovely*.

But his experience with the succubus, Siri, still filled him with dread. Dropping into the glade, he tested the pebbles through the stream's rippling current. They felt solid, wet . . . real. He splashed the water over his face, felt the icy spray of contact, the refreshing sensation on his skin.

He forced himself to remember Qwenqwo's words: *Look for the shade of one whose fate it is to linger there.*

What was really going on? Was it all just a dream – or some kind of hallucination? It felt too real to be either of these. He was conscious, able to question what was happening. Somehow, in spite of the fact it was completely impossible, it was real.

'Will you share the joy of the forest with me?' The girl's voice rang out through the wonder of the woodland scene.

Laughing hoarsely, his happiness cutting through any lingering disbelief, Mark threw off his boots and axe to run with the girl through the soft meadow, loving the soft feel of the grass and loam under his feet. Mark knew he was looking at the girl queen, Nantosueta. But she didn't seem evil as Qwenqwo had described her. Even her voice was girlish. *Lovely!* Mark thought it again, blinking several times in astonishment at himself, at his own reactions.

How could he be imagining anything like this?

Through an arbour of blossoming trees, he saw the great ascending spiral of stone steps rising from a mountain meadow as they must have appeared two thousand years ago, those steps above what was now the plateau of Ossierel, climbing to the great pentagonal tower on the summit of the tor. That tower, in this vision, had no figure on the pinnacle. He recalled Qwenqwo's words: *Discover what lesson, if any, is to be learnt from it.*

What could he possibly make of this?

Two thousand years ago the young queen, Nantosueta, had faced the same forces of evil that they faced today. A desperate war had been fought out in the forests and on this plateau. The enemy forces had broken through into the cloisters and cells below this very chamber. They had murdered everybody and destroyed the spiritual centre of the temple complex, then battered down the doors to get to Nantosueta herself. What must have gone through the mind of the Queen in those final desperate moments?

Mark thought that he knew now what Nantosueta would have considered. One last act of defiance . . .

The will to defeat those forces of evil would have

overwhelmed everything else until, however brutal her actions now appeared, to her in that moment they became her only hope. Something terrible, something extraordinary, had been invoked by Nantosueta in those final minutes, as the enemy battered their way through that final bronze door.

Mark emerged, blinking, from the vision. 'You were always a step ahead of me, Kate.'

Kate gazed back at him without replying as the crystal matrices metamorphosed from moment to moment in her eyes. A power was controlling Kate, one that Mark didn't understand. Then she was directing him back into the vision, as if she had conjured up the greatest thrill of all.

Mark was back in the summery glade once more, aware of the young woman who had danced with him only moments ago, but who now stood among the trees, silent and still, as if observing him. Her hair was a downy cataract of blue-black and she was dressed simply in a white linen gown and sandals. Her face, bare of adornment, was terrible with purpose, her left hand splayed towards the ground and her right arm raised to the sky. On her brow she bore an oraculum, an inverted triangle of the Trídédana, similar to Alan's, but where Alan's was a ruby, her oraculum was black.

He didn't dare to blink, so arresting was the realisation that was now running through his mind.

There was barely time to take in those gesturing hands

– the one, as it seemed, stretched to the heavens, and the other, with its fingers and thumb extended over her beloved valley – and then she was gone.

It was as if the sun had set over the valley. The image of the woodland scene faded at once. Mark and Kate stood in the thick dust, facing each other beside the crystal window in the empty chamber. Kate looked bewildered, but Mark was relieved to see that her eyes had returned to normal. He took her shoulders between his own trembling hands.

'Did you see . . .?'

Kate nodded, tears rising into her eyes.

Mark helped Kate to climb the final narrow spiral of steps. They stood on the platform cut from the rock of the crag, above which the gigantic statue stood sentinel over the pass. Their gazes lifted skywards, to discover that the beautiful face of the girl in the glade had been replaced with a mask of fury. In her brow was the triangle, black as obsidian.

The Fall of Ossierel

With night already closing around them, the elders welcomed the returning Mark and Kate to an urgent gathering about an open fire on the flagged floor of the great hall. Alan, who was sitting between Qwenqwo Cuatzel and Bétaald, smiled at Kate as she joined them. But his face was pale and his eyes animated. Kate realised it could only mean one thing. It frightened her so much she chose not to sit with Alan but between Ainé and Milish, while Mark took his place next to Mo, taking the hint from the Kyra to remove his axe from his back and place it in front of him, one blade resting on his thigh. Each took a drink from a porcelain cup provided by Bétaald, a herbal tonic prepared by the Aides to refresh and clear the mind. Incense and aromatic spices were added to the flames to banish the stale odours of the old building. Qwenqwo explained Alan's desire to explore the memories of this war-ravaged citadel. At this many eyes fell in mute reflection on the flames; Milish was the only one to look directly into Alan's eyes, with a hint of concern for him, before her eyes also gazed into the fire.

'I know there are those among us who will counsel against this action, yet still the Mage Lord is faced with a grave and difficult problem.' Qwenqwo spoke quietly, but could not conceal his own anxiety. 'He believes that he and his three friends were brought to this world for a specific purpose through a voice of enchantment. That very purpose is the question that must be answered, and answered soon, for great danger threatens us here, where so much blood has been spilt in recent and ancient times.

'The Mage Lord senses that the key lies with the death of Ussha De Danaan, last High Architect, within these sacred walls. Why should the De Danaan, widely renowned as the bravest and most prudent of leaders, abandon the ancient capital to the forces of the enemy, commanding the defenders to flee and thus ensuring her martyrdom, along with her council, and abandoning Monisle and its peoples to the ravages of the Death Legion?'

Ainé spoke tersely. 'Not all the defending forces abandoned the High Architect. Many of the garrison of Shee refused her order and remained true, as, from childhood memory, I recall.'

The dwarf mage bowed. 'I am aware that the Kyra's mother-sister, herself the Kyra at that time, remained to save what lives she could, ultimately at tragic cost to herself. Nevertheless, I must caution that this dream journey, if indeed we follow it, will be perilous. It will demand much of the heart and mind of the Mage Lord himself.'

Alan nodded to the Mage of Dreams, a look that valued his integrity and his concern for him. He then addressed the entire circle. 'You all know that I wouldn't do anything to hurt or threaten you. But I know that the voice that called me and my friends into this world is close to us here. We all sense it among these ruins. If the voice really is that of the High Architect, Ussha De Danaan, then I need to know why she called us here. But I'm not forcing you to take any risk. If you don't want to join in the dream journey, I'll go there on my own. I won't blame anybody who wants to pull out.'

Kate felt strangely debilitated since coming down from the Rath, but she also saw how nervous Alan looked. She said, 'I agree with Alan. I'm coming with him.'

'And me,' added Mo.

'Mark?'

Mark shrugged.

Kate saw Alan frown at the sight of Mark's battle-axe – he hadn't been present when Qwenqwo had presented Mark with the weapon, though she presumed that Qwenqwo must have told him about it – and his eyebrows lifted, as if seeing Mark anew. 'We need a definite answer, Mark – yes or no?'

Mark nodded, his face slightly flushed. 'I'm coming. I agree that we need explanations.'

Alan looked at the Kyra. 'What do you think, Ainé?'

The Kyra's large blue eyes looked directly back into his. 'The course you undertake is filled with peril. The dwarf mage admits he cannot guarantee your safety.'

Qwenqwo said, 'It is true that, in normal circumstances, a dream journey would involve little risk. But the Kyra is right. These are not normal circumstances.'

The Kyra shook her head. 'And the "chosen" are not normal people.'

Alan turned to the chief. 'Siam?'

'Where the Mage Lord leads, so shall I follow.'

Kate saw how deeply Siam's words affected Alan. She also noticed the frown now crossing the Kyra's features. Alan nodded, his lips pressed tight.

Bétaald agreed with Ainé. 'It cannot be prudent to go against the counsel of the Kyra. For all its defences, this fortress may prove a fragile refuge. We are greatly outnumbered. The Legun is still within the forest and the Death Legion is armed with new malengins of war and accompanied by fearsome allies from the Wastelands. If your dream journey should fail, or if it should imperil the soul spirit of those who take part in the journey . . .'

Murmurs of agreement arose from others among the elders around the fire.

Qwenqwo, who had seemed lost in concentration until now, spoke out in Alan's defence. 'The Kyra questions the purpose of the Mage Lord. But what would a Shee-witch know of this young man's valour! Has the Mage Lord not explained his reasons to you?'

'Hark at the wisdom of a fallen mage!' Ainé countered. 'Was your power not corrupted by the warlock in Isscan, where you were held in its thrall for five-and-twenty years! How do we know you still retain the power of dreams? Worse still – how do we know that what small power you may still retain has not been perverted by malign influence?'

'Ah, so there we have it!' Qwenqwo growled. 'At last we hear the suspicions that have darkened your mind since we met.'

'Please! We must remain united,' urged Milish. 'We cannot allow internal divisions to distract us from our purpose.'

'You speak sense!' growled the dwarf mage. 'However, since my power has been questioned let me assure this company that to reveal what is buried in the very rocks and bowels of a place such as this, as what is buried in the inner labyrinths of the mind, remains within my lore.' Those sparkling green eyes lifted to the vaulted roof, and his voice softened as he confessed his fears. 'Yet though the power to do so still rests within the runestone, I freely admit that I cannot evoke it without help from the Mage Lord.' His eyes stared obstinately into those of the Kyra.

Ainé barked, 'All men are foolish, but a dwarf it seems has wits commensurate with his stature.'

Qwenqwo jumped to his feet. He slammed his foot down on the flagged ground and his eyes protruded round and glistening as he pointed with a stubby left hand at Ainé, who was taller when seated than he was standing on his toes. 'The honour of your house was abandoned in the vale of Gadhgorrah, where the ground is paved with skulls!'

All four friends gazed, wide-eyed, from Qwenqwo to Ainé. Was the dwarf mage suggesting that once there might even have been war in the distant past between the Shee and the Fir Bolg?

With a raised arm, Milish halted Ainé's angry reply. She urged Qwenqwo to sit down. Then the diplomat spoke calmly, reassuring all around the fire. 'We all share Ainé's concern. There is none here who wants the Mage Lord to suffer risk. Yet the Mage Lord proposes to enter dreams, not reality.'

Ainé countered, 'Do not underestimate the peril of dreams.'

'What peril is Ainé talking about?' Alan turned to the dwarf mage.

'In entering such memories, the soul spirits of some of those who participate might manifest within the dream and thus be exposed to potential injury.'

Ainé's head jerked back, as if her face had been slapped. 'There! It is exactly as I thought.'

Kate's widened eyes, as those of the entire company, were now turned to the Kyra. She dreaded to think of what Ainé was implying.

Alan shook his head. 'Ainé, I really don't want to take any unnecessary risks. But I sense that I have to do this. I sense it here.' Alan touched the triangle in his brow. 'I wish I had more of a choice, but I just can't see any other way.'

The Kyra gazed stonily into the flames. 'I have made the Mage Lord aware of what this place, and its history, may provoke. Yet still my duty bids me stand by him in all that he ultimately decides.'

As Qwenqwo left to gather the materials he needed, Alan walked out alone into the night, finding a refuge on the rampart that looked out over the uppermost fosse. Gazing down onto the winding valley, shadowed under a night sky and obscured by mist and cloud, he couldn't help but wonder at the nature of the powers that still fought to control this world. *Fate!* In his mind he recalled that day fishing the Suir, when the swans had attacked. He heard the homp-homp beating of their wings. He was gazing once more into those eyes, all-black with rage . . .

'Alan, I'm here.'

He spun around to see that Kate had come out onto the rampart to join him. He threw his arms around her, hugged her fiercely, feeling a tide of love and relief flood his body.

'You didn't sit by me. I kept an empty place for you.'

'Oh Lord, I'm sorry.'

He sighed. 'You know, Ainé's probably right in her worry. That business with the Legun, it scares the hell out of me.'

'Then stop it right here and now. Say no to this dream journey.'

'I can't. I wish I could, but I can't.'

She held him tighter. She kissed his throat, feeling the tension that consumed him at the thought of what he was undertaking. Cloaked and silent, the Shee were out there in the dark patrolling the walls. There would be no calls from the watch to declare that all was well.

'Alan, I need to talk to you. It's been such a strange day. We climbed to the top of the tower, Mark and I. You wouldn't believe what we saw. If only you'd been there to see it!'

'We'll talk . . . soon. I promise.' He cupped her face with his hands. 'After this is done, we'll stay up and talk all night long.'

He kissed her closed eyes, tasting the salt of her tears, and hugged her to him with all of his strength. He so needed Kate, with her love and her closeness, that he resented it when Milish appeared, calling him back to the fireside. 'The dwarf mage is ready.'

'Okay – just give us a few moments.'

When Kate and Alan returned to the fire, they sat side by side, his arm around her waist, and they watched Qwenqwo place a small bronze vessel into the heart of the fire. They saw how something within the bronze vessel glinted and flashed with spectral potency. Qwenqwo stood erect, with his uninjured arm stretched before the flame, as if shielding his eyes from its heat and light. Then he hesitated for several seconds, gazing at Alan, as if allowing him a final chance to change his mind.

Alan nodded.

He felt the oraculum begin to pulsate, then flare to full power. He couldn't suppress an involuntary shiver. 'If anybody has last-minute doubts, this is the time to leave the circle.' He waited until it was clear that nobody was going to leave. Then, his face set with purpose, Alan let go of Kate and focused all of the power of the oraculum onto Qwenqwo.

The huge and sustained charge that entered the figure of the dwarf mage caused his wiry red hair to stand on end. From the bronze pot, he lifted something heavy and glowing, an object he treated with great reverence, which sparkled in the firelight a deep and perfect blue. Alan knew it was the runestone, although it was already changing in Qwenqwo's hands, becoming a wide-rimmed goblet, pentagonal in its outer surfaces above an ornately carved base, yet a perfect half-globe in its interior. Symbols glided around the vessel walls, eliciting gasps from the people sitting around the fire.

'Such rapture,' murmured Qwenqwo, 'is it to gaze at last into the chalice of Urox Zel, grand Mage of the Fir Bolg.'

The dwarf inhaled the aroma from the goblet's contents, an elixir that condensed the light like quicksilver and smelled of a pungently aromatic fragrance. Then he chanted a series of incantations in which Alan caught only a single word, which sounded like the name of a deity, before Qwenqwo added a pinch of powder, sniffing again, holding the goblet over the flames, mixing the elixir with a gentle rotation of his hands, until with a final sniff he was satisfied it was ready.

With a fierce pride in his eyes and bearing, he passed the goblet to Alan.

Alan didn't take an immediate sip but looked deep into the swirling contents. He inhaled its heavy aroma, already falling under its hypnotic spell. The oraculum was pulsing powerfully. Suddenly a massive surge of power flashed from his brow and the goblet blazed, its contents a rubicund glow, and eldritch light spilling out into the air about them, invading the minds of everybody gathered in the circle.

For a moment Alan glanced at Qwenqwo, his grip upon reality already tenuous. Then he drank the contents in one swallow.

Under a sky dark with smoke, and crimson in its reflection of flames, they saw Ossierel burning. They were aware that they were gazing through the eyes of dream, and yet in their hearts and minds they felt the anguish and pain as if it were really happening all about them. They shrank from the thunder and cascading of stone as the city's beautiful towers and minarets tumbled about them, its gilt-frescoed domes ribboned in smoke and flames, its hallowed walls holding still a while, against the brutal frenzy of attack. Even now they couldn't help but be awed by the spiritual beauty of the world that lay ravaged around them, as if in the worst of the horror and despoliation its splendour grew all the more wonderful by contrast, even as the gardens of exotic herbs and flowers withered and died, and the libraries of knowledge crackled and erupted into pyres among the ruins.

The citizens of Ossierel lay dead in thousands among the broken walls, where blood and terror ran side by side in the ravaged streets and courtyards, while an army of warriors, drunk with slaughter, fought hand to hand with outnumbered Shee.

Alan, Kate, Mark and Mo experienced a nauseating sense of dislocation, as their soul spirits alone emerged into the dream landscape, where an old crone appeared to guide them, her grief evident in her crumpled mouth. Leaning for solace on a staff of power she led them out of the pillaged streets and through an underground labyrinth to a place before the palace gates. Here she hung back from them in a grove of trees with silvery seedpods that chimed even as they tossed with the hot breath of the flames.

In a momentary silence between thunderous detonations, Alan heard Kate sob. His eyes swept upward to see the cause of her distress.

A woman hung crucified before them: a tall Shee, with white hair spread about her face like a halo, her limbs splayed to either side and nailed to the decorated panels of the gates, her blood running over the whorled and spiralling patterns of ancient silver laid on black oak. She had a long, expressive face, tapering to an almost pointed chin under a wide, intelligent brow. Her eyes were ash grey, strangely calm amid the agony and the violence. In the centre of her brow was an oraculum of power, circular and silvery as a full moon. Everywhere they saw evidence of torture on her body, with its tattered remnants of a formal white dress, gilt-seamed, and streams of blood ran from multiple wounds to flood the cobbled entrance. Bolts of matt-black metal transfixed her arms in their outstretched posture, and similar bolts bisected the bones above her ankles. But her weight would have ripped the iron bolts through the flesh had it not been for the shackles of spiked strapwork that pinioned her thighs and her trunk between the chest and abdomen, fettering her body to the gates.

They knew immediately who she was: Ussha De Danaan, the last High Architect of Ossierel. And they knew now that it had been her voice, across time and worlds, that had called them here. In profane mockery, her crown of power had been impaled on her brow, a golden corona with a tall vertical crescent, the symbol of a quarter-moon.

In the courtyard behind the gates columns of women wearing gowns of lime-green were compelled to kneel with their heads bent. They heard a blare of trumpets, strident and alien, and in a moment the women were beheaded, their blood soiling the sacred ground.

A thunderous detonation shook the wall in which the gates were embedded. Lightning tumbled in its wake, so charged it could not be extinguished through striking the ground, but, crackling and spreading over the ruined gardens, it ignited the trees in its path. Wave upon wave of ebbing power emanated from the crucified woman. Then, as if through an extraordinary effort, the oraculum on the De Danaan's brow became alive. As if only now aware of their presence, the grey eyes of the giantess moved from face to face among the four friends. In the focus of her gaze, an intimate communication flickered through their minds. They heard her address them in turn as 'Chosen', as if each one of them was special to her, in representing some individual window of hope.

'We have precious little time. Yet I know that you have questions you wish to put to me.'

Through his own mounting terror, Alan found his voice. 'Ma'am!' The truth was, he didn't rightly know how to address her. 'We don't know how, or why, you called us here.'

'Like you, the Tyrant came from beyond our world, albeit a world of darkness. To my predecessors, his purpose appeared merely that of conquest and despoliation. But then, as I watched his powers grow, a new understanding dawned. He seeks absolute mastery of the Fáil. We who were born under its influence cannot defeat him.'

'What is this Fáil? I ask people about it, but nobody will answer my questions.'

'The Fáil is a malengin of magic. It was constructed long ago by a race of magicians known as the Arinn. Its purpose was arrogant beyond measure, a quest for immortality among those who made it. Great danger arose from such aspirations.'

'But why choose us? What can we do?'

'Fate, not I, did the choosing.'

'Fate?' Alan couldn't keep the disappointment from his voice.

A wave of weakness shuddered through her. Her eyes closed. But then, as if she had summoned the last vestiges of her faltering will, they flickered opened again.

'In time, if you live, you will come to understand how fate and the Fáil are interwoven.'

Alan stared up into her ravaged face, bewildered. 'What are you saying – that everything that has happened, our coming here – it was all decided by the Fáil?'

'That . . . That is for you to discover.'

'But how?'

'Its makers constructed three portals, through which its mystery may be confronted. One of the portals was destroyed long ago, in the battle that ended the Age of Dragons. Two portals survive, one that was formerly here in this very sanctuary but has now been transported for safety to Carfon – the other, alas, is already in the possession of the Tyrant. Already he has begun to corrupt its original purpose.'

With her dying breath, her face fell into a mask of grief,

as if she pitied them the burden she had placed on their youthful shoulders.

'He cannot be allowed to subvert it to malice. If – if you should fail – if all should be lost – well, better this tormented world should end rather than succumb to the hegemony of evil.'

The implications of her words stunned the four.

As the De Danaan died, an immense shockwave struck the ground, sweeping outwards through the despoiled landscape, extinguishing the runestone of the dwarf mage of the Fir Bolg, and with it the dream journey of all who sat around the fireside in the great hall of Ossierel. In that same moment, Kate faltered and slumped to the ground. Even as a wave of darkness engulfed Alan, he fell down onto his knees beside Kate, holding her close to him, calling her name.

The Legun Incarnate

Alan was a prisoner again in the snow-bound wilderness, his limbs stretched on the rack of the springy poles. Agony tore apart his bones and joints. The pain was unbearable. Yet a part of him whispered that this was not real pain, this was the past. He had survived that – had been saved by the arrival of the Shee. He was surviving still. With his lips drawn back and his teeth bared, he roared his defiance with the last breath of his tormented lungs:

Nooooo!

Then, as if from a great distance, he heard a voice whispering in his ear. A voice he recognised. His confused mind seized on that voice. He heard other sounds from far away in the distance, sounds carrying from where there should be no sounds. Desperate shouts, moans . . . screams. Who else could be screaming? Who was enduring this same hell?

'Alan! *Alan!*'

Was Kate calling him?

No – impossible!

His eyes were blinded by madness still. His arms were curled against his chest, his fists clenched so hard that his nails were cutting into his palms. He was shaking his head furiously, shouting his defiance into another world. A world racked by moans and screams. Was Kate hurt . . . unconscious? A memory cut deep into his brain by terror . . . terror so great . . .

'Alan! Wake up!'

With an effort of will he forced the terror out of his mind, the nightmare visions out of his eyes. With his head weak on his wobbly neck, he peered around from where he found himself, on the paved floor beside the now spent fire in the great hall on the temple plateau. He really was here – Ossierel – where he had shared his dream journey with his friends!

'Alan!'

He saw her now, her face full of concern for him, her hand touching his face, brushing the sweat from his eyes.

'Mo!' He sighed with relief.

Her face was anxious and drawn, thinner, seemingly more waif-like, than when he had last seen her. She was kneeling beside him, her dark eyes peering out of a face that appeared to be a mask of soot. She screwed her eyes shut as a thunderous explosion swept through the hall, peppering them with fragments of stone. They both coughed in the wake of dust.

'What's going on?'

'The Death Legion is attacking. It started while you were still trapped.'

'Trapped?'

'In the dream.'

They had to shout to each other just to be heard above the fury of battle.

He blinked, trying to come to terms with what Mo was telling him. *Trapped in the dream* . . . 'How long?'

She crouched down again, cowering from another explosion. 'All night,' she said, 'and all through this morning.'

Alan's head fell back in confusion. It must be early afternoon, although it seemed like twilight because of the smoke. 'Kate?'

Mo shook her head.

He struggled onto his feet, tottering against the wall for support. His head reeled with dizziness. 'What's happened to her?'

'The Aides took her to safety.'

'She's not dead? Tell me the truth, Mo.'

'She isn't dead.'

'What happened to her?'

'She was hurt by the dream. She remained unconscious, as if she couldn't come out of it. Kemtuk says that her soul spirit was wounded . . . by what happened. As if she was especially sensitive to . . . to the death of the High Architect.'

Alan stumbled out of the hall, followed by Mo. Above them a tempestuous sky tossed and howled over the shadowy outlines of the ancient capital city. The acrid smell of fire and smoke choked his nostrils.

The whole plateau was in tumult.

A continuous rain of livid green missiles deluged the ruins from the surrounding slopes. Every few seconds the shadows were lit up by explosive flares as heavier missiles struck. Even the sky flashed and glowed as if illuminated by flickering searchlights. It took several moments of reorientation before he realised that the light was coming from the burning forests. Currents of hot wind lashed his skin, accompanied by the harsh detonations of exploding missiles, the crackling and splitting of masonry; and everywhere his nostrils registered the dank musky odour of slaughter.

'Ainé? Siam? Milish?'

Mo's eyes fell as he took hold of her arm. 'They're out there – fighting!'

'I have to help them!' With a groan of pain, he exercised his right shoulder. 'My weapon, Mo – the Spear of Lug?'

'Alan, you're not fit to fight.'

'The spear, Mo – I need it.'

As she ran back into the chamber, Alan searched for a better position to look around and see what was happening. He had to wipe dust and splinters of stone from his face and hair.

Then, through a gap in the smoke and flames, he

glimpsed Death Legion troops moving through the streets. *They've broken through – they're among us!* But there was something else he detected nearby: a menace he could not see, although its presence assaulted his senses. In his brow the oraculum flared, sending a thrill of alarm throughout every nerve of his body. He knew what he was sensing, and this time not in a dream but in reality: the awesome malevolence of a Legun incarnate.

The attack was so violent that the streets and buildings were glowing with that foul green lividity as Alan turned slowly about to probe the confusion of battle with the oraculum.

He could detect no clear sign of the Legun nearby but he could sense its influence. It mocked him from the forested slopes on the western bank opposite the island. This was where most of the missiles were coming from.

What must have been the heavy cost of such a breach in the defences? Yet still every sacrifice would be for nothing if the assault succeeded. He had to force his own recovery – to help.

Mo returned with the spear, so heavy for her small frame that she had to carry it two-handedly.

He accepted the spear and exercised his right shoulder again. 'How long, Mo, since they broke through?'

'At first light this morning.'

Their voices were torn away by the hot wind of another cannonade, then the clamour of a fresh attack, the defiant battle hymn of the Shee rising above the crackling of the flames. Ainé, if she survived, must be there, at the very heart of it, shoring up what she could of the breach in the face of overwhelming odds. Suddenly there was a lull, in which he could hear the broken stonework crackling. Mo's voice fell to a whisper. 'It's the Legun that is making you sick.'

Alan looked at her. Was Mo capable of sensing the Legun? He felt a stab of concern for that small, grimy face now puckered in concentration, her lips trembling. He whirled around, spear at the ready, aware of a shadow approaching, then felt relieved when the shadow revealed itself to be a smoke-begrimed Milish. There was no time for discussion. She clasped his shoulder, wordlessly lifting the flask of healwell to his lips.

With gratitude, Alan accepted the elixir. Within seconds he felt the reviving of his strength and spirits.

'Milish – where's Kate? Mo said the Aides have taken her.'

'She has been moved with the children to a place of safety.'

The memory of what happened to Kate, her face pale as a ghost's, made him panic. 'Where have they taken her?'

Milish looked at him.

'Take me to her.'

'I understand how much you want to see her. But I cannot take you to her. I am very sorry, Alan, but neither you nor I can spare the time. You must trust the shaman and your friend, Mark, who has been instructed to guard her.'

Alan shook his head, disbelievingly. Mark helping Kemtuk to guard Kate? He couldn't credit what Milish was telling him.

Milish's voice cut through his thinking. 'Oh, Mage Lord – can't you see what's happening? We face a dreadful disadvantage in forces. We are besieged not only by thousands of legionaries . . . new malengins of war. An army of Gargs!' She groaned aloud. 'The forest about the southern slopes is in conflagration. Soon the entire Vale of Tazan will be consumed.' Milish shuddered. 'Perhaps it is too late even now. We should find some means of helping you to escape.'

Conflict raged in him. He couldn't bear even to think that he wasn't going to see Kate. He so desperately needed to be with her, to see her, to hold her. His teeth clenched.

'I won't . . . I can't!'

'If you are determined to risk your life, then help the Kyra. If she falls, the Shee will have lost their leader.'

Milish's words made sense, though it was a sense he didn't welcome. Then, glancing at Mo, he hesitated in the act of leaving them, and returned to hug Mo, brushing his hand over her brow. He called to Milish as he passed out through the doorway:

'Take Mo to Kate! Take care of them both!'

Readying the Spear of Lug, he headed to where the sulphurous explosions were hailing down on the closest section of the fosse. If Ainé was to be found anywhere, it would be here.

Arriving at the breach he saw that fighting extended for at least fifty yards through the broken wall over a wrack of bloodied bodies, fallen masonry and guttering flames. Here and there Alan recognised men of the Olhyiu, stabbing furiously with their whaling lances. Shee fought alongside the Olhyiu in human form while others prowled the streets and buildings as great cats. He could hear the growls and roars that signified new attacks everywhere, accompanied by screams. As he looked about him, his nostrils sickened by the stench of the green slime, a detonation struck close enough to singe his eyebrows and burn the skin of his cheeks. It was followed by a screeching sound, as if the air was being tormented by the passage of the incandescent mass that tore an arc thirty yards over his head. The missile exploded with a thunderous impact against the side wall of the great hall.

The building was already pitted with gaping holes. Where were the elderly and wounded? Where were the children?

Alan shook his head, not wanting to imagine the injuries and terror confined within those ancient walls.

'Ainé – Qwenqwo!' He shouted their names aloud.

An unseen Shee, bloodied from several wounds, sprang to intercept a shadow that appeared suddenly out of the smoke. Alan started back from a grotesque shape that fluttered through the air, suspended on vast leathery wings. He was so horrified by his first clear sight of a Garg close-to, he stumbled and nearly fell over a dead body. The Garg had gigantic blue-grey wings, stretched in sinewy membranes across attenuated fingers. Its skeleton was drawn out to grotesque proportions, with a powerful scaly tail, so it could not only glide but fly, with great flapping movements, through the tormented air. He glimpsed a face equipped with fangs, and hugely elongated toes, from which needle-sharp talons extended, livid with poison. The Garg would have clawed his eyes out if the Shee had not taken it by one leathery wing and smashed its skull against the broken fosse.

Alan barely had time to recover from his shock before the same Shee, bleeding from mouth and nostrils, was fighting hand to hand with a massive legionary.

The soldier's helmet had been partially cloven in some earlier confrontation, yet still he engaged with the Shee, his teeth clenched and a fanatical hatred in his eyes. Taking advantage of her distraction with the Garg, the legionary had taken a fierce grip of the Shee from behind, his left arm encircling her throat and his sword burying itself deep in her flesh, rooting for arteries and windpipe.

Alan plunged the Spear of Lug into the legionary's side, but only managed to wound him. With a howl of pain, he continued his attack on the Shee. Alan twisted the blade deeper, even as, with a deft twist and sidestep, the Shee twisted her own sword backwards and upwards, piercing the legionary's throat. Without waiting for the corpse to fall, she stepped forward to place her body before Alan's as another shrieking Garg plummeted down through the air, its taloned feet directed at his heart.

The strike was lightning quick, with no time for the Shee to protect herself. She took the venomous thrust, impaling the creature with her sword even as she herself was killed.

Stumbling sideways, so he didn't make such an easy target, Alan was confronted by another unequal struggle. A lone Shee fought two legionaries, striking sparks from their swords with her glowing blade.

With a roar, Alan struck the spear against the helmet of one of the legionaries, but his strike rebounded with barely a dent in the matt-black metal. At the same time as the Shee gutted the legionary in front of her, the second brought his short sword upward in a two-handed lunge, piercing the woman in the small of the back and then tearing, rending, bisecting bone, flesh and spinal cord, yet still continuing the upward lunge, tormenting the Shee in the very moments of her death with its hacking, ever-deepening wound.

Alan gritted his teeth. He was so confused by events, he was behaving stupidly. The oraculum pulsated in his brow. He closed his eyes for a moment, directing its pulsating force to his right hand. He felt the union of power with weapon. Anger rose in him.

With a throaty moan, the legionary was dead at his

feet, the Spear of Lug transecting helmet and the head within.

Suddenly two Aides were by his side. They tried to fit him with armour, capping his head with a helmet of steel and attempting to sheathe his body, from shoulders to knees, with mail. But he tore off the helmet and thrust the Aides away. The armour would only have weighed down his spear hand. Alan heard his own voice roaring in his ears as he stumbled forward, forcing his way deeper into the conflict, gaining strength with every step as the oraculum blazed to white power, the swell of his anger ramifying and spreading into his muscles. Dead bodies of Shee lay scattered about him now, intermingled with lesser numbers of the Olhyiu, their flesh overrun by the green slime, which flickered and danced over their wounds as it devoured their tissues.

The oraculum registered Ainé somewhere to his left. He spun in that direction, through rubble and carnage and the oppressive closeness of evil.

Before he had taken twenty paces he heard the screech of tormented air as another sulphurous missile cast its foetid arc to crash into the ancient walls somewhere behind him. He cast a wave of power to avert the concussion of thunder and flames from his face.

Two legionaries materialised out of the smoke to challenge him. Alan touched the metal head of the spear against the oraculum in his brow. He felt the shockwave as the amplification of the power descended into his arm and infused the Ogham his grandfather had cut deep into the cutting edges of the blade, causing the spearhead to blaze with power. In an explosive blur of motion the legionaries were lying dead at his feet. Finding a small mound of broken wall, he sprang up onto it, standing above the drifting smoke and flames, and he peered about him through the continuing clash of swords and armour.

An old Aides woman with a twisted spine was crouched over a dying Olhyiu, offering him healwell. A moment later she uttered a dull cry and fell like a sack of bones, half her chest destroyed. He saw how her body was already oozing the slimy glow of the Legion's poison. Rage took possession of him, roaring through his mind and honing the speed of his thinking.

Alan held the Spear of Lug aloft, its blade effulgent like a miniature sun. Through its aura, he searched for Ainé and Qwenqwo, the two other oraculum-bearers, finding them fighting back to back in the smoking ruin at the bottom of the breach. They were trapped within a throng of legionaries, grossly outnumbered.

A pulse of force erupted from the oraculum in Alan's brow. With a surge of his mind, he made contact, power for power, with the Kyra's Oraculum of Bree. He used the direction of contact to lead him to her, sweeping the blazing spear through the cordon of enemies. The flame of his rage consumed them, danced in an instant from helmet to helmet, passing through shields and armour until their bodies burst into flame.

Ainé and Qwenqwo, shocked, peered about themselves, unable to believe what had happened, but then they sprang to join him, where his spear was still held high above his head, its pulsating light reflecting off the corpses.

The weariness of Alan's limbs was forgotten as he grasped Qwenqwo's shoulder, the dagger of Magcyn trailing from the dwarf mage's bandaged left arm and the bloodied battle-axe trailing from his right. Qwenqwo returned Alan's hug. Ainé stood back, staring at him in open astonishment. He felt the quick probing of her oraculum, assessing the power that must be visibly glowing on his brow. Then she did him the greatest honour, offering him the fleeting wrist and arm embrace, in the manner of an intimate Shee greeting.

'Our cause is grave. Already there are a great many injured and dead. Our scouts believe that all the southern battalions of the Death Legion are close by in the forest, and the Gargs are attacking from the opposite side of the river. Our enemies outnumber us perhaps fifty to one. But most grievous of all, our enemies are led by a Legun incarnate.'

Alan nodded, recalling Ainé's earlier advice when they were resting close to the waterfall. *In spirit we may fight it. But if it attacks in the flesh no mortal force will prevail against it.* His voice was tense but controlled. 'You were right to fear the dream journey, Ainé.' He couldn't help but blame himself for what had happened to Kate.

Ainé shook her head. 'This is not the time for

recriminations. One more cannon hit and the hall will be destroyed. We must return to the plaza and organise a new defence.'

The scene, when they got there, was desperate. Alan wheeled about, taking in the brave fighting against increasingly overwhelming odds. Into his consciousness came a dreadful foreboding. Before he could see it through the green pyres and the smoke and the stench of death, he heard its obscene growl, as if the veil of light and air had been rent apart and something dreadful was willing itself into physical form nearby.

Duuuvaaalll!

A storm of malice flickered and swirled about the smoking ruin that surrounded them. Ainé began the chanting battle hymn of the Shee, calling back the survivors of her scattered army through the breach.

Duuuvaaalll! I, the humble servant of my immortal master, challenge your feeble powers in combat!

Alan turned to Qwenqwo, who was standing to his right, his feet wide apart, the battle-axe spinning in his right hand. 'Go, Qwenqwo! Run! I want no foolish sacrifices here. Find Milish. Help her to protect Kate and the others.'

'My friend – I will not desert you!'

'If you truly are my friend, you will do what I ask of you.'

For just a fraction of a second the disgruntled face of the dwarf mage glared back, furious at being dismissed from the field of battle. Then he disappeared, as if the smoke had swallowed him. Ainé remained, crouched to his left, with her oraculum blazing power to her sword arm. He sensed the malevolence of the Legun nearby, probing his inadequate defences.

Then Alan saw it – a dreadful creature, gigantic in size, with a skull-like face, sat astride a giant battle charger, horse-like in its form but with fangs for teeth and a frame as powerful as an elephant. Though its rider had the skeletal leanness of death, the spine of the charger was bent under its weight. Alan guessed it had to be the same Legun that had killed Ainé's mother-sister and scarred her face.

He hoisted the Spear of Lug level with his shoulder, its Ogham ward pulsating strongly.

The charger reared in front of him, half emerging from the flames and ruins. Talons sprang from the Legun's claws, raking the sweat-streaked flesh of its steed in a brutal determination to force it under control, and now the red gleam in its eyes was wholly directed at Alan. Power glimmered and streamed about the Legun, as if a dark sun were continually reforming out of the voids of space. Splinters of loathing glinted in the red pits of its eyes.

Alan held his ground.

Through the white flare from his own brow, he searched the enemy for the vestige of a human heart. But he found none. From this close, the issuing voice was an assault upon his hearing, a harsh hiss, like red-hot lava polluting fresh water.

Put aside your pathetic probing. You cannot hope to comprehend my master through me.

Ainé took advantage of its focus on Alan to attack. Crying, 'De Danaan!' she sprang high into the air, her sword extended, every ounce of strength in her tall frame directed at the shadowy region of the Legun's throat. But the blade, even though glowing with all of her power, made little impact. It struck the dark form with a blaze of green sparks, but there was no pause, not even a shudder in her terrible enemy. The Legun struck out with taloned claws while she was still in flight, catching her shoulder with an immense reach. Alan watched Ainé fall against the wrack of bodies. Then, with a growl of glee, the Legun reached down and picked her up by the hair, dangling her body high above Alan, as if she were no more than a figure of straw, then cut deep with an extended talon, reopening the scars on the left side of her face.

I tire of such trivial digression. Again I challenge you, Duuuvaaalll, vain hope of the Witch of Ossierel, to mortal combat.

Alan's oraculum blazed. Assuming the First Power, he held steady against a second wave of the Legun's malice, directing his own powers into the Spear of Lug, so that the weapon forged by his grandfather, Padraig, metamorphosed into a conduit of power beyond any that could be contained by any ordinary weapon. It became the force of his will.

'Come on then. See if you can take me!'

Moment by moment Alan felt the power expanding

within him, finding consummation with his anger, ramifying to fill his entire being. If the Legun was truly an integral part of its master, then he could hurt the master through its physical being. He clenched his teeth.

'This is for Mom and Dad!'

With all of his force he hurled the Spear of Lug into the figure of darkness. The flame of contact exploded to the right of its chest, below the shoulder that held Ainé's battered body aloft, the point of impact shimmering in a rainbow-hued implosion, issuing wave after wave of shock into darkness. The spear burst back out of the vile flesh, returning to his arm in a matrix of aftershock, recoiling further, like a counter-blow, causing Alan to reel backwards.

With a roar, the Legun dropped the Kyra. Alan could see that even though he had attacked it with all of his power, he had not destroyed it. But he had hurt it – and hopefully its master.

You dare to profane the Almighty One! You are no more than a speck of dirt in His eye.

The Legun struck back, a glancing stroke of effortless ease. Alan attempted to parry it with the spear, but he hadn't the strength to completely deflect it. A crushing pain exploded in his chest. He was tossed backwards, landing with a bone-jarring concussion on the pile of broken stone and bloodied shapes. The Legun expanded until it became a thunderhead of power, above which the red splinters of eyes gloated in triumph.

Be assured I have a relish for inflicting pain that is beyond your imagination. On your knees and pray for death to release your torment.

Alan had to find some way of playing for time. Ainé needed to recover from the concussion. He struggled back onto shaky legs yet still challenging the Legun, keeping its murderous focus upon himself.

'In your dreams!'

Is this your measure, Duuuvaaallll – insufferable True Believer. I might have extinguished your mortal existence at a stroke, but you have insulted my Liege, so I am inclined to sport with you. I shall scourge you first through those you fawn over, so my ultimate satisfaction will be all the sweeter.

So saying, the monstrous form reached out and, picking up the still unconscious Kyra, it extended two talons at her eyes.

'Stay your malice, Septemvile!'

Through a mist of pain, Alan saw the petite form of Mo insinuate herself between the Legun and himself. In her right hand she held her bog-oak talisman aloft. He heard Mo speak, although her lips were not moving. Her voice sounded an octave lower, no longer girlish in its intonation.

'Mo – get out of here! Save yourself!'

Her show of force was foolishly brave in these circumstances. Mo couldn't hope to defeat the immense power of a Legun incarnate.

What pretty spoil are you?

Through the oraculum Alan glimpsed the triangular shadow that silhouetted Mo's figure from behind – a figure,

impenetrably dense, cowled in spiders' webs. *Granny Dew!*
Against the shadow, Mo's face glowed, spectral with light.
The voice appeared to come from Mo but it was too deep
and calm for the friend he knew. 'Your master will know
me by my true name. I am Mira, *Léanov Fashakk* – the
Heralded One.'

Ahhhhhh!

Alan found himself ignored as the gigantic shape
shifted its focus to the diminutive figure of the girl.

This spectral Mo confronted the Legun and spoke calmly
again. 'Let him live. Let them all live and I will surrender
to you.'

'No! Mo – get out of here!'

Thrusting all that remained of his faltering power
between them, Alan was once more struck aside, hurled
against the broken stones, the Legun barely registering
his intervention, so absorbed was it with Mo's challenge.
Yet still the Legun made no attempt at a physical attack
on her. Alan sensed a lightning-quick probe of the small
figure, both in the Dromenon and in the flesh. And in
the image in the Legun's consciousness he saw a new
image in the place of Mo, a figure tall even for a fully-
grown woman, and strangely, hauntingly, beautiful. He
sensed great power within the figure. He also sensed the
Legun's desire to possess her, covetous beyond limit.

*Why would I bargain with you, little sparrow? Your strength
is but a sigh in the storm of my hunger. I shall take you and
sport with them also.*

Rage blazed in the triangle behind the girl. The Legun drew back from the challenge, as though reconsidering the nature of this new threat. Alan heard new words invade his mind, words that seemed to come from Mo, although he knew that they were really coming from a much older and wrinkled presence. Granny Dew was speaking through Mo's mind.

Mira is but a child. She can but distract it briefly. Yet for such an eventuality did the De Danaan sacrifice herself. There is one among you whose destiny is manifest.

The Blood Rage of a Kyra

Mark was watching over Kate's unconscious body, with *Vengeance* unsheathed, when he heard the words of Granny Dew invade his mind. He knew that the words were directed at him. But what did they mean? He couldn't abandon Kate. Even so, the wider implications were abundantly clear. The battle was being lost in the streets of the ruined citadel. With a sudden dread, he also sensed another presence. The succubus was nearby. Leaving Kemtuk to nurse Kate he ran up the steps to the side-alley entrance and peered inside. His heart faltered. The three Shee who had guarded the entrance lay dead, their bodies hacked to pieces.

Immediately he heard the hated whisper. 'My lovely boy!'

Her voice came from the air above his head. His eyes wheeling skywards, he witnessed an incredible sight. The succubus was floating down through the tormented smoke and green lividity of attack, her hair clasped by an enormous bat creature. Mark thrust *Vengeance* aloft.

Mocking him with the tinkle of her laughter, she alighted just feet away from him. 'You will not harm me, my heart. Have you forgotten your promise?'

'You tricked me. Seduced me.'

She preened in front of him, her lips pouting in the doll-like face. Her scent was in his nostrils. She was already brushing her face against his, her pink tongue nuzzling against the cold, wet skin of his ear. 'You will find that the promise is binding.'

'No!'

He pushed her away from him. Though his left arm trembled, he pressed the battle-axe against her breast. Behind him he heard the sound of fluttering leathery wings. The Garg!

Her sigh enchanted him. 'A promise is a promise!' Her body curled around him, her warm softness overwhelming all of his senses. Mark felt faint with the promises she was whispering into his ear. But then, as her beautiful mouth, lips parted, extended towards his, he imagined her face replaced with the ugly snarl of his adoptive father. He imbued that face with the pain of every unwarranted punishment, every mocking insult that had been directed at him and the sister he loved – the sister he had been unable to protect. His heart filled with a bitter guilt, a guilt that filled his entire being, the guilt of self-loathing. He no longer cared what happened to him. As her mouth closed on his, he thrust *Vengeance* through the heaving breast, burying the blade right to the hilt.

In death, the power of the succubus was broken, and Mark found himself in the embrace of a wizened creature centuries old, the mouth toothless except for the four fangs of needle-sharp canines. As he shook this obscenity off the blade, he felt a piercing pain in his back. He twisted his head around to see the Garg's wing-talon withdraw, still dripping venom. Immediately he felt the poison enter his flesh and begin to spread. He wheeled through half a circle with *Vengeance* extended, severing the gargoyle head from the creature's shoulders, a good two feet higher than his own. But in that same moment he heard the scratchy patter of more talons on stone as other Gargs descended the stairs into the cellar.

He rushed to follow them, but a blow from the hilt of a heavy weapon struck hard against the back of his head.

He turned again in falling. Three legionaries had appeared behind him, together with a smaller, evil-looking man holding a dagger with a twisted blade. It was the heavy hilt, black metal decorated with glowing silver that had struck his head. With horror, Mark recognised the sigil of Grimstone's beloved master. As he struggled to get up off his knees, the man pressed the dagger into his throat and Mark felt a second poison burn into his flesh. But then the small man hesitated, his attention distracted by the spectacle of Kate's unconscious body being carried up the cellar steps over the shoulder of a Garg.

Mark tore himself free of the man with the dagger. He pushed himself upright, struggling to stop them taking Kate. But the legionaries still pinioned his left arm so he was powerless to strike. The small man turned back and smiled, his red-veined eyes wide with anticipation. He wriggled the tip of the blade deeper into Mark's throat, while relishing his anguish at the sight of the Garg taking flight with Kate's auburn hair clasped in its feet. With a great clattering of wings it soared skywards, wheeling through the smoke and missiles.

The small man continued to torment Mark, preparing to deepen the wound and twist the blade. But a sudden blow from a heavy blade clove his head in two. All of a sudden, the area was empty of Garg and legionaries. A helmeted and mailed figure stood over Mark, battle-axe twirling.

'Qwenqwo – is . . . is that you?'

The emerald-green eyes fell on him, their gaze melting from battle rage to concern. The dwarf mage fell to one knee, supporting Mark with an arm around his shoulders.

'Aides!' he roared.

Suddenly others appeared. Two Aides helped Mark to stand, though he was tottering from the poisons spreading from the wounds in his neck and back. He couldn't bear to face Qwenqwo, who had put him in charge of protecting Kate. His head fell. Despair was like an iron fist squeezing the air from his lungs.

'I failed you!'

'No, my friend! You did not fail me.' Qwenqwo spoke softly, taking a flask of healwell from one of the Aides and lifting it to Mark's lips. 'But there is little time – if you would claim your destiny!'

Overhead, more and more Gargs were circling. The sky was filled with the beating of their leathery wings.

Mark swallowed, feeling the healwell penetrate the membranes of his throat. He felt a little revived, although the poisons coursed through his blood. Yet he had heard Qwenqwo use that same word as Granny Dew – destiny! Was it possible that even in despair there was a last ray of hope that remained open to him?

Thunderclouds lowered over the blazing citadel as Alan gathered what strength he had to confront the Legun. Mo, with the help of Granny Dew, was somehow holding it, absorbing the greater part of its malice. But Granny Dew had already warned him that Mo couldn't hold out for very much longer. He felt a heavy hand clamp his left shoulder and he whirled around to find the injured Ainé once more on her feet, her right arm dangling uselessly by her side. She tottered, the matrix in her oraculum pulsating weakly. He could see that she was mortally wounded.

'There is little more I can do for you,' she panted, her pallid face awash with sweat. Then her blue eyes widened and a spark of awe lit them, as if from her inner spirit. 'Yet I thank the Powers that I should have lived to see the arrival of the Heralded One!'

Her left hand moved to touch his brow, and her oraculum began to pulsate more strongly, as if drawing spiritual strength from him for a final act of defiance. 'Help me.'

Alan gazed into Ainé's eyes. 'How can I help you?'

'Preserve these, my memories, for my daughter-sister.'

He shook his head. 'No – don't say that!'

'Give me this comfort.'

He lowered his head, nodded.

'I would enter blood-rage but my body is too weak. For this I must draw power from you – from the First Power.'

He glanced where the Legun, high on its charger, had eyes only for the tiny figure of Mo. He focused all of his power on Ainé's Oraculum of Bree. The explosive union threw them both backwards. Alan's arms rose, in a reflex action, to protect his sight from the blinding cataract of light that emanated from the Kyra.

Only now did the Legun refocus on them.

A single lightning bolt erupted upwards from Ainé's soul spirit of the white tigress and struck the thunder clouds overhead, spilling out far and wide, like an inverted tree of power, its roots dividing and cascading over the sky. Then it reversed, condensing centrally, as if to massively concentrate its energy, after which a twisting, spiralling vortex of lightning descended, followed by an almighty crack of thunder, to strike the crouching tigress, the spiritual energy imploding to a soul spirit of fire and lightning. Each movement of the tigress's limbs caused arcs of lighting to spill into the adjacent ground, and its eyes radiated light, like miniature furnaces. With a roar that shook the ground, it pounced, its huge weight and energy tearing into the body of the Legun, its terrible maw aimed for the throat.

The flaring oraculum in Alan's brow continued to supply every mote of his power to Ainé's spirit until she retained no vestige of life. But still the Legun prevailed.

Gathering whatever strength he could as the healwell dampened the poisons in his blood, Mark broke into a staggering run, hammering the ground with his booted feet as he climbed above the broken fosse and the burning buildings, above the fierce battle that continued over the plateau. A roar of fury from the Legun below revealed that some new struggle was distracting it. Lifting his face, Mark gazed up at the pentagonal tower, raised like a fist above the tor.

He began the ascent.

As he climbed the first dozen steps of fissured stone, the malevolent reek followed him. He sensed that the monstrous enemy had become aware of him. While confronting others it could still cast its malice in a second direction. He felt it invade his mind, looking for weaknesses. It was attempting to control him. Almost immediately, the shadow of a Garg fell over him. The Legun had summoned it to attack.

Unbidden, into his memory came his tormenting by

Grimstone: the earliest recollections, when he was no more than three years old, of the mocking jibes about his true parents and origins – the first wounds.

Your father was a drunk and your mother was a whore. What does that make you?

He couldn't hide the hurt deep inside him, no matter how hard he tried to dismiss it.

It had taken the Legun mere seconds to discover his weakness.

At once, into his consciousness came wounding images, memories of other hurts, failures on his part. Mark shook his head from side to side in a determined effort to keep to his purpose.

Still he continued to climb.

A screech cut through the air and a shadow loomed. Mark whirled, with *Vengeance* raised to strike out at the attacking Garg, whose talons almost raked his hair. The rasping voice of the Legun echoed inside his mind. *Deny, then, that darkness rules you, Mark Grimstone!*

He ignored its taunts, pressing higher, playing for time, all the while wondering why the monster did not tear him bodily from the rock.

Suddenly the Garg attacked again. It was more cunning this time. Its talons raked his scalp, and blood ran down over his forehead and into his eyes. Mark couldn't see the rock in front of him. He was forced to stop on the dizzying height of the staircase to wipe clear his eyes with the back of his hand. Even then he could barely feel the steps under his flagging limbs, though they continued to climb.

He turned around. The valley already seemed so far away, so distant. The entire world appeared to wheel around his dizzy head as he drew back his arm, hurling *Vengeance* at the descending Garg. He buttressed himself against the stone with his right hand, watching the twist and arc of the glittering battle-axe discover its mark, cutting through the main wing bone like butter, the Garg fluttering desperately as it plummeted down a thousand feet. With his left hand upheld, he waited. The central hilt struck his wide-open palm and he closed his fist tight about it.

Weapon and warrior were one.

Blinking the continuing trickle of blood from his eyes, he found a new strength to attack the stone steps.

My master need teach you nothing. The darkness is there in you already, Mark Grimstone!

'Not true!' he muttered.

The answering stench of wickedness, of the putrefaction of its hate, almost threw him into the abyss.

As its malice wore at him, the Legun diverted more of its concentration to the lonely figure climbing the steps. Still he opposed it, keeping his face turned into the mountain, his legs climbing, climbing. Against the fury of its spite, he was horribly exposed. But he thought about his love for his sister, Mo, and his friendship for Kate – even Alan. In love and friendship he found the strength to endure the torment that clawed at every lift of his agonised ankles and the scorn that tried to weaken his resolve.

What do these wretches mean to you, fighting their miserable skirmishes in this alien world? Reflect! How easy it would be to relieve your pain!

Mark wrenched his head up to stare up at the looming pinnacle. It was closer now. A couple of hundred feet. But that small distance seemed huge in front of him. And the light was ebbing from the afternoon, as if a terrible darkness beckoned.

The flailing wind numbed his fingers, and he began to lose his footing on the stairs. Still he forced his exhausted limbs upwards, fighting each individual step at a time, while a tormenting giddiness made his senses spin, and in his mind the malignant probe dissected and pried, hunting for the secret places, reaching back into the memories of the maturing boy, discovering the pain.

Grimstone's voice: *You failed again!*

'No!'

A weakness invaded his heart and he fell against the cold stone, feeling its edges bite into his body, tearing at the flesh of his hands and his knees. *What else are you cut out for but failure! Your father was a drunk – your mother a whore!* The belt rose, hesitated at the top of its arc, before coming down with a hard crack over his naked skin.

'No!' Every breath was a groan. 'My real father cared

about me. He tried to show me he cared . . . when he gave me the harmonica.'

He stopped, striking his forehead against the rock. He couldn't climb another step. He had to cling dizzily to where he had stopped. Staring back over his shoulder, unable to resist the impulse that was invading his mind, there was no doubting the allure of letting go, of allowing his pain that final release in the tumble, that sheer fall through crackling wind and howling abyss, to end his life on the rocks below.

The Legun was expanding its power over him. In his mind it cackled with increasing confidence.

You were weak. You sold yourself body and soul to the succubus. You betrayed Kate.

'I was stupid. The succubus tricked me.'

You failed her again when she needed you. You were meant to guard her and you lost her. The Gargs have her now – can you imagine the sport they will have with her?

Suddenly his hands froze on the step in front of his eyes. His feet would not budge. 'Yes – *yes*! I failed her. I failed her.'

Take but a single step into the embrace of darkness. There you will discover the end of your miserable existence.

Mark thought about that. Just one step off the edge of the staircase and it would be over. No more torment. But the Legun didn't care about ending his torment. Mark's head lifted again to the wheeling clouds, to the few steps above as they turned abruptly leftward, the final ascent.

Above him was the pentagonal tower, a black monolith thrust into the stormy sky. His teeth chattered in a bitter exhaustion.

Something came to mind: a memory of climbing these same steps just the day before. He recalled his conversation with Kate about the statue of Nantosueta that adorned the summit. And the centuries of dust in the highest chamber. For some reason, the Death Legion hadn't dared to climb these steps, not in two thousand years. He took heart from it to shout his defiance at the Legun.

'I've had a worse monster than you on my back all of my life. So you can go back to hell!'

Then, sliding *Vengeance* back into its sheath, he used both hands to climb. He forced himself onward clinging to the next step, pulling his shuddering frame eighteen inches higher, although the pitch of the staircase seemed almost a vertical climb, with no handholds other than the cutting edges of the steps.

The chasm yawned below him, giddy and nauseating, drawing his will back, pulling him off the face.

He felt a sudden intense stab of despair. It came from outside him, from somebody else . . . In his confusion, he thought this came from Mo. But how could it come from his sister?

Mark was so worn out he was climbing on hands and knees. Blood oozed from around his fingernails and mixed with the sweat that was dripping from his face so that his hands slipped on the smooth-worn stone.

The darkening sky was suddenly lit up with a flare of lightning. An ear-splitting crack of thunder boomed. The lightning erupted in a great cataract around the tower, and then it coalesced and struck back down to earth somewhere below. Mark heard a roar so violent it shook the tor. He felt the stones shift and grind under him, as if they had been struck by an earthquake. But then – suddenly – release. Something new, a massive blow, had weakened the Legun. The miasma was gone from his mind.

Groaning aloud, he forced himself on. Suddenly, the going was easier and he fell over the topmost step. He staggered through the inwardly sloping jambs of the ancient portal and further into the atrium, there to pause, to gather his breath and allow his heartbeat to settle.

A twist of staircase led up into the projecting pentagon of the tower.

Ignoring the pounding of his heart and the wheezing of his lungs, he ascended the staircase until he emerged under the vault of the sky. He stood on the flat pinnacle, surrounded by a low wall beyond which the Vale of Tazan stretched in a dizzying panorama from horizon to horizon. Here, in the howling of the wind, so high up the tempestuous sky seemed to press down on him like a ceiling, he slumped against the gallery wall, looking down into the despoiled valley, at the pall of smoke and ruin rising from the temple complex far beneath him. Islands of orange flame licked among the great sweep of forests, feeding the black mantle of smoke that rose into the air.

From the sloping forest across the river a grey-speckled mist was rising into the sky. He realised what it was: thousands of Gargs joining the attack. His limbs trembling with urgency as he turned to look up at the colossus that surmounted the pentagonal Rath. Nantosueta! How different she looked from the beautiful girl in the woodland glade. This figure was ten times life size, struck from the same enduring granite as the tower that bore it. His limbs trembling with exhaustion and poison, Mark gazed up into that grim face.

'Help me now, Granny Dew!'

Abruptly, he felt a new force intervene. With gritted teeth, he suffered the dislocation as he was torn away from this stony platform and returned to the cave of sulphurous lava. Here the cobwebbed figure loomed over him, her black eyes peering intently into his. She was tapping a knobbly stick against his ankles as she urged him to follow her, a flaming firebrand in her other hand.

The Third Power

Granny Dew led Mark out of the cave of lava, which now appeared to be an antechamber to an enormous new chamber. As if ignited by the firebrand's flare, light, brilliant and multicoloured, swept through it in motes that spiralled and flickered like starry galaxies throughout its great spaces. The colours ignited a Milky Way of flickering reflections in the walls, in the quartzite floor and the kaleidoscope of ceiling. In their progress they brushed by straw stalactites, as delicate as ivory hair, glittering with diamantine refractions. From the floor, giant stalagmites sprang up in beautiful reds and oranges, some striated and polished like marble. As if in answer to Mark's weakening gaze, the glitter of iron pyrites seemed to metamorphose into the glory of a peacock. He saw the bird fan its tail, as if for a moment it had come to real life, and then it reverted to crystal.

'I don't have time for fireworks!'

'Time does not exist here, child!'

What did that mean? Mark felt the poisons surge and swell through his blood, weakening him further from moment to moment. Now that he was dying, was he being given some sort of a final lesson?

He sensed forces, powers that went beyond any normal comprehension. There was sound too, like musical chimes and harmonies, as if the labyrinth were vying in song with the beauty of vision. Mark caught the scents of spring in his nostrils. But all the sights and sounds were doing was wasting vital seconds. When he waved it all away, the movement of his hand evoked a cloud of damselflies, metamorphosing into being from crystalline motes; a second wave brought into life a hummingbird, with its whirring hover; the fall of silver dust became the glory of a leaping salmon, arcing full-bellied through the rainbow spray of a mountain torrent.

Even as he gasped for breath, the brilliance that seemed to exude from the very molecules of air was extinguished, and he was being directed towards a single focus. In the light of the firebrand, still held aloft by Granny Dew, he was drawn through the entrance into a third cave. This was smaller, more intimate, and dominated by what appeared to be a circle of stalagmites. As he struggled towards it, the stalagmites took on the appearance of petrified trees. Standing in the centre was a single stone column, vaguely human in shape, as if a cowled and shawled figure brooded there. Closer to, the figure loomed, blue-black in density and flickering in its depths, as if dormant with inner life.

The old woman inched her way forward, entering the circle of petrified trees, her face downturned and averted. When she reached the central pillar, she began to anoint three faces in the stone with some kind of oil.

Her dirt-begrimed fingers traced the delicate lines of the faces with devotion, her voice growling incantations. Abruptly her task was finished. She drew back from the pillar and fell onto the dusty floor with her face still averted, skulking into the background. Mark felt compelled to turn his attention from Granny Dew to the column of stone.

Conflicting emotions swept through him: annoyance that nobody here seemed to give a damn that he was dying, along with fear of what felt like the potential for almighty good or malice.

He felt imprisoned there, his own will taken away from him, as if his being had become trapped by his own terror. But then hands, grimy and powerful, took hold of his elbows and propelled him forward, into the maelstrom of power. Her words growled in his ears. 'Qurun!'

Into the spinning vortex those gnarled hands guided him.

'Daaannngerrr!'

The whispering of a name . . . *Qurun Bave*. Had her words been leaves, they would already have dried and decayed to powder in his mind. And then even in her voice there was a tone of caution. *Qurun Macha*.

One of the faces in the stone appeared to have come alive, a feminine presence. In the quaver of dread in that old voice, he felt a powerful reinforcement of her warnings.

The old woman was dragging herself back a pace from him, still hugging the ground on her age-old knees. Mark realised that he no longer needed the light of the firebrand. He was standing between two members of the petrified circle of trees, the upstanding trunks and branches lambent with an inner radiance. His guide was urging him deeper, yet she withheld herself with hisses and moans. Studying the stone figure at the centre of the circle, he saw how its surface was deeply etched with grooves, as if hands of knowledge from ages past had scored some forbidding runes over its surface. Compelled by forces he was unable to resist, he stumbled closer to the cowled figure.

'Daaannngerrr!' He heard the old woman's urgent whisper, as if she were reading his mind.

He glimpsed her at the margin of his vision, frantic with worry, scurrying about herself, dragging her finger in the damp earth, drawing at a furious rate, faster than he could register. As if incanting some spell.

Compulsion overcame dread, forcing him to stagger forward again until his outstretched hand could reach out and touch the surface of the luminescent figure. He pressed his finger over the runes. He couldn't read them but instinctively he sensed their incredible power.

The old woman hung upon his progress, murmuring, incanting, despairing at his incomprehension in the presence of the powers that now confronted him.

'Mark, abide! The test – *the test!*'

What test?

But there was no time to wonder as he faced the figure, which had several faces above a body that was a conflagration of glowing runes. Falteringly, as if struggling through a mixture of faintness and dread, he forced himself closer. Standing before the triple-headed being, he forced his arms through the blizzard of force, so that he embraced its glowing outline. Distantly he registered the shriek of outrage as the old woman, who had been trying to wrestle him back, was herself thrown backwards, forced to prostrate herself once more two paces beyond the circle.

Mark felt a shock of fright: there was no air in his lungs as, with clumsy fingers, he ran his hands over the first face. It was a stern yet not unkindly face. His mind opened, however timidly, to question it. The voice of Granny Dew was no longer in his ears but in his head. *Qurun Bave!* He was gazing at the ruby triangle on the brow of stone, even as the old woman's voice was cautioning him, growling at him, to move around the obelisk – as if questions could be dangerous, and hesitation more dangerous still.

A ruby triangle – the First Power!

He was allowed mere moments to confront a second face – a much younger face, with lips parted in a seductive smile. This being aroused him far more deeply than the succubus with the merest wisp of touch, then shimmered away, as if reacting to his presence with a mocking laughter. A whispered name, like a sigh against his ear: *Qurun Mab!* Cold sweat drenched his brow. Yet still, seduced by the voice, he couldn't resist the urge to place his kiss upon those second lips. Even as he was drawn to do so, a family of lovesome shadows danced and gyrated about him, brushing against his flesh, sighing and whispering, as if he only had to free his will, to lose himself in pleasure beyond imagining . . . Sibilant peals of laughter. *She is the One, we are the daughters.* These daughters were in competition with each other for winsome seductiveness. *Come sport with us and you will know paradise . . .*

Mark's head spun, causing him to totter, almost to fall.

Child – heed the brow!

At the last moment, before his lips met those of the figure, he saw the triangle in the brow: a metamorphosing matrix of meadow-green, in which arabesques of gold ebbed and spiralled – Kate's crystal.

With even the thought of Kate, the memory of failure rose in him. He was only vaguely aware of the voice of Granny Dew in his mind, growling, at the same time as her head was bowed to the floor – and her hand was reaching down, slowly, carefully, to throw a cooling handful of dirt on the second face.

Now, foolish child – back!

Only with all that was left of his will could he tear

himself from their embraces, the temptresses that reluctantly drew back from him and faded into the sighing figure. He forced his legs to move on muscles of lead to the third face, hidden from the light of the atrium in shadows so dark it seemed that it could not even be illuminated by the firebrand's flame. His fingers recoiled in dread. The third face was cowled in a hood, the face within it, however beautiful – and beautiful he knew it was, deeply, instinctively – felt colder than winter. Her perfect teeth parted in a smile.

Mórígán!

Terror threw him back against the ring of trees, his jaws chattering, his limbs weak and trembling.

Through his dread, he heard the old woman speaking. Her words addressed the third entity, whose icy lips he had refused to kiss.

Stay your fury over this frail coracle. Let failure or success now condemn or succour him through the peril that lies before him.

A wave of force caused Mark to wheel about, to stretch his arm towards Granny Dew. She attempted to come a yard closer to help his progress, her lips moving in a growling mantra. Then suddenly, with her eyes widely staring, she thrust her hand through the fringe of trees, pressing something hard and burning against his forehead, impressing it there, her lips writhing against each other, as if both an immense duty and a terrible sacrifice had been set in motion.

My crystal!

Pain exploded in Mark's head. He was flung back against the circle of petrified trees, his eyes wide and staring. A potent force was assuming form in the pillar before him. For a moment, in place of the cowled figure of the third face, he saw a constantly metamorphosing matrix of dark and light, before the cowled face with its icy beauty returned.

His brow, with its obsidian crystal, was forced into intimate contact with the brow of the face. He could smell the oils of Granny Dew's anointing. He could feel the area of contact condense to form a triangle. An inverted triangle – he knew it would be black. The sensation of fusion was so agonising that for a moment he lost consciousness, but the strength of attachment wouldn't allow him to fall. Without the strength to hold back any longer, his lips pressed against the icy lips, tasting the old woman's earth-encrusted fingers, the sweet aromatic oils . . .

A new shock of union rippled through him, scoring throughout his mind and spirit like an electrical discharge, thrilling to the very tips of his fingers and toes. A deep, animal part of him exulted. A whisper entranced his mind. He was aware that it entered through the burning triangle in his forehead, though he was no longer in contact with the being.

So the De Danaan blasphemy is now challenged? Yet is such an ordeal warranted? Are you worthy?

What was he supposed to reply to that? The question was too vague, too fantastic, for his comprehension.

He felt certain that it was from this dreadful face that the dark shadows crept, to wheel and gyrate over the walls of the cave.

He heard the old woman reply on his behalf:

Mark is afraid. He has known fear of rejection for a very long time. Yet he will assume the powers of True Believer.

With his heartbeat roaring in his ears he heard the reply of the Third Power, like glaciers grating over the rubble of landscapes.

Does he understand that something which so terrifies him in ignorance will become a thousand times more terrible through understanding?

He murmured, 'I'm here too, you know.'

The shockwave of direct communication threw him onto his knees. *And so understanding, will you, Mark Grimstone, accept your destiny?*

'I'll accept it. Whatever you want of me.'

There was a pause in which that chilly face appeared to assess him anew. Then, as if to scorn him, he was shown a pinpoint of light in the darkness. A terrible despair cut through his awareness as Mo's voice rose, like a plaintive cry, on the wind. 'I am losing my strength, Alan! Leave me!'

Mo – Mo was in danger. Concern for his sister flooded Mark's mind. 'All I ask is that you let me do it quickly enough to make a difference.'

He knelt before Mórígán, trembling, in a dreadful silence. Then he felt a powerful throbbing from his forehead which spread so that his whole mind seemed probed. There was a quickening in him, as if a little of his strength was returning, barely enough to enable him to stand on his own and endure the shock of being cast out of the labyrinth.

Back on the pinnacle, and gasping once more for breath, Mark saw how the Legun had expanded its power. The sky was a maelstrom, ravaged by lightning. He swayed back against the rail, staring up at the gigantic statue far above his head. He sensed his newly acquired oraculum blazing darkness rather than light, focusing all of his concentration on the figure of Nantosueta, marbling its surface with rivulets of fiery luminescence which sparkled and cascaded in a dense web of runnels and matrices throughout the crystals of the rock.

Moment by moment, as the figure grew ever more incandescent, weakness invaded Mark's heart. Icy sweat dripped from his face. Yet still he held his trembling body erect as the Dark Queen blazed brighter – as if the crystals of granite took fire.

When she spoke, it sounded like the rattling of a sea of bones.

Speak – and quickly before you invoke my wrath. Why have you profaned my age-old slumber?

'Don't you remember me?' He had to hurl his words with all of his strength from mind to mind, and even then they sounded like a whisper against the battening storm of force that whipped and tossed about the tor. 'We met in the chamber – in a kind of dream.' He panted for every breath now, trying to overcome the growing giddiness in his mind.

Silence.

'I don't have time left for explanations. Look at what's going on around you!' His breath was shallow, rapid. 'Down there . . . on the temple plateau. Innocent people are being murdered by the same evil you fought long ago.'

Weariness again, in a great wave of sorrow, swept through the very atoms of his spirit as that great head turned.

Mark's teeth were chattering from the poisons coursing through his bloodstream, yet he refused to shift his gaze from those all-black eyes now beholding him from their wrinkled brow. He summoned up every last fibre of his reserve. 'They're my friends. Can you remember what it was like to have friends?'

A shudder moved through the figure. *Pity? Is that what you expect of me?* A groan, like the susurration of a dried-up ocean, buffeted Mark's spirit. *Would that I could feel pity!*

His throat was dry. His tongue felt so swollen it was hard to speak. 'I remember how lovely you looked . . . when we met in the dream.'

He sensed a pause for reflection in the figure of stone. *Great anger at injustice was my undoing. Pride became my blood, and it hardened my heart to stone. Wrath has become my fate, and I must endure it until the end of time.* But then her voice softened, so it sounded more human. *Yet to communicate with a caring heart, though brief unto a single moment, is such sweetness.*

His heart was misfiring in his chest, his body sliding down the parapet until he was slumped against the low wall, *Vengeance* a discomfort against his spine. Through a mist of confusion he thought of the real Nantosueta – the dark-haired girl laughing as she pirouetted among the slender trunks, as free as one could only wish to be. He tried to lick his lips with a useless tongue. 'We held hands. I . . . I know you're no older than I am. I know what it feels like to be that lonely.'

The voice fell to a whisper. *Who are you?*

'Mark . . . Mark Grimstone is my name . . . '

You could not love me, such as I have become?

His limbs shuddered. His body trembled so it took all of his strength just to lift his face up to look at her.

'I do – I do love you. I've loved you since that moment . . . In the dream, when you held my hand.'

A sigh fell from the figure, like the patter of spring rain entering a forest that had known only drought. A girl's soft voice spoke to him then, gentle and lovely as he remembered her: *In two thousand years, yours has been the only heart brave enough to love me.* She sighed again, but this sigh had the sibilance of joy. *How could I not love you in return!*

Mark's heart lifted with what felt like an impossible mixture of joy and hope. 'Then prove it by saving them . . . Save my friends!'

So let it be! Yet avert your senses lest dread rather than desire is the memory you would keep of me.

Mark found himself falling into darkness, melding into consummation with Nantosueta, mind for mind and heart for heart. He refused to avert his senses, gladly sharing her gaze as her right arm drew its awful force down out of the heavens, and that single white-marbled left arm extended with the fingers splayed to a spider-shape of bleached ivory. Suddenly, those fingers exploded in blue-black lightning. Her accompanying words were a summons that swept far and wide over mountain and river and through the forests . . .

Guardians of Tazan – awaken!

Resurrection

Qwenqwo Cuatzel felt the power descend over the plateau as if a sudden static charge of electricity had crackled over his skin, lifting his hair so it felt as if his helmet had risen half an inch higher on his head. After Mark had left him, the dwarf mage had gone down into the cellar to discover the shaman, Kemtuk Lapeep, dying from a wound inflicted by the Gargs that had taken Kate. There were children here too, many sick from a poison cast into the air of the chamber. The council woman, Milish, had arrived to join him in tending the children. Now she too lifted her head, startled: 'What is it?'

'Salvation – by the merciful gods!'

The dwarf mage hugged the tall statuesque woman, and then ran for the steps. He came lumbering up out of the cellar, passing several Aides on the blood-soaked paving stones, then burst out into the alley with his eyes thrown wide open, singing a battle hymn he had thought forgotten. In his right hand he held aloft the runestone, which pulsated and glimmered with power.

'What's happening?'

He didn't have time to hug the spiritual guardian, Bétaald. He ran towards the central plaza, where he heard the unmistakable roar of a grizzly in blood-rage. Other sounds he heard over the din of battle: the roars of the enemy and a muted cheer from Olhyiu throats. With the oraculum cradled in his injured left arm, and the Fir Bolg axe twirling in his right, he hacked his way past Kehloke, who stood wounded and exhausted among a small circle of Olhyiu that fought alongside the giant grizzly bear against hundreds of legionaries and swooping Gargs. Qwenqwo Cuatzel ignored them all. He forced his way through soldiers and Gargs, until he reached the fosse and turned his face up to view the Rath of Nantosueta. Then he turned to peer down into the Vale of Tazan.

With tears filling his eyes, he murmured, 'Ah, bravely done young Ironheart! For so long have I endured to witness this!'

Gigantic cataracts of blue-black lightning arced through the air, provoking luminescent rainbows throughout the valley, even as dazzling flares of light expanded and fused in the statue of the Dark Queen high overhead, transforming her figure into a furnace of dark power. The avalanche of ur-lightning separated into myriad feelers and rivulets as it struck the slopes, where the thunderous reverberations seemed to go on and on. Vast and wide, a terrible constellation of stars, dark as gunmetal against the light, began to glow in the war-ravaged valley. Tears made tracks down the cheeks of the dwarf mage as he saw the lightning bolts strike one stone head after another. On the forest floor a reluctant movement began. Here and there, sheathed in crackling spiderwebs of power, the horned heads of the Fir Bolg war beasts ripped a passage out of their snow-covered graves.

Armoured with their thick hides, on their backs they carried the heavily muscled drum masters, bronze-armoured and helmeted. Straddling their pommels, in a semicircle of diminishing size, were the six great kettle drums. The eyes of the drum masters were all pupil, black and bulging as beetles. From the broad flat feet of the war beasts, claws extended to take firm purchase on the slopes. Steadily, purposefully, the drums began to call out . . .

Boom-boom tan-tan . . . Boom-boom tan-tan . . . Boom-boom tan-tan . . . Boom-boom tan-tan . . .

The drumming of the masters set up a coordinated signal throughout the valley, discovering everywhere a second wave of response, as the war beasts held their ground, standing eight feet at the shoulder, tiny grey eyes of malice looking for bodies to toss with their triple horns, huge jaws open to snap and tear, while the black-eyed drummers beat out their rhythm of awakening into every nook and cranny, so that not a single warrior, other than the few heads destroyed by the Legun, would fail to heed the call.

Death Legion and Garg alike hesitated as the drumming expanded, patiently, remorselessly, until it became an omnipresent thunder sweeping through the valley. And soon the first among an army of fifty thousand broke free of the grave, with a rattle of stones and a scattering of insects and worms, their eyes beetle-black, their shoulders weighted with heavy armour, struggling out of their entranced slumber to answer the call of the drums.

The emerging Fir Bolg warriors were giants among the race of dwarfs, the tallest no more than five feet, yet they were shouldered like oxen, with arms and legs muscled like roots of oak. They bore a great variety of weapons, swords, spiked ball-and-chain, and double-headed battle-axes with hafts bent and twisted for sigmoid patterns of flight and their blades embossed and silvered with runes of power. These terrible weapons were now rediscovering the bonds of weapon and master, turning, swirling, glinting ominously in the blue-black lightning that ran and hunted for the great stone heads close to the ground. In a continuously flowing machine of war, the arriving warriors were aligning to columns on either side of the war beasts. All in that same flow, the drum masters began to press forward, hammering out a new rhythm, some leading their columns down into the valley heading for the river, others wheeling their war beasts upslope, the clawed feet, sharp and strong as steel, biting deep into the slippery ground.

Immediately the slaughter began.

A Garg in mid-flight was bisected by a twirling battle-axe that curved in its flight to return to the hand that cast it. A Preceptor leading a platoon of Death Legion reached a Fir Bolg warrior, only half emerged from a muddy stream, and sank his twist-bladed dagger straight into the warrior's throat. The legionaries cheered and chanted the sacrificial hymn to their master. But as the blade emerged from the cold, pale flesh the wound self-healed. At the same time those all-black eyes opened on the Preceptor and an armoured fist reached out and crushed his throat.

Above the third fosse, surrounded by a renewed intensity of battle, Qwenqwo Cuatzel, Arch Mage of the resurrected Fir Bolg, held the runestone aloft and whispered a message through the oraculum to Alan:

'Bear it a little while longer!'

Alan received the message, but couldn't reply. He stood, with the incandescent Spear of Lug extended, his teeth clenched and his feet splayed. Mo lay unconscious by his side. Ainé's remains lay nearby, her body cremated by the fury of her own attack on the Legun. Her ashes were mixed with those of the Legun's charger, which had been immolated in the same attack. Even the immortal Legun had been weakened and maimed, and was leaking foul green slime from the terrible wound inflicted by the Kyra. Yet still it confronted Alan, battering down his last reserves of strength and spiritual energy. Suddenly, as if detecting his exhaustion and anticipating victory, it roared out a call to all of its forces. Legionaries turned, urged on by their Preceptors. Gargs wheeled about in mid-flight, heading for the single focus of the Legun amid the wreckage of bodies and broken masonry on the great Plaza of Ossierel.

Glancing backwards, Alan saw that he and the small company of Shee that still fought around him were surrounded by legionaries, and the focus of an approaching swarm of Gargs. The Legun reached out an enormous fire-scarred hand and, with a venomous claw, rapidly closed on Alan's brow, determined to quench the blazing oraculum.

From nearby, Alan felt a small whisper of support enter his being. Qwenqwo was fighting his way closer. The runestone! Alan sensed the message of the runestone, the Mage of the Fir Bolg calling for help.

Taking a new comfort from the closeness of his friend, Alan poured his last reserve of resistance into the spear. He plunged it yet again into the flesh of his monstrous adversary. But the approaching hand hardly faltered, redoubling its purpose, forcing its talon closer. Belatedly, Alan realised the implications of the Shee having lost their leader. He sent a call to every Shee still living, directing them to fight their way here, to where the oraculum-bearer was losing his battle with the Legun.

At several breaches in the fosse, great cats appeared from the flame and smoke of the nearby slopes, leaping out of the shadows to tear out the throats of the legionaries attempting to hold their ground.

But the Shee were fighting overwhelming odds. The legionaries were armed with steel-mesh nets and long-bladed battle forks, and the numbers of tigresses were dwindling, the survivors tiring. Suddenly, through the same breaches, the war beasts now clambered, their drum masters swaying in the saddles, all the while implacably calling on the warriors to rise and follow, the drum beat never faltering.

Boom-boom tan-tan . . . Boom-boom tan-tan . . .

The rhythm of the drums rolled out over the plateau, sending a wave of alarm through the enemy. Gargs fell on the emerging Fir Bolg, to be met with a rain of heavy arrows, javelins, battle-axes. A big centurion dropped from an upper window, his sword held aloft in two hands, intent on bisecting a marauding tigress with a single stroke. But a whirring black battle-axe clove deep into his chest before he reached the Shee, skimming the ground before rising up to find the armoured fist of its master.

As if sensing the changing tide of battle, the Legun hesitated, but then, drawing deep on the malice of its master, it lunged at Alan a final time, accepting a wound the full depth of the spearhead, yet still pressing through every wave of his resistance. As if in slow motion, Alan could only stare at the approach of the venom-dripping talon, resisting with all of his might the imminent moment of his death. The talon was only an inch or two from his face when he heard a sound in the distance, like a humming from thousands of low-pitched throats at once. A whirling entity was approaching, directed at the intersection of his oraculum and the talon.

A sudden roar of pain filled his ears – but it wasn't Alan's. It came from the Legun, whose taloned hand had been severed by the wyre-glowing battle-axe of the Mage of the Fir Bolg, who had placed all of the power of the runestone into the stroke.

Boom-boom tan-tan . . . Boom-boom tan-tan . . .

The drumming now filled the air, approaching Alan and the Legun from three separate directions, as the Fir Bolg adopted a triple-pronged attack formation, each prong led by the trapezoidal spearhead. At the tip of each spearhead fifteen war beasts formed a cutting wedge, the drum masters beating out a new tactic, the warriors swaggering from foot to foot. Their shoulders swayed in their ponderous ballet of combat, bodies twisting and rotating, their positions never still, so as to deflect any arrow or spear, their armour so dense and heavy that not even the fiercest thrust of blade could penetrate it.

At an unspoken command, a hail of battle-axes fell on the encircling legionaries, while another tore into the descending cloud of Gargs. Flying clusters and ground formations disintegrated as the bodies fell, with heads detached or wings disintegrated, and all the while the drumming continued, as the three-pronged formation closed around the central focus of the Legun, the runed blades whirling and returning, to be cast again and again and again.

Alan, his spear arm shaking with exhaustion, watched in disbelief as a flurry of battle-axes struck the Legun. The glittering blades tore deep into the malignant flesh and then, strangely, horribly, continued to spiral deeper, burying themselves entirely within the monster. A second wave struck, a third – and then it became a hailstorm, thudding into the vast malignant being, until a deluge of green gore covered the surrounding plaza. It altered focus, pouring its malice into the nearing columns. But the warriors who fell, consumed with livid green fire, simply rose again. No power, no matter how dreadful, could kill those who were already dead. With an explosion of rage that shook the ground and echoed in the ruined walls, the Legun was gone.

Alan's ears were deafened by the drums as Qwenqwo appeared by his side. Then Milish arrived, kneeling by the unconscious body of Mo, her regal face awash with tears. 'What are we to do?'

Alan blinked, unable to speak.

Qwenqwo spoke softly, reassuringly. 'It's over. Everywhere it is as you see in these streets. The guardians of the Vale of Tazan are at large in its ancient forests. They will continue to hunt until not a single enemy remains.'

In the hours that followed, the surviving Gargs took to the air, a great cloud dispersing into the gloom of the Eastern sky. The survivors of the Legion fled to their ships in the river below. Yet even here there was little respite from the Dark Queen's vengeance. A great commotion, too far away for Alan to see it clearly, thrashed the water, smashing one of the ships and tossing the survivors into the moiling river. The soldiers clinging to the wreckage screamed as a gargantuan shape rose out of the water – even from such a distance he imagined it might resemble the gaping jaws of a titanic serpent. Its hunger appeared to match its size, for it rose and snapped again and again, as if filling its belly for a hundred years.

The Cost of Battle

Alan stood in the rain on the elevated platform of Nantosueta's tower, heedless of the storm winds blowing from the southeast, from Carfon and the sea. How he had made his way here – how long he had stood here – he didn't recall. The battle was over. And now the implications were only beginning to sink in to his mind.

Ainé and Kemtuk dead. Kate lost – taken! And Mark . . . Oh, sweet Jesus, what had happened to Mark?

'Mage Lord!'

Qwenqwo's face looked up into his, the dwarf mage's stout body wounded in several new places. Alan became gradually aware of the sky, the hard, high green sky of early evening, with its wrack of storm clouds, wheeling over him. His jaw ached from being clenched in anger and sorrow as he gazed up at the entwined figures of stone towering above them. His friend, Mark, bearing obvious wounds, embraced the smaller figure of the Dark Queen, the two locked in an embrace, as if for eternity.

'What does it mean, Qwenqwo?'

'Mark saved you – saved us all.'

'Is he dead?'

'He is not dead. Though dead he most certainly would have been, in flesh and spirit, had his iron heart failed him, for he carried twice a death sentence of poison in his blood.'

'I don't understand. How can he not be dead?'

'Look at their brows.'

Alan stared more closely at the faces of the entwined figures. Each brow enclosed a black inverted triangle.

'It's an oraculum, isn't it?'

'The Third Power – the fates protect us!'

'Mórígán's power . . . Death itself?'

Qwenqwo's face wrinkled into a frown. 'Yes.'

'If Mark isn't dead, where is he?'

'Subsumed, body and spirit. He is now bound to the Third Power, as was the Dark Queen.'

Alan shivered, staring up at the entwined figures, a fateful realisation flooding his mind. As bound as he was himself?

'If my ruby triangle is the First Power and Mark's is the Third, what happened to the Second Power?'

'If I interpret rightly, it should have been Kate's.'

Alan reflected, with a dizzying resentment, on the complex pattern of what had brought the four friends here – of what still directed, perhaps even controlled their very lives and actions. 'What is the Second Power?'

'Perhaps the power of new birth – but also that of healing – of healing, perhaps, that which was thought to be unhealable!'

Alan sighed. So that was why the dark forces had so focused on Kate. What more would the Tyrant fear and hate than the power of new birth, of healing, in such a ravaged world! And how he wished Kate was still here! Her loss brought a terrible sense of emptiness.

'And Mo?'

The dwarf mage said nothing.

Alan recalled Mo in that awful moment, when her tiny figure had confronted the Legun, with the shadow of Granny Dew supporting her like a guardian angel. What did it mean? How was he expected to make sense of any of it?

Grief rose in him again, that same grief that he had felt with the loss of his parents, but now it boiled within him, as unbearable as madness.

Qwenqwo preceded him down the winding staircase cut into the sheer face of the rock until they emerged onto the battle-scarred ruins of Ossierel. Here, amid the rain-washed ruins and flagstones, the smell of death hung in his nostrils. The dwarf mage took him to Mo, who lay where she had collapsed after the Legun had fled. Mo was still being nursed by Milish. Alan knelt beside her petite body. With gentle hands he touched her face, the matted black hair. He heard Bétaald's voice, an anxious insistence from the background. 'She will live. There are others, more desperate, who need our help.'

He didn't like to leave Mo. But Bétaald was right: the need for ministering to the survivors overrode all others. Alan stood shakily erect to face the dark-skinned spiritual head of the Shee, noticing that her arms were streaked with her own blood.

'I'm sorry about Ainé. She was incredibly brave.' He inclined his head.

Bétaald's yellow eyes searched his, as if searching for some additional explanation, or words of comfort, before she replied. 'A great many of those who answered the call to arms lie dead among these stones.'

So he became aware of the gravity of the catastrophe that surrounded him; in addition to the losses of the defending Shee, many Olhyiu were also dead. And many of the survivors lay injured among the ruins. Even the survivors, haunted by grief and loss, faced an uncertain future. Where would they go now that the Temple Ship had been destroyed?

He walked among the wounded and the dead, witnessing the price paid by those who had sacrificed so much to help him and his friends. He didn't have far to wander. At every step, pools of blood, broken bodies – and worse – met his gaze. The groans of the injured scourged his ears as, one by one, he came upon their pain-racked figures, often in small huddles, blood-soaked and pitted by livid wounds. On and on he wandered among them, absorbing the blankness of shock on their faces, the ebbing of life from their eyes.

A hardening of purpose established its hold on Alan Duval's heart on this wet and bitter evening.

He stood aside to allow two survivors to pick up one of the dying Shee. He watched them carry her through the wisps of smoking ruin, heading for some vestige of cover. A rank pestilence still seeped from the earth, as if the darkness still struggled to seed itself everywhere. The shadow of that darkness mocked him still with the evidence of murdered innocence, of so many faces that had once smiled at him, looked to him for hope and protection, the precious life now taken from them. It was difficult to conceive that any of the more vulnerable had survived such a pitiless assault. Yet the Aides were opening up avenues into subterranean passages and cellars, from which the surviving children and elderly were being assisted into the light. Others were tearing apart the rubble to discover still more dead and wounded.

Milish left Mo to the ministration of others and sought him out.

Though every bit as exhausted as he was, she insisted on walking beside him. 'The wounds caused by sword and arrow we can repair. The Aides will stitch sinew to sinew, or set broken bones. And healwell will support the loss of blood and the shock of scorched flesh. But some bear wounds worse than those struck down by sword or even the foul green flame of the legionaries' weaponry.' Outrage pained the diplomat's voice as she led Alan to the entrance of one of the underground chambers, where a dozen or so of the youngest children had been hidden. The Aides, assisted by able-bodied Olhyiu, had carried them out of the cellar and now they lay in the cobbled alley, every face pallid and feverish. It was here that Alan found Turkeya, kneeling in grief by the body of Kemtuk.

Alan fell to the ground beside Turkeya and embraced him, tears welling up in the young Olhyiu's eyes.

Milish spoke softly, with a comforting hand on both their shoulders. 'A group of Gargs, led by one so powerful it may have been their leader, forced entry here, though the portal was guarded to the death by three of our bravest. Here it was that your friend, Mark, was wounded by a Preceptor even as Kate was taken. And it was in this cellar that the shaman was himself killed while attempting to protect Kate. The leader of the Gargs was killed by the dwarf mage, who arrived too late to prevent their purpose. Its remains, together with those of the Preceptor, are nearby. Unfortunately, the dwarf mage arrived too late to prevent the Gargs from spreading their poison among the children.'

Alan climbed back onto his feet and examined the children where they lay, eyes glazed and red-rimmed, the cherry-red lividity on their lips, that same glow aflame in their cold flesh. One of these innocents he recognised: it was Amoté, the little girl who had danced to Mark's harmonica on board the Temple Ship and pulled Kate's hair.

'Oh God, Milish!'

In the first glimmer of dawn, Alan wandered alone to the easternmost reaches of the third fosse, where a thousand feet of sheer cliff face bolstered the defensive ramparts. Here, the air was cold and refreshing. The cyclopean stones of the fosse supported him, standing high on a promontory and gazing out over the spectacular panorama.

The Vale of Tazan yawned before him, too colossal in its wandering valleys and soaring mountains to take in with his tired eyes. How serene it must have appeared in the eyes of the young queen before war and death had invaded that tranquil scene. Even now thunder still rolled among the distant calderas, charging the air with casts of lightning, and an icy rain squalled among the trees, quenching any remaining flames, with palls of mist blanketing the ground where ash and embers had been most extensive. Here and there, in the distance, the drums of the Fir Bolg reminded him that they had not yet completed their terrible purpose, a purpose that would continue until not a single legionary or Garg remained within the sacred valley. And even then, as Qwenqwo had explained with a look of outrage, the warrior guardians would be condemned once more to their living graves. Alan felt the grief of the dwarf mage like ice in his heart.

Had he, and his friends, caused these terrible events? Was vengeance enough to make all of this worthwhile?

Alan turned his face up to the cleansing rain, washing away the reek of death. In the rumbling detonations that still shook the tor under his white-knuckled fingers, he sensed the same relief in the very rock. Evil was receding, although its defeat could only be temporary, and even this victory had been bought at a very great price.

Kate was somewhere out there, unconscious and taken away from him. Yet even in that situation there was a small ray of hope. The enemy had some purpose in keeping her alive. If all they had wanted was to kill her, the Garg would have left her dead in that cellar. The swell of grief within him peaked. From his brow a pulse of light flared, and a signal surged out of the valley and far beyond, until it located an unconscious mind caught in the soaring flight of a gigantic V-shaped cloud over the Eastern Ocean. He sensed the tens of thousands of leathery wings flapping and gliding on the prevailing currents of wind. He had no way of knowing if Kate could hear him as he cast his promise, carried upon his pent-up anger into the universe of morning.

Only survive! No matter where they're taking you, I'll find you.

Alan was still standing there at full daybreak when Qwenqwo returned with a flask of liquor.

'My friend,' he said, his voice hushed. 'A man's drink.'

Alan was too grief-stricken to face Qwenqwo. His feet were frozen to the rampart of stone, his mind still locked in the direction of the Eastern Ocean. Qwenqwo squeezed the flask into his fingers. The dwarf mage spoke gently, insistently. 'Yet still there is Mo who needs your help – though darkness appears to have taken hold of her very spirit.'

Communion

During the long night, Alan had done what he could to help Mo, but no probing of her body or mind using the power of his oraculum made any difference. The confrontation with the Legun had destroyed something subtle and personal in her, in her soul spirit perhaps, that Alan could neither understand nor restore. Milish had kept her going physically with regular sips of healwell, but mentally she remained unresponsive. Meanwhile, the people rested before beginning the descent to the causeway at first light the following morning. There were so many injured and sick among them that all able hands, including Siam's and Kehloke's, were put to carrying and stretcher-bearing.

Alan and Milish took the stretcher carrying Mo, though she appeared to weigh no more than a feather, and her face was wasted almost to a skull. Much easier going downhill than it had been in the ascent, they made good progress following their own trail through the dense forest, hacked out only days earlier. The Fir Bolg heads were still and brooding again, while the mist-wreathed grandeur of the valley appeared to weep in its desolation about them. Alan was silent throughout the journey and, from time to time, Milish glanced at him, as if fearful of the anguish she already sensed there and uncertain of his additional reaction when they reached the shore. When finally Alan saw the wreck of the Temple Ship coming into view, its great masts reduced to stumps, and its timbers and decks reduced to charcoal and ash, her fears proved justified. A heart-wrenching sob shuddered through him, a grief that was suddenly unbearable, as much through remorse at having abandoned the ship as at the implications of that abandonment.

The stench of burning was acrid in their nostrils as they laid Mo down among the many wounded on the shore. Meanwhile Alan left Milish and headed into the shallows beside the wreck.

Close to, he wept openly and silently. The ship had given them its protection throughout their journey, but nobody had protected it from the Legun as it vented its hate over every inch of her flame-raddled superstructure. From behind him he heard the empathic voice of Turkeya, their new young shaman, in a piping hymn of woe so reminiscent in its cadences of Kemtuk on the frozen lake, as he went down on his knees and lifted a handful of embers. Ash spilled from his fist, forming a sorrowful plume in the gusting air, drifting down and about the pebbled shore and the river's edge.

The ruined ship lay unnaturally low in the water, as if in its suffering it had sought some small comfort from burrowing into the river bottom. Siam's voice, joining them in offering his respect, was breaking with emotion. 'Surely we may attempt to rebuild her. Is this not the greatest forest in all the land?'

'I don't think so, Siam,' Alan spoke. 'Nantosueta has been woken from her sleep. She guards her forests again, and long may she do so!'

'But if the ship cannot be made sail-worthy, all is lost. With so many sick and wounded we cannot travel overland.'

Alan turned to Siam, noticing the left arm and shoulder bloody with wounds, and still that old hat was twirling about in his hands. Minute by minute, the survivors began to gather around them, the exhausted Olhyiu and even the Shee. Bowing his head, Alan scratched at the wispy dark beard that sprouted over his cheeks and chin, and then, taking a deep breath, spoke hesitantly, awkwardly. 'I want to thank you all. Heck, I don't even know how to begin – how to say how much we owe you.' He shook his head.

Siam replaced his battered Pilgrim hat and with a defiant stance he turned to face his people.

'In his modesty, we see the brave heart of our friend, the Mage Lord, clearer than he sees it himself. What if we had stayed among the Whitestar Mountains – what then would have become of us? Had we not sacrificed all dignity and hope when we surrendered our fleet to that desolate place? What else but a slow and bitter humiliation confronted us? The Mage Lord came from another world, yet he took the burden of leading us out of winter. He battled the malice of a Legun incarnate. Would we not follow this man, the Chosen One of the De Danaan, to the gates of Ghork Mega itself?'

Alan was embarrassed then by Siam's lofting of his hat and by the strained cheer that sounded from these brave and injured people.

'Though our sacrifice has been great, we thank you and your brave friends, three of whom have suffered in our cause. What greater purpose might befall the Olhyiu people than to help you in such a quest? And that quest has not ended. It still leads us to Carfon by the Eastern Ocean. And there, if I have to drag this hulk by its keel along the bed of the great river, is where we shall take you.'

Taking heart from the chief's words, Alan addressed them all in reply. 'Siam is right. We've got to do the best we can – use whatever presents itself to us. His courage should be our guide.'

They prepared a meal from what was left of the dried fish and ate it together on the riverside, in the shadow of the hulk. Over this frugal fare, they debated what best to do. In the situation that faced them there really wasn't much alternative: their only hope, no matter how desperate, remained with the Temple Ship.

They resolved to find out if it could be made to float, even if it was rudderless, like a raft. Ropes were passed about the trunks of the trees on the bank so that using this leverage, they could attempt to drag the hulk into the deep water of the central stream. A party of Olhyiu went out into the forest and returned with long poles, taken only from trees already fallen. If it was a hope at all, it was a very slender one. Even if they succeeded in refloating the ship, a Herculean task awaited them, since they would still have to pole their way all the hundreds of leagues to Carfon.

Some of the fitter men took up key positions, a leg clinging to a beam or inside a crumbling porthole. Shouts of encouragement willed on the tired limbs and sweat-drenched brows. They strained and pulled with every ounce of strength until the muscles of their brawny arms and shoulders bunched like the gnarled roots of the encroaching trees, and the veins on their brows swelled like hawsers. The labour continued until the midday sun broke through the wintry mists that still bathed the valley. Alan, who had climbed onto the fire-ravaged deck, was watching out for the slightest response.

'One more time!' He waved to the chief in the thick of the struggling figures on the aft deck.

But the enormous ruin would not budge an inch: it was stuck fast, resistant to every effort.

'It's no good!' Siam shook his head. 'She's dead in the water.'

Alan flopped down onto the charred deck. He didn't notice Milish climb onto the deck, but now her hand found his arm, and she sat down beside him as they gazed around them at the demoralised Olhyiu.

'I have to do something, Milish.' His eyes met hers. 'I know it's going to look kind of desperate – but the situation is desperate.'

He climbed to his feet, then called out to Turkeya to throw up the Spear of Lug. Turkeya did as he asked, casting the great spear so high it went through a parabolic arc and impaled its head in the centre of the middle deck. Alan went over to stare at the spear.

But Milish clutched at his arm, as if to stop him. 'What is it? Tell me what you're planning.'

'Remember when Valéra was dying? Do you recall the cure for the poison that threatened her unborn daughter?'

'Mage Lord, no! It is much too risky.'

'I have to try, Milish. Please don't try to stop me.'

Milish stared at him as he fell to his knees on the deck before the spear, running the flesh of his forearms against the cutting edges until blood welled out of the cut veins and ran onto the spearhead, where he clasped it with his hands.

Milish called out to Siam, 'You must stop him!'

The chief ran forward from the aft deck, arriving by the kneeling youth, whose head had fallen onto his chest.

The oraculum was throbbing powerfully in Alan's brow as the blood ran over the Ogham-glowing blade and seeped out into the ruined timbers.

Siam put his arm around Alan's shoulders. 'My friend, have there not been deaths enough in this accursed place?'

'She isn't dead, Siam. She can't be.' Alan took his blood-soaked hands away from the blade and spread them, with splayed fingers, on the charcoal-grimed wood. He implored the ship, through the oraculum, 'Show us there's even a spark of life left in you!'

Siam exclaimed, 'What's dead is dead! Come, let the Aides bind your wounds. Then let us attempt the long and perilous way on foot. I cannot promise deliverance, but we must take whatever measures are available to us, no matter what the risk.'

Alan allowed himself to be helped to his feet. He turned around through half a circle, facing the bulk of the ship, as if wishing his final farewell through the oraculum. Then he sensed the faintest tremor.

'Siam, did you feel that?'

'What is it?' Siam still kept a firm hold of Alan's shoulders, as if to make sure he didn't bleed himself again.

Alan probed again, this time more purposefully directing his oraculum into the depths of the ship. He felt it again: a weak response.

He tried harder. The oraculum flared, throwing Siam backwards so he almost fell. Alan poured all of his concentration into the hulk. He maintained the pressure of force until his head felt giddy. Suddenly, there was a muffled implosion as part of the superstructure fell in, showering them in charcoal and ash. Siam gaped, as if fearful the remaining structure was about to collapse.

On the shore below people started to back away from the hulk. But Alan stood fast.

Siam, reading Alan's mood, looked over the remains of the rail towards the milling crowds and bellowed, 'What has become of the proud Olhyiu, who respond to every groan and shiver with startled eyes! Is the Mage Lord not here among us? Above all we must keep faith.'

But it wasn't easy to keep faith against the groans of resettlement that were now taking place. All eyes were fixed on the region in the foredeck where the superstructure had collapsed. Yawning there into the dusty light was a gaping hole. Probing it with the oraculum, Alan sensed a responding shudder, like a moan issuing from deep below. Cautiously approaching the hole, he peered inside. He could make out little at first beyond the immediate opening, yet he sensed that a natural passage lay there, as irregular in its lining as a mountain cave.

'A torch – somebody!'

Siam got hold of a brand, lit it and then joined Alan by the opening. 'I shall be your torchbearer!'

Alan shook his head, taking the firebrand from Siam's hand. 'Go back to the shore. Get everybody else to stay clear of the ship. It could be dangerous.'

'I am no stranger to danger.'

Alan shrugged. 'Okay. But stay behind me.'

He was barely a step inside the portal when he recoiled from the odour of rot and decay. He was glad of the breeze that entered with him, fresh air rushing in as if to fill a vacuum, fluttering the firebrand as he held it aloft before him. Taking a second step into the tunnel, which led away into darkness, he descended, spiralling down ten or twelve feet, to a level where the lowermost hold of a normal ship might be. But clearly this was no ordinary ship. Here a cobweb-encrusted portal led into a new passage. As Siam probed it with the torch, wraiths of darkness appeared to swallow the light, as if darkness had become a force here, born out of misery. Caution ignited the oraculum so that it added the rubicund glow of its light to that of the firebrand as, with tentative steps, they continued their passage onward.

An eerie silence pervaded the gloom. Side tunnels confronted them as Siam held the firebrand aloft to inspect their organic walls.

'By the great Akoli, we have entered the throat of a dragon!'

Alan understood what Siam meant. They might be exploring the internal passages of some vast creature, with ridges at intervals like the rings of cartilage supporting a gigantic windpipe, but one that had long since ceased its expansion and contraction with the act of breathing the primal air.

The main throat – for throat was how Alan also thought

of this passage – twisted and turned on itself, with many diverging branches, often multiple, opening to either side, or to above and below, so that he had to be careful to circumvent the pitfalls. He grasped what he could of the wall or the ceiling with his free hand. Yet though he had wandered a hundred paces into this labyrinth, still nothing looked familiar. The inner spaces seemed to defy reality. He counted his paces from that point and soon registered another hundred, yet as he could determine from the absence of footprints in the grimy floor, he had never once retraced his steps. Stumbling to his knees over a protruding rib, he sensed how darkness closed about him, as if to devour him.

Panic yawned around him, an inchoate fear that caught his breath, yet, gaining his feet again, he asked Siam to loft the firebrand so that its glow reassured him, and then he paused in order to regain his composure. He was certain now of that answering tremor.

The ship is answering me, as if reading my innermost thoughts, my innermost feelings.

Now and then he detected new odours, sometimes pleasant – the scents of flowers – and at other times unpleasant, bog-tars and sulphur. And he heard the clashing sounds of distant upheaval, as if he were close to the embryonic forces of creation. He felt a shudder in the heart of the ship, if 'ship' was an appropriate word for the real nature of this mystery. There was a feeling of being watched, and he almost shouted aloud, so overwhelming was it. Yet there could be no need to shout, even to whisper, only to think.

Then immediately, as if it had sensed his thrill of communication, he sensed a change. Slowly, almost imperceptibly, he was aware of the metamorphosis of its elements, although, from moment to moment, there was little visible change. 'Siam – if what I'm sensing is true, it's wonderful beyond belief. Maybe I just want to believe it. If only the ship would give me a sign so I know I'm not mistaken.'

'What you feel is true!' Siam's growl sounded out from somewhere very close to him, yet lost in the dark.

'Then you sense it too?'

'I feel it.'

My God! He hardly dared to think what it meant.

Question after question thrilled his mind. But there was one he hardly dared to articulate. Then he made himself ask it, excitedly, falteringly, through the window in his brow, 'Are you alive?'

There was silence for several charged moments, and then there could be no doubting that he had his reply. Although he hadn't moved a step, he found himself within a chamber with walls that glittered faintly as if made of gold. But their surface was too soft for metal. When he reached out to touch them they had a heavy liquid feel, as if he were pressing into a lake of mercury. There was no clear reflection in this dully glittering substance, not even when he shone the firebrand's light against it. It absorbed light as, presumably, any energy that was directed towards it – yet still it glowed with a soft and ancient light, like a heart of liquid gold.

'Siam, what do you make of it?'

Siam stared back at him, a mixture of terror and wonder in his eyes. 'Mage Lord, do we not sense it, even if we have nothing else to go on other than our feelings?'

Alan's eyes widened. He ran his fingers over the giving surface of the walls – the liquid softness of organic being – uncertain if they were changing even as he looked at them, while observing for the first time that in cross-section they formed a pentagon. The ceiling was faceted also, the natural drawing together of the lines of the pentagon.

'She's grieving with us, Siam. I know it, absolutely, though I can't explain how I know it.'

Siam nodded.

Alan's heart beat too fast for comfort and he struggled to catch his breath. 'We've got to find a way to help her.'

'She is beyond any help that I might conceive.'

Alan stood at the dead centre of the golden heart of the ship. He called out, 'Show me what to do. Guide me!'

Siam's eyes were wide and staring as he held back in the entrance, the firebrand trembling in his hand. Alan stood with his feet wide apart as if to give his giddy head balance, then placed a blood-covered hand on each of two opposing walls. The oraculum pulsated.

He maintained his position, the oraculum throbbing

powerfully and insistently. Then he thought he saw something, a faint flickering in the walls of the chamber. His heart pounded as he realised what he was seeing. However faintly, the walls had taken on a background ultramarine, through which a rippling of stars, as complex and beautiful as a clear night sky, came and went from view. The pulsation of stars suggested an answering heartbeat. The heart of the Temple Ship was beating again, however feebly.

Alan's face was a mixture of exhilaration and exhaustion. His lips moved, as if attempting to speak the words that were entering his mind from his communion with the ship . . . *Remember the frozen lake . . . The lightning!*

How could Alan forget their escape from the Storm Wolves? He recalled looking up into the thunderheads, seeing the lightning, his left arm tensing against the sky and his white-knuckled fist bringing it down and directing the lightning at the ice . . . No – not directly at the ice, but first directly through the ship!

'I used the First Power to revive the ship.'

That was what the ship itself was telling him. Abandoning all defences, Alan opened his mind completely, through the oraculum, focusing on the pulsating matrix.

Oh – wow!

Extraordinary sensitivity combined with immense raw power. Not the patronising voice of command he had anticipated, but the invitation for him to be one with her in love and fellowship. A wave of new vigour tingled through his mind and body.

With all of his mental strength, he poured the First Power into the golden heart of the Temple Ship. The tingling surge was so exhilarating he was forced to clench his teeth – or he would have shouted out like a drunken man. The wonder, the joy of it, coursed through his blood and spirit. The ship was returning what he had asked of it. It gave it to him with such joy – more freely than he could ever have hoped for or dreamed.

Communion!

Alan and Siam headed back the way that they had come, stumbling as they retraced their steps through the dusty labyrinth, slipping around the pitfalls until they emerged, blinking, into the daylight. They didn't look back as the portal closed itself off behind them. Leaving Siam kneeling on the deck, and extolling the great Akoli, Alan rushed to the charred rail on the foredeck, waving his arms at the startled people who had been standing around, confused and anxious, waiting for him. He saw how their expressions changed from fear to hope, sensing the change in him.

Alan turned to the kneeling figure of the chief and shouted, his voice ringing with elation. 'Go gather everybody together and bring them up on deck. And Milish!' His eyes searched the huddled groups already on board and found her. 'Get the Aides to bring up all the wounded. And Bétaald – gather together the Shee. We must get everybody up onto the deck.'

'But is the deck safe to bear such weight?'

'Trust me! I have something important to tell you all.'

With caution still, the wounded were lifted up the makeshift ladders onto the fire-ravaged main deck. A Shee carried Mo on board, then left her to the Aides, who oversaw a bed of furs. Others stitched Alan's arms, where he had cut them with the spearhead, then dressed them. Suddenly a woman screamed as the cinders of an oak bulwark disintegrated in a shower of dust. 'The ghost of the ship will devour us. See there its very bones are gleaming!'

And in the gap it seemed that she was right: the skeleton of the ancient vessel did seem to protrude through the ash, like a rib of ivory.

'Stay calm!' Alan called out, to settle their fears. 'No harm will come to you!' He could hardly contain the rapture that glistened in his eyes. He stood erect, feeling the reviving spirit that amplified and crackled about him. He knew that Qwenqwo had come to stand beside him.

'What is it, Mage Lord? What did you discover in the depths of the ship?'

'Something wonderful!'

'Tell me more, or I shall die from curiosity!'

Qwenqwo turned to Siam a face so full of pleading that the Olhyiu chief laughed and picked him up in a bear hug. 'Do not expect a simple man, such as me, to explain what we saw. Not if I lived a thousand years!'

Alan couldn't help but laugh. 'Patience, Qwenqwo! We'll talk about everything later. Right now I have things to do.'

'Mage Lord!' It was Siam who now approached him, Siam whose eyes were still wide with shock at what he had witnessed, as he waved at the groaning superstructure with his hat. 'For all the wonder we have witnessed, yet still I cannot see how we are to escape this prison of ash and peril.'

Alan led Siam to the remains of the rail that separated the aft section from the broad middle deck, and from where they could address the gathering crowds.

'Don't be afraid of the changes you are about to witness.'

'Changes, Mage Lord?'

More cries were sounding out. Yet excitement surged ever higher. For with a shimmer about the very fibres of its structure, the ship was metamorphosing. 'Look about you,' he shouted to them. 'The ship is healing itself.'

He could feel his own sense of wonder spread among them. He called out, so they could all hear him, 'The dwarf mage has asked me to explain what is happening. But I'm struggling to put into words the miracle I have just witnessed. The Temple Ship has been more than our refuge. Believe me when I tell you that it isn't just a vessel constructed out of oak. It's alive! I know how incredible this must seem to you all. And yet it is true. It knows the delight of joy and it knows the anguish of despair. It mourns the loss of friends, just like we do.' Alan looked at Siam, whose eyes were jumping here and there, as changes were taking place around them.

'Siam wants to know how we're going to make headway in this sunken wreck, whether it be alive or not, the several hundred miles of distance that still separate us from Carfon.'

Alan shrugged at Siam, then lifted his eyebrows at the equally incredulous Milish, who had left Mo to come and listen to him. 'I don't have a clue as to how it will happen. But my guess is that for the moment we don't need to understand, only to be patient. To believe!' Then, with rising excitement, he watched how the ash was peeling from the underlying ivory: it was showering skywards, contrary to wind or gravity.

'Trust the Temple Ship. It will take care of us during this journey.' He nodded to Milish, adding in a softer voice, 'Now let's try again and see if we can help Mo.'

Alan accepted the limp body of his friend. Mo appeared so frail, so weightless, he might have held a ghost in his arms. He remembered Qwenqwo's words in the story he had told them on the river: he had called the ship the Ark of the Arinn. It seemed that no one other than he and Ainé had heard Mo challenge the Legun . . .

Your master will know me by my true name. I am Mira, Léanov Fashakk − the Heralded One . . .

My God!

Mo, who hadn't needed a crystal to hear the thoughts of others! It seemed to Alan, standing on the deck of cinders, that there was a mystery to his friend that was every bit as strange and wonderful as the Temple Ship.

Nothing in his power could cure Mo, any more than it had healed the ship. The Legun, through its malice, had damaged both of them. And yet now, after he had set the ball rolling with his oraculum, the ship was healing itself. Was this the lesson he needed to help Mo? The spellbound company saw Alan's body become one with the oraculum. He made contact again with the ship, being to being; his figure radiated light.

There was a long and strained silence. But Alan endured it, standing with his head bowed. Then, when it appeared there would be no response, they heard a faint tinkling sound, a sound that was strangely comforting. With much whispering and nervousness, people rushed about the decks or gathered in protective clusters about the wounded, as moment by moment the ship melded its powers with Alan's. The oraculum flashed from Alan to the ship, and at once a new force took shape in the air above them, a force that took myriad youthful female forms, spiralling and revelling about the ruined superstructure. In the wake of their sweeping movements Alan saw rainbows of light, in their voices he heard the birdsong symphony of spring, in their fragrance he sensed the intoxication of a child dancing through a summer meadow dense with wildflowers.

'You're beautiful!' he exclaimed, his vision, all his senses, compelled to wheel and turn, bedazzled.

The playful forms consummated to a single focus that became a being of impossible voluptuousness, shimmering in the air before searching out the figure in Alan's arms. Her eyes were the green of a summer meadow, with dancing motes of gold. With a curve of great tenderness, her body stooped until her lips brushed Mo's brow. For a moment, Mo's body took on the same radiance as Alan's. In that moment, he sensed the spirit revive in her, just as he had sensed it in the ship.

Mo's eyes opened and she looked up into his smiling face. He hugged her gently before passing her back into the welcoming arms of Milish.

Moments later, the whole ship shuddered, then lifted a yard out of the water, and almost immediately began to inch away from the shore. Slowly, haltingly – as if needing to accustom itself to its new form and purpose – it assumed a new course against the centre stream.

On the Wings of Angels

For the first ten miles or so it gathered a slow and steady pace. All the while the cloud of ashes billowed from the dissolving timbers, following in their trail like a plume of smoke. Then it first became manifest on the port side, a spar as if the bud of a great wing, extended outward, sparkling over its ivory surface like starlight.

Kehloke, her wounds bound, came to stand within the embrace of her husband. 'Look!' she exclaimed. 'It flies through the water as a bird through air – see even the prow has become a great beak!'

Little by little, as the forested slopes glided by, the form of the Temple Ship emerged more clearly, and it was not as a bird but the delta shape of a great manta ray, with vast wing-like extensions of its pectoral fins. The prow assumed a dome and then a streamlined head, the breadth of its wings brushing the waterside foliage of the narrow channel with each upswept tip, and sweeping round to fashion the living quarters within twin-horned fins to either side of its head, some thirty feet above the waterline.

Past the divergence of the waters about the island and into the great swell of the river, there was a new urgency to the ship's movements. A quickening of pace, as if it were impatient to leave this haunted valley in the cradle of its smouldering mountains.

All but the severely wounded stood on deck to watch the island of Ossierel with its distant Rath of Nantosueta pass them by on their starboard side and then recede into the mists of early evening, a lambent energy still flickering about the dreadful tor, as if in passionate farewell.

Meanwhile structures continued to evolve over the smooth hill of body behind the head, rearing high, as gill slits, then arching over until they became shelters for the convalescing wounded.

There were no doors or portholes any more, no masts or spars for sails, no bell tower or staircases leading below. Instead downy combs extruded, like living stalactites under these beautiful roofs, raining down a gentle mist of nectar. The Olhyiu women tasted it on their fingers, and then quickly began to gather it up in vessels and hats, so parched lips could be refreshed by it. The men began to construct primitive nets from what cord and material they had retained. They cast these from the stern and drew them in, heavy with salmon. As the great volcanic mountain chains moved by on either side, the Olhyiu were so overcome with awe they watched in reverential silence as Tazan's formidable valley closed its fist behind them, passing out of a second winding pass of cliffs that soared above them and echoed the farewell to their passage.

Past the cliffs, they felt the slowing of current as the river widened again and the landscape broke down into smaller pinnacles, a broadening valley of rocks in place of the giant redwoods.

By first light the next morning they were moving swiftly south, carried by the confident swell of the great river. Alan was comforted by the sight of Mo, her hair now trimmed in the fashion of the Aides, being helped to stand at the very apex of the prow, supported by Milish.

A creative ambience trilled the air, as if the ship communicated its joy of recovery with the mountains and the thinning trees, with the water that moved slower than they did in its swirling currents. The first of the seabirds wheeled overhead, delighting in the chase of their passage.

On the second day of their southbound journey, the late afternoon sky cleared to a beautiful eggshell blue from which a light fall of glittering snowflakes imbued the air with loveliness.

Mo was strong enough to join Alan on the foredeck, standing unaided, but still watched assiduously by the caring Milish. They talked about the deaths of the Kyra and Kemtuk, and the loss of Kate. They also grieved over Mark, and the sacrifice he had made.

Mo whispered, 'I know he isn't dead. I feel it.'

Alan put his arm around her shoulders. Her words had echoed the advice of Qwenqwo on the Rath, but these were words he didn't pretend to understand.

She asked him, 'Will we ever see him – or Kate – again?'

'I don't know, Mo. I really hope so.'

Together, they gazed into the desert landscape, where time had worn a fantastic geometry of stone and sand in which delicate shades of lilac, gold and lavender curled about the natural sculptures: cones and pyramids of stone in gorgeous shades and shapes, as if they had been moulded from the primal landscape by the playful hands of children. There were thousands of configurations – tens of thousands. They shimmered and sparkled in the sun, like mother of pearl.

'What do they call this place?' Alan asked Milish.

'In Carfon they call it "The Painted Desert".'

The following morning, like the ghost of a bygone age, the broken dome of a great vault rose out of the haze of scrub and sand: a monolith at least two hundred feet high. By its left side a single wall survived of what must have been a great palace of stone, with level upon level of pillared porticos and romantic arches surviving, through obstinacy, the millennia of dust-blown time. It seemed much older and finer than the walls of Isscan. Alan, who found himself alone on the prow, wondered at the great antiquity of the civilisations of Monisle and the city state they were now approaching. About its hinterland he saw clusters of beehive shapes, tiny in the distance, yet they must be two storeys high and of the same hues as the rocks.

Milish took Mo back to rest, but joined him a little later, standing silently for many minutes, as if she were deep in contemplation.

Something is troubling her, he thought to himself.

He kept his own silence for a while as the ship hummed to itself, against the complex rhythms of its bow wave against the rocks.

'Carfon,' she spoke at length, 'will appear a strange city to you. Of all the city states, it was the most ancient in its lineage, and so the most elect within its boundaries. The fall of Ossierel changed everything. It made Carfon the final repository of the truth and wisdom that was our world.'

Something is frightening her!

Alan watched how mists coiled from the bow spray over the water and, like sprites of mystery, still seemed to follow their passage.

It was many minutes before she spoke again. 'In Carfon, the ruling families cannot help but resent the transformation. First the Council-in-Exile demanded territory within the oldest walls – and in arriving there became a power within a power, subject to no laws of Chamber. Since then a generation of refugees has swelled its population to eight million frightened souls.'

'Don't worry,' Alan replied. 'I'll look to you for advice.'

She hesitated again. 'I may be less useful than you anticipate.'

Next day, the passing landscape gave way to the great alluvial plain that fed the city and its hinterlands. Piñon and juniper scrub took root in the desert, and then trees. Broad-leafed trees. To Alan they looked familiar from Earth, but sufficiently different to be vaguely alien. He recognised oaks, but these were blue-leafed rather than green. At first these appeared in isolated clusters but they soon became denser copses, and then woodlands – the remnants of great forests that had once cloaked the land. Soon they came upon the first evidence of cultivation, a warmer land with fields of corn, like mile-square rugs laid to dry in the warming sun.

It was on the fourth day after leaving the forbidden valley that people came out to welcome them in the waters below. They approached in small boats and canoes and tossed aloft garlands of flowers or fresh loaves of bread. Others threw lines, at the end of which were baskets of fruit and vegetables. The food lifted everybody's spirits, since they had tired of the monotonous diet of fish. Still the great winged shape, the ivory of its coat taking on the rose of sunset or the gold of morning, coursed swiftly along the centre stream as the crowds became ever more numerous along the banks, as if word of their coming preceded them in every hamlet.

And soon a cry was heard from the banks to either side,

the same phrase, like a hymn of thanks for their safe-coming: 'The Angel Ship – the Angel Ship!'

It was another day before they first glimpsed the city walls, straddling the great estuary on the shores of the Eastern Ocean. Reflecting the low sun of evening, they soared two hundred feet above the rocky shore. Crowds lined the battlements. They were holding lighted candles in their hands and, as the ship drew level with them, people performed a ritual, fashioning a triangle from right to left shoulder and down to the inverted apex of heart.

Milish took her place on his left side, dressed in the formal regalia of silver plume and ornate gown and dress. Mo, with head bowed, hunched silently to his right.

The Temple Ship coursed by a deeply recessed and ancient gate in the high walls. It appeared a half-pentangular arch within an arch. Above it was a tablet of stone carved with inscriptions about the edges of its weathered stones. The gate and the walls that enclosed it gave the impression of great antiquity, older by far than the cyclopean walls of Isscan – older perhaps even than the Rath of the Dark Queen in the Vale of Tazan.

'Why are you so tense, Milish?'

She hesitated before replying, as if troubled by the fact that he sensed her every mood. 'It is the Water Gate, which leads into the Old City. It troubles me that the High Council-in-Exile has kept it closed against us. Do not underestimate their capacity for mischief.'

He looked up with interest at the massive walls, and at

the people with their lighted candles. 'I know what's hidden inside those walls, Milish.'

'Hush – hush! I beg you. Do not speak openly thus. It is blasphemy even to speak of it.' Her voice fell to a whisper, her presence suddenly frail and vulnerable beside him.

'I sense it, stronger than any force I have ever felt through the oraculum. It's like it's calling out to me – as if I were sensitive to its calling in every particle of my being.' He put his arm around Mo's shoulder.

'For all your power, will you not heed my counsel? Do not talk about such things in such unguarded circumstances! Do not even think of it!'

But how could he not think of the Fáil when he knew that it held the answers to the challenge entrusted to him and his friends by the High Architect as she was dying. The continuing purpose of that quest still faced them. Soon, though it might be the most dangerous force in the universe, he would have to confront it. And Milish was right: even thinking about it, he felt its terrible awareness focus on him.

'First we rest,' he said, quietly, calmly, his words addressed more to Mo than to Milish. 'Then we organise.'

Milish's brown eyes assessed the waiting crowds. 'For the moment let us give thanks that fate has preserved us. Let us not look grim and whisper.' Milish lifted her arm to wave, and her face was smiling at the fluttering ribbons and the dancing lights.

The Temple Ship then heeled about a buttressed corner

of the ancient walls, where a tall tower hovered a hundred and fifty feet above them, and it approached a second gate, more openly constructed than the Water Gate.

'This is the Harbour Gate,' said Milish. 'And I am pleased to find it open to us. It would appear that the Prince Ebrit, the Elector, has seen fit to welcome us. But be warned – this is a city that knows only intrigues.'

The Temple Ship halted a hundred yards out, in deeper water.

Soon a barque of state, of gilded and tapestried finery, emerged through the wide-flung gates, and many oars dipped and pulled in perfect harmony as its shallow draught skimmed over the waves. A great cheer sounded from the Shee and the Olhyiu on board, to be answered by the thousands of people holding aloft their candles of welcome.

On the dock, as if disdaining to join those aboard the approaching vessel, Alan sensed a powerful mind. He searched the distant mass of figures until he found its source: a very old woman who stood alone in the shadows of the gate, her toothless mouth collapsed and wrinkled, her back stooped and bent over a staff of power. For a moment he was shocked to sense her warning:

Beware the object of your quest. It may prove a poisoned chalice.

A second presence, a good deal more hostile, caused a thrill of alarm to pulse in the oraculum. Alan glimpsed a tall man with a bearlike head, one of his arms replaced by a false limb of matt-black metal. *Could it possibly be*

Snakoil Kawkaw? Alan shook his head, keeping a protective arm enfolded around Mo.

He would face any new challenge when it arose. Today Carfon welcomed them like the buds of spring after a famine winter.

Acknowledgements

My sincere thanks to my agent Leslie Gardner for her encouragement and advice in writing this book, and to Dr Hilary Johnson and her agency and my editors, Dr David V. Barrett and Laura H. Booth, for their courtesy and thoughtful contribution to the final script. It is also a great pleasure to thank my artistic collaborator, Mark Salwowski, whose cover illustrations for my books have been an inspiration over many years. I also want to proffer my grateful thanks to Brendan Murphy, whose belief and practical support was greatly appreciated. Finally, I am indebted, as always, to my wife Barbara for her patience and indefatigable support.

The story continues in

THE
TOWER
OF BONES

Coming November 2012